TEN SHOES UP

A NOVEL

GARY L. STUART

Ten Shoes Up

Copyright © 2015 by Gary L. Stuart. All Rights Reserved.

No part of this publication may be reproduced, stored in a retrieval system or transmitted, in any form or by any means—electronic, mechanical, photocopying, recording, or otherwise—without prior written permission from the publisher, except for the inclusion of brief quotations in a review.

For information about this title or to order other books and/or electronic media, contact the publisher:
Gleason & Wall Publishers
7000 N. 16th Street, Suite 120, PBM 470, Phoenix AZ 85020
www.garylstuart.com
gary.stuart@garylstuart.com

ISBN: 978-0-9863441-0-7

Printed in the United States of America

Cover and Interior design: 1106 Design, Phoenix, AZ

Other Books by Gary L. Stuart

The Ethical Trial Lawyer

The Gallup 14

Miranda—The Story Of America's Right To Remain Silent

Innocent Until Interrogated—The True Story of the
Buddhist Temple Massacre and The Tucson Four

AIM For The Mayor—Echoes From Wounded Knee

Anatomy of A Confession—The Debra Milke Case

CHAPTER 1
Angus–New Mexico Territory–1881

I WAS RIDING LOW in the saddle toward the last stand of aspen on the south slope of Ten Shoes Up. We'd forded the Rio Chama's north bank about two hours earlier. The Utes named this mountain. Something to do with five braves chasing a lion. Story was the lion won. I'd heard talk the government wanted to change it to Osier Mountain, but that's getting ahead of my story.

The boys hard on my trail were a half-mile downslope. The tracker in the lead was good at his game, but even a squinty-eyed ranch hand could have followed my big bay's track through this snow. Hoping to ease the weight on Tucson's back, climbing up a steep rocky incline, I leaned down over the saddle horn and let him have his head.

"All right, Tucson," I said to him, giving him a rub on the neck, "keep diggin'. Know you're tired. Last push. We'll be shed of 'em when we reach the cut."

There'd been times riding this mountain, on the backbone between New Mexico and Colorado, when I'd gone for weeks without hearing a human sound. I've heard talk that, by 1890, these mountains will be full of flatlanders from Kansas. God help us. Maybe that's why talking to Tucson is a comfort. He's big, nigh onto seventeen hands, surefooted, with a neck as thick as a one-hundred-pound sack of grain. I figured he'd save me again.

The cold, high mountain air turned my breath to white fog as we pushed up a slope too steep for a man wearing chaps and spurs, but Tucson was bred to climb these mountains. Behind me, the constant crunch of hooves crashing down into the crusted snow and the swooshing of rock sliding downhill gave those boys away. Doubt they could see me in the quarter-mile stand of aspen, but unless they were deaf as river rocks, they could hear me, too. The gravel scattered downhill behind Tucson like a sluice chute. Since there were at least three, maybe four, I heard more than they did. Leather slapping, horseshoes clanging on granite, and far-off cussing. When I stopped to let Tucson breathe, I heard muffled talk. Most likely about me. Probably looking for a clean shot.

The wet October snow bent the tree branches below, but the wind up this high blew the snow off steep slopes like this one, just shy of the tree line. We were close to topping out at nine thousand feet, and the noonday air was thin.

Tucson stopped when we came to a small flat space, stomped his feet and snorted upwind. Tugging up a tad on the reins, and leaning back into my saddle, I let him blow after climbing hard for the last fifteen minutes. Reaching down to check my latigo, I cupped my other hand to my ear. Nothing. Then something faint. Not a voice. More like a growl. I suppose I could have yelled down they had the wrong man. Wouldn't have made a spit of difference. They were sighting me in. I could feel it on the nape of my neck, those little hairs standing up like spikes on a porcupine.

Laying my right glove on Tucson's mane with my reins loosely twirled through the two middle fingers on my left hand, I patted his sweaty neck.

Half a minute to suck up some high air, that's all I can give you, son. I'll need a fast trot out to get us over the top.

Snorting into the frigid air, Tucson tensed up and gave me a good shake. Then, still blowing, I eased him into a switchback to get us up to a flat granite shelf forty feet away. From there, the level shelf wound through the last quarter-mile of this old Ute warrior trail. The elk hide saddle horn dug into my gut as I leaned forward trying to keep my profile down. Twisting to the offside of my saddle, I caught a glimpse of the boys behind us. Tucson paid me no mind and pushed the trail behind us.

The snow had become steadily wetter over the last four hours. As the sun filtered down through the gray clouds, I could feel the muscle strain coming up through Tucson's withers. He was sweating up some, mostly out of nerves. Natural, I supposed, since he could hear rough stock behind us, running hard to catch up.

Yeah, old son, I hear 'em, too.

Narrowing my eyes at the broken trail up ahead of us, I tried to reckon the trail up the granite slope on the other side of the aspen stand. Utes, riding bareback, notched this trail for more than a mile, topping out just below the granite reef. This was a damn fine high-ridge trail to ride on a summer morning, but with winter coming down and a posse coming up, I felt like a skitter fox being tracked by a mountain lion.

Pushing the brim of my hat back, I craned my neck up, trying to distinguish the black granite spire on top of the mountain. Its crevices splintered the gray sky. Those boys on my trail likely saw the mountaintop as a Conquistador's iron helmet. But, from a quarter-mile away, the jagged outcroppings looked like stone panthers struggling to escape the mountain's grasp. The closer I got, the stronger the pull. The first settlers down below had called it God's magnet, sucking in the north wind. Blue-black ice spewed back out at any man who rode this trail from the south side. I gathered my duster and notched a tighter knot in the wool kerchief at my throat.

"Boys," I said aloud, knowing they were a quarter-mile down the mountain from me, "I can live a mite longer up here than you can." Tucson just kept on digging.

I could melt snow for water, my .30-40 Krag rifle would drop white-tailed deer. My saddle bags were chuck-full of coffee, hardtack, jerky, and salt. My oiled canvas tarp and two heavy saddle blankets sheltered me from rain and wind. My edge was simple. I was patient. They weren't.

The tree line was clear now. Up this high, the rocks took over and sometimes rained down on you when you least expected it. Four hundred yards to my left, over there by the black rock face, I thought I spotted it. At first glance, it fooled me, looking just like another crevice draining ice and snow down from the peak one thousand feet above us. I knew better. The Ute Cut. The only way to cross over to Colorado.

All right, son, we're close enough to smell the crack in this old mountain now, just you keep on digging.

The black hole in the south face of Ten Shoes Up was more than sixty-feet tall. It would fool most because it looked shallow, like all the others. But this one dived into a split in the bluff. Barely wide enough for a horse. In a storm, the crack carried water off the bluff at flood speed, raining gravel down the mountainside. A southeast wind would drive the water over into Colorado. A northwester blow would drown New Mexico. But, on this gray day, the snow wasn't melting, and the wind was only ten miles an hour, tops.

"God damned railroad," I said. As usual, Tucson ignored my muttering. But, he rattled me in the saddle, shaking off the sweat of the hard climb.

CHAPTER 2
Captain Standard H. Plumb

WE'D BEEN TRACKING the big bay horse since yesterday morning. Now we had him in range, quarter-mile above us. Me, Undersheriff Joe Pete, his part-time deputy Bo String, and Branson. Four to his one; my kind of odds.

"Well, can you see the sumbitch or not?" I said to Branson, the tracker and shooter from Trinidad. *What a goddamn mess,* I thought. The man spurring his horse up ahead of us had it coming, whoever he was. Even up this high, in damn cold weather, I was sweating so much it made me itch. I hated feeling wet under a heavy wool shirt. Mud all over the horse, plus my best boots, wasn't my style. I waited for Branson's answer. As usual, he took his time before paying me proper attention.

Branson was a dark-skinned breed, with coal black hair tied in a single braid hanging halfway down his back. His shoulder blades poked up out of his shirt like they were pointing at a pair of vacant eyes. The man never seemed to look your way. Somehow, he still bored a hole in you if you looked at him long enough. He wore two or three dirty buckskin shirts, depending on weather. He favored an oily sheepskin vest, mule-hide chaps, Mexican spurs with over-sized rowels, and a two-foot long leather quirt strapped tight to his right wrist.

"Why we tailin' this fella?" Branson had asked me when he saw me waiting for him as he stepped down off the train and unloaded his horse yesterday morning in Chama. I'd been the head of railroad security for the AT&SF for four years. No ridge rider on a mountain horse would screw up my deal. They did not call me Captain Standard H. Plumb for nothing. Branson, as usual, did not understand. He was a fine gun-hand and not half-bad at nosing out track. But I had to do all the thinking.

"'Cause I told Mr. Steen he's the one that's been robbing our trains, that's why."

"You sure he's headed north?"

"Sure enough to wire you over in Trinidad. Sure enough to pay you and these two other men twice what the Territory of New Mexico pays. And, sure enough to send you packing if you don't quit asking me surly questions like am I sure? Damn right, I'm sure!"

"Captain Plumb," Branson said, "just you let me be," as he worked that big .50 caliber Hawken from the sheepskin scabbard strapped to the rigging on his horse.

"He's zigzagging back now toward that black crevice. I figure him at seven hundred yards, but the wind's tricky up here, so I mean to give him a two-notch leeway."

Branson chambered a round into the thirty-six-inch barrel, and thumbed the rear sight up into place for long-distance shooting. We'd spotted the sumbitch just as his big bay edged out from an aspen stand up ahead about a quarter-mile. We jumped off our horses near the edge of a thick stand of Ponderosa pine.

In my haste to dismount, I'd hooked my right spur on the dang bedroll causing my fool horse to rear up just as I swung my right leg over the cantle. The iron shoulder guard on my .30-30 Winchester smacked me on the nose, opening an old cut in my left nostril. It hurt to talk. Hell, I could hear my own wheeze as I tried to stanch the blood spewing into the handkerchief I always carried in the flap pocket on my canvas duster. The blood looked black against the red-checkered cloth.

We'd heard the man before, twice in the last four hours. Undersheriff Joe Pete told me his name was Angus. Unclear whether it was his first or last. No matter, I told him—we're gonna catch him, and the AT&SF Railroad would charge him with train robbing. Branson knew better. "Don't catch him, kill him," I'd ordered. "There's an extra hundred dollars in it for you if we take him back slung over his saddle."

But, the only glimpse we'd caught this far was of his horse, a big muscled bay, coming out of a stand of red cedar. About a half-hour later, we got a backwards look as he crossed Whiskey Creek. We'd picked up his track yesterday and found the small fire pit where he'd camped last night; this was the first time he was within .50 caliber range. But, now he was close enough to shoot. Sumbitch was just shy of the lower edge of the bluff. Out in the open—too far away for a .30-30, but just right for Branson's big .50 caliber Hawken.

Using the pommel of his saddle as a barrel rest, Branson licked his thumb, tested the wind direction, and moved the notch wheel on the back gun sight three clicks.

"He's gonna get his ass knocked halfway down the mountain firing that big gun off the back of that little horse," Undersheriff Joe Pete said.

"He ain't," I said. "Branson's trained that little Morgan to stand while he's firing. Why don't you shut up and let the man work?"

The barrel angle, at a little north of thirty degrees, made the shot even harder. Branson took in a half-dozen slow breaths, his chest pushing out against the stirrup leathers. Leaning his cheek into the polished walnut six inches behind the two-inch hammer, he slowly closed his left eye, squinted with his right, and tensed on the first of two cold steel triggers.

Gripping the stock of my .30-30, I jacked a round into the chamber, which irritated Branson. He eased back, shook his head at me, and leaned back into the gunstock. I could feel the cold moving up through my boots. It settled in with the twist in my gut as I anticipated the kill shot coming. But, Branson just kept on aiming, holding his trigger finger a fraction off the trigger curve.

"Goddamn it all," Branson said, "I'm close enough for a shot, but maybe too far for a kill. I might only hit his leg, or nick him somewhere that won't slow him down."

"Then kill the horse, you fool. If he reaches that shelf, he'll get clean away."

I was guessing. Truth is, almost everything a hundred yards away was blurry as hell. Unbeknownst to my railroad bosses, or Undersheriff Pete, I'd seen an eye doc in St. Louis six months ago.

"Early onset cataracts," he'd mumbled, before taking another swig from his whiskey-smelling coffee cup. "You'll be able to see blurs at a distance for another year. Then you ought to get a job sittin' on the porch."

Branson knew. That's why I'd hired him, even after he put it unkindly, "Captain, you can't see for shit. Without my eyes, you couldn't track a pig through its own holler."

"Goddamit, Branson, can you sight the sumbitch or not?"

"Yeah, but your pestering me don't help none. And, don't be jacking rounds into your rifle, you might shoot me."

Undersheriff Pete and his deputy moved up closer to us. "You boys had best stay mounted," I said.

Pete and Bo String paid me no mind, but it wasn't the time to exercise my authority. They eased their horses into a small level place five feet behind my horse.

"Sounds good to me, Captain," the undersheriff said, "but I think our horses need a rest, too. We'll be dismounting."

"Suit yourself. You boys are gonna get some reward money with a single shot from Branson's big gun."

I watched the young deputy, Bo String, lean into his horse as he nudged her to the flat part of the trail. Undersheriff Joe Pete had guessed Bo String's age about twenty. He rode with the ease of a man who'd spent every working day on horseback since he was nine years old. He struck me as an amiable man, with little ambition. I figured he'd signed onto the posse more out of boredom than an interest in the reward money. But, by the look of his clothes, he could use the five dollars a day, plus coffee and biscuits in the morning.

Branson inched up the business end of the big Hawken. "I'm going to wait until he reaches that next switchback," he said, back over his shoulder. "I want a broadside shot. I'm sure I can kill the horse. But, he'll present a much bigger profile sideways. Then, we climb on up there and pack him out."

"How come the railroad is offering a four-thousand dollar reward? Is what they say about him true or not?" Bo asked as he swung to the ground. He got off a horse effortlessly. Like a storekeeper stepping off his front porch.

"Never mind about that," I said. "Just you shush while Branson's drawing a bead."

Joe Pete looked at Bo and held his forefinger up to his lips. Branson waited two minutes before leaning in against the side of his little Morgan. The bay up ahead was just turning to his left, giving Branson a wide-angled look.

Bo, settling back on his heels in a cowboy squat, watched Branson sight in the target. He reached inside the duster for his pint bottle of warm-up whiskey. Turning his back to me, he held it out in front like it was bonded whiskey, instead of local brew. He wrenched the stopper out of the top of the bottle with his teeth. There was just enough sunlight to send a glare off the glass bottle up the mountainside. Just then, Branson held his breath and pulled the trigger.

CHAPTER 3

Angus Heads for the Ute Cut

I SAW THE FAINT GLINT in Tucson's eye, and felt his neck twitch, as he tensed up and strained to look downhill to our left. Wham! He bolted on me; jumped damn near a foot. I gathered the reins, gripped the saddle horn, and heard the crack of a big bore rifle downwind. A split second later, I felt a sharp pain in my foot. My right boot came out of the iron stirrup just as Tucson's right foreleg buckled. He righted himself, but I was afraid he'd taken a bullet. I jumped off and saw that the shot had hit my right boot, below the spur strap, and then sliced along the outer skin of Tucson's thigh, tearing skin and maybe a little muscle, but missing the bone. Sucking in my breath, I jumped back up on him and bellied down over the horn. Tapping my left spur lightly against his ribs, I moved him into a trot along the uphill side of the trail.

Sorry, Tucson, I'll check on you in a minute. This is no place to dismount.

Thirty seconds later, a second shot boomed. It missed me by ten yards, clanging off the granite wall behind me, and then ricocheting to God knows where. Three minutes later Tucson topped us out of the last switchback. I wedged him into the cut forty yards to the west, and we disappeared.

CHAPTER 4
Captain Plumb Regroups

"YOU MISSED THE sumbitch."

Branson glared at me with his right fist raised. "No, by god, I did not. Something spooked that horse just as I got a broadside look at horse and rider, damn it to hell! My round hit either his horse or the man. My second shot was like shooting in the goddamn dark. I ain't gonna waste no more lead from here. Let's go get him. He's down on the ground, and his horse has run off somewhere."

"No." I knew it'd be no use. I hadn't seen exactly what happened, but I was sure the sumbitch was up into that Ute cut now. Technically, Undersheriff Joe Pete was running this posse. He looked doubtful about charging up the damn mountain. So I decided for him.

"It'd take us twenty minutes to get up there, and by then he'll be halfway to Colorado. Or, worse, the sumbitch could stop fifty yards from that shelf, draw a bead, and drop all four of us. Once we're on that switchback, we'd be as open as the man you just missed. He ain't shot no one so far, but no one's backed him into a corner, neither. Let's get back to Chama. I'll wire ahead to Montclair and warn the sheriff there he's headed their way."

The breeze picked up some, and swirled the loose snow around us. The snow had melted some, but up here, the loose ice was making the trail dangerous.

I turned my attention to Bo, thinking I ought to take my quirt to him for spooking that big bay and causing Branson to miss a clean shot. But he stood his ground and took my stare.

"That's what I was asking about before, Captain," he said as if nothing had happened. "I mean if what they say is true, it don't make no sense to offer a small reward for the man. They oughta be more respectful. He's worth over four grand."

"What 'n hell you jawboning about, Bo? The man's a train robber. Now, tell me straight, what have you heard about him?"

"Jus' that he ain't no damn train robber. Folks know him. Maybe he don't think it's rizght your railroad is taking every other section of land along the track. He ain't the only one thinks that's wrong."

I did not have time to explain to this damn fool cowboy, playing at being a deputy sheriff, that the United States Congress had granted the Atchison, Topeka and Santa Fe Railway Company, ownership of land alongside the track as compensation for building the transcontinental railroad system. So, I turned to Undersheriff Joe Pete.

"What kind of deputies do you hire in Chama, Sheriff? Ones that don't respect the law? You didn't tell me this bag of bones was in sympathy with train robbers and anarchists and such. You get him the hell out of my sight 'cause he's off this posse right now. And, his pay comes out of your pocket—I'll see to that."

"You can have your posse, Captain Standard H. Plumb," Bo said. "The man you're chasing lost his young wife some years back, but that don't make him no damn train robber."

Before I could quirt the little bastard, he swung around and pulled his cow horse out of the line. Jumping up onto that double-rig saddle without sticking a boot in stirrup leather, he put the spurs to her. Him and his horse headed straight down the mountain.

Joe Pete shook his head at me and then touched his right index finger to the tip of his hat.

"Well, Captain Standard H. Plumb, there you have it. According to my deputy, which you just fired, the wrong man is heading north over the mountain into Colorado, and my deputy is headed south down to Española . I expect you'll be the talk of the whole dang Española Valley by sundown tomorrow."

CHAPTER 5
Addie in Montclair, Colorado

"**A**DDIE MORTON," I said to the full-length mirror in my bedroom, "you are never going to get to San Francisco looking like you *belong* in Montclair, Colorado!"

"Addie, is that you talking to yourself in the mirror again? I thought we talked about that. Besides . . ."

"I'll thank you not to eavesdrop on me, Robert," I said, with a little stomp of my foot for emphasis. Not that it would do any good. Robert was kind, thoughtful, maddening, and stubborn, but he was the only family I had.

Why does he act like our father? Why can't he see that Montclair, for all its grassy-plains beauty, is not the place for me?

Montclair, Colorado, faced the giant green upswing of earth that separated it from the New Mexico territory. Granite-topped peaks loomed up into the sky almost forty miles across the plains. Between here and there, the seemingly never-ending plains formed a blanket of color in the spring. They sheltered a windy green and yellow plain, vast as the Sonoran Desert, but channeled by innumerable streams. Ten Shoes Up was the highest peak we could see from this part of Colorado.

We only had one street; the other two were more like connecting alleyways. The man who elected himself mayor of Montclair, because he was the first settler here, claims we have over three hundred residents. I suppose his count might be accurate if you made the tally on a Sunday morning, when the ranching and farm families came to church at First Presbyterian. Oh, yes, Mayor Shanley was a Presbyterian and he started the church, too. Probably before sundown on the first day, his little wagon train stopped and he declared Montclair as their final resting place.

Let's hope it's not mine, I told the mirror as I pressed my skirt down with the palms of my hands.

We had the only church, the only bank, and the only school for seventy-five miles in any direction. So, I guess three hundred residents could be true. I knew them all, liked most of them, and wished deep in my heart I wasn't here. Robert and Mayor Shanley insisted that Montclair gave every living soul something to smile at—the white-topped peaks separating us from New Mexico. Like everyone else, I smiled at those peaks every morning. But, like every other day for the last four years, my brain buzzed at what might be beyond them. Far enough south and you'd hit the Gulf of Mexico. Far enough west and the Pacific Ocean would welcome you with wind in your hair. And, just beyond the wind was San Francisco Bay. At least that's what it said in Mr. Robert Thomas's 1880 *Farmer's Almanac*.

But, nobody except me thought about such foolishness as moving to the Gulf of Mexico, not to mention San Francisco Bay.

Montclair's other civilizing claim was that it had the best bank for one hundred fifty miles around, in any direction. Of course, my brother would say that. He founded it, with the small inheritance our parents left to us. But, my favorite Montclair fact, at least for the last two years, was the stagecoach stopped here, twice a week.

Our house was just across the road from the stage stop. While sweeping our little front porch, I heard the Cumberland and Overton's big, five-passenger coach clang its way around the town's water cistern.

Someday soon, I'll climb aboard you and make my way to San Francisco; just you wait.

Just like always, there wouldn't be no one new on the stage, at least anyone who intended to stay awhile. There were young men my age in town. Two to be exact. And, there were a half dozen more scattered out on the small ranches that dotted this part of southern Colorado. But, they all shied away from me like a skittish horse. Or maybe they were all just nervous nellies. Maybe I was shying away from them. I'd confided my concerns to Robert, but he was no help at all.

"It's your smile," he joked. "You've got a fifty-dollar smile and a five-hundred dollar brain. These Colorado ranch hands are working for forty a month and found. Besides, you can waltz. I may never get you married off."

"Not your place, Robert," I reminded him. "Your job is to make sure I've got enough money for a new start in San Francisco when I'm twenty-five. By then, I'll have helped you establish your own social life in small-town Colorado."

My brother, who used to be fun when he was "Bobby," switched to "Robert" the day he opened the front door of his bank, The Bank of Montclair. That was four years ago, when he was only twenty-four and I'd just turned eighteen. Our wagon train had stopped for supplies before pushing on for Oregon. It looked like a good, solid place to start afresh, our father said. And, with that simple observation, he immediately abandoned the family plan to move to Oregon from Dayton, Ohio. Both our parents died of the ague six months later. Robert and I were on our own, and I was only sixteen.

Every time I thought of my mother, whom I adored, and my father, a stern but well-intentioned man, I went rigid. Like now. My fists curled, and my head nodded forward. That awful fever felt real to me. No one ever even tried to explain inexplicable death. Of course not. It is death and it's always close by, they said.

Dying is abandonment. Why, God, if you are a god, did you abandon us in such a godforsaken place as this? My brother loves it so, but I, by god, do not.

"Brother," I called out through the porch window, "the stage's coming."

Despite his youth, Robert was set in his ways. He closed the bank every day at noon for two hours. It was more a New Mexico custom than a Colorado one, which is why he did it. He had as many customers from New Mexico as he did here.

"Big baggage on top, or outriders alongside?" he asked, over my shoulder.

"Come see for yourself. I can't make out what's on top. Old man Spencer's riding shotgun this week. With the same greasy duster and the neckerchief with the holes in it. The man smells so. I hate to wait on him."

Robert walked up behind me, holding his coffee mug in both hands. The dust from the heavy coach swirled behind the five-foot iron-rimmed, spoked wheels and over into the town's rain cistern.

Squinting in the late afternoon sun, Robert gave the matter his usual careful observation.

"They have at least two passengers; one's a man who's lost his horse. See the big saddle up on top, and a flowered suitcase. A man and a woman—but not traveling together. No outrider—means they aren't lugging a strongbox this trip. You'd best get over to the café and make sure Maude's got a late-lunch ready."

Stage travelers liked Montclair. A nice warm café in the Montclair Hotel, a large, well-built stable, and two saloons. Even though the stage always got to town by three o'clock in the afternoon, they stayed overnight. It was a ten-hour pull from here to Alamosa. No one wanted to show up in that sleepy little town after midnight. Only one hotel and it was smaller than ours was.

Robert was right. The middle-aged woman belonged to the flowered suitcase. I'd seen her before. She had kinfolk at one of the ranches north of here. The man was a complete stranger. I watched him drop down out of the coach, then step up onto the leather strapping, which formed a small rear deck on the coach. He effortlessly swung his saddle down. Then, picking up heavy-looking saddlebags, a thinly rolled canvas tarp, bridle and rope, and a rifle snugged inside a deerskin scabbard, he walked over to the boardwalk in front of the hotel.

He did not look around at the town, or the people. Been here before, maybe. Even now, I don't know why, but I studied him more than I do most men who get off the stage. Something about him. But, then he brushed through the swinging doors and into the lobby. He's just another stranger, I thought, on his way from somewhere to somewhere else.

But, he's got an interesting look about him. I'll give him that.

It took me no more than three or four minutes to take off my house apron, walk to the café, and don my café apron. He was still in the lobby and I got a better look over the half-wall separating the café. He looked to be maybe five years older than I was. I mentally measured him at six-feet two, but underweight. He'd dropped his gear down on the floor at the foot of the stairwell. Now, turning away from the little registration desk, he walked like his arms and legs were made of loose rope. As he was facing me, I could see his face and the droop in his shoulders; he looked as tuckered out as any soul I'd seen lately. Bushy eyebrows, a ruddy face, and gray-green eyes, but with a sculpted jaw made of wrought iron.

Not your usual stage passenger, Addie Morton.

Later, after he'd checked in and hauled his kit upstairs, I walked into the lobby to look at the register blotter. "Angus" was the listed name. The lines for home city and how long he'd be here were blank. I suppose most little hotels had registration desks. But ours was different. A polished oak pedestal, with a leather ink blotter, a small bell, and a quill with its own crystal ink barrel.

Orlando Johnstone, slicking down his receding hairline, came into the lobby from his small office behind the registration desk. I hated his pencil-thin mustache, although it matched his smile. As the hotel owner, he was my boss, although I worked for the cook, Estancia Ortiz. It bothered my brother that I worked at the café, now that he owned the only bank in town. But, working gave me a little nest egg—for when I stepped off that stage coach in San Francisco. Some day.

No harm in asking for his name, I thought.

"Mr. Johnstone, what did that stranger say his last name was?"

"Angus," he said, looking down his beaked nose at me. "Angus. His first and last name. Beats all. Ever heard of a man with only one name, Addie?"

"Yes, but only Indians. Could be he was just joshing you."

"No, he's not a joshing man."

Mr. Johnstone had that little smile on his face when he said it. The one he thought everyone would take as friendly. It was merely duplicitous.

"Angus, whatever his last name is, kept that big rifle nestled in the nook of his arm as he signed in. I could see a gun belt under his sheepskin coat. Like I said, not a joshing man. You'd best get back to the kitchen, Addie."

At six that evening, Angus came into the café, looked at me, smiled, and asked where he should sit. Confident man, I thought, but not arrogant. I smiled at every customer—it was how my mother raised me—but with Angus, it was real easy.

"Over there by the window, the small table, or if you're expecting someone, you can sit at the round table in the center. We're not too busy tonight."

After settling himself into the cane-back chair at the table by the window, and carefully placing the dark blue napkin on his lap, he settled himself and turned to me.

"Can I have a beefsteak, done all the way, fried potatoes with onions, please, two fried eggs with the yolks looking up at me, and two bowls of vegetables, please?"

He said "please" twice in one sentence.

I wrote his order down on my tab sheet, looked back at him, and gave him an assessment, hoping he'd take it as a compliment.

"Hungry man," I said. "We need more of you in here."

Silence. Then, as I turned toward the kitchen, he acted as if he was waking up from a short mental nap.

"And a pot of coffee. With toast. Honey for the toast, but no sugar for the coffee."

"Before your steak or as dessert?"

"Before, during, and after, if you don't mind."

With that, he looked down at a small notebook, fished a pencil out of his vest-pocket, and stopped talking. Not exactly smiling, but with the hint of a grin on his face.

I noticed something else, besides the fact he said "please" twice. A fresh smell; something rare at dinnertime.

I'll be damned. This man's just come from the Chinese bathhouse down the street. Hand-cranked soap and a fresh shave, but no bay rum.

Later, when talking to my brother, I recalled his neatly combed hair, and the dark red curls reaching his coat collar. It bothered me he didn't remove his hat. He just ate his meal, slowly cutting each piece of steak and setting his knife on the edge of the plate before putting the food in his mouth.

"Well, that's something," Robert said the next morning at breakfast, showing little interest in a stranger stopping overnight with the stage. No account at the bank, not interested. That was Robert.

"And, he chewed with his mouth closed. Now, that's something," I offered Robert as a retort.

"What else did he say, Addie?"

"Nothing; nothing at all. He ordered his dinner and looked down at a little notebook he'd fished out of his vest-pocket. I was more or less dismissed. So, I just let him be."

I didn't work breakfasts, so I didn't get the note until after my lunch shift. Mr. Johnstone motioned from his perch at the registration desk as I served the only three customers in the café, all at the same table.

"That tall cowpoke you were curious about last night might've taken a fancy to you, Miss Addie."

"What makes you think so?"

"First off, all our customers take a liking to you. Second, he left you a note."

"A note you say? Why would he do that? He never said a word except to order dinner. A dinner with no tip, I might add."

"All the same, he asked me your name, and then used the desk pen to write *Addie* on a little brown envelope. He licked it shut, laid it down, and hauled his kit out to the waiting stage. Didn't say a word, either. Suppose he knew I'd hand it over."

Mr. Johnstone handed me an odd-shaped, beige-colored envelope, smaller than a letter and narrow, like the ones my brother used for change at the bank. He waited for me to open it, but I took it back into the café. I stuck it in my apron pocket and finished clearing the tables and moving the pies around in the glass-fronted cabinet. Estancia was in the kitchen, pouring something from one bowl into another, back and forth. I filled a glass half-full with fresh buttermilk, and sat down at the built-in counter.

He'd written my name on the envelope in a rough, but firm hand. At first I thought the two-inch square card inside was blank. But, when I turned it over there were three neatly printed words, *"Thanks, good dinner."* It wasn't signed. It touched me, but not like you'd think. I'd been here in Montclair for four years.

This is the first note or letter of any kind that I've received since we left Ohio.

There was something else in the envelope. Fishing it out of its tissue paper, I found a Double Eagle, brand new Liberty Head, stamped 1879. For a three-dollar meal! I held it up to the light. It looked real.

Robert will know. If I show him.

I didn't see Angus, the man with only one name, for a month.

CHAPTER 6
Captain Plumb in Santa Fe, New Mexico

SANTA FE SUITED ME just fine. Those who didn't know me on a personal basis addressed me formally—Captain Standard H. Plumb. No one called me Mister. My friends called me Plumb, although I admit there weren't all that many of them. When I checked into the Exchange Hotel, the staff treated me like all the other important men who, from time to time, lived there. It beat the hell out of my other life—riding trains, stages, horses, and sleeping on the ground or in rented rooms at boardinghouses up and down the railroad track. From Chicago to Santa Fe. On the AT&SF, on-the-job, all the goddamned time.

I knew this was an important day for me and I dressed for it. Walking up the central staircase to the Presidential Suite, I felt like I belonged there. I was mighty proud of my brand-new, shiny black, bluchers—a true gentlemen's boot. That's what the salesman thought I was when I paid for them. I reached the third floor's outer lobby and noticed a speck of lint caught in the heavy tongue of my left half-boot. I was wearing these for show—they looked good indoors, but were worthless in the saddle—no big heel and no rack for my spurs. Whisking the speck off, I squared my shoulders and moved toward the guard standing beside the massive double doors to the only apartment on the top floor.

Like all railroad guards, at least at this level, this one wore his best suit. He had a shiny face and smelled like a gentleman ought to smell. Wanting to appear important enough to be recognized, I waited for him to address me. He didn't. He just pointed at one of the two Victorian comfort chairs in the wide hallway. There was a little spindle table between them so I put my hat there. This was good, as it meant I was the only man honored with an appointment this morning.

Without a word, he poured me an Irish whiskey, neat in a cut-glass snifter. He kept his face tight, his jaw shut, and the riffraff out. Good man. He studied me carefully. Expect he was looking for a bulge under my suit coat. Seeing none, he returned and resumed his post beside the entry doors. Looked like a white man trying to mimic a cigar-store Indian. I turned my attention to the little sip of whiskey. It was another suitable gesture, befitting the great man who'd invited me to the best room in the house. I admired the four-wheeled cart, all polished and sparkling, with finely chiseled, little inlaid boxes holding decanters of whiskey, sherry, and chilled water. The mustachioed guard had poured my whiskey without asking whether I wanted one. Gentlemen did this in preparation for important meetings, even if it was ten o'clock in the morning.

"My name's Captain Standard H. Plumb."

"Yes sir, I know."

All railroad guards were armed. This composed man was no different. And, like all the others, he presented the picture of a private security guard who would kill you to keep you from irritating the man inside. He wore his Sam Browne belt, with its checkered cross-strap, dual holsters, and a cast brass buckle with military precision and shine. His left side holster housed a black snub-nosed .32. The right side holster, more a sleeve than a full holster, displayed an eighteen-inch, yellow maple stanchion, with a one-inch-wide wrist strap. Cartridge loops and a special black leather holster for a shiny set of handcuffs completed the rig.

He looked down the hall, never at me. I studied my bluchers and the rim of the crystal glass in my hand. The ritual drink had been dutifully handed off. Protocol demanded we ignore each other. As I sipped the whiskey and let the aroma tickle my nose, I could not help but think my job might be on thin ice. Best to be well-dressed and confident at a time like this. A hand-painted plaque, with no room number, proclaimed in gold gilt, *The Presidential Suite.*

A knock came from inside the room. Nodding slightly, the guard growled, "He'll see you now."

Standing up, I set the whiskey snifter down, squared my shoulders in the gilt-edged mirror, and stepped into the suite. This was my second meeting with one of America's richest and most successful men. The first time had been in his private railcar at night. The dark elegance of that eight-foot-wide space paled in the grandeur of this huge room in the bright sun of a New Mexico morning. Six-foot tall bay windows, on three sides of the room, overlooked San Francisco and Shelby streets, with the Plaza open to the third side. A Spanish *fonda* or boardinghouse had occupied this corner since Santa Fe's founding in 1607. It would later become *La Fonda*.

The country was marching westward and Santa Fe was right smack dab in the middle of things. Back then, 1880, Santa Fe was bigger than Los Angeles. The railroad track might have stopped at Lamy, twelve miles to the east, but Santa Fe was the official terminus of the *Atchison Topeka and Santa Fe Railway*. The track would soon run all the way to Los Angeles, by way of Albuquerque, where the AT&SF made good on its boast of joining the Midwest to the Pacific Ocean. That's why the President of America's second largest railway company, Thomas Jefferson Nickerson, was here. I squared myself knowing he would soon be demanding straight answers from me.

Two men were on the far side of the room. One, sitting on a double leather sofa, didn't look up. The other, a short unbalanced man with a slight limp and a droopy left eye, moved toward me. The finely polished oak floorboards were dressed with oval shaped, deep maroon and black carpets. As he walked in my direction, Arthur Steen, general counsel for the AT&SF, addressed me in that deep baritone I'd come to know well.

"Mornin', Captain. Have a seat over here, if you don't mind."

"I don't mind atall. And, thanks for the hallway whiskey—always a nice way to start the morning."

As though he were a tour guide instead of one of America's smartest lawyers, Steen said, "This room's forty-foot square. This furniture is from Mr. Nickerson's Chicago home. Do you favor antiques, Plumb? If so, you'll want to look around and pay special attention to the frescos on the Roman fireplace there." He pointed to the far end of the room where Nickerson maintained his focus on the papers in his lap.

I figured either Steen was marking time until Nickerson was ready or this was a staged entrance to unsettle me. It did. Following Steen's pointed finger, I sat on one of three sofas facing the Piñon logs burning in the fire pit. Sinking back into the brocaded seat cushions, I cleared my throat, intending to make a comment to Steen about the wrought iron fire stand.

Nickerson, without looking at either of us, held up his hand and motioned for us to quit talking. For two full minutes, no one said anything.

"All right then," Nickerson said, putting the sheaf of papers on the low table in front of him, and stroking his Van Dyke beard.

Turning slightly in his chair to face me, he continued, "Plumb, your handwriting is atrocious. Steen here must have your reports typed by my secretary before they are legible." Then, turning his attention back to Steen, he lifted his first finger up, as though he was conducting the first violinist in his own personal orchestra.

On cue, Steen turned. "Captain, you missed him. What's your excuse?"

"Well, Mr. Steen, you see, my man Branson must have flinched at the last second because the shot careened . . ."

Steen waved me off. "No, Captain. What Mr. Nickerson and I want to know is why *you* missed him. We have your written report, with your discourse on a seven-hundred-yard shot into the wind, uphill, at a moving target. It would have been a miracle if the shot *had* got him. What we need from you is why he got seven hundred yards away from you. You'd been right on his tail for seven weeks, although if I'm reading your report correctly, you were not even successful in learning his name.

"Here's the thing, my good man. No one, despite a considerable investigation, has ever seen the lone man who robs our trains at will. No one can say anything about him, except he's a passenger. He gets on, robs without anyone noticing, gets off, and then leaves the train at will. It was sheer luck the conductor, on this last embarrassment, gave you a clue to the man's name. Angus, is it? A Scot, you think. You chased. He escaped. That's the nut of it, Captain. Why can't you grasp this?"

"He is the robber! I'm sure of it—"

"Your report says the man you chased for two days *might* have been the man who robbed the train," Steen interrupted. "But no one saw him. No one identified him as a robber, or a passenger. He was just a man standing by a railroad trestle in Colorado, who may have been from somewhere in New Mexico. That's all you know about him."

"He's the man, Mr. Steen. If he's innocent, why did he run? We tracked him from that trestle to a camp three miles away. He had a horse there waiting for him. We tracked that horse for a day and a half and caught up to him as he tried to elude us by using an old Indian trail over a ten-thousand-foot mountain."

"Ah, Plumb, he did not *try* to elude you; he plainly *did* elude you."

Nickerson looked up, raised his cane a few inches off the floor, and then tapped the end softly on the oak.

"Captain Plumb. You're a fine man with a secure future. But, your grasp of what is at stake here worries me. Do you even know our business? It's not just a railroad. We are selling vision, you fool!"

Nickerson commenced a coughing spell and pulled a brown silk handkerchief out of an inside pocket. Dabbing his mouth, and taking a sip of water from a half-full glass on the table, he continued.

"Vision of the West. Our vision, with every other section of land adjacent to our tracks. Do you realize the price, the gain, the vastness of the thing?"

Steen reached over and stirred another spoonful of brown sugar into his tea. Nickerson walked over to the fireplace as the lawyer continued, "Do you know, Captain, how much land Congress allotted to us to build the transcontinental railway? We own every other section on the line. A section of land is six-hundred-and-forty acres, man. Multiply that five thousand times. That's the vastness of the thing. We will be transporting new settlers to the West by the tens of thousands."

"And, every one of those new settlers rides our train at a discounted price," Nickerson chimed in, looking only at the fire. "They buy a parcel of land from us; we give them a free ride. They see new lives for their families in the magnificent American West. That's what I mean by the vision business, Captain."

"This man, Angus," Steen said, "a man with no known last name, could become to us what the Russian winter was to Napoleon. He's just dabbled so far, three robberies with only thirty-thousand dollars to show for it. But, what if a dime novelist, or a cheap yellow journalist, gets ahold of the story? What if he were to write a story about this Angus fellow? That could undo all of it, man. And, if you do not resolve this, he will be the end of you!"

"Me?" I stammered.

"You. And, my good man, I don't mean just your job."

Nickerson left the fireplace and walked behind my sofa, tapping his cane on the floor, and whooshing away the smoke from Steen's now smoldering cigar. "So, get him by the spring thaw, Plumb. You can count on a generous bonus. I expect you'll need to hire some other good fellows to track him down. You do know where to look, don't you?"

"Yes, sir, I believe I do. He's from Chama or thereabouts. He hides out in the canyons along the Toltec Gorge. He's mostly on horseback, which makes him hard to track, and . . ."

Nickerson banged his cane hard down onto the hardwood floor.

I jumped. Twisting my head back toward him, I faced the brass tip of that cane pointed square at me.

"Good Lord, man! You didn't think I was talking about geography, did you? He's taken thirty thousand dollars from us, some of it in gold coin. Follow the money. The man won't be far away. Don't all detectives know that elementary protocol?"

Nickerson left the room, with Steen and me sitting in silence. My first thought was that Steen would hold it against me for not standing when Mr. Nickerson left the room. But, I was rattled by the sound of that brass-tipped cane slamming down on the oak floorboards. Steen got up, came over, and took hold of my elbow—gentle, like I was an elderly aunt. Steering me back to the double doors, he stopped just in the lee of the left-hand door and said, "He's got a bank, man. Find it and you'll find him. He's not the kind to bury it in a gunnysack. He's too smart for that. How do I know he's smart? I can see the question on your face. Hell, man, he just steals it out from under our noses. A man that resolute will want good interest on his account."

CHAPTER 7
Angus in Alamosa, Colorado

I GOT OFF THE STAGE in Alamosa after the daylong ride down from Montclair. Gathering up my kit, I crooked the Winchester in my arm, swung the saddle and tack over my shoulder, and headed inside the livery barn. As I lugged my way through the fifteen-foot-high double doors, Aposto, the barrel-bellied livery keeper, gave me a big-toothed grin, and rushed to take the saddle off my shoulder.

"*Me alegro de verte otra vez*, Señor Angus. But I'm sorry to see you afoot. I'm right, *si*? Where's that big bay gelding I sold to you, what, maybe four years ago? I think you named him Tucson, is that right?"

"Good to see you too, *mi amigo*, but we had a little wreck on Ten Shoes Up, and Tucson took a big cut in his shoulder muscle. So, I left him with a rancher east of here."

"Left him? Watch you mean, Señor? Left such a fine animal as Tucson? I dunno about that."

"Tucson's the best horse I ever rode, Aposto. But, it'll take six weeks for that tear to mend. The rancher will board him until I can get back that way. Don't worry yourself about it. I expect to be astride him before the spring thaw."

"OK, Señor, I guess you came here on the stage, or maybe the railroad."

"I came in on the stage. You ever ridden one of them damn things? Like a bad trot downhill, riding with a loose cinch, on a cheap saddle."

Nodding his head, Aposto said, "I got horses to sell. You need one, right?"

"Right. And supplies, too. I was thinking of maybe packing, so maybe you've got a good pack mule, too?"

"Sí. I have a small mule and two burros. But, Señor, I have something also that you should see. I have a mustang, a long-legged buckskin that a vaquero rode here from Texas. I had him five months now, but he will take a real hand to line him out. You, of course, are just the hand. And, I also have a big gelding; got him last week from a silver miner up in Wolf Creek Pass. He has coal black feet. You know what that means when you're packing a heavy load of supplies. Look at these horses."

As we were walking to the corrals behind the barn, Aposto asked, "Hey, Señor, you know a Pinkerton is looking for you, que no?"

"Which one?"

"It's the Capitan but I don't know his name. He don't give up so easy, que no? I heard he was in Chama last week or sometime and was not happy about something. I dunno what. But, a cowboy from the *Dos S* was in here just yesterday to bring me five horses for the stage line. He told me the Capitan was still looking for you."

"Looking where?"

"He don't know. But, he says if I see anyone that wants to know, I tell them to stay away from the *Dos S* brand, also. So I'm careful not to sell you horses from down there. You know those *Dos S* cowboys are some mean hombres. Except this boy, he seemed OK."

"Ask about me by name?"

"*Si*. Angus."

"And his name?"

"Bo. Bo String. I dunno about a name like that. Watch you think?"

We talked a little more, and then Aposto cut out the mustang and the big stout bay I could pack on. He declined to make me a dirt price on one of the mules. He called them burros, but they were mules. Never took to mules. I bought the buckskin-colored mustang to ride, and the big bay to use as a packhorse, horses for thirty-five dollars, cash. A bargain, I thought. So did Aposto. Once I'd brushed them out, they looked like easy keepers, although the buckskin took to twirling.

"I appreciate you telling me and keeping your ear to the ground about the Pinkertons. *Gracias por el caballo*. That little mustang looks like he's a mountain climber. And, Amigo, I left something on the shelf for you."

He smiled, turned his back and walked back to his room inside the big open area of the barn. I watched as he reached up to the shelf above the door. He shook off the dust, mouse

turds, and a spider web, and then carefully opened the little
envelope and removed the wrapped twenty-dollar Liberty
Head. Smiling back at me, he tried to bend it with his teeth,
spat on it, and rubbed it on his leather apron. I knew he'd be
a little drunk by the time I reached the south fork of the Oso
Negro creek, ten miles south of town. I also knew he'd keep
my business to himself.

An hour later, I brushed and saddled the five-year-old
mustang, picked his feet, and had to reset the left front shoe.
I'd brushed both horses, but I gave the big bay a strong back
rub with a little molasses drip and a gunnysack. I bought a
forked packsaddle, two canvas tarps, packing ropes, tie-downs,
and enough grain for two horses from Aposto, along with a
quart jug of cane sugar. It took purtin' near an hour's hag-
gling in Spalding's Dry Goods Store. Course, some of that was
drinking coffee time in front of the potbellied stove. I bought
a month's worth of food stock, bacon, beans, coffee, and two
pounds of fresh elk jerky packed in waxed paper. Old man
Spalding sacked twenty pounds of grain for the horses in
one-pound sugar sacks. He stacked three boxes of .30-40 rifle
cartridges, two .45 boxes for my Colt, and a can of gunpowder
along with fifty feet of fuse line, on the counter. I stuffed all
of it into two strapped canvas bags so I could diamond hitch
'em to the packhorse.

My new mustang was a little tight—a barn will sour a
good horse in five months. The big bay packhorse paid no
attention to the nearly one hundred pounds of supplies tied
down with a diamond hitch over the canvas tarp. I swung a
leg over the mustang. He gave me a little Texas spin causing
me to miss the offside stirrup. Snatching the lead rope from

Aposto, I turned south, ponying the packhorse, and feeling loose in the saddle for the first time in three days. Crossing the river south of town as the sun dropped lower over the horizon, I started talking to my horses.

"Well, boys, we're headed for good grass, clear water, and maybe a storm. Antonito is over that way. Long ride. We'll take our time, but stay away from things that might bother us. People, mostly."

Rubbing the horse's oversized neck, I commenced to putting him through gaits, changing leads, and checking his trail manners. After long-trotting him for three miles, I said, "Well, son, let's see if we can get the notion of that warm barn out of you."

Shifting my pelvis forward in the saddle, I pressed my thighs down on his withers. He surged forward. I held him in a long, easy lope that stretched him out, without straining him, or pushing his knees and hooves too hard. We were running in tall grass bordering a prairie stream. I was paying attention to avoid anything that looked like a bog. The mustang took to ponying the bay easy. He'd been used as packhorse. From his steady gait, I figured the boys using him must have been in a perpetual hurry. He long-trotted easy like, keeping the pack centered on his back. As I leaned into his neck, with the reins held high in my left hand, I dallied the mustang's lead rope one turn around my saddle horn with my right hand. He took the cue and moved from a lope to a full gallop.

Making sure my boot heels were well behind the stirrup, with my spurs pointed out about thirty degrees, I ran him flat out a quarter mile. Then, slow-like, I backed him down to a long trot.

"Easy, son, that'll do it."

The mustang chinned up and twisted his head back a time or two, keeping a nervous watch on the packhorse behind us. During the run, I felt his raw muscle thunder up through his withers to my legs. Soon enough, my lower back argued with me. But, if I rode easy off the cantle, I could keep my weight centered above the cinch.

At the end of the run, he started to wheeze, and lather up. I knew he'd be slick as a fresh-caught trout under his saddle pad. So, as I eased back on the reins, tugging him down, I watched his neck muscles settle. The packhorse snorted behind us. Then, easing down into a walk, I gave him another fifty yards to cool down, before walking him over to the small stream.

Dismounting from the offside, I tested the last cowboy to ride this young horse. He did not flinch as I reached up and flattened first one ear, then the other. He held his chest steady when I pulled up on the onside D-ring, and loosened the cinch. Then, loosening the breast collar, and tugging his chinstrap just a little, I watched him watch me through a big copper eye. Feeling comfortable with the horse's manners, I dropped the split reins flat to the water and watched his head drop back down to draw on the cool water. I let him suck up half-a-belly full, and then pulled him back out of the streambed by the front saddle strings. No shying away. Ears up and straight.

The packhorse paid no attention to either of us, as he sucked as much water as he thought he could hold. Packhorses and camels, I thought—*smarter than town folk.*

"Damn fine ride, son," I said, stepping out in front of him, just a little, and scratching his forehead. Using the backside of my glove, I wiped off the salt-colored sweat all the way down his head to his long jawbone and around his nostrils. Not a ripple, although he gave me the copper eye the whole time.

"OK, Horse. You're a keeper. Come winter, or maybe spring, I'll give you a name. None that fits you comes to mind. So, for now, I'll call you Horse."

The long gallop had loosened Horse's girth, the tie-downs on his saddlebags, my rifle case, bedroll, and my duster. So, I loosened the stampede string on my hat, pushed it back, and retied and rechecked every part of his tack.

Then I double-checked the diamond tie on the bay. The frame had moved back four or five inches. Loosening both cinches, I centered the load. Then, hitching up my chaps, I walked back to the bay, jumped my left boot into the stirrup, swinging my right leg over the cantle as fast as I could. He didn't spin. Cooing to Horse, I neck-reined him away from the creek bed and steered him south in what seemed his natural long walk gait. Clamping down inward ever so slightly with my knees, I tapped my left boot to his underbelly, moving Horse into a steady trot.

We trotted for almost an hour, and I paid close attention for signs of nervous sweat along the edges of the saddle blanket. Nothing to bother him. Then, just as I thought I had a real dream of a horse, the damn fool bolted five feet to the right at the sound of a faraway gunshot. I stuck, but had to grab the horn. I spun a quick look over my shoulder at the packhorse. He was tense, but not spooked. I'm guessing the shot was a ways off, probably over the next ridgeline to the east. It wasn't aimed at me, but since I'm the cautious sort, I headed the other way—due west.

CHAPTER 8

Captain Plumb Heads Back to Chama

MR. NICKERSON'S SPEECH about catching Angus before he could mess up the AT&SF's vision of the West was still causing me a gut pain something fierce. The only thing worse than a gut ache is having one on horseback. Truth be told, I hate long horseback rides. The morning after Mr. Nickerson and Mr. Steen checked out of the La Fonda, I took the stage-coach from Santa Fe up to Raton. Spent the night in a Mexican boardinghouse. Dreadful. Yesterday, I took the next stage to Antonito, Colorado, where I switched to the Denver & Rio Grande railroad back down to Chama. All that just to avoid a two-day horse ride from Santa Fe, direct to Chama. I love trains and hate horses.

Two drummers, one hawking cooking pots from Chicago, the other selling olive oil-based medicines, pitched a cattle buyer from Texas for thirty-odd miles as the train slow-poked its way from Antonito to Osier. The first thirty-mile stretch of track is most interesting. Winding all the way through the Toltec Gorge, a man can look up and see mile-high mountains on both sides.

"Could you gentlemen hold your pitching for a while? Lots to see out those windows beside you," I said.

They paid me no mind. I tried a diversion. "You boys ever wondered why they call this part of the trip the whiplash?" I asked. No answer in my direction.

"Well, let me tell you," I said ignoring the fact that they were ignoring me.

"It's an interesting engineering story. You see, we're at an elevation of nearly nine thousand feet through here. Trains slip a lot on steep hills. To gain altitude, the railroad track must be made to loop back on itself. Isn't that interesting?"

They just kept jabbering about their cooking pots and how olive oil made medicine nearly goddamned perfect. I had the *Denver Post*, but it lost my attention when we got to Osier, because of forty miles worth of jabbering from the damn drummers.

"All right! You boys best listen now. I am Captain Standard H. Plumb, chief of railroad security on this line. There's railroad families living here, and they are all a wantin' to buy your goods. So, either you get off here and sell something, or I will have to shoot you for talking me to death."

They shut up. Never made another peep, even when we crossed over Cumbres Pass, the highest damn point on the line at over ten thousand feet up into the sky. Cold, too, on account of twenty-foot high snowdrifts, right here on the track.

They got a snow blower engine with a big-ass propeller on the front. But, no need for that today.

A mine guard sat across from an Indian agent in opposing seats at the front of the car. They glared at each other for thirty-five miles. For part of the way, I tried to give them a talk about President Nickerson's vision of the American West. No one seemed interested. So, I studied the hundreds of side canyons that had dug their way down from the tree line into the river. We crisscrossed over trestle bridges every mile or so. Good place to hide if you're robbing trains, I thought.

"Evening, Captain," Undersheriff Joe Pete said, as I stepped off the end of the train and took in a lung full of Chama's crisp mountain air. "How was your ride?"

"Excellent, Sheriff, thanks for meeting me. Were you able to locate that posse man, Bo String, like I asked in my telegram?"

"I sent word, but his new outfit, the Long Jake, is on fall roundup right now, so I doubt he'll be here for another two weeks or so."

Just as well, I thought. I had in mind offering him another chance at posse work. Because I had a feeling he knew something he wasn't telling us. If I could have got him out of town, I'd have had Branson beat the shit out of him.

"I thought he rode for the *Dos S* brand."

"He did. But, he up and quit right after we lost your man on *Ten Shoes Up*. I suppose you're here to talk about that."

Lowering my voice, as we passed a small crowd of locals standing between the café and barbershop, I said, "Sheriff, do you mind waiting to talk business till we get to your office?"

"You're the boss, Captain."

"As long as we're just shooting the bull, Sheriff, tell me something about that huge gorge I just came through, the Toltec. Looked to be some damn fine trout holes down there in the river. Saw some elk and a fair amount of bear sign when we topped out at ten thousand feet over the Cumbres Pass. You live in a fine place, even if it's hard to get to from Santa Fe."

"Well, thank you, Captain, that means something from a man as well traveled as you. The gorge is a wild place. Hard to get out of, except by riding from one end to the other. The train has made it easy, but back in the day it was one hell of a ride by horseback. "

The Chama Sheriff's office looked like every other sheriff's office in the 1880s, on both sides of the territorial line. Colorado achieved statehood in 1876, but I knew it would take New Mexico a lot longer. There was not all that much to Joe Pete's office. An oak desk cluttered with ashes, glasses, and paper filings. Four sturdy wood armchairs, a round table for writing. One cane-back armless chair, a bookcase one-third full of stacked paper, two cells with two bunks, a pair of chamber pots, and a cast iron sink. But, on the south wall, facing the street, Undersheriff Pete had something slightly richer than any other town this size I'd ever been in. He had a finely crafted Walnut, twelve-slot gun rack, with a locked ammunition drawer at the bottom.

"You got a fine collection of guns there, Sheriff. Is that a Model 1873 you got?"

"No, sir!" he beamed. "You are looking at the Winchester Model 1874, the finest shooting rifle ever made. That's a .40 caliber but they make it in a big fifty caliber, too. This one here's especially good for shooting from horseback. Expect you already know that, though."

"No, can't say that I do. What makes you think it's better on horseback?"

Taking the gun out of the rack, Pete pointed to the hammer. "Because this model holds a stack of pelleted primers and when you flip this over...see right there? It flips over this little nipple each time you pull the trigger, making the hammer fall quicker and smack-dab on the casing. Beats all hell out of most everything else. Most others employ individually loaded percussion caps."

"Well, don't you go telling my man Branson about that. He thinks his .50 Hawken is the finest long-barreled gun ever made."

Pete smiled, "Well, Captain, your man Branson is living in the stone age of long-range shooting. These new guns came out of the Civil War, where the world's best sniper shooters perfected their skills. Was Branson part of all that?"

"Does he look like he's that old?" I said.

"Suppose not, but he's not a man to stare at, if you know what I mean."

A long hat rack on one wall, wanted posters nailed to the opposing wall, and a picture of President Rutherford B. Hayes filled out the rest of the office. Pete took his seat behind the desk and got down to business.

"How can we help you today, Captain?"

"It's that damn Angus, Sheriff. He's still loose and that means my employer's trains are at risk. You interested in making more money helping me find that bastard?"

"So, you and your shooter, Branson, didn't find anything the other side of the mountain last month?"

"No, nothing for sure, that is. A rancher down the other side told the sheriff in Montclair that a man walked into his place leading a bay with a big cut on his hip. He worried about laming him, so he walked the horse in. Then he asked the rancher to take care of the horse—a big bay, he said it was. He left two Double Eagles for feed. How about that? Then, the man walked a half-mile to the main road where he must have hailed the stage into Montclair. By the time we got there, he was gone. They said over to Alamosa. I believe that man was Angus."

"Yep, figured that."

"Can you help me some more?"

"Yes, sir. How much more did you have in mind?"

"I reckon about two, maybe three weeks."

"I meant money. How much more money?"

"Ten dollars a day. And they've upped the reward. Angus is getting under their skin. The AT&SF is willing to pay ten thousand dollars for him and the Denver and Rio Grande is thinking about adding to the pot. They want me to take a share of the new money. I'll be taking half. The other half goes to you. Hell with Bo String. Hell with Branson, too, unless he comes through, and actually shoots the sumbitch. Course, we'd want you to get us a fresh warrant. You can do that, can't you?"

"A warrant? Well, let's see. Judge Bickel ain't particular about those things. He trusts me. If I say Angus is a train robber, he'll sign an arrest warrant. But, Captain? I'm wondering if there is hard evidence that Angus is your man. No one saw him do anything except stand by a train trestle after a robbery. Even then, you said the witness was not all that sure. And there's another thing. It's fall round-up time. They are moving cattle from high meadows down to lower ground. There's few unemployed cowhands out there right now. If I'm not asking too much, what's the burr under the railroad's saddle? Hell, he's just one man and he ain't hit you all that hard, has he?"

"Sheriff, you and I don't get paid to think. But my boss, Mr. Thomas Jefferson Nickerson, the by-God for damn-sure President of the AT and the SF Railroad is a thinking man. He asked for my opinion. I'll tell you what I told him. You see, this one man could not have pulled off three train robberies unless he was real smart and had people helping him. He does not have a gang, but someone's helping him. Hellfire, he never blows anything up. So, I figure I'd better outsmart him. I know how to catch him."

"Well, I expect you're right. But, that don't tell me why the by-God president has to fret over one man. You'll catch him. Winter's coming. He'll settle in somewhere. You can look for him come spring."

The tin-glazed coffeepot on the wood stove in the far corner of the room hissed a little as I helped myself to a fresh cup. Taking a firm hold on the ragged, fold-over leather glove, I moved the pot handle and used my bare hand on the metal hanger. "You make good coffee, Sheriff. Tastes like last's week brew. Strong as a Mexican blood bull. You wouldn't have a little bottle of coffee sweetener, would you?"

"Bottom drawer of the gun cabinet, in there with my ammunition, Captain. Help yourself."

I poured two dollops from the quart bottle.

"Now would you look at that? *Jas. E. Pepper*, of Lexington Kentucky, bonded bourbon. You are drinking above your pay grade, Sheriff. Now about this man, Angus, I think we'll catch him, but not in the usual way. See, he's not going to stick his loot in a sack and hide thirty thousand dollars in gold coins under the floorboards of his shack. He's going to put it in a bank. Hell, he could probably live off the interest, don't you think?"

Joe Pete started to laugh, and then thought better of it. "You want to raise a posse to check on bank accounts?"

"No, Sheriff, I do not. I want you to help me find people with connections to bankers or land agents. They know where this man is. Hell, he's got to come see them sometime; otherwise his ill-got gains from robbing my employer ain't going to do him no good."

Pete could not hold it back any longer. "Hoowee, Captain, that's a story I thought I would never hear! You mean to tell me he's robbing you and then putting the money in the bank? Don't that beat all. Bo String was right."

Just then, two middle-aged men with matching aprons spilling over their belts, pushed open the door and marched in like soldiers. One wore gold-rimmed spectacles. Other than that, they looked identical. Ignoring me and the coffee cup in the sheriff's hand, they yammered at the sheriff, both speaking and neither listening to the other.

"Sheriff Pete, my brother's at it again!"

"I ain't either!"

"He's taking orders meant for me."

"They're mine!"

"We have got to put my brother in his place and you need to tell that railway agent, or his deliveryman, to take better notice when delivering goods to our store."

"Ain't nothing wrong with him delivering to my side of the store."

"Ain't your side!"

"Is too!"

"No, it ain't . . ."

The brother with the spectacles finally ran out of breath. The other one kept muttering, almost to himself.

"I ain't doing no such thing . . . my order, not his . . . he has no use for flat tin or baking soda."

Undersheriff Pete must have heard it all before, but it struck me as interesting. As I heard the twins banter, I gathered that Chama had a dry goods store *and* an outfitters' supply store. Most places this small would only have one store for both trades. Finally, when they'd had their say, Undersheriff Pete moved his boots off the desk and leaned forward in his chair.

"Morning Tom, Ed. How's business down at the store? Sounds like you should have kept the family business intact instead of splitting it up into two competing stores."

The brothers argued with each other for the next couple of minutes. I sipped sweetened coffee in the corner. The sheriff gave them a lecture.

"Of course, the law should allow a man to order goods and not have his brother take delivery. That's what I told you last time you came stomping in here. Now listen to me. I could ask Judge Bickel for a hearing on this dispute. I could tell him that Tom's ordering tin goods for his dry goods store. Ed is taking delivery of the tin goods over on his side—in what you boys call the outfitters store. I could tell him the brothers ain't all that brotherly. You boarded up the family store right down the middle, which confuses Arturo Chavez most every time he tries to deliver your stuff from the railroad shipping office. But, the judge might want you boys to take down that wooden siding you put up in the middle of your folks' old store. Is that what you want me to do?"

The Wall brothers were not one bit satisfied with this kind of justice. Nonetheless, they thanked the undersheriff for listening. Separately, they toddled back down the street to their one-door store with two cash registers and a five-foot wall down the middle.

"Coffee holding up OK, Captain? I could put some fresh grounds in the bottom of the pot, and you're welcome to as much sweetener as you like. Gives your belly a warm feeling, don't you think?"

I took his fresh remarks as a reminder to get things ironed out, nice and flat. "Sheriff, we have it on good authority that Angus is a risk to our enterprise. The railroad that employs me wants me to make it clear to you we are serious about our president's vision. He's opening the American West to every right thinking easterner who can afford a ticket west."

Pete pushed away from his desk and headed for the ammunition drawer. "I believe I need a little sweetener, myself." He poured one dollop into his mug. "Captain Plumb, I do not know anything about these visions of the American West. What is your exact point here?"

"Just this: Angus is smart. A lot smarter than the average storekeeper, like your Wall brothers. And, he might be just smart enough to know how to cripple our enterprise. If we cannot catch one man robbing the train at will, what's to prevent a dozen men robbing all the trains whenever they get the urge?"

"Well, Captain, how do I catch somebody who's smart enough to do that?"

"You do not need to pay any mind to that. I have confidential information on this. What I need from you is Angus's background, where he's from, who he can count on, and where he banks his money. You can ask questions and get answers. This is not horseback work. It's talking work. You can use the teletype at the station agent's office for free. So, ask around, because what we need now is information. I'm authorized to pay you for twenty days' work at eight dollars a day. If you want the job, just nosing around, I'll get the money wired to you. You probably won't be out in the field until we get a reliable sighting on him. Winter's coming, so he's got to land somewhere."

"Maybe not, Captain. Winter don't bother a mountain man like him. He's a plenty tough hombre from all I hear. But sure, I can use eight dollars a day, plus a cut of the reward. And, when I see Bo String, I'll send you a wire. Meanwhile, I'll nose around for bank accounts. You staying over to the Chama Hotel?"

"Just for the night. I'm going to follow the Rio Chama on down to Santa Fe on the stage. Let me know what you find out."

CHAPTER 9
Angus in the Toltec Gorge and the Rio Los Piños

I TIED HORSE TO A FORTY-FOOT tall blue spruce, snugged back from the rock face, two miles above Osier. Seemed a fine spot to watch the train crew stoke the coal bin and fill the water tanks.

The train took close to six hours to haul itself up from Antonito in Colorado to Osier, which was but a mile or two north of the New Mexico Territorial line. Steep inclines made for a long hard pull up to Osier. Then there was slow going through Sublette, before the steam engine puffed across the Cascade Creek trestle. In most places, there was no way for a man to ride his horse alongside the track—just wasn't wide enough because of the granite cuts coming out of the Toltec Gorge.

I squatted back on my heels next to a moss-covered rock the size of a bull. Easing my Warner & Swasey prism binoculars, I was careful to protect the lenses from sun glare. Sighting in on the water tower, even from two miles up, I could see the twenty-foot diameter tank, built on twelve-foot railroad tie stilts. The tank held almost five thousand gallons of water from a ground well on the slope just above the tank. Nobody around. I figured the train would chug in there 'bout noon.

Studying the ground, I tried to reckon out the distance from my little looking spot downslope to the coal bin and from there to the closest stand of aspen and birch. It was less than two hundred yards. Open range, tall grass, no covering trees. From the closest cover to the northern edge of the forest was a good quarter-mile. Seemed a right-fine place to rob a train.

An hour later, I heard the engine and saw a faint trail of black smoke billowing to my left down toward Rock Tunnel. Ten minutes later the engine inched into view. As it topped the meadow, the engineer blew his steam whistle to let the guards in the caboose know they were approaching their first and only stop on the daylong run. On some trips, the train would pick up miners needing a ride down the mountain to Chama. I couldn't see any movement around the water tower, or close to the lumber stacked on the far side of the track.

As the train slowed down, the engineer squealed his brakes, and then eased off the big handle, letting the train continue rolling toward the tower's water chute. The smokestack quit billowing, and I could see the engine and all three hooked cars. Naturally, the engine was first, and then came the mail car, followed by the passenger car and caboose. I'd been on that caboose once—a small kitchen, two tables, and seats for guards, or train employees moving from one job to another. I spied out several empty seats. Looked to be several men, one in overalls, and the others in traveling clothes, standing on the gangway between the mail car and the passenger car.

The engineer stuck his head out. From this distance, it looked like he was studying something on the ground below the engine. I panned the binoculars down and adjusted the dual lens wheel slightly. There was a dead animal, probably a young fawn, alongside the tracks. As the train passed by, the engineer tipped his hat. Good man, I thought.

The crew spent a scant twelve minutes to fill the water tanks. Seven passengers, dressed mostly in city clothes, suits, ties, low boots, and various hats, got off and wandered up and down the short train, stretching their legs, and lighting up cigars. Only two of them seemed interested in the terrain, and no one paid any attention to my little rock ledge a half-mile up.

Training my binoculars on the mail car, I realized that no one had opened the door, and no one passed from the passenger car forward from the gangway into the mail car. No one stepped down from the caboose. I could not tell how many guards might be in either car. Based on my experience with the AT&SF line running through Trinidad, I guessed one guard in the mail car, and another drinking coffee in the caboose.

The tin chimneys on the tops of the cars looked like little top hats from where I was. Each car had a small wood stove. Their stacks were only about ten inches above the top of each car. The fourth tin stack was a reliever from the toilet room at the front of the passenger car. For the sake of the women who used the toilets, the passenger car designers included a small grate in the ceiling to suck up any noxious air left behind by gentlemen travelers. Leastways, that's what a conductor told me once.

Horse whined. I looked back to the tree where I'd tied him, and clicked at him. Then I scanned the crowd of men to see if any of them had heard Horse. No sign. No one looking our way. Of course, we were nigh onto two miles distant, but sound carries a long way at ten thousand feet. Up this high, train smoke floats in the air. The icy water sluicing down the chute into the big tank sitting on top of the engine sounded like the paddle wheel on a riverboat.

The *Rio de los Piños* runs west before emptying into the *Rio Chama* alongside a good part of the train track. Before the train arrived, I thought I could hear a faint ripple of water from the river below me, almost three miles from my squat point.

This was the third time I'd scouted the twenty-five mile run from Chama to Osier. I was sure that no posse from either side of the territorial border could get up here unless they added a horse car to the train.

CHAPTER 10
Angus in Antonito, Colorado

I LIKED ANTONITO, which was saying something, seeing as how I wasn't all that fond of towns. This one had something to brag about. It was the eastern terminus of the *AT&SF Railroad* and the southern terminus of the *San Luis and Rio Grande Railroad*. And, like every other visitor in a small town, I was there to go somewhere else. They all looked at me with either suspicion or kindness as I hobbled from the stage stop 150 feet up the muddy road to the railroad station.

No one back in Chama would have recognized me today. I looked thirty years older, walked on crutches, wore rags I'd picked up in a trash bin, and carried a bright red gunnysack. Most folks looked at me and turned away, except for those that zeroed in on the red gunnysack. Either way, I'd be remembered for something I wasn't. That's the way disguises work. I read that in a dime novel I bought in Denver. *Angus, ain't you a sight?*

My old man smell came from a generous lathering of talcum powder, Epsom salts, and vinegar. I'd mixed it up after I got off the stage from Alamosa, where Aposto was kind enough to let me have one of his famous red gunnysacks. I'd aged myself properly in the change room at the Chinese bathhouse on the edge of town.

The ticket booth in the Antonito train station was exactly like every other booth on the railroad—small, drafty, but sporting well-swept pine floorboards. Station agents always swept their floors when they weren't selling tickets, and they only sold tickets once a day.

"Where you headed, old timer?" the needle-nosed clerk on the other side of the brass ticket window asked.

"Chama," I mumbled, talking out of the side of my mouth. I'd stuck a marble in the right side of my mouth, creating what looked like a tumor on my jawbone. That and the two-week old beard, aged by gray powder mixed with foot oil, made folks want to be shed of me as quick as possible. I used the sleeve of my ragged wool coat to muffle a sneeze and I narrowed my gaze at Needle Nose between the bars.

"One way or round-trip?"

"What say?" I asked, cupping my dirty right hand up to my ear.

Louder, the ticket agent said, "Are you coming back or stopping over in Chama?"

"Not your business. I got the money for the ticket."

"Three dollars. One-way," the agent said, pinching his nose with thumb and forefinger. He did not want this old coot standing there any longer than need be.

I'd ridden this train twice before, but not looking and smelling like a broke down man just shy of the cemetery. The last time this same ticket agent saw me, he thought I was a young deaf-mute. I'd handed him a printed card confirming I could neither speak nor hear. Next, I pushed under the brass rod a piece of butcher paper with my destination scrawled on it and paid my fare in rumpled up notes for a round-trip passage.

My first trip had been a hoot—the passengers saw me as a fat-cheeked storekeeper with a long black beard, short scraggly white hair, and a bulging belly. Some would have described me as about average height, or tall, or hard to say because I only had one arm. Had anyone noticed, on any of my other trips, they'd have spotted something odd about me. Something to remember me by. On one trip, I'd drug an old Army saddle on board with me, shy any kind of rigging, which I insisted on placing in the seat beside me. In another, I wore a heavy leather raincoat, even though the day was bright and sunny.

The point was, hell, I wanted to be noticed. Especially at the Osier water stop.

The train pulled to a stop at the Antonito station. Five or six passengers got off. The little crowd of new passengers huddled together as the engine let off steam. It chugged like a giant horse straining to jump out of an iron chute. I stood off to one side. I'd wrapped my left ankle with canvas strips and cut down an old boot as I hobbled on the boardwalk alongside the train. Nearly everyone looked at me like I was part of a traveling circus. First, they studied my foot, then my face. I'd gussied myself up some—dark lines, like little blood veins, thanks to a little watered-down India ink. My eyes were not clear to anyone because I was wearing spectacles with one dirty lens, and one coal black lens, making me the only one-eyed man on the train. The other passengers were seven men, and two tired-looking women with three kids. One of the kids had a snot-nose and shied away from my smell. Everyone noticed my red gunnysack. It had bumps and holes, and poked out at odd places. I could see them wondering what I had in it. And, it smelled, too.

I took a seat up-front by myself, with the gunny in the next seat.

"You might have to share that seat, sir," the conductor said, as he punched my ticket.

"Might not," I said, looking out the window as the platform pulled away. I picked the front right-hand seat because it was next to the toilet. I bent over, holding my knees and tightening my gut. As soon as the engine pulled us out onto the main track, I headed into the toilet. The conductor came down the aisle taking tickets from three new passengers. I heard him ask someone, "Where's the old coot?"

"In the toilet," someone said.

Twenty minutes later the conductor knocked on the toilet door panel, "Is everything all right in there, sir?"

"I got a ticket. Just let me do my business."

I went to the toilet four more times before we began the long pull up toward Osier. Back at my seat, I saw a man dressed up in a fine three-piece suit saunter through the car as if he was important. He'd come from up front—the mail car. Reckon he'd been there all the way from Antonito.

"Morning," he said to the passengers behind me, as he passed by my seat.

The two women behind me said something like, "And to you, sir." He was too dressed up for either the engine or the mailroom and was too impressed with himself to be a conductor. And, he didn't sport a black cap with gold braids. He wore a stiff bowler and a black string tie over a ten-button vest. The dead giveaway was that there was no mud on his boots. *Gotta be a railroad detective*, I thought. He passed on through to the caboose.

An hour later, the conductor came through again. "Approaching Osier," he announced.

"Will we have time to step off the train for a little air?" the women with the snot-nose kid asked.

"Regular water stop is fifteen minutes—don't wander too far off the station landing."

Now I cannot say whether they got off or not. I was busy watching what happened on the offside of the train while the water tower did its work. I left my gunnysack in the seat, lumbered over to the toilet, and locked the door once I was inside. Then I wormed myself outside, squeezing through the little window and dropping to the ground just as the train was slowing to a stop under the water sluice.

Once outside, I moved behind the pile of timbers and set to watching the front door of the mail car. The engineer and the brakeman were attending to the important business of taking on water—paying no heed to the mail car. A man I'd never seen before stepped through the mail car door, and out onto the front landing. Then he jumped off the train onto the ground on the creek-side of the track. I watched as he skedaddled down the slope to a small stand of trees. He had an ordinary looking black duster and his hair looked oily. But, what stood out was a white canvas bag he'd strapped over his right shoulder with a leather halter. He scrambled downslope and moved into the scrub oak blind. From there, he moved on into the covering trees.

The other passengers milled about on the other side of the train. No one paid any mind to me, or the man scooting down the slope with his canvas bag. One of them asked the conductor where the old coot had gone.

"Is he still using the facilities?"

"Can't say," he answered.

The train pulled out of the Osier water stop exactly twelve minutes later. Right on time. It would be another half hour before the mailroom guard would regain consciousness and struggle through the mailroom door, cross the gangway, and tell the conductor that the train had been robbed.

All they'd find of my presence was that ole red gunnysack, full of week-old garbage from behind the Chinese bathhouse in Antonito.

By then, I'd climbed a mile and a half up the slope to the little stand of blue spruce where I'd hobbled Horse the day before. I saddled up and rode downslope to pick up the trail of the man with the canvas bag strapped to his back. The trail was easy to pick up and follow as the man headed south by southwest along the banks of the Río Dos Los Piños. I tracked him for two miles, and then he turned his horse into the streambed. There were no hoof prints on the other side. I knew then he'd cut into the middle of the stream and was headed downstream. It's powerful hard to track a man riding in a stream. 'Bout all you can hope for is to find where he decides to get back on the bank. That means you need to watch both sides of the bank. I found two places where he'd come out and rode alongside the stream. Both times, he meandered back into the streambed for a quarter-mile. Eventually, I lost his track when he came out onto a limestone slab. He ditched me there somewhere. So, I headed back upstream, toward Antonito.

CHAPTER 11

Captain Plumb in Santa Fe, New Mexico

THE VERANDA OF THE Exchange Hotel in Santa Fe faced north, toward the plaza. My ground-floor room faced San Francisco Street. Good view of the Governor's Palace, across the plaza. I'd just finished dressing, and was admiring my shiny new suit coat in the ornate floor-length mirror when I heard the knuckle wrap on the door.

"Captain Plumb. It's me, the front desk clerk. Got a telegram here. You'll want to see this right away, sir."

"Well, what 'n hell you think you're doing, son?" I growled as I opened the door. "Telling my business in the hallway! Give it and be on with you."

Steen's telegram soured me.

TO CAPTAIN STANDARD H. PLUMB—HOTEL EXCHANGE—SANTA
FE NEW MEXICO TERRITORY—STOP—DENVER & RIO GRANDE
TRAIN ROBBED YESTERDAY, WEST OF TOLTEC GORGE NEAR OSIER
COLORADO—$21,000—FOUR PAYROLLS HIT—ONE MAN JOB—THIS
IS NUMBER FOUR—PRESIDENT NICKERSON NOT HAPPY—REPORT YOUR
PROGRESS INSTANTLY—GO TO CHAMA IMMEDIATELY—FORM POSSE—
RPT ON ARRIVAL CHAMA—STOP—FROM ARTHUR STEEN—GENERAL
COUNSEL—AT&SF—CHICAGO ILLINOIS—STOP

Flipping open the cover piece on my gold-covered pocket watch, I realized the morning stage would leave for Chama and points north in thirty minutes. I shucked the suit, put on knee-high boots, and grabbed both my guns, my badge, and a travel kit. Storming by the front desk, I saw the pimple-faced kid who'd delivered my telegram.

"Get over to the stage station, tell 'em to hold the stage for me, I'll be there in ten minutes."

I ran to the train station to talk to the telegraph office. There were five more messages about the robbery at the Osier water station above the Toltec Gorge. All of them from Mr. Steen. Three to the AT&SF business manager, one to the paymaster for the *Dos S* brand, and one to the Stockman's Bank of Santa Fe, where most northern New Mexico silver mines held trading accounts. I told the station agent to resend all five to Undersheriff Joe Pete's office in Chama and to direct him to gather a posse.

"Tell him I'm a coming."

Remembering Branson, I said, "And telegraph Branson in Raton. Tell him to meet me in Chama tomorrow. And to bring his Hawken. And, hells bells send him that telegram from Arthur Steen, too."

They held the stage. All six horses in harness were restless, jerking against the yoke, and raising a nervous sweat because they'd been standing in place for thirty minutes. I was unhappy to see that two women and a small girl were on the stage. They'd want to talk all the damn way to Chama. I had to think of a way to give Angus a .50 caliber end to his miserable life. Sumbitch. This had gone, by God, far enough!

CHAPTER 12
Marse Shelters Angus in Montclair, Colorado

MY LIVERY BARN HAS A big sign over the big double doors leading out onto the road: MONTCLAIR LIVERY BARN— PUBLIC ACCOMMODATIONS—HORSES AVAILABLE— MARSE BINKS, PROPRIETOR.

So, when someone banged on my back door at four o'clock in the morning, I figured he knew me.

"Who's out there?" I bellowed as I headed through the barn to the door leading to the outhouse.

"It's me, Angus," came a muffled voice on the other side of the door. So, when I opened the door, I took note that Angus, bundled up tight with a muffler around the lower part of his face, looked like a pilgrim lost on the prairie.

"Angus, have you forgotten where the front door is? Or, are you in need of using my facilities?"

"Can you open the side door so I can get Horse inside? He's cold, too, and we'd like to come in private-like, if you don't mind."

After Angus led his horse into one of the inside stalls, I gave him a few seconds to adjust to the blackness of the inside of my fifty-foot-long barn. My seventy-odd years in the horse business was plain to anyone in need of my services. My blacksmith forge was in front, and my ten-stall walk-through was in the back. I fixed loose shoes, broken bridles, and wagon wheels. And, I supplied the best working stock and, no doubt about it, the finest saddle and tack in southern Colorado. Most people knew my real secret—I was privy to most everything that happened in the town my daddy started in 1844.

"Mornin', Angus. You come in quiet like. Suppose you're as cold as you are hungry, from your look. I'll finish hanging your tack and give that mustang you're riding some grain and a good brushing. You go on inside and get out of this Colorado cold."

"Well, it's your barn and Horse here has been under me since noon yesterday. I expect he'd enjoy your company right now."

After tending to Angus's horse, I came back into what I called a kitchen—even though it was more office and storeroom than kitchen. I stoked the fire, added grounds and water to the coffeepot, and lifted an almost warm biscuit from the covered tray on the warming rack above the stovetop. Angus came in the other door, smiled and stuck out his hand. Shaking hands with me was something you did carefully. Sticking my hand into Angus's rock-solid cowboy grip, I crunched down hard. Every friend I ever had counted on my blacksmithing skills, and they came from hand strength. You can only trust a smithy if he had a grip like an iron vise—that's how my daddy put it.

"I see you're riding that mustang out of Aposto's barn over to Alamosa."

"Yes, Marse, that's exactly right. He's steady and an easy keeper. You like him?"

I filled my own cup, and popped one of the suspenders over the heavy, oiled pants I'd put on over my nightshirt.

"Hell, Angus, I started that horse three years ago and traded him to Aposto last summer for a draft horse I needed for a farmer in Pueblo. I'm happy to see his big copper eyes back in my barn. Will you be here for a few hours? Or is this just a stopover?"

"Need to talk to Robert. Down at the bank."

"No, son, I think maybe I ought to go down to the bank for you. I'll tell Robert you're here. They're looking for you."

"Pinkerton man?"

"Yeah. He came in on the afternoon stage—a man named Branson. Ugly man, I have to say—greasy hair—never took off his black duster. He left out of here on one of my long-walking horses last night, but he made no argument about paying my price for the horse. Hell, Angus, he didn't even stop at the saloon. Headed in a hurry for Antonito, he said."

"What makes you think he's looking for me?"

"Ain't he?"

"Hard to say. Could be he is. What points you in that direction?"

"Well, lemme see. You're a horseman who likes riding alone. You have left me a big ole tip a time or two; twenty-dollar Liberty Heads. Those signs point somewhere, don't they?"

"Sure. They tell you just what you said. I like horses and feel generous around those I like and trust will mind their own business, just like I mind mine."

"And, you're right about that. I ain't fond of the Pinkertons, or the way they treat their stock. It's no never mind to me who he's looking for. But, he's asking questions about someone that puts me in mind of you. That's all I meant."

Angus unrolled his tarp in the stall I'd directed him to. I went back to bed. Three hours after sun up, with Angus still asleep, I walked down the street to Montclair's Dry Goods and Pharmacy. I bought a sack of fresh bread, ten bags of carrots, and five cans of peaches, then walked across the street to the Bank of Montclair.

"Morning, Marse," Robert Morton said when I opened his door. "Glad to see you so early of a morning. What banking can I do for you today?"

There was no one else in the bank that early. But, Robert Morton, a punctual man, opened his front door at nine o'clock sharp, customers or not.

"Morning, Robert. How's the banking business? The horse business is a mite slow, mostly because it's cold outside."

"Well, you got a point. Money doesn't flow well in cold weather. Come springtime, we always do a little better. How about a cup?"

Like every other business in town, the bank had a wood stove in the corner, a coffeepot, and a shelf full of cups for customers. No biscuits, though. I helped myself and Robert looked down at his lists and figures.

"It's about Angus, Robert. He's over in my barn. Came in quiet like about four. He slept in a stall with his horse. Thought

I had better come in since there's a commotion about him. You know, that train robbery down to Osier. Said he needs to see you."

Robert looked up at me, nodded his head, but didn't say anything for a minute. He got up, went to the front door in his little one-room bank, and stepped outside onto the new boardwalk that connected his building to the tin maker's shop next door. Apparently not seeing anyone headed our way, he stepped back inside and slid the day-latch closed.

"Seems nobody needs banking this morning, Marse. So, tell me, old friend, how much did Angus tell you about his banking business? Little, I expect."

"Not anything is more the case. I met you when you first came to town six years ago. Met Angus the year before that. I guess I know you and him are friends, but he don't know about my banking business and I ain't asked him about his."

I spun around a little in the big cane-backed armchair by the fire, twirling the coffee grounds in my tin cup.

Robert sat down behind his desk, clasped his hands behind his neck, and looked toward me without looking right at me. The bank got little foot traffic, but Robert wanted privacy.

"Good. My idea of a good customer is one who knows his money, keeps his banking business private, and can be trusted to keep his word. Angus is good that way."

"Yeah. He is."

We used silence as a way to inch our way into something we both suspected. Was Angus the good man I knew him to be, or was he the dastardly train robber the Pinkertons thought he was?

"You know, Robert, it's much the same in the horse business. 'Cept that everybody in town knows what you're riding and how you treat your stock. Angus is a good judge of horse-flesh, and I reckon he trusts you a lot. But, he's asked me to keep an eye out on the Pinkertons for him. A week back, after the stage pulled in, I seen that railroad captain, the one in the three-piece suit with the fancy shoulder holster, coming out of here. I just figured he was asking about Angus. Don't know why a Pinkerton man who does his business mostly down in Santa Fe would be bothering you up here. And then, a day ago, another Pinkerton man, named Branson, came in the stage, but rented a horse from me to ride south. I believe he's headed for New Mexico. He asked about a man that fits Angus's description."

The coffeepot hissed on the stove, and a gust of wind rattled two of the windows on the east side of the room. Morton didn't seem bothered by either. Scraping his chair a little closer he said, "Marse, you've always had a good eye for this street. I expect you know a lot about everyone who lives here just by observing who goes into what store and when. And, you're right about Captain Standard H. Plumb. He's got his eye on Angus."

"I already know that. He thinks Angus is robbing trains. Hell, maybe he is. But, there's more to it than that. Angus might be hitting the AT&SF where it hurts, but he just ain't no common, by-God thief. So, since Angus is friend to both of us, and Plumb is not, let me be square with you. Angus is not afraid of anything and if he takes a mind to, he'll walk in your front door this morning. Folks will remember that, especially if our town marshal puts up a wanted poster on his front door. Somehow, I think that would not be a good thing for you or him. Am I right?"

Robert said nothing. But, he got up, walked over to the stove, stuck in two sticks of kindling, and shook the coffee pot.

"My coffee is designed to keep people from drinking too much of it. I'll close for lunch an hour early today. Addie always fixes noon lunch for herself and me, except when the stage is coming in."

"You're lucky to have her. Is she still all dreamy-eyed about California?"

"I am, and she is. But we're talking about Angus. Now, he's a man who lives on bacon and beans cooked over a one-man fire up on some ridgeline. Don't you suppose he could use a home-cooked lunch?"

"Probably could."

"So, if you don't mind, ask our friend Angus to walk over to our house before noon. We're on the end of town, and if he walks the footpath behind Main Street, with his head down and his collar up, no one is likely to see him, as he'll be coming from your barn. You watch out for the Pinkertons, and I'll watch out for whatever money our friend Angus might have; no matter where he gets it."

CHAPTER 13
Angus at Addie's House in Montclair

I TOOK MARSE'S ADVICE and waited until the stroke of noon on my dad's pocket watch. Then I took the back way out of his barn and followed an arroyo around the town about a quarter-mile on foot. It gave me a chance to think some but the sweep of the prairie in four directions got in my mind. While I hadn't noticed before, coming in on horseback, the little town was surrounded by dozens of small creeks and ponds. It had natural cisterns, arroyos, and dry riverbeds. A man could sneak up on a town like this, even though it was smack in the middle of a wide-open prairie.

I came up out of the arroyo about forty yards behind Robert Morton's house. The cloudy sky, coupled with the ten-mile-per-hour wind, and a temperature of about thirty degrees kept most people inside. I walked up to the back door, knocked lightly, and Addie opened it immediately.

Smiling, she said, "Well, this is a surprise. It's you. Thanks for the tip," and waved me into the room as she headed for the stove.

Robert's sister? "You're Addie from the restaurant?" I asked lamely.

"I am. I could put on an apron if that would help you remember me."

"Oh, I remember you all right. You were on my mind for a . . ."

I couldn't finish the sentence, but she took mercy on me.

"Come in and we'll start anew. Robert says you're a mystery with a head on your shoulders."

I stepped through the door into the kitchen, smelled wheat bread from the oven and chili from the stew pot. And coffee. The room was hot, at least for me, seeing as how I spent almost every day on higher ground, in colder temperatures. Talking to her back, I said, "A mystery? That's what he thinks of me? Maybe he was describing my horse; he has a good head on him."

"I'll get Robert. Why don't you sit down right there?" she said, pointing to the small round table covered with a bright blue oiled cloth. She'd set two places, with her best China, forks on one side of the bone white plates, spoons on the other, and a small bread knife running crossways to the plates on top. There were two small porcelain bowls filled with salt and pepper in the middle of the table. A larger bowl filled with small nuts nudged up against a Denver Iron Works nutcracker in the shape of a beaver.

"Good to see you, Angus. You look well," Robert said, when he appeared a few minutes later, offering me his hand.

As we shook, Addie turned to the stove and poured two bowls of chili. She sliced four slices of stone wheat bread, put them in an Indian basket, and cut two chunks of butter from the icebox beside the sink. She set all of it on the table, took off her yellow apron, and smiled at both of us.

"Eat. It's not there just for looks."

Robert waved me over to the little table.

"Thanks for coming to the house, Angus. I just thought it'd be easier to talk here."

Addie walked over to the coat stand beside the front door, put on her overcoat, and wrapped a big wool scarf around her neck. With one hand on the door handle, she glanced back at me.

"Don't mean to intrude, but is there any small chance that you would sit and eat with us? It would be real civilizing for me, although probably not all that interesting for you. I live in the mountains, and I could tell you some things about the big rocks and maybe bears, if you're at all interested."

No one spoke for a few seconds. Robert grinned. Addie narrowed her eyes and nodded in my direction.

"No, but thank you, Angus. Robert says he has business to discuss with you. And I have an errand to run. But after, if you were of a mind, I'd love to hear something about bears and mountains. We could sit in the parlor, when Robert goes back to his bank."

With Addie gone, and Robert feeling a little ashamed for not introducing his sister, he told me to hang my coat on the hook and sit. I nodded and took off the sheepskin mountain coat; underneath I wore a mid-calf canvas duster with four large flap pockets in front. Reaching first into the left side front pocket, I took out a cardboard bound notebook and a pencil. Digging down into my inside chest pocket, I pulled out a well-worn leather pouch with a small bear claw that kept the pouch flap closed. Robert watched me as I patted the jacket and found a small waxed paper package tied with strong brown string. I set them on the table and motioned to the leather pouch.

"Can you put that inside your safe for me?"

"Sure. And, I suppose you want me to deposit the other package, the one with real money in it, in the trust account? Right?"

"Yes, sir, please."

"Angus, seeing as how we're about the same age, why do you always call me sir?"

"You're wearing a suit, starched collar and a black string tie. Makes you entitled."

"Well, I don't mind a title at the bank; I suppose it helps when it comes to collecting the annual interest payment on a mortgaged farm or ranch. But, here at home, I'm just plain Robert. OK?"

"Suits me."

"Is that a pun, Angus?"

Over chili, bread, butter, and coffee, we talked about what I needed from him—money for supplies. He asked if the two accounts he'd set up at my request were what I needed.

"Yep," I said, giving him a careful look.

"One in my name; the other in trust."

He dunked an end piece of toasted stone bread into his chili before looking up at me.

"One in your name—Angus Esparazza, and the other in trust. If you don't mind my asking, are you a Scot? Angus is Scottish, you know."

"I am."

"And Esparazza? Is that Mexican?"

"No, my mother was Spanish, and she never lived in Mexico. When I was born my parents followed what I'm told was the Spanish custom—first name was my father's family name—surname was my mother's family."

"Probably complicated your life as a kid, didn't it?"

"No. Everyone in the family called me Razza for short. It stuck until they died."

"Oh, I'm sorry to hear that, Angus," Robert said, leaning back in his chair. "How old were you when you lost your parents?"

"My uncle, who took me in after the fire, said I was three. But, I don't remember any of that. I was raised by him—a bear hunter, mostly for grizz, and the best tracker in New Mexico."

"So, you're half Spanish and half Scot, is that it?"

"Could be. Ain't important now."

We finished lunch, not talking about much. Robert poured more coffee for us. He stirred little sugar cubes in his. I put one in my mouth and sucked a little coffee through it.

"Is that a mountain man's trick, Angus—sipping coffee through a sugar cube?"

"Sugar is hard to come by up high, so I got in the habit of rationing them, and most everything else. One cube a day makes a bag of sugar last two months."

"Well, Angus, let's do some business here. As I mentioned when you first came to the bank, it's unusual to have a trust account with a blank name for the beneficiary."

"And, like I said then, all you have to do is mail the monthly statement on the trust account to the postal box number I gave you."

"Yes, the one in Denver. I've been doing that. That suits the banking regulators from Denver, although they are curious about it. By the way, Angus, how did you pick me to hold your money?"

"Well, Marse is my friend. He says you're an honest man, and never foreclosed a man's loan."

"Yes, but, if I had no choice, that's what I'd have to do. I have depositors to protect."

"Well, fine. I'm a depositor, too."

Robert looked at his pocket watch once or twice. We'd spent almost an hour talking about his business, banking, and mine—riding high ridges, frothy rivers, and the plains that made this part of Colorado a nice place to visit.

"If you don't mind my asking," Robert said after the second bowl of chili, "the money in your account seems to favor depositing, but not many withdrawals. Are you a frugal man by nature, or are you saving up for something?"

"Well, it does not cost much to feed a horse you already own, and I can live off what I shoot or catch in the mountains. But, I suppose I ought to credit my uncle for keeping a tight hold on my money. He said a dollar saved is worth two spent. Took me awhile to get his meaning."

"I wish we had more like your uncle in Montclair. Folks here don't save much. But, some stick coin money under the floorboards in the barn."

He talked some about himself and his bank, and their little town. I asked why Addie was waiting tables at the restaurant instead of teaching school.

"Addie's a dreamer, Angus. She dreams of places that no one around here has ever seen. Places with new faces, as she's fond of saying. Places with beaches, seashells, and music. How about you? You ever dream about a new life?"

"I dream about waking up alongside a cold mountain stream and riding young colts with their heads up."

Robert gathered my envelopes and took them to a little box on a shelf. The wind was blowing hard against the window glass in the front room when he stopped mid-stride.

"How about new faces, Angus? I mean, doesn't it get lonely riding alone and living off whatever the mountain provides?"

Truth be told, I couldn't recall a conversation about new faces in my life.

"New faces are what most people look for, but I like the faces I see in the clouds and the hard rocks that spew out of mountains after a hard rain."

Feeling like I was overstaying my welcome, I reached for my hat off the peg on the wall. "I'd best be getting out of here. I'll be over to Marse's if you need me this afternoon. I'll likely head out when the sun goes down."

"Angus, you'd best stay a bit and tell my sister something about those mountains and bears you favor. She could use something new to dream about."

Just then, Addie came back in the front door—cheeks flushed with the cold. We moved from the kitchen to the parlor. I spent two hours with Addie after Robert went back to the bank. She never asked me about my business with Robert. I never asked her about how she liked working in the café, or why she wanted to know about mountains or bears. She smelled nice, even though I was five feet away on the facing sofa.

Addie's touch was everywhere in the small room. Three windows faced the little porch in the front of the house. All three were draped with lace, a dark blue velvet side-panel, and white curtains. The L-shaped room featured an eight-foot ceiling. In the middle, they had a hanging kerosene lamp, with four small brass oil chambers, and bright pink cylinders covered by brass cups. Directly below was a round table about the size of a buggy wheel. The top was multicolored marble, set on a polished enameled, three-legged stand. A lace covering allowed the orange and silver marble strains to highlight the room. A small silver bowl of water was in the table's center, with finger-length pieces of splintered wood floating on the surface.

"Do you know what that bowl is for?" Addie asked, watching me trace one of the wood splinters.

"Don't think I've ever seen such a thing. But, my guess is the wood peels off vapors because of the kerosene lamp up there," I said, pointing up to the ceiling. Addie's kerosene lamp was different from the one my folks used when I was a kid; she had a mantle wick. My mother's was tin, and used a flat wick because she moved it from the front room to the bedroom we all shared. The glass chimney on Addie's was made of brass, and looked to be a foot-and-a-half tall.

"Yes, you're right. It keeps the room moist in the winter, robbing the cold of its hold on your throat. Some think vapors remove stress. I'm not sure about that myself, but it makes my skin feel better."

I moved away from the table to the glass-fronted bookcase on the west wall.

"I'm glad that works for you, but my skin needs toughening, not soothing out. I prefer living outside most time. Even when I'm up at my cabin on Ten Shoes Up, I sleep outside most nights. There's one thing for sure about stars—they never bore you."

"Outside, all winter long?"

Squinting at me, she tilted her head to the side and hunched her shoulders up.

"I'm serious, Addie. There's shelter no matter how high you go up the mountain. When I'm on a hunt, or just exploring a new canyon, I build a lean-to or a snow fort. Sometimes I live under overhangs built by nature to protect man and beast. It's a good place to think. Up high, crags and rocky crevices interrupt sad thoughts and skies change color every few minutes. There's a lot to look at and ponder. If you're in the mood to do that."

"What do you like best about being alone up there, Angus?" she said as she leaned back into the cushions on the sofa across from me.

"Every day is different. That's what I like about it. You may think it's the same flight of birds, or even forest critters padding across your path, but life changes every minute up there. One minute, the air calms everything around it, the next it's blowing at you with a fierceness that makes you feel as alive as the storm that's heading your way."

"I love looking at the mountains, Angus, but I must confess that I've never been up to the top of any of them. I sit here reading most afternoons, but I take great comfort that those mountains are there."

Nodding, I walked over to the black bookcase snugged up against the center wall of the room.

"Could I look at one of your books? The only collection of books with leather binders like these I ever saw was in Denver two years ago."

I told Addie I'd read about a dozen books in my life, left behind in my mother's trunk when she died. She listened to me talk, not so much to hear what I had to say, but more likely because she suspected I rarely talked to anyone, including her brother.

"Angus, please excuse me a minute, I want to show you something from my bedroom. It won't take a minute."

I watched her walk from the front room to the little hall-way that led to three closed doors. She stopped at the first one, opened it, and went inside. She went out of sight for a moment, and then, to my surprise, appeared again, from across the room, standing in front of a full-length upright mirror on one of those swivel stands. On the other side of her bedroom, an oval-shaped mirror hung from a brass chain. I could see her back in the full-length mirror and part of her face and head in the other mirror on the opposite side of the room. I hoped she couldn't see me, but I just could not take my eyes off her. She moved both hands to the back of her neck, fluffing out her hair. Then she pinched first one cheek and then the other, and smoothed down her dress. Reaching down to what I assumed was a table next to the mirror, she picked up a small crystal jar of something, and put her finger in it. Then she dabbed at the freckles on her nose. Turning sideways, she brushed her hands down her hips and took a deep breath. She went out of sight again and I heard the distinct creak of a stubborn drawer being pulled open. She came back in with a black velvet sack tied at the top with a thick piece of dark red ribbon.

"Here's something I bet you've never seen on one of your beautiful mountains."

She opened the velvet sack and handed me a seashell the size of a small watermelon.

"This is one of my most favorite possessions, Angus. Have you ever seen anything in your life like this?"

"No, can't say that I have. Looks like a rock that came from the bottom of the ocean. Right?"

"It's not a rock. It's a conch shell. If you're real quiet and don't breathe too hard, you can hear the ocean, right inside. Try it."

"Well, Addie, I'll take your word on it. You probably don't want me handling something like this. What if I dropped it?"

"Well, Angus, I'd have to shoot you, with your own gun. But, don't be silly—just hold it a little above your ear. I want you to hear the ocean so you'll know my secret."

It was lemon-colored, but had splashes of green and blue and was shaped like a small mesquite burl from the base of an old withered tree. It twirled up from the bottom like smoke from a fire does when there's a wind hitting it. And, it felt a lot lighter than it looked. She held it up to my ear with her fingertips, not letting it touch the palm of her hand.

"Hold it here, lightly, not actually against your skin."

I felt a little faint, with her so close and all, but then I heard it. A whooshing sound, faint and then coming back at me. We stood still. After a minute, I realized I was holding my breath. She laughed when I let out a big breath.

"Hell's fire, it does sound like the ocean, well, at least as far as I can guess what an ocean sounds like. I've heard people describe ocean sounds, but this is close as I will probably ever get."

"Oh, Angus, I'm so sorry to hear that. You can't imagine seeing the ocean? Or hearing it? I can feel an ocean breeze on my face every time I hold this beautiful conch up to my ear. The ocean is not for everyone, but I will get there someday soon—to San Francisco—by the bay and by the ocean, too. Maybe you'll change your mind about mountains and give the ocean a chance to talk to you. Now, enough of my dream. Tell me about the bears up in those mountains."

"They are there because without bears, the mountains would not have a natural leader. Bears are the biggest, fiercest animal we have. They take what they want, but only in proportion to what they need. And, they will let you alone if you respect their territory. Flatland folks could learn a lot from bears."

"How many winters have you spent in the mountains?"

"Nine."

"Not to be too personal, but Robert mentioned that you lost your parents a few years ago. Did you escape to the mountains after that?"

"My mother died when I was six. My dad was a traveling man—traveled all over the west as a surveyor for the railroads and for mining companies that needed roads to haul ore down to smelters. I lived with what you'd call distant relatives, mostly because they needed help around their ranch. But, I traveled a lot with my dad and he taught me everything about difficult terrain. I was fascinated by places that no one else seemed interested in."

"Please forgive me, but it sounds like high ground is as much an escape as it is an adventure. What were you escaping from nine years ago?"

"Well, yes. Escaping is a fair call on my life. I married when I was eighteen. Mazy was sixteen. We lived up high, just on our own. Then her appendix burst when we were in a place that took some hard riding to get out of. Nothing I could do. But, I still see her up there, no matter which mountain I'm on. She comforts me. "

"I lost my parents, too, Angus. But I still have Robert. I'm sorry you're alone in this world. Excuse me, while I put the conch shell back."

She put the shell back in the velvet sack and went back into her bedroom. When she came back, neither of us wanted to talk about dreams anymore.

I wanted to say something about losing her parents, but it got twisted up in my head.

"Well, I got close to the ocean once. I made it as far as the confluence of the Columbia River and the Spokane River. I rode a boat with fur trappers for almost two hundred miles. We ferried horses for trips off the river. It was a government party, charting the river. They hired me to wrangle the horses. We stopped about a hundred miles shy of the Pacific. They said we were close enough to smell salt water. They were joshing me."

We seemed to run out of things to say, like there was a mountain *and* an ocean between us. Addie sat sort of primly on a brocade sofa with ornate carved arms. While she was in her bedroom, I'd moved to a high backed red-leather armchair that felt stiffer than most rocks up on Ten Shoes. I must have looked uncomfortable, because she said, "That's an awful chair to sit in, isn't it? Robert bought it two years ago out of a catalogue. I make him sit in it once a week, for his penance."

When I left, she stood formally at the back door, and offered her hand. I'd only shaken hands with a woman once or twice in my life, so I was unsure just how to take it. I held out first my left hand, and then quickly offered my right. As it ended up, I took her small hand in both of mine.

"Don't suppose it would be proper to leave a tip for the lunch, like last time, but you'll never know how much I enjoyed both the food and your talking to me."

"No, Angus, a tip is quite out of the order, even in Colorado, where gold and silver are the staples of our lives. But it's a kind thought. Why don't you just save your Double Eagles and buy me dinner in San Francisco some time? I'm bound to go, you know. Just ask Robert. I'm saving the coin you left. Maybe I'll use it to tip a handsome waiter in San Francisco."

Your presence will be his tip, I thought, but could not muster the courage to say anything like that.

"All right, then. Maybe I'll be back in the spring."

"All right, then," she echoed. "Make an excuse to come back in the spring. Good bye, Angus."

CHAPTER 14
Angus Riding South

AS THE SUN DROPPED in the west, I turned due south. We rode all night. By dawn, I'd reached the prairie that stretched down into Antonito, the last town before you cross the territorial line into New Mexico. Horse was up on his toes during most of the night, nervous-like. He'd spent the better part of a month in a fifteen-foot stall in Marse's barn. Now, at first light, we heard a wail from a wolf pack yip-yapping a quarter-mile away. He paid no attention to them.

A half-hour after sunrise, I found a protected draw and built a small fire. For me, there were bacon and beans with two cups of black scalding coffee, and, for Horse, grain. After a three-hour rest, maybe two hours before the sun reached its high noon, I headed due south for Sublette. From there, I figured on dropping down into Toltec Gorge. The draw led down into a small canyon, with a covered brush opening.

We rode the afternoon out and then found an overhang that would cover me and the horses. The packhorse followed the lead line like a kite in the wind.

I figured we were twenty miles from Sublette. Horse was turning out to be a damn fine animal and seemed like he could read my mind. He took easily to my preference for night riding, then sleeping in the morning. He liked late afternoon feedings, munching a feedbag of grain. I always dolloped in a little cane molasses. Made every horse my friend, even on the first ride. A three-quarter moon and a starry night at eight thousand feet had given us an easy ride.

"Well, Horse, would you just look at that," I said, in the slow and low voice I knew was calming to animals of every kind. There was no one around to hear me talk, or Horse whinny. Suited us. We pulled up on the edge of a watery sinkhole and took in a powerful sight. The West's biggest solid granite mountain, not more than twenty miles away. Its massive cracks and fissures loomed up out of the prairie, the glare of the sun rose on my left flank sucking away the cold night air. I flattened the high collar on my sheepskin. Horse's breath still fogged out in front, but the morning sun warmed both his back and mine. I gave him his head, and let him pick his own way down among the boulder-strewn trail.

Moving carefully down the gash in the rock, it took Horse about two hours to reach the bottom of the gorge. Then, finding the D&RG tracks, we commenced the climb up the other side. I knew the train would not come through here until midafternoon. That'd give me plenty of time.

I'd thought the route through, as we picked our way around boulders bigger than a barn and a damn sight heavier. As long as we stuck to the south side of the track, I knew we'd top out high over the tunnel they called "Mud Tunnel." Never knew why they called it that. Anyhow, from there it was twelve or thirteen miles south to my cabin. There were a dozen or more box canyons off the creek. The only sure way to get there was by following the creek all the way up from Cascade Creek Trestle. The railroad work crew, mostly Chinese labor, had finished the trestle two years ago. From there it was downhill to the depot in Chama.

There was still snow up this high. Horse knew how to break trail with the best of 'em.

All right, son, get us on up there.

CHAPTER 15
Captain Plumb at the Osier Water Station

"**D**AMN YOUR HIDE, Branson. Where 'n hell you been for two days? You were supposed to be here yesterday afternoon," I yelled.

"Well, Captain Standard H. Plumb, you ain't an appreciative man, are you? Getting here was no easy feat. I'm near tuckered out as you are. I rode like hell to get from Montclair to Antonito yesterday. Then I spent last night in a cheap boardinghouse with no whiskey. I was up early this morning and spent all day on the train just getting here to Osier. That's where I've goddamn been for two days!"

"Well, never mind. Just get your gear and your Hawken off the damn train. We got you a horse, and daylight's burning out from under us. Alfonso, this here's Branson. Branson, Alfonso is the man that's gonna track that sumbitch Angus.

You got that? He tracks. You shoot. No more flinching at the last second."

Branson ignored the insult. And, as usual, he poked a question my way that showed he had no confidence in me.

"Captain, what makes you think this Angus character was ever here in the first place? Tell me that. Hell, we chased that ghost once before. It was not me who flinched. It was that fool kid Joe Pete brought along. I'm right pleased to see that he ain't here this time."

"Ain't your place to question me, Branson, but I'm happy as all hell to put your mind at ease. Two railroad men spotted Angus jumping off the train day before yesterday. The engineer was sure he robbed the train. The brakeman showed me a red gunnysack he left behind. Seems he weaseled himself out of the widow in the facilities room. This man, Arturo Ganado, is a tracker who can follow anyone. They say he can follow two-day old track like it was fresh blood out of a chicken shack, with fox prints in the mud."

"Alfonso Ganado, Captain," the Mexican man interjected, speaking deliberately and slowly.

"OK, Alfonso Ganado, then. Let's get horseback." Ganado and Joe Pete badgered two fresh horses down the ramp of the horse car and onto the cindered side of the rails.

"Why two horses, Captain Plumb?" Branson asked.

"One for you, and the other to use as a packhorse for that sumbitch's body when you blow a hole in him with your Hawken."

The boys busied themselves testing stirrup leathers and tightening cinches. I moved the jug-headed horse ten feet away from them. My saddlebags weighed more than thirty pounds, and it was a struggle getting them centered. The fool horse just would not stand still. Had to give him a crack on his behind with my quirt. That got his attention.

"No, goddamn it, Sheriff, I don't need no help with the bags. These here bags are railroad property and are none of your business; nor that of your new deputy, Alfonso Gando or Ganado, whatever his Mexican name is. You see this here lock? It's there for a reason. Stay away from my property."

Finally, Sheriff Pete, Branson, Alfonso Ganado, and I mounted up. Alfonso took the point, leading us south, downhill, along the track headed for the Los Piños River. We hit the river two by two as the icy water splashed up on man and horse alike. This was snow run-off water, and it bit little holes into my cheeks. Horses gave it no attention at all. Coming up a steep bank on the other side, we headed west again toward the Cascade Creek trestle three miles away. Once there, Alfonso jogged his horse on out ahead, talking back at us over his shoulder.

"Best you men stay back, at least a hundred yards. I got to sniff and smell and don't need your noise in my head when I'm tracking," he warned.

After we dropped back, I asked Sheriff Pete, "What 'n hell does he mean, he's sniffing and smelling?"

Over his shoulder, Pete hollered back as best he could, as we were in a hard trot.

"Tracking's best done alone, Captain, with no one yapping at the man. Just you leave him be. I've hunted with him before. Let's hang back, he'll holler if he needs us."

Cooled off by brush whacking for an hour, in and out of Cascade Creek, Branson rode up alongside me.

"If you don't mind my asking, what makes you think our man is fishing this creek this time of year? Doesn't he know winter's coming? Just 'cause this is where he robbed the train a few days ago does not mean he's dumb enough to hang around waiting for your hired track dog to sniff him out, does it?"

I knew that next to Alfonso, Branson was the most important man in this four-man posse. And, I accepted that the shooter had made good time getting here in two days. So, I backed off my mad and cut him some slack.

"Glad you asked, Branson. I have it on good authority that Angus was up to Montclair last week sometime. He run off from there headed south. I figure he's coming here."

"You figure? How's that? I thought no one had seen this Angus sumbitch for two years."

"Could be. But, a muleskinner, interested in the reward, saw a man head out of the livery stable two nights ago just after dark. He was riding a young bay horse. Coulda been a mustang, he said, and he had a kit like the one we saw the sumbitch had when you missed shooting him six weeks ago."

"I remember shooting at a man on a big bay, but he wasn't a mustang, nor young. You think he switched horses?"

"You hit the horse, goddammit; not the man, the horse! A Pinkerton man from Alamosa says the man was riding a big bay, but he coulda been a mustang. Anyways, he was outfitted in a sheepskin coat and a big-brimmed black hat. That remind you of the man you missed on Ten Shoes Up? I believe he went to Montclair to do business at their bank. I'll deal with that uppity banker after you shoot the sumbitch name of Angus somewhere up this creek."

Two miles down the Cascade Creek streambed, Alfonso spotted the trail coming up out of the creek bed onto a bluff from a hundred feet away. He stopped, turned around, and waited until we trotted up to him.

"We got him now, Señor Plumb. Let me go ahead two hundred feet. Don't make too much noise behind me. Just follow me. I'll be following and listening for this man you want to shoot. I get the same reward as your shooter, *que no?*"

"It's Captain Plumb, not Señor Plumb. And, no, goddammit, you don't get the same share of the reward money. If you find him and shoot him, I'll double your share. But, if Branson here does the job, he'd get a bigger share than anyone. You savvy that, Señor Ganado?"

Three hours later, it was too dark for us to see Alfonso's tracks in and out of snow patches. So, Pete galloped ahead and got Alfonso to turn back. I called a halt after we hit dark. We camped in the middle of an aspen grove with a small fire and a quart bottle of drinking whiskey. Pete passed around a sack of buffalo jerky and a tin full of hardtack biscuits, more or less for supper. But the whiskey did the trick. It was too cold to talk so we, except for Alfonso, fell asleep within the hour. He'd moved away from the fire, and sat back on his boot heels against a big tree, smelling and sniffing the night air. Pete said something about how he could hear through his nose, or some such nonsense as that.

Next morning, we ate a cold breakfast with hot coffee while Sheriff Pete brushed and watered the horses, except for Alfonso's little black gelding.

"Dammit, Sheriff, why in hell didn't you bring some fit horses for this posse?" The two horses we'd off-loaded yesterday from a special cattle car hooked onto the caboose looked beat after just one day and a night tied to a tree. Alfonso's horse looked fresh and squirrel-tailed.

Pete brushed my horse, and then his, while Alfonso and Branson tended to their tack. "How come this guy, Angus, is ponying another horse? Anybody got an idea on that?" Pete asked.

Giving him a dismissive look, Alfonso answered, "Two horses, one carrying a man, the other a heavy pack."

"How you know that?" Pete queried.

"From the depth of the hoof prints coming out of the creek, yesterday. It means a horse under pack when I see track like that."

"Don't give a damn about the packhorse. Is it that sumbitch or not? Are we on his trail again?"

"Well, maybe so," Branson said. "I noticed the depth of the hoof tracks, too. But, the horse that's hauling a man, not a pack, is a different horse than the one we tracked on Ten Shoes Up. This one's got a shorter stride, but I suppose you already knew that, seeing as how we found his big bay healing up on that ranch this side of Montclair. Right?"

"Right, we found the horse you shot instead of the sumbitch riding him. Don't be reminding me of that."

Alfonso was not listening anyhow; he'd mounted up and was long trotting that big stallion of his, leaning off to one side and then the other. Hell of a rider, and a tracker. But, his pace made it hard for Sheriff Pete, me, and Branson to keep up. When Pete first introduced me to Alfonso, he looked to be a hard man. He had a face that looked like a pan of hot oil had hit it. Streaks, crevices, and holes everywhere. And, he was bald as river rock, with tiny little eyes, so small you could not see their color. He answered to Alfonso, but hadn't said two words in ten hours of riding.

"A cabin in the high country, you sure about that?" I asked as I spurred my horse up alongside Joe Pete.

"Captain, that's what Alfonso said. I paid him twenty dollars in gold coin, just like you said I could. He used to work out of the livery stable at Fort Garland, hunting lion and bear on Ten Shoes Up. He never knew Angus, but he knew the liveryman down there in Fort Garland. He said Angus bought heavy axes, ropes, two buckets of tar, and a block and tackle rig. He hauled it out of there, with supplies for the whole winter. He loaded all of it onto a three-mule pack train. All by himself. Two summers ago."

"Hell yes, I can believe it," I told Sheriff Pete.

"That sumbitch, whose name I ain't gonna dignify by saying, is a mountain man for sure. That explains why your paid informer and tracker brought that extra horse I asked you to get for us. We're gonna need that horse. You make deputies too damned quick, and you follow orders too slowly, to my way of thinking."

"I can't say about the extra horse. But, for one thing, he knows about Angus, so he can identify the body if your man Branson can get a clean shot this time. For another, there aren't too many men unemployed right now. You know?"

"So you're sure?"

"Well, why 'n hell would he be hauling that much stuff out of Fort Garland? The man's not a nester, or a five-cow rancher. He's a loner. Hell fire, even loners get cold this high up on the mountain. He's built him a wintering cabin, to my way of thinking. And that's where he's headed."

We crossed the third little creek as we topped out of one canyon and headed down into another. The weather was brisk, but not hard on the horses. I pulled my duster string a little tighter around my chest.

Joe Pete rode silent for ten minutes. Then, he suddenly picked up the thread of the conversation. "He said Angus let it slip that he was headed for Cascade Creek."

"And when did your man say it happened, last spring?"

"Hell no. This was two years ago. I believe the man's been living up there alone for two years now. That's why no one around here remembers seeing him. Word is he grew up in the Chama valley. A homesteader's brat, that's what they say about him."

"Well, if he let it slip, it was the first slip I ever heard the sumbitch make. But, Undersheriff Joe Pete, you just might have cottoned onto why no one's seen him of late. He's got a hideout."

"And, Captain Standard H. Plumb, that reminds me of another reason to bring Alfonso on this posse. He lives over near Dulce. That's forty miles due west of here. He's been tracking from Dulce to Trinidad his whole life. Not much escapes his eye in the high country."

"I'd love to catch the sumbitch all warm and cozy in his hideout. Let's put the spurs to these horses. We got a track to follow."

Joe Pete pulled his horse up at a little flat place. Wrapping the reins around his saddle horn, he twisted back and commenced to unwrap his saddle tarp. Pulling out a heavy wool scarf, which he threw around his bony neck, he said, "Goddammit, Captain, winter's coming on. There's already snow up there. If Alfonso ain't fit to find two horses, one under pack, crisscrossing creeks, across patches of fresh snow, then we are on a fool's errand."

"Don't you fret about fools, Sheriff. If your man can track this Angus sumbitch to his hideout, Branson can blow a .50 caliber hole in him. Then we got us a reward to split."

CHAPTER 16
Bo String Crossing the Rio Chama

I'D USED A BRANDING IRON on my saddle and lettered my name, Bo String, along the stirrup leathers on both sides. Most cowboys could tell their own saddle a hundred yards off, but, for some fool reason, I wanted my name on mine anyhow. It sure didn't matter to the little cow pony I was riding today. Sierra danced up on her toes and kept twisting her neck back at me. We were just crossing the Rio Chama on the low side of the river. She jigged sideways a little as we trotted up the short winding road into Brazos.

"Looks peaceable don't it, Sierra?" I said to the little black mare I'd been herding cattle on for the last six months. I'd picked her out of the Long Jake string. Jaramillo, the round-up foreman for the Long Jake Ranch, had taken a liking to me. He said the mare's name was Sierra because that's Mexican for saw. That seemed fitting, seeing as how the mountains up ahead of me looked like giant saw blades cutting into the low hanging clouds on the far side of the river. "Tell you what, Bo. If you'll come back to the Long Jake brand for spring roundup next year, when we need your roping skills, I'll let you take Sierra, that little black mare you favor. Consider it a bonus for hard riding for us this last three months. She sucks up grain like a sluice from a gold strike. I'm thinking grain in the Long Jake barn might be a mite scarce this winter. So you take her. You're a man that hardly ever uses his spurs, and she's a horse that never needs one."

I was right pleased with this little horse. Mostly, I rode good cow horses, moving as I did from one ranch job to another. But, a little mare like this one, with a perfect nose for herding cattle, was something I'd never had before. High white socks, a rump stout as a chuck wagon, and a white star on her forehead gave her a proud look. Hell, she carried my Texas Jack roping saddle like it'd been made for her. She had narrow withers and took a short cinch girth. At only fourteen-and-a-half hands, she was easy to step up onto. Hell, I was but five foot six myself.

It was just coming on dark as I rode through the old part of Española before reaching the five new buildings just across the Brazos ditch. In the old part, they claimed to remember why this village was named after a ditch. The old men smoked, drank a little Mescal, and talked about the Conquistadores they claimed spent a winter here, three, maybe four hundred years ago. I doubt that. Anyways, the ditch drained off the Rio Chama, a mile away, and provided good irrigation to the two hundred acres of grain and yellow corn under cultivation in this little farming village.

"Evening, young man," my uncle, the liveryman, said, as I dismounted on the offside. "That's a fine looking animal you're riding. Looks like a cow horse."

"You betcha she is. I'm riding for the Long Jake now, but they don't need me in the winter. How you doing, Uncle Emiliano?"

"I'm fine. Your ma's fine. So's your aunt, who's still mad at me. That woman can keep a mad on longer than any man in the valley. But, welcome home, son. Everyone will be glad you're back. Just put that fine little black in the corner stall, where it's quiet. I'll give her a half-sack of grain."

"If you don't mind, Uncle, she sucks up grain. Maybe a full sack?"

"All right. You go on and wash up in the back. Then, head on over the footbridge to the house. I think your ma's over there trying to cheer up her sister. Woman just won't cheer up hardly at all these days."

Ma had moved back across the footbridge eight years ago, when I turned sixteen. That was the year Pa lost the little ranch I'd been raised on near Dulce. The bank took the ranch, and Pa died of the shame of it. Some said his heart gave out, but I knew the ranch was his heart. The bank took both.

The little adobe cookhouse was our family's gathering place. Lit only by candles, it boasted a stone fireplace in its center. What made it different was a round stone chimney, enclosed on all sides by what Uncle said they called a skylight down in Santa Fe. My grandfather built the house, one adobe brick at a time. He started with a stone chimney, and built the walls next. He was the first man to have a glass ceiling in a house in this part of the country. Everybody who passed by marveled at the four double-glass sheets, in eight-inch square frames. Set up high on a brazed pipe frame, it was a sight few had ever seen in a small village. Grandfather even took the weather into consideration, Pa said. He told me it sloped down in all four directions. Didn't matter which way the rain came. Rain sluiced off it like a big old duck atop the roof.

Three other smaller adobes formed a half-circle around it. My aunt and uncle lived in one, Ma in another. The third was a bunkhouse for whoever needed a bed. I'd slept there between ranch jobs for the last nine years.

"Okay, Bo," Ma said, after releasing her bear hug, "are you in trouble, or are you home for the winter? It's got to be one."

"No, Ma. I'm not in trouble. The girl, she's in trouble. So I need to hide out for a while."

"If you don't quit telling those lies to me, I'm going to give you a big whoopin'. Girl! Ha. No girl would look at you; skinny like a sugar sack with a half-pound of kindling. And you smell like a hired mule. How long have you been riding around without a bath?"

I washed up, but didn't take a bath. A fifty-year old serape draped the big copper tub in the bunkhouse. No one took a bath until Saturday afternoon. The other two guys there, my cousins, would have made life hard if I'd listened to Ma.

Dinner was noisy, and slow, like always. "So, Bo String, you still look like your name," my Aunt Josefina said, as she flipped tortillas in a cast iron pan. She was the best cook in the village. The smells in her kitchen could make a cowboy cry.

"A string bean, not a pinto bean. My sister says you looked like a fiddle string when you were born, so they named you that. Sit down and we'll make you look like a rope, at least.

Emiliano, who sometimes thinks he's in charge around here, thinks you will stay here all winter. I hope so. We'll turn you into a sausage by Easter Sunday, Nephew. Maybe they'll change your name to Bo Sausage."

I sat and ate with my cousins at the long table. There was no tablecloth, but Aunt Josefina scrubbed the wood slats every morning with soap so harsh, it would take the hide off a wild boar. Brightly colored ceramic bowls of chili sauce, onions, pickles, and day-old bacon bits formed a little circle in the middle of the table. Next to them, three large, glazed pitchers waited patiently every morning. One for well water, another with homemade wine, and the last with a kind of yellow tea mixed with milk, honey, and melon juice. Fried meats, pork or chicken, came in smaller bowls. But, best of all was the big wicker basket. It was as round as Emiliano's belly, and filled with hot tortillas.

First, you went to the stove and filled your bowl with beans from the cast iron pot. Then, you added what you wanted from the center of the table. But, before anyone could take a single bite, Uncle Emiliano had to say grace to the Virgin Mary. Then, everyone ate as fast as he could, before the food ran out.

The next morning, I saw a rider on a black stallion stop at the livery barn. He was talking to my uncle. There seemed to be an excitement of some sort. I couldn't hear the words from the bench where I was working on my tack, and my guns, but my uncle was waving his arm and pointing back down to the river. Ma had taken my small roll of clothes and both of the felted wool blankets that held fast inside my canvas bedroll. I was cleaning and oiling the Colt revolver and the .30-30 rifle that Pa had left to me. No money, but a damn good rifle. I was using a wire brush to buff the hard iron spurs that every vaquero worth his salt wore in New Mexico. Gringos wore silver spurs. Vaqueros wore black iron. Pa was a German immigrant, but Ma's family went back two hundred years to Hidalgo Spain, Aunt Josefina always said. My cousins kidded me by calling me a German-Mexican string bean.

The gringo on the black stallion spurred his way back down the slope to the river. About an hour later, Uncle crossed the footbridge for lunch. I went to help him carry a big sack of onions. "What was the ruckus this morning, with the gringo on the black studhorse, Uncle? I was thinking at first I'd better come save you. But, I already cleaned my gun and didn't want to shoot anybody, and then have to clean it again."

"Ah, Bo, you remind me of your dad. He was funny, too. But, no, it was not a ruckus. Just a small disagreement. I know that guy. Riding a stud is a show for him. But, we got two mares in heat in the barn. He was smelling them and starting to get a little crazy. That guy's from Dulce. You might have known him, too. I think he knew your dad."

"What's his name?"

"Alfonso Ganado. You know him?"

"No, I never seen him before. He looked like a gringo to me, but his name is Alfonso Ganado?"

"He is not a Mexican, but he's not a gringo, either. Ganado is a Navajo name; don't know his family origins. But I know this about him. He's a tracker. Mountain lions, wild boar, and men on the run. I don't like men who track just to kill, not to eat. He's a hard one, that *hombre*."

"Well, Uncle, as long as he's not tracking you, or me, I guess we don't have to worry about him."

Over lunch, which was more beans but less chili, the subject came up again. "So, this man-tracker, Alfonso, is he on somebody's trail? What's he want from you?" I asked.

"He wanted me to give him dried beef and some bacon. And, of course, he wanted a jug of our wine—that's what he wanted most. But, he did not want to pay for any of the things he said he needed. He said the railroad would pay me later."

"The railroad? One of their workers died, but they need a tracker?"

"I dunno. Alfonso's been by here before. He's hunted Mexicans, Texans, and all manner of animals. I don't like him."

"Did he say he was riding for Captain Standard H. Plumb?"

"Didn't say a name. Just that he was told they were bringing a spare horse for the body. A posse from Chama. That's where he's going to now. Chama. You know, somebody robbed the train up there by Osier, maybe it was last week. They will get him. I feel sorry for him, even if he's a train robber. And, I'm afraid I know who it is."

Bo was almost afraid to ask. "Who, Uncle? Who do you think it is?"

"A man named Angus. I know him and he's a good man. Used to come by here sometimes. I help him sometimes. I know his eyes—they don't lie. He's just lonely because his wife died, not too long after they married—when they were both just kids, really. You ever heard about that?"

I saddled my little mare, gathered up my clean blankets, both guns, and borrowed a heavy felt coat from Uncle Emiliano. Filling a gunnysack with food from Aunt Josefina's kitchen, I fretted about telling Ma I was leaving again. I got that sad job done, and took my mare to the horse trough. Sierra drank her fill, so I jumped the stirrups and trotted back across the ditch, and headed north, the way Alfonso Ganado went. Somehow, without knowing why, I was on Angus's side this time.

CHAPTER 17

Angus Riding South Down Bear Mountain

WO DAYS OF HARD RIDING, but Horse and I felt mighty good to be five, maybe six miles away from my cabin. I'd doubled back twice, watching my back trail. They were there, maybe three hours behind me, following Horse, that steady old packhorse, and me from Aposto's barn. Nothing to do now but let those boys come on in—maybe close up—where I'd have an advantage.

Five miles north of the cabin, we'd slogged up a long sloping canyon through a foot-and-a-half of packed snow. But, once we topped out, there was but a few inches of fresh, crisp snow, and clear blue sky on the horizon. There were deer signs aplenty, some bobcat tailings, but no horses, mules, or sign of humans, Indian or otherwise. The bears were all in hibernation by now. But, red-tailed hawks, a few eagles, and a pair of Peregrine falcons kept track of us the whole run up the mountain.

Checking the shadow of the sun on the downslope side of the big pine trees, I reckoned we'd made the pull to the top in just over four hours. It was not yet noon when we started down the south slope of the mountain. I figured we'd make it to the cabin in a couple hours. And we did.

If a man was paying close attention, even from twenty feet away, he wouldn't have seen a thing. Nothing but a dense stand of spruce and fir. What looked to be a game trail around the stand headed down to a fast-running stream two hundred feet downslope. If you were real still, you could hear it from here. Anyone following my track would've passed by the cabin thinking I was headed for the stream downslope. That's where my track would peter out. They'd follow the stream down a mile or so, and then figure it out—I'd doubled back on them. They'd turn and come back up.

That little stream ran year around, except when it froze over in the deepest part of winter, but that was two months off. Right now, it was running smooth and clear. Unless I had a fire inside the cabin, there was nothing to signal anyone that it even existed. Even a Ute wouldn't come on it accidental-like. Heavy twenty-five-foot tall spruce trees, mixed with red fir, pushing forty feet up into the sky, and wild oak brush created a tight wall of native timber. That's all you could see if you followed either of two natural trails up the mountain on the south side. My cabin was in the middle, completely obscured by timber and dense undergrowth.

Two years before Mazy died, I'd dug deep into the side of the downslope. That made more than half the cabin below ground level. It had taken me almost a month to dig a twenty-five-foot square hole directly down into the black earth. On the north side, I'd notched spruce logs back into the up-mountain slope. The effort broke two new pickaxe handles. It took near a hundred hours of hard banging on the business end of the pick just to get down five feet into a mix of granite shale, sandstone rock, and clay. Then, I sloped her back ten feet. The front width was almost twenty feet. The entire back wall was exposed earth, with mud plaster over gunnysacks. The front foundation was pure caliche mudpack. The pack was four feet tall in front, with vertical log poles from there up to the roof. Inside the single room, the stone floor kept out the mountain, and the mud roof kept out the sky. Altogether, the space just plain ignored harsh weather outside, and kept a body snug—cool in the summer and warm in the winter.

I'd hauled the flooring stones two miles by mule. Their strength made the job possible, but their constant braying persuaded me never to own another mule. The log walls, five-inch diameter fir trees, came from a dozen different stands each more than a mile away. The vertical cracks between the walls were mud and tar. Inside, it looked like any other log cabin. But, from outside, it looked like part of the mountain.

There was no front door, but there were four vertical slits about five inches wide facing downslope. Both had whole fir logs, with split-pine edges. I'd left the bark on the whole logs facing out, and covering the narrow openings. When closed, the slits looked like trees. But, when open, they gave me soft light and cool air of a summer morning. If there was any danger, from hostiles or other undesirables, these slits became gun ports. I'd built two slits on the east-side wall, and on the west, a door large enough to bring two horses inside through the west wall.

Just like the first trappers did up this high, I planned to share the inside space all winter with my horses. No need for a horse shed. Nothing from the outside suggested the place even existed. Took two months to finish took the job. When done, I figured I had what no other fool on the mountain had ever even thought about—a wood and mud cave for humans and horses.

The best part was the stone fireplace in the back wall. My pa had picked up some masonry skills, before he began survey-ing the western half of the country. He must have passed them on to me. I took naturally to cutting the stone and caulking it in real tight. I ran a tin chimney, surrounded by stone, up through the mud and natural earth roof. Once there, I ran the pipe flat along the roof, then another twenty feet uphill before it let the smoke out slow and easy. To get that, I cut holes in the pipe along a six-foot section.

Thinking Ma would have been proud, I dug a root cellar directly into the mountainside. The only way anyone could ever know it was there was to see it from the inside. Making two trips down to Brazos, I hauled enough dry stores, salted meat, and grain for the animals to last three months. Two eighty-gallon tanks stored enough fresh water for three weeks. Course I'd never thought about a posse tracking me up here. I'd worried about marauders, hungry miners, and even that rare Indian who was up to no good. But, if Robert Morton was right, the Pinkertons were after me again. And, if he was wrong, and those boys were not hard on my trail, I'd spend the winter alone. As usual. But, as I thought on it, Addie came to mind. Probably take me all winter to sort my thinking out on her, I figured.

CHAPTER 18
Bo String Riding North Up Bear Mountain

I REMEMBERED THE SAD LOOK on Ma's face when I crossed the Brazos's ditch. Now, hunkered down before a small campfire, I was thirteen miles away. Reckon it was near three-fourths of the way up to the top of Bear Mountain. Good decision? Hope so. Ma had worried about winter coming on and me heading up mountain. I'd wrapped two felt blankets and a canvas tarp tight around me. The November cold, at almost eight thousand feet, seeped down into my bones as the night sky gave way to gray and the frost turned to ice.

Sleeping upright, in a sitting position, cross-legged, on my saddle pad, was something I'd learned while on night herd duty with the *Dos S* brand. That way, my butt was off the ground, and the rest of me was upright against the tree. I could see my little black pony, hobbled and rubbed down with buffalo grass. Her nosebag was near clean of the double handful of sweet grain I'd given her. My saddle was horn down next to the rock-sheltered fire pit, with only small embers left of the dead log I'd busted up for kindling. My rifle was upright, leaning into the tree beside me. I was in for a long night.

My plan didn't seem all that sound after a long day's ride up the mountain. I guess I thought I'd just luck onto something that would clue me. As far as I could tell, no one had been up here for years.

"That damn posse has to be ahead of me. If that's the case, why haven't I cut their trail yet," I asked Sierra. Bending one ear toward me, but otherwise paying no attention, she chomped on the last few specks of grain in the bottom of the nosebag. I was riding northeast and knew that if they'd chased Angus from Cascade Creek, they'd have taken a line southwest. I'd come across their back trail somewhere on this trajectory. Unless I was ahead of them. That was a worry, but I knew they had a day's head start on me, so I was near certain that I'd cut their trail somewhere. Several long trotting horses in the snow would show up a quarter mile away.

I'd wiped down my rifle, snugged the six-shot double action Colt into my loose belt, and tried to outguess both Angus and the posse. If they are up ahead of me, I should cut their trail somewhere before hitting Cascade Creek on the other side of the mountain. But, if they are already on this side of Cascade Creek looking for Angus, I might meet them coming head on.

"Dang it," I mumbled to Sierra. "We've come this far, might as well go over the top and drop down into the Los Piños valley on the other side. They gotta be ahead of us still."

CHAPTER 19
Angus Hunkering Down on Bear Mountain

U NSADDLING HORSE, getting him brushed down and settling him inside the cabin took a good half hour. Another
half hour breezed by while I settled the packhorse in. Figured
it could be a long stand. So, I poured each one a coffee can of
grain in the feed trough and filled the two-sided water bucket.
Closing the half-door between the stone floor and the outside
door, I opened the wall slits on three sides of the cabin. The
midday air rushed in, and the musty room began to air out.
I left the horse door open and made sure both animals had
tie-downs on their lead ropes and butt ropes keeping them
in their spaces.

I thought I'd best check the chimneystack so I walked up around the cabin and pulled my way up the steep hill that formed the cabin's north wall. Twenty feet uphill, I reached the end.

Everything was still, on first reckoning. But, once you get still yourself, the forest comes alive. That comes from being fifty miles away from people. If you quiet your mind enough, you'll hear birds chirping, wind blowing softly in the pine-cones, and critters everywhere, scurrying about their business.

Four large boulders that leaned against one another, just twelve inches off the ground, but on a higher plane than the cabin roof, hid the chimneystack. They helped flatten out the smoke from the wood stove twenty yards downslope inside the cabin.

The temperature was in the low thirties when full dark came, but the wood stove quickly warmed the fifteen-foot-square room. No danger of smoke attracting anyone in the dark, I thought. The cabin showed signs of pack rat activity, and maybe something larger. Raccoon, probably.

Using my jackknife, I opened a can of peaches and some tinned meat for supper. I'd already made a small pot of cowboy coffee, and it was hissing on the little iron stove. Then I laid out my bedroll on the makeshift bunk, more a platform than a bunk, on the far side of the room.

There were no chairs or other comforting things in here, but I'd made two split-pine benches, and a small eating table in front of the stove. The benches served two purposes—one for working leather and tack, and the other to sit on, in front of the window slits.

The five-foot-long, belly-high workbench sat to the rear of the room, close to the wood stove. The other bench, chest high, was two feet higher than the workbench but narrow, and less than a foot across. That made it easy to move with one hand, from one window slit to the other. Its three legs, tied in the middle with rawhide, supported a smooth leather pouch at the top. I'd carefully measured its height to make sure that I could sit in front, lean my forearms and head on it, and still see downhill.

I buttoned up the window slits and the east-facing door at dusk. Shortly after dark, Horse's breathing changed. Both horses slept standing up. I slept fitfully. Dawn came, but I thought better of restarting the fire. The packhorse, unburdened by one hundred fifty pounds, stood his ground alongside Horse, but paid no mind to him, or me.

CHAPTER 20

Bo String Finds the Posse on Bear Mountain

COME FIRST LIGHT, I unwound myself up out of my cowboy squat, loosed the felt blankets, and stretched my knees out. Pulling my near-frozen boots on, I tugged my hat down, which I'd worn all night, so far it squashed my ears. Pure quiet. All around me. I relieved myself on a barberry shrub, which attracted Sierra's attention. She gave me the evil eye, not liking being both hobbled and tied to a tree all damn night. Not giving it enough thought, I restarted my little fire, thinking I'd make some cowboy coffee. Just as quick as I'd started the fire with my store-bought wood matches, I realized the smoke would carry for miles. It was too good a sky to mess up with smoke, so I drowned the little flame with a double-handful of dirt. Then I brushed off my saddle, and chewed on a stick of deer jerky while I studied the clouds.

Taking off the hobble rope, I brushed Sierra. She nibbled on my arm, signaling her forgiveness for tying her to a tree all night. I saddled up, and headed north. I'd ridden about a mile through rough brush when faint sounds up ahead got my attention up ahead. Something breaking through scrub oak bush? Or last year's pinecones cracking underfoot? Dawn wasn't more than a few minutes old, so everything was fresh. Ground frost was disappearing, dew taking its place. The air, crispy still, was just starting to warm up. Every bird within a quarter-mile flitted around. Whatever I'd first heard went quiet. So I just sat there, snug on my saddle, knees loose, and waited.

CHAPTER 21
Angus Hears Something

THE WINDOW SLIT ON the downhill slope of the cabin had come to be one of my favorite places to sit and take in the morning air. I heard the horse first and saw birds flying around looking at something I couldn't see. But, the sounds of the horse got louder as I imagined it digging in to climb up my direction on snow-crusted ground. Horse sounds carry more than a half-mile in air this thin. And, birds, coming in and out of view, give the sky a little sense of movement. Somebody was close. Just one horse. Made no sense. But, no matter, I closed the slit, barred the door on the inside, and hunkered down. Sound would tell me a whole lot more than sight would inside my wood cave. Forests muffle sound, but rocks carry it. So, I listened for the clang of iron horseshoes on hard granite rock.

Hunkered down inside my own cabin listening for sounds of danger ain't my way of doing things. It came to me that a duck floating on a pond feels just like this before the shotgun blast. You never hear it coming. The trees out there in front of me were watching with me, and the rocks were listening, too—all of us waiting for something. One horse, I thought, coming into view through the trees any second now. Or not. Seems as if we were caught in a spider's web—me, my new mustang, the dependable packhorse, the trees, rocks, and whoever 'n hell was picking his way up the trail to us.

CHAPTER 22
Captain Plumb's Posse Pushing Hard

Alfonso Ganado had good ears, too. He rode back toward us, not because he heard a horse, but because he wasn't hearing anything.

"Something is moving, Capitan Plumb," he whispered and pointed down at the fresh tracks, as I rode up next to him.

The trail was still clear—two horses headed downslope, but not sliding, and there was no fresh ooze. These were yesterday's tracks, not today's.

"I thought you said you'd lost the trail about a mile back, Alfonso, but my good man, you've obviously found it again."

"*Si, Señor,* I did. Your man tried a gringo trick by dismounting and crossing a fifty-foot wide sandstone shelf on foot, leading both horses. But, then he had to tie them to a tree on the other side while he brushed some scrapes from the horseshoes on the rock. I found that place because there was a rope burn on the backside of the tree. The packhorse reared up, because the tracks were too many for just standing. He's close."

"Or," Branson said, "he might be twenty miles down the mountain headed for Brazos."

"You two had better keep your mind on our business and quit snipping at one another," I said.

I dismounted, headed for a big flat rock, and sat down. Inching a toothpick out of my felt vest, I watched as the three of them came over, got off their horses, and loosened their cinches.

"OK, Alfonso, you're doing a good job. You think we should ride hard now? Or, can you tell anything about how far he might be from us, based on his horse tracks in the snow?"

"No, the tracks tell me which way, and they tell me how long ago he was here. He was here yesterday. But tracks don't tell how close he is. The air tells me that. Let me ride ahead for a mile. You wait here ten minutes, and then you follow my track. Don't listen; just follow my tracks. I can hear you behind me, but I will also hear what's up ahead. If he's close like I think he is, and if he makes some noise as he's going down toward Brazos, I'll hear him. He'll go slower on the downslope because the higher the sun gets, the muddier the trail will be."

"Brazos?" Joe Pete butted in to the conversation. "Captain, I thought you had some information about a hideout up here somewhere. But your man smells out that Angus is headed to Brazos?"

"Don't matter," I said. "Either way, we're on his track. Ganado is right. He can scout out in front of us a mile. He'll either find a hideaway, or the slick track will drop off down the mountain toward Brazos."

Branson did not like this and said, "But, damn it, Brazos is only a little farming village. It's about thirty miles that way. If he's going there, he will be out in the open for over twenty miles. We got two pairs of good binoculars. Ganado has his track. Let's get horseback and thunder on ahead. I want another shot at him."

Waving Branson off, I turned to Pete and Alfonso.

"All right. Pete, you and Branson stretch your legs and empty your bladders. But, don't go sipping on those warm-up whiskey pints you law boys keep in your dusters. We got ourselves a train robber up ahead. Don't let me down again. Branson, maybe you'd best loosen your Hawken out of its scabbard. I can smell the sumbitch."

CHAPTER 23
Bo String
Makes Contact

SIERRA WAS FEELING HER OATS as we kept climbing up another half-mile, snorting and striking rocks through the snow. I'd pulled up to let her blow on a little shelf at the edge of a thick stand of fir. As I hooked one knee over the saddle horn, I saw a lone wolf lope off ahead of me, about two hundred yards upwind. Because I was downwind, he didn't smell me, but he heard my horse sounds. You don't usually get this close to a full-grown mountain wolf—damned impressive creature. I watched him stride up the hill toward a rocky outcropping. High in the sky above me, two red-tailed hawks circled and made long sweeping turns gliding in the updrafts coming from the top of the mountain. Then, clawing me out of my revelry, I saw horse tracks, fresh ones, not forty yards in front.

Taking the slack out of my reins, I swung my leg back down off the horn and snugged my boot back into the stirrup. From this vantage point, I couldn't see much in the tracks other than it was not just one horse. There were two horse tracks, close together, like the back one was on a lead rope. Headed south on an almost parallel track from my northward heading. Someone had passed by me real close—headed back down behind me. But I couldn't tell when.

Easing my rifle out of the scabbard, I sucked in a big breath and eased my horse over closer to the tracks. Looking back and forth and up and down the track, I could see no signs of anything moving. Stopping the mare with an easy rein, I got off, but held tight to the reins. I took off my left glove and felt the edges of the front track with my fingertips. Frost. So, these horses had come through here, headed south sometime yesterday. The tracks were deep into the ground below the snow. Fully loaded packhorse in back. And, they were evenly spaced; a man wasn't in no hurry.

Jumping the stirrup, I mounted as still as I could. Listening. Smelling. Thinking. If the rider was Angus, why was he headed south? It could not be the posse; it was just two horses. I walked my horse fifty yards to my right, then turned downhill, looking for an outrider. Nothing. I did the same in the other direction, walking slowly past the double-track. Nothing.

Not a hard decision, I thought. I'd best follow these tracks downhill. Back the way I'd just come. The tracks had the same even spacing. Whoever this rider was, he was riding at his own pace. Didn't look like he knew anyone was chasing him. Not in a hurry. No sliding or sloshing around the hoof prints.

I needed to get my bearings. Seeing another high outcropping on my left, I moved behind the horse track in the snow and rode for higher ground. Binoculars would not have helped, even if I'd had any. I was in a deep stand of mixed fir, spruce, and pine. Not seeing was a hindrance, but I could hear.

I swung my leg over the cantle when, of a sudden, I heard breaking brush up the trail to the north. The distinctive sound of small acorn branches breaking, and rawhide chaps sliding along boulders came from the north, in front of me. Someone was upwind—headed my way.

Keeping still in the saddle, and holding my gloved hand over the mare's nose, I leaned forward on her neck. Right at the point where I left the track up ahead, and had turned off to my right, I could see a black horse, a helluva big black horse. The rider leaned way off the side of his saddle, head down, studying the ground. Then he stopped and tugged his horse's head up high, lifting it with a gentle pull on the reins held up over his own head. He was moving his horse's head out of my line of sight.

As I stared at the rider sixty yards ahead of me, I realized what he was looking at. He was studying Sierra's tracks, the ones we'd made just minutes ago. Not taking the time to think it through, I wheeled Sierra on a tight loop.

He was now only sixty yards away, on a clear line of sight for both of us. Except I was up on a bluff, probably twenty feet higher in elevation than he was. The rider, dressed in a black duster, with his hat pulled down low over his eyebrows, held a long-barreled Sharps rifle across the crook of his left arm. He and his horse stood their ground for about two minutes. I froze still, hoping he wouldn't look my way. Then, slowly scanning the ground beneath him, in an arc from left to right, the man took off his hat and leaned his ears one way, and then the other. While I could see him clearly, it was obvious that he hadn't spotted me. He'd just started wheeling his horse around, when Sierra shook loose of the nose hold I had with my glove, and whinnied into the cold mountain air.

Swinging back in a tight arc, he spotted me up on the outcropping. Dropping the reins, his horse stopped. In a flash, the man jammed the rifle into his shoulder, and slid his left hand up the stock. I could see the muzzle end of the barrel swing and then stop dead on me. I could not see it clear, but I knew he was about to adjust the rear V notch. He was sighting me in.

I could almost feel the bullet coming my way as I dropped my head down and to the right, spurring the little mare with my left boot into a tight downhill turn. She leaped off the outcropping an instant before I heard the sharp crack of the bastard's first shot. High and wide, but not for lack of skill on his part. Sierra had just saved me by leaping off the outcropping and dropping us both three feet below the trajectory of the bullet.

Skidding forward, her front knees buckled down into the snow. I lurched forward onto her neck but kept my seat, pulled back on the reins, and somehow fished my .30-30 out of its scabbard. Sierra righted herself, throwing her head back and digging her rear hooves deep into the snow, rock, and mud. We slid downhill another ten feet completely out of the shooter's line of sight. The boom of the gun meant it was a heavy-bore hunting rifle. Sliding low off the saddle on my right side, I held tight on the reins with my left hand, gripping the rifle with my right. Skidding to a halt, as Sierra gasped for breath, I slid my left arm under her neck, soothing and taking control at the same time.

"There you are, girl. Steady now, we're out of it."

It sounded like the tracker made a bad guess of it. The loud cracking noise of his thrashing horse was now on the down side of the outcropping, which would keep me on higher ground. I jumped off the saddle, threw the reins over a low hanging spruce limb, and crawled on my hands and knees to the edge of the outcropping. And there he was. In plain sight, not more than fifty feet downwind, downhill, and unable to see me because he was studying the trail, looking downslope to where he thought I was.

Taking in three measured breaths, just like Pa had taught me to, I calculated the downward angle, figured in the absence of any wind drift, and sighted my .30-30 on the man who'd just tried to kill me. Aiming at the ass end of his horse, but guessing I'd shoot high, I held my breath and pulled slowly on the trigger, trying hard not to alter the sighting. I felt the subtle push back of the trigger as the firing pin hit the bullet casing, visualized it dead center on the brass casing, and then felt the little pop upward towards the tip of the barrel, followed by the hard slam of the stock against my right shoulder. As I heard and saw the fire blast out of the muzzle, I saw the man's big black duster collapse onto the horse's neck. Then, in a rush of energy, the black horse pitched backward, spinning around, trying to dig his hooves down into the mushy snow.

First, the black hat, then the rider fell off the right side of the horse. I watched the Sharps hit a boulder and clang off into the rocks. The horse, now shed of its rider, loped off up the trail with stirrup leathers slapping against his belly and loose reins dragging in the snow.

CHAPTER 24
Angus and Bo String

CABIN FEVER MAYBE, but I felt the need for a little outside air. So I eased open the horse door and stepped out under a mostly clear blue sky with a slight wind bearing north by northwest. That's when I heard the first shot. A few seconds later an answering crack, with a different whine. Not the same rifle. Two different men firing. At one another, or at something upwind from me? No doubt about the sound—first a big bore blast and then the whine of a .30-30 carbine. To the north. Behind me, I thought; they're coming. But, who's shooting and why two different guns? *Someone shooting back?*

I ran uphill to the chimney and pulled the flat rock over on top of the tin chute. Then I scrambled twenty feet east, circling back around on the west side. Nothing coming, so I went back inside, pulling the door shut behind me. I hoped no one would see my boot tracks at the chimney hole.

Barring the door with the hickory branch I'd cut to fit smoothly into the flat iron L bars, I struggled to catch my breath. Patting Horse on the rump, and giving the packhorse a hand along his back, I clicked at the mustang, "Horse, you be still now."

Pulling the wood stove's iron cover off to the side, I poured the rest of the coffee on the smoldering coals. There was no smell. Good.

Taking a long listen first at the east window slot and then at the two in front, I decided no one was near the cabin. Three or four Mexican blue jays sat on two thin branches of a fir tree fifteen feet downwind of me. Horse was standing stock still, with his right eyelid half closed. Right, no one close by. But they're coming.

I checked to see that the breach load of my Winchester .30-40 Craig held the maximum five rounds. Then I slid a sixth brass cartridge, three inches long, into the firing chamber. Standing the long barrel gun up against the wall six inches from the window slit, I pulled the high bench over to the front slits. My .44 Colt, which I carried with five rounds and an empty chamber under the firing pin, was still on the shelf below the first slit. I pushed a sixth round into the revolving chamber and eased the hammer down. This was a double-action Colt, and was mighty comforting to have, since the coming fight might be close in. Leaning on the oak bench, I listened carefully. Not a sound except for birds, wind, and the comforting rustling of tree branches.

Reaching up to the top shelf behind the stove on the rear wall of the cabin, I took down the four-foot leather casing holding Pa's eight-gauge scattergun. Loading both barrels with double-ought shells, I used an oilcloth to wipe down the barrels. Using a dry cook rag, I spat on the short walnut stock and gave it a little spit and polish. I was careful to finger around the brass trigger housing. Then I stood the eight-pound turkey killer up against the west wall's vertical slot.

Breathing in deeply, I took another listen. Breathing out as slowly as I could, I bent over at the west window for two, maybe three minutes. Nothing. Opening the uphill facing slit, I peeked out. Two black-tailed jackrabbits nibbled at the leavings under an acorn bush ten feet out from the cabin. There were squirrel droppings and mouse tracks on the pine needle ground, and a slow-moving cloud cover coming in up above me. But nothing moving close in. No sounds.

Opening the inside door to the root cellar, I eased a small pouch of venison jerky out of a mason jar. I could almost hear my father saying, "Son, if you can't shoot, you might as well chew. It makes the time pass and will settle the bees in your belly." It's what he always did while waiting for a deer to cross the creek and come within firing range. But, this time, I wasn't waiting for a five-point buck.

Nothing happened for the better part of an hour. I sipped water from a tin cup, rechecked the cylinder on my .44 Colt, and quietly walked from one gun slot to another, listening and watching the birds for any movement outside. Then, as faint as a rainbow trout flopping in a stream, I heard the intermittent clop of a horse coming down the slope from behind the cabin. Then came the sound of branches being swooshed aside, followed by a horse's snort, signaling that its rider had just tugged him up. A chain chinstrap will do that.

I could not see man or horse, but I could feel him. If I couldn't see him, I'd be invisible to whoever was out there. He had not discovered the cabin, or I'd have heard something. Too much heavy underbrush out there to move quietly. Hiding my cabin in the densest part of the forest worked to his disadvantage. But, I couldn't see him any better than he could see me.

Horses ain't human, but they make most of the same sounds we do—snortin', fartin', wheezin', and stumblin' through brush. Their iron shoes clang something awful on rocks and thud when hitting hard dirt. Those sounds were coming down at me from the north. Just one horse. The horse coming at me was nervous. I could tell because when a horse is up on its toes, the thuds on the ground take on a different sound. It's hard to hear from atop the animal, but from twenty-five feet away, at near ground level, it was clear. A nervous horse carrying a settled man? Not likely, I thought.

I could faintly hear the horse's heavy breath pushing air out into the cold morning air. I sensed movement, like a rider tugging back on the reins and inching his mount along the broken ground west of my cabin. Bet he was listening as hard as I was. Could be he was just careful, moving down the mountain trail, knowing he was upwind of me.

Then, just for a moment, I saw the horse and its rider. Thirty seconds later, they reappeared, and stopped not twenty feet from me. I cupped one ear at 'em. I could see through the branches that he was listening, too, leaning over the offside of a little black mare. Then, faint as a whisper in the dark, I heard what they heard. More horses, more men, someone yelling, probably a quarter-mile away. Sound carries a good distance on a crisp, winter morning.

"Captain! Captain! Over here. I got a track."

That had to be the posse. I looked back at the rider as he dismounted. He'd lost his hat, and a wet mop of black hair stuck up every which way. He wore a heavy felt coat slick with wet snow and mud. He was favoring his right shoulder with his left hand and sideways to me. His face wasn't all that clear on account of the tree branches between us, and he had a dried cut along his cheekbone. It looked like dried blood or maybe mud—hard to say from here. I'd never seen him before, but somehow I had the feeling I ought to know him.

Covered with snow, the man's bedroll hung halfway off the little black mare he was riding. I could see the top of a saddle sheath on the far side of his horse and a looped rope slung careless-like around the horn.

Then, as though he had nothing better to do, he tried to reattach the bedroll to his saddle strings and recenter the full, double-sided saddlebags. But, I could see he was having trouble using his right arm, even though his left hand held fast to the .30-30 rifle in the crook of his right arm.

I'll be damned! This boy out there is what the posse was hunting, not me. The boy's back was to me now, as he struggled to recenter the load on the back of his horse.

Hoping the posse couldn't hear me, but the boy could, I hissed at him,

"All right, stranger. I got a bead on you. Just you lower that .30-30 to the ground right now. Keep facing your horse. Don't turn around. You move and I'll drill you where you stand."

He froze. Dropping his .30-30, he leaned into the little mare, as if he was weak.

"Angus, is that you behind me?"

Horse whinnied to the mare, and I said, "Just you stand where you are. I'm gonna come out and walk up behind you. Real slow, now. Just stand where you are."

CHAPTER 25

Captain Plumb Finds Alfonso Ganado

I WAS FURIOUS WHEN WE caught Alfonso's horse running up the trail toward us.

"Goddamn, Pete, that's your tracker's horse a-runnin' up to us. Damn fool must have got himself shot. Go get that horse!"

Ten minutes later, following the track downhill and leading Alfonso's horse, we found him. He'd crawled forward from the place in the snow where his horse had thrown him. He was leaning up against a forty-foot Ponderosa pine. He had taken a bullet in his left thigh, and had lost some blood, but he wasn't unconscious.

"Who shot you, Alfonso? Was it our man? Goddamn, why didn't you wait for us? We heard two shots—did you drop the sumbitch?"

I was still horseback, firing questions to Alfonso. He was splayed out on the ground with his neck and head partway propped up on the tree trunk. At first, he didn't recognize us, giving me a vacant stare. Pete dismounted, tied his horse to a sapling, and looked at Alfonso's wound. "He's torn up bad, Captain, but the bullet came clean through. He ain't gonna die now, but he's bleeding some, and we got to get him down off this mountain. Hell, Captain, he'll bleed out if I can't stanch the flow."

Turning to Branson, Pete asked, "Can you get down here and help me? Fetch that little kit out of my saddlebag. And bring me your bottle of warm-up whiskey, too."

"You hold on there!" I screamed. "We got to move forward. Our man is out there—not far away. Branson, you take the lead; get your Hawken out. I can smell that sumbitch. We can't take no time for doctoring."

Joe Pete ignored me. Branson got off his horse on the right side, took the Hawken out of the scabbard, and leaned against his horse.

"Captain Plumb, you're a dead-on bastard, aren't you? You'd leave a good man down, let him bleed out, or freeze before nightfall? Just to catch a train robber? My god, man, I'm wondering if you got your faculties about you. You get down. Let's fix this man up. If he can ride with a busted leg, he can track. If he can't, then I'll track. But first we got to take care."

I argued my case, but staring at Branson's .50 caliber killing rifle calmed me down some. Dismounting, I reached for my water jug. I let them be while they doctored him. He continued to seem disconnected from us, but over the space of five minutes of doctoring and jabbering, Alfonso gave us an accounting.

He said he'd come on a man on a horse, who he assumed was the man we're tracking. He fired one shot with his Sharps, but missed as the man's horse jumped near off a little cliff. The man was more than two hundred feet away, uphill from him. Somehow, the man got behind him a few minutes later and fired down on him as Alfonso was short-stepping his horse down the mountain. Then, taking a short swallow from the water bag, followed by a long pull on the warm-up whiskey, he finished the story. He got shot, the other man got away. The cold was settling in. He answered Pete through pursed lips. The man who shot him was young, mounted on a little black cow pony.

He didn't think it was Angus.

"The little man was acting odd, Señor, like he was hunting us. He was a cowboy, not a train robber, Señor."

This was not welcome news. I glared at Alfonso and then turned to Joe Pete and Branson.

"Do either one of you know what 'n hell this man's talking about?"

Neither one answered, but just busied themselves tending to Alfonso's shoulder and left leg. Then Branson offered, "Captain, no sir, no I ain't got the slightest idea who 'n hell shot him. But, study on this. Last we saw our man, Angus, he was riding a bay. A gelding. Maybe he got a new horse somewhere. But he's no boy. He's a big man, well over six foot. Alfonso shot at a young man, a boy, he says, on a little black horse. Sounds like an innocent stranger, although God knows what he's doing up here. I think he's been eating too many beans and panicked. But, I'd say, now we got his wound stanched, he's gonna live this day out. We can get back on the trail, and let this ignorant tracker mend his self, best as he can. Let's tie his horse to a tree and worry about him later."

Turning back to Alfonso, I said, "Shit, man, you shot at the first man you saw. You were supposed to ride back and get us. Those were your orders."

Alfonso paid no mind to me. He would live, but I could see he'd had his fill of posse work, and me. Joe Pete fashioned a canvas splint out of pine branches and cut bedroll strips. They stopped the blood flow by pressing down hard on his wounds.

"Get him on horseback, Pete. Branson, you help Pete lift Alfonso up on his horse."

Branson took the lead, following the track down the mountain. We'd lost nearly an hour.

CHAPTER 26
Angus Gets Ready

"**B**O STRING? That's your name?"

"Yes sir, it is," Bo said, sitting on the long pine bench inside my cabin. I checked him for bullet wounds, even though he assured me the shooter on the big black horse had missed him by a country mile. But, he'd banged up his right arm some during the commotion.

"And, you're sure you hit him—you saw him go off his horse on one side and lose his rifle on the other?"

"Hell yeah. I wasn't but seventy-five feet away. I got him all right. But then I skedaddled downhill. I knew there was more of 'em close by."

"But you did not see any other riders?"

"I heard 'em. Calling out and all."

Slowly, I pulled the story out. He'd lost interest in posse work after that first try at it, when Branson missed me with his big Hawken on Ten Shoes Up a month ago. Then, he'd heard something about me robbing trains; he didn't recollect where he heard that.

"I ain't no train robber, son," I assured him.

"Why n' hell you running then?"

"Not running so much as they are chasing. Maybe you ought to go out there and ask them why they're chasing me."

As he chewed on my venison jerky, drank my water, and fought his shoulder pain, he gave me the rest of his story. When he was halfway through, I believed every word. This boy was not a liar. So, when he heard about a new posse forming up in Chama, and that they would track me down from Cascade Creek, he just decided to ride up here, and help me out. Simple as that.

"You just decided? How'd you figure that? You had no way to even find me, much less help me. Just blind luck—that's all. Jesus, Bo String, you got a crazy name. Maybe that's because you are crazy."

He continued to massage his shoulder and I could tell it pained him, but he was not the complaining type. He gritted his teeth when he had to move, but he was settling in and breathing normal.

"I believe your shoulder is just bruised; it ought not to affect your aim. The man you hit is not Plumb's pet shooter. I'm guessing he's a hired tracker."

We drank more cold water, chewed on venison jerky strips, and shared two hardtack biscuits. And, we waited for whatever might be coming our way.

I reckoned they'd come here the easy way. Just follow Bo's snow track, see the spot where he dismounted, and realize from the boot tracks somebody had drug him off the trail. That would tell them that Bo and I were close by.

"They'll find my horse," Bo said, rubbing his shoulder with a salt, sugar and molasses solution I'd mixed up for him.

"Yeah, they will."

"Should we set up outside, shoot 'em quick-like, before they shoot us?"

"No."

I asked him to sit still awhile. Looking out the gun slit on the west side, I shook my head up and down, motioning with my palm down at Bo. The way I figured it, the posse would either see or hear Bo's mare tied outside. The fight would be on then.

"Best to fight from inside, don't you think?" Bo asked. "Beats me. Ain't never been in a gunfight," I said not looking at him and shushing him with a downward wave of my hand. I was straining to sound out whatever was coming down the mountain at us.

"Never? You ain't a train robber, and you ain't a gunfighter? Jeeze, Mr. Angus, what are you?"

I moved away from the west gun-slot and checked the view to the south. My horses had quieted down, but his little mare was stomping and snorting outside, tied to that pine tree. Turning back to him, I said, "Let 'em shoot all they want into these six-inch fir logs. My logs are notched in with black, frozen tar. They'll hold. When they come, make sure you don't stick your face in front of the window slits. If you do, they'll give you new holes to replace your nose. But, they

have to get in close before they can fire a shot. Kneel down
and hunch over. Keep your eyes down at the bottom of the
sill. Got that?"

"I reckon, but there's four of them and only two of us."

"You put one of 'em out of commission. That's just three
against us two. And we've got the high ground. If a man comes
in sight, light him up. They ain't here to kill *you*, but I doubt
if they will be all that particular now."

When they came, they were noisy. Trotting horses, snorting
in the cold air and fighting their bits, causing bridle chains
to ching and leather to slap in the crisp air. Even going slow,
following the track, iron horseshoes were clanging down on
rocks. While we could not see them, the noise they made
told their story. Every so often one of them would slip on the
messy trail. I sensed they were constantly moving forward
with spurs to the horses' belly, then tugging back on the reins
to reconnoiter the trail. We could hear it all.

"Bo, listen tight, with your mind as well as your ears.
Saddlebags flapping. Branches cracking. These men just cannot stay quiet on the hunt. Can you hear voice sounds over
the clanging? Yammering back and forth about us, I expect."

Bo cupped his chin in hands and leaned out through the
gun slot.

"Yeah, Angus, I hear faint voices but can't make out no
words."

The voices became clearer. Then, finally, I could hear
separate men, filtered by the trees, and not more than fifty
feet away. The first voice, gravelly like a man who smoked too
much, asked, "See anything, Branson?"

"Not yet. But, there's some damn funny tracks up there. Let me get a better look. Hold up, boys! I believe our man got off his horse just ahead. There's boot tracks leading into the trees over here. And something else. Can't tell from here. Hold up, I said!"

"Is there blood?" another man hollered.

"Ain't gonna say. Plumb, maybe you'd best send Joe Pete up around that big rock to your left. Maybe they got a cave up there. Don't bunch up through here."

"Who's Plumb?" I whispered to Bo String.

"He's the Pinkerton man that works for the goddamned railroad."

"Oh, yes, that would be the famous Captain Standard H. Plumb. And, Branson must be his pet shooter. Undersheriff Joe Pete—a decent man, I thought."

"Yeah, except Plumb told him, and me, that there's a big reward out for you, preferably dead. And, Branson is the man that shot your horse on Ten Shoes Up. That was you out in front, right?"

"You were with them, Bo String? How'd that happen? You're a long way from collecting a reward now, son. What's your take on why Undersheriff Joe Pete is riding with Plumb?"

"Well, it ain't just for the money. He probably believes you actually did rob the train. As a lawman, he ain't got no choice. He has to make himself available to the railroad's Pinkerton agent."

Five minutes passed. No horse sounds. No more yelling. Then from the east side of the cabin, "Captain, there's a little black mare over here. Just tied to a tree. No rider. He's got to be close by. I cannot see anything on this side."

Another five minutes. Colder now, like losing a blanket off your bedroll. Four men, I thought, leading their horses, straining to see through the tightly bunched Ponderosa pine, scattered Douglas fir, and thick acorn brush. Bear country, boys; lucky for you they are hibernating this time of year.

Then, from Undersheriff Joe Pete, "I'll be goddamned. There's a log cabin, or shack. Something. I dunno. Could be the front of a mineshaft. Never heard of any mining up here. You boys hold on that side. Let me take a closer look."

I knew he could not see us through the slits until he moved directly in front of us—only ten feet away. And, by then, he'd be on the downhill side, looking up at my front wall, and staring at Pa's eight-gauge shotgun.

"Hey Captain, it's a cabin! Don't see no sign of life, though. No horses here. You want me to look inside?"

Before Plumb could answer, a different voice warned from the east side, "You'd best hold up where you are. I can see it now. It's the front of a mine dug into the mountain; something 'n hell like that. No windows. But, there's trees right up against it. Never seen anything like it before. It looks like a goddamned bunker, 'cept made out of trees."

Bo String whispered, "That's Branson. He's got a huge gun that takes bullets near as long as a dollar bill."

"Shush," I said.

From the downhill side, Joe Pete spoke up, "Captain, that ain't no mine. It's a fort. I can see two slits from here. They looked like trees at first. But, now I'm closer, maybe they're little skinny windows. I'm gettin' closer. It's uphill, smack dab in front of me."

I watched from the bottom windowsill as Undersheriff Joe Pete slowly advanced through the trees twenty feet directly in front. Bo saw him, too, and carefully pushed the front of his .30-30 out the slit, thumbing back on the hammer. I laid my hand on his arm, whispering, "Don't shoot him. Just let him inch his way to us. I'll handle it from here."

Pulling his rifle barrel back inside, Bo leaned back on the pine bench. I moved to the other front slit and stuck the double-barreled scattergun all the way out in front. Undersheriff Pete climbed over the last boulder on the downhill in front, about twelve feet away, straining to make sense of what was dead ahead of him.

He heard a sound no man ever wants to hear. Click. Click.

I eased back both hammers when he got to my twelve-foot range. He went quiet, and pale, and looked like he was gonna pass out. He was close enough to hear me whisper. In as low a voice as I could muster, I said, "Freeze, Sheriff. This is Angus. I've got two barrels of eight-gauge double-ought aimed at your belly. Freeze and you live. Move and I'll gut shoot you where you stand."

Only then did Pete's focus narrow in on what he thought was a big knot in a dead aspen. Twin bores of a shotgun barrel, and he'd stepped right into its line of sight. Laying his rifle down slowly, he froze like a big-eyed fish caught in a block of ice.

"Better. Now, just you kneel down."

"I ain't here to kill you, Angus, if that's who you are."

"Shut up," I said. "I don't want to spill your guts on the snow. You do as I say."

"Yes, sir."

Two minutes passed. No sound from the others. Pete looked like he was gonna wet himself. I listened for birds, but heard nothing.

"Okay, Sheriff, ease that six-shooter out of your holster. Left hand. Fling it in front. Now!"

From the east side, "Pete," the gravelly voice snarled, "where 'n hell are you? I'm over here, on the upside. I can see logs, looks like a well-tarred wall, but I don't know what it is. Are you close in yet?"

Now that both of Pete's guns were on the snow, I whispered to him, "Crawl, man, crawl on your belly, man, real slow-like, to your right, around to the side of the cabin."

Bo and I watched the sheriff crawl. Moving to the door, I inched the oak plank out of the L-shaped bars on either side. Bo signaled when Pete got as far as the corner. I jumped out, grabbed his coat collar, and drug him inside. The horses butted back nervously, but I calmed them by leaning against Horse and cooing to the packhorse. Once I'd flung him on the floor and motioned to Bo to keep him there, I went back outside, gathered up his rifle and revolver. When I got back inside, he hadn't moved an inch. Looked like he wanted to throw up—all pale and shaking like he had the dysentery.

"Sorry to do that to you, Sheriff. I know this's not of your making. I'll get you some water and a blanket."

Prodding Pete around Horse, past the grain box, and into the main room of the cabin, I nudged him onto the backbench, next to the still-warm stove. Pete was dumbstruck. He was still alive and Bo String was in here with me.

"Howdy, Sheriff Pete, how's your posse holding up?" Bo said grinning from one ear to the other.

"Bo, take that rawhide strip off the hood next to the stove. Tie the sheriff's hands to his gun belt, and then run it back under the bench, while you're at it."

He started to explain his presence to Joe Pete, but I shushed him, "How many men you got out there?"

"Just two. Captain Plumb and his man, Branson. But Branson has a .50 caliber Hawken. Almost got you when we tracked you on Ten Shoes Up. We had a tracker, name of Alfonso Ganado, but you shot him out of the saddle about an hour ago."

"Sorry, Sheriff, it wasn't me."

"Sorry, Sheriff Pete, it was me," Bo String said, as though he couldn't wait.

"Your tracker and I damn near bumped into one another a mile up the trail. He tried to kill me, but my horse jumped and then she knocked me plumb off the saddle. I don't lose my seat that easy. Downright embarrassing. So I shot back."

"Quiet down, the both of you," I said, "This ain't over."

I stuck the shotgun back out the slit and aimed up at the sky. Pulling the trigger, the right barrel blasted the top of a tree. Moving the angle higher up, I fired the second barrel. For a weapon of pure terror, there is no other sound to compare with an eight gauge shotgun. Then, as loud as I could, I hollered, "Captain Plumb, I just gutshot your sheriff. And, I got another man in here with me, name of Bo String. I believe you know him. So it's down to this. We got more guns, higher ground, and food for the winter. You ought to remove yourself while you can still breathe."

Five minutes went by.

Sheriff Pete could not stand it. Almost crying, he whispered, "Angus, I'm regretting I ever got that first arrest warrant out on you. We had no evidence on you then, or now. But, this time, we ain't even got a warrant. The judge refused me. When I told Captain Plumb, he said it did not matter. He's not here to arrest you. He's here to kill you."

"Well, don't let it bother you none, Sheriff. He ain't going to do either one. Be quiet now. Let's see how much sand Captain Standard H. Plumb's got in him."

Another ten minutes passed with no movement and no noise from inside, or out in the snow. Then, "Sheriff Joe Pete, where are you? We cannot see you."

The wind, picking up, carried Plumb's voice. I just leaned back on my boot heels, being careful not to sit on my spurs. Pa's reloaded eight-gauge set easy across my knees.

"You there, in the cabin! Can you hear me? I am Captain Standard H. Plumb! We have a warrant for your arrest. It's for robbing the AT&SF railroad and the Denver and Rio Grande. If you have harmed Sheriff Joe Pete, then it will be the rope for you."

I let it pass. It was getting cold out there, and in another few hours, it'd be dark; sundown comes early this time of year.

We could hear movement in the trees in front. In as low a voice as I could muster, I said, "You've got no warrant, Plumb. You ain't even got a sheriff no more. I gutshot him with one barrel, filled with bird shot. He's in awful pain, but he'll live to tell the truth about you. He's inside with me, getting warm. I'm thinking of giving him a sip of whiskey while we wait for you to do something stupid."

Joe Pete looked at me like I was a crazy man, whispering, "Angus, why'd you say that? You never even fired at me."

"'Cause I want him to believe I'm a man-killer. Puts him on guard. You be still now."

From down below, "Sheriff, that right? You inside? He ain't killed you?"

I motioned at Undersheriff Pete with my palm facing upward. He got my drift and hollered out at Plumb, "No, he ain't killed me, not yet. But, I got a bad wound, and he's hogtied me to boot. And, he's got Bo String in here. That's two guns facing you. You ought to go on now; this is over."

On cue, Bo sang out, "Captain Plumb, remember me? I'm the guy that left you behind on Ten Shoes Up. And, I'm the guy that shot back, in self-defense, and blew your Dulce tracker plumb off his horse. I'm siding with Angus now. He's an innocent man, I believe."

I crawled over and untied Joe Pete. Reaching up and opening the root cellar door, I motioned him inside. "Stay on the floor inside there. Flat as you can."

Then I signaled to Bo to do the same.

"They'll try to blow out a hole in this place with that big .50 caliber. It won't work, but he's got to get in close to make the try. We'll see. Men with long rifles sometimes ain't brave up close."

Five minutes later, his shooter let loose. Pistol rounds or even .30-30 bullets would bog down in tight-bound fir logs, but a .50 caliber round is a small cannon. I spoke low to Bo and Joe Pete, "It'll go through. That Hawken will penetrate the upper half of the front wall."

Then I crawled in there with 'em.

The Hawken shooter took his time about it, firing eight shots, and spacing them thirty seconds apart. The boom of a .50 caliber blast coming your way from a thirty-six-inch steel barrel turns your knees to jelly. He fired into the slits, front and side, low on the floor, and up high, trying to chink a hole. I figured he must have moved up the slope, because he fired two more down into my mud roof. From the east side, he pushed three rounds into the side horse door. But, inexplicably, he aimed high, above the heads of both horses. The horses thundered back, kicking at the door, squealing and thrashing about. Then he stopped.

I could hear high-pitched voices outside in the snow, but couldn't make out their words. The wind had picked up, rattling the horse door, and pushing cold air through the gun slits. As the temperature dropped, the sky got grayer. I was guessing it would be flat-out dark in thirty minutes.

"What'll they do now?" Bo asked me.

"They'll try to burn us out."

"How do you know?"

"That's what I'd do."

"Oh, God, I don't want to die in a fire," Undersheriff Pete moaned.

"You won't. They'll have to move in real close to throw a torch. Either that, or lay a fire on the horse door over there. But, long's I'm in the root cellar, I ain't gonna see them, whichever way they come."

Pete and Bo String looked at one another, but offered no solution. Feeling the quiet outside, I began to crawl across the stone floor and over to the horse door on the west side. Picking up the eight-gauge, I said, "Boys, I'm going outside to wait for them. You stay in here. Bo, soon as I close the horse door, you give the sheriff my .30-40 Krag. I'll take the scattergun. I ain't all that good a shot, you know. Don't come outside. I'll either get them, or I won't. You can't change nothing."

Pete, the sound of surprise in his voice, said, "Hell, Angus, are you saying you don't have a lot of experience in gunfights?"

"This is my first."

I took off my heavy sheepskin coat, unbuckled my spurs, and laid my right glove on the bench. Hanging my hat on the ten-penny nail by the horse stall, I wrapped a blue-black oversized neckerchief around my head. Shedding my gun belt, I pocketed six extra .44 pistol rounds in my back pocket, and stuck my pistol in my pants, where I could get to it easily, if I got hit. Finally, pulling four yellow shotgun cartridges from the paper box on the floor, I stuck them in my front vest pocket. Then, giving the mustang and the packhorse a pat on their rumps, I squatted down beside the horse door.

"Open her easy like, Bo String, and don't spook my horses."

Once outside, I could feel the storm gathering. It was twenty degrees colder, and the wind had come at us sideways. The fir trees were dropping snow from branches, and every few seconds I could hear small pine branches cracking up and down the slope. Moving up the hill on the west side, I crouched over, hunkering down as far as I could get and still move uphill. A low profile is a bad target, I'd once heard from a loudmouthed gunfighter in a bar.

When I got about twenty feet above the cabin and near a small opening in the tree line, I heard the crackling of an acorn bush. Stepping into the dense forest a few feet, I stopped to listen. The movement I was hearing wasn't coming from up above; it came from where I just was—behind me. Turning around so I could look downhill, I saw them step into view. The first man parted the thick brush and moved into the ten-foot flat area I'd cleared for the horse door. Be damned if it wasn't that prissy feller I'd seen on the train. The one in the three-piece suit, saying good day to the other passengers as if he owned the railroad. I remembered that he paid me no mind, thinking an old coot did not deserve a howdy from a man like him. Captain Standard H. Plumb, in the flesh. The other man was big. Hatchet-faced, gaunt, but determined, from the set of his jaw. He had a dark wool scarf wound around his neck and wore a black bowler that'd seen better days.

Plumb, bundled up in his long, leather coat, followed this feller. The big man had no trouble carrying a four-foot long heavy pine branch, matted with dead, wet leaves. And, he carried a Hawken .50 caliber, slung over his shoulder.

Plumb had a small pistol in his hand which looked to be a .32 caliber storekeeper's gun. And, he had a .30-30 Winchester over his shoulder on a military sling. The leather band across his chest put the gun on his back. *Won't be no use to him there*, I thought.

This was the first time that I'd seen that cannon of a gun they called a Hawken Fifty. Its walnut stock looked recently oiled and the curved, cheek piece was shaped like a beaver's tail. With a twenty-inch shoulder stock, capped in iron, and a thirty-six inch barrel, it probably weighed close to twelve pounds. Like I'd suspected from the spacing of the shots into the cabin twenty minutes ago, it was a single-shot, bolt-action. When chambered open, the cartridge delivery chute was over six inches long. That's why the big man blasting away at my cabin had taken so long between rounds. It takes a good twenty seconds to fish out a fresh round, wipe it off on your sleeve, and then slide it down the chute into the firing chamber, lay your cheek to the stock, settle on an aim point, and squeeze that big iron trigger.

I held my breath as they walked toward me. Because both were hunched over studying the ground, they couldn't see me. When they got to the west-facing horse door, the big man unslung his Hawken and leaned it against a rock. Plumb moved up alongside him. They'd figured out what I'd been afraid of. They knew they could not be seen, or shot, from inside the house, as long as they stayed on this side.

Working together, quiet-like, they maneuvered the four-foot-long branch up against the west-side door of my cabin, causing a stir inside from the horses. Plumb holstered his .32 and dug in the saddlebag slung over his shoulder for something. Looked to be a small can of kerosene. Oddly, I felt relieved. Kerosene was something lazy men used to start campfires. It would take them a minute or two to set up a fire hot enough to burn us out. Plumb started to unscrew the cap, while the other man dug in his coat pocket. He'd taken off his right glove. I was close enough now to see him pull out a flintstone and a steel striking tool.

Easing up to a standing position, I commenced to move slow and careful down the hill to close the distance between us. Since they were focused on the horse door, I was on their blind side. From six feet away, I aimed the scattergun straight at them, and one by one, cocked both hammers.

At the first click, the big man jerked his head to his right, looking downhill, not fixing the right compass on the sound. Plumb didn't react to either click, but he was startled by the look on the big man's face.

Knowing that someone is hammering down a shotgun in your direction is frightful. But, the important thing is figuring out exactly where it came from. They froze.

"You boys thinking 'bout buildin' a campfire for your supper?"

Neither uttered a word. Plumb dropped the kerosene can. The big man slowly lowered the branch, keeping his hand in the big flap pocket of his canvas coat. I was not all that surprised to see that the man with Plumb was the same scoundrel I'd spotted jumping off the platform of the AT&SF train three days ago. This was Plumb's pet train robber, coal black pigtail and all.

"That's right, boys. It's me. I'm outside, right behind you. You just heard a welcome from my Pa's eight-gauge scatter-gun. I got an itchy trigger finger and could blow both of you to smithereens from here. You'll be dead before you hit the ground. So, it's your call, gents. Make your move."

Nobody moved. But, seconds later, the horses started kicking at the door again. And, all three of us heard noises coming from inside the cabin. But, neither man moved a muscle. They stared at the door with me at their backs. Like two dead men waiting to hear Gabriel's horn.

"Unload them guns and that fire log. Now! Then drop to your knees in three seconds. One, two . . ."

Plumb dropped his little .32 and unslung his Winchester. Pigtail sucked in a gulp of cold air, dropped the tree branch, and turned to face me. Then, with a wild jerk inside his vest, he pulled a short-barrel .38 out of his waistband. Leaning back and sticking his chest out, he swung the pistol my way. He was six feet from me when he snarled, "You sumbi . . ."

I squeezed the right trigger on the eight-gauge. The power of the blast blew him back hard against the horse door, but his grip on the .38 held fast, and his trigger finger clamped down as his rib cage blew apart. The .38's short barrel was less than two feet away when it spat fire and blasted a twenty-grain lead slug directly into Plumb's mouth.

Pigtail was dead before he hit the ground.

Plumb died when the back of his skull exploded.

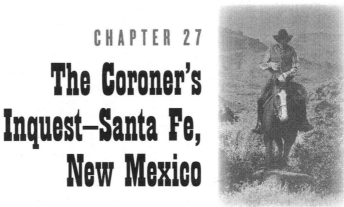

CHAPTER 27
The Coroner's Inquest–Santa Fe, New Mexico

IRST TIME I'D EVER BEEN in a courtroom. The judge, a man named "Hon. A. Craig Blakey" had his name engraved on a brass plate he carried around with him. A kindly man, he tried to put us at ease. It was what they called a "Coroner's Inquest," and it was the first for almost everyone there. It'd been seven weeks since the shootout up at my cabin on Bear Mountain and one day short of that since I'd seen the two men now sitting beside me—Joe Pete and Bo String.

"All rise, please," the bailiff, a small man in a brown tweed suit, bellowed out to the crowd behind us. He was looking hard at us—Undersheriff Joe Pete, Bo String, and me when he talked. Probably thought we might not get up.

We'd been told where to sit—on a little bench he said was for witnesses. The judge had a big desk set atop a platform so he could see everybody. There was a chair inside a railing, which he'd told was the witness box. So, there we sat, betwixt the box and the bench, waiting for him. The spectators' chairs were crammed behind us.

"You will be first to testify," he said, aiming a bony finger at Joe Pete.

Tony Neis, Chief Deputy US Marshal—New Mexico Territory, sat in front, at a long table directly in front of the bench. Pete wore his Sunday-go-to-Mass suit. Bo String, sitting on the end, looked mighty uncomfortable in a starched shirt he said his ma made him wear just for this event. Once everyone was on their feet, a little narrow door opened behind the bench and a man carrying a little stack of papers and a gavel made his way to the seat of honor.

"That's the judge," Joe Pete whispered to me, earning a frown from the bailiff.

He was a tall, bearded man, dressed in a black funeral suit with a big chest pocket holding a pair of spectacles, a long fountain pen, and a small book. By the look of him, he wasn't one to fool with. That was plain from the stern gaze he gave us as he pulled a high-backed chair closer to the bench. A man of substance, he walked with a purposeful stride, spun the cane-back chair to his liking, Then, waving his hand at us in a downward motion, he plopped down and arranged the papers he was carrying with others already up there. There was a quiet whoosh as folks in the back sucked in a short breath, then everything got still. Next, fetching the spectacles from his vest pocket, he centered them onto the thin bridge of his nose. He broke the still of the room with a big ole wheeze.

"All right, settle down all of you. This is a coroner's inquest into the deaths of two men in a remote cabin on Bear Mountain. It is just south of Ten Shoes Up, and is on the New Mexico side of the Toltec Gorge. The events transpired on, let's see now, here it is, November 30, 1880. They died, more or less in the presence of three men who are here today to give testimony about exactly what happened up there. Captain Standard H. Plumb, of Chicago, Illinois, died of a gunshot wound from a .38 caliber pistol, not his own. He'd been living here in Santa Fe over at the hotel. Chester Branson died of an eight-gauge shotgun wound to the chest. It says here he lived in Raton, New Mexico, but the report also has an address in Trinidad, Colorado. Never mind that. We are late in getting to this hearing because winter set in up north and some of the witnesses to these deaths had wounds to recover from and business to settle in Colorado. But, we are all here now. Right, Undersheriff Pete?"

Undersheriff Joe Pete stood up, "Yes, Judge, I think you got all you need to hear from right here," as he waved his hand at Bo String and me.

The first row behind the court rail in the territorial courtroom in the Palace of Governors was reserved for special guests. That's where Thomas Jefferson Nickerson, president of the AT&SF railway company sat with his general counsel, Mr. Arthur Steen. Next to them sat a man named Escalante Henderson Davis, who, the *Santa Fe New Mexican* reported in yesterday's paper, was the railroad's new chief of security. Gawkers from the Plaza filled the rest of the rows, all the way to the back of the courtroom. Joe Pete said three of them asked him questions when he came in this morning; two newspaper reporters and a dime novelist from El Paso. Said he didn't tell 'em a thing. The jury box was empty.

This was also Undersheriff Joe Pete's first time inside a real courtroom. They did not have one in Chama, he said. Didn't need one either, he said. But, he was comfortable in the black suit, string tie, and a starched, add-on stiff collar, because he was a Methodist. I wondered whether anything up in Chama compared to the way they did things down here in Santa Fe.

"Mighty fine," the Judge said. "Since this is just an inquest and nobody's liberty is to be bothered, we don't need jurors, lawyers, or such. That all right with everybody?"

Not waiting for anyone to object, Judge Blakey turned to the little sheaf of papers spread out in front of him.

"Says here that these men were under your jurisdiction, Undersheriff Pete, so we'll commence the proceedings with your testimony. Come up here and swear yourself in and I'll put some questions to you."

Pete took the oath, sat in the creaky witness chair, and waited for the first question. The judge shuffled the papers around. After a minute, he looked up, seemingly surprised to find Pete not talking.

"Well, get on with it, Mister, don't wait for me. Tell us what happened."

Pete could talk in a bar, and on the trail, but he did not sound all that convincing in a courtroom. He plodded through things that were, he said, "troubling" to him.

"Well, you see, before the shooting started, we did not have a warrant to arrest anybody, leastways for the second posse,

the one the Captain led us on, up and over Bear Mountain.
But, Judge, we did have one the first time we took to the chase,
when we tried to arrest a man on Ten Shoes Up. Judge, do you
want me to go into that anymore?"

"No, Sheriff, we are only concerned about the deaths on
Bear Mountain, unless of course you shot somebody on some
other mountain—you didn't, did you?"

"No, sir, but you see . . ."

"Ain't no need for that, then. Just get on with it," the judge
said, returning to his paperwork.

"All right, then," Pete said. "But, I did not do any paperwork on this, on account of . . ."

"Sheriff, you are here to testify. Not to write things down.
I have two detailed written reports on this matter right here
in front of me. I'm hoping you will just tell me what happened
so I can get on with the business of this inquest."

Pete twitched and sucked in a big gulp of courtroom air. He
leaned in and out from the back of the chair, as though he were
hoping it would move him clean out of here. He did his best to
state the essentials of the chase up from Cascade Creek. In the
space of two minutes, he explained the run over the top of Bear
Mountain and down the other side to my cabin. When he got
to the part about what happened when he first approached my
cabin from downslope, he said he was "downright embarrassed"
that I'd captured him. Then, he said, he figured everything out
and was "downright happy." When the judge quizzed him about
what happened outside the cabin when my shotgun blast went
off, he said Plumb and Branson "got their selves killed."

Judge Blakey nodded, but then shook his head from side
to side.

"Yes, they did. But, what do you know about how their killing occurred? Just summarize it for us."

"I dunno. I was on the other side of the door."

The judge looked up from his papers.

"Undersheriff Pete, it matters not which side of which door you were on. What matters is whether you believe their deaths were caused by felonious means. These reports confirm that Angus shot Mr. Branson in self-defense. Is that the nub of it?"

"Yes, sir, that's exactly my opinion, even though I was on the other side of the door."

"All right Sheriff, you can step down. Now, for the benefit of everyone in this courtroom, most of what Undersheriff Joe Pete knows is set down in the written report. I've read it carefully. What Undersheriff Pete said here on the witness stand is what we call "'supporting'" evidence. It's necessary when conducting an official coroner's inquest to do this in public. That's why we have an official court reporter. Mr. Sharp is writing all this down. Now we're gonna hear from Mr. Bo String."

Bo got up, stepped up onto the little platform beside the judge's bench, and waited, looking down at his muddy boots as though he'd never seen them before.

"Is that your given name, son, Bo String? If so, tell it to the bailiff and he'll swear you in for your testimony on this affair."

He looked at me for permission. I motioned to him to go on. He said his name, then assured the judge he'd been given that name by his pa, and was right proud of it. The judge asked him if he was part of the posse, which he denied. Then he asked him if he shot one of the posse members, "a man name of Alfonso Ganado."

As Bo commenced to build an explanation, the judge interrupted, "No explanation needed, son. That is not before me today and you are not charged with anything for it. I just wanted to see if you'd confirm the written report I have here in my hand from the sheriff's office in Española , which covers the town of Dulce. And you've done that. So, just tell me what you know about the deaths of Captain Plumb and Mr. Branson, which are the subject of this coroner's inquest."

But, Alfonso Ganado was in the back of the courtroom. He'd already talked to the bailiff, who told him that unless he knew for certain what happened at the cabin, his testimony was unneeded. At least that's what the judge told Bo when he tried to explain what had happened between him and Mr. Ganado. Wagging his finger, the judge said, "just get on with it, son, we do not need to examine Mr. Ganado's role here."

Bo said he was right there on the other side of the door with Sheriff Pete when the shotgun boomed, followed by a pistol shot.

"And so, Judge, I can't rightly say with my own eyes what happened."

"But, you asked Angus what happened, didn't you?"

"Well, sure we did, and—"

"Did you believe what he said and did it sound logical based on what you heard through the door?"

"Well, yes because . . ."

"Thank you, Mr. String. You may step down."

As he came back to his seat, the judge turned back to his sheaf of papers. A minute or two passed before he looked up. Then, nodding his head in my direction, he said, "Now, I believe that it would be in order for me to explain our process before

I call the next witness. This is a court of law, and it is my job to decide whether a crime has been committed or whether the shooting on Bear Mountain was a lawful act. If I find that a crime might have been committed, then I'll invoke a proper charge for the prosecutor to mull. It will be up to him whether we have a trial or not. You've just heard from two witnesses that can't be all that helpful because, as they said, they were on the wrong side of the door."

The crowd rustled some because one of the spectators in the back row, a woman with heavy skirts, left and apparently caught her skirt on the bench. The judge was patient. When she finally made it to the door, he returned to his speech.

"All right. The court has a copy of a statement by Mr. Ganado, taken by an officer of the law. It is not helpful because he was two miles away when Captain Plumb and Mr. Branson got 'their selves' killed, as the Undersheriff put it. For the record, I did not learn all that much from Mr. Ganado's report."

This caught the attention of a bearded man in a fifty-dollar suit sitting just behind me—Thomas Jefferson Nickerson. Standing up as a courtesy to the court, he said, "If it please the court. Your honor, if there are questions about just who was robbing our trains here in the New Mexico Territory, then you ought to hear from my general counsel, Mr. Steen. He's sitting here alongside me. He knows what happened."

"Mr. Nickerson," the judge drawled, touching his right index finger to the side of his head, "I think that could be a mighty fine idea, seeing as how your lawyer's name comes up in the official written report, which I was just about to explain, before you interrupted me. So, just you let me get to that."

The courtroom buzzed a bit, then settled when the judge turned his attention back to his sheaf of papers.

"Now, I'm the United States Magistrate here in New Mexico; that's on top of my appointment as a Territorial Judge. And, that's why I'm conducting this inquest, on account of there is no other federal magistrate between here and Denver. On matters where the territorial line gets blurred, like it does through the Toltec Gorge between Colorado and New Mexico, federal jurisdiction is appropriate. Now, gentlemen, there is one more written report, prepared by George Ramsey, the United States Marshal in Denver, Colorado. Marshal Ramsey knows all the facts relevant to this inquest, because it involves one of his own men."

The crowd behind me stirred. I turned around to see the commotion and saw Mr. Nickerson shaking his finger at his lawyer. The judge paused, and then looked at the president of the AT&SF.

"In answer to the question I see coming by the look on your face, Mr. Nickerson, you'd best know that I've already talked to the next witness. I'd arranged to talk to him in my chambers earlier this morning. Before this hearing started. I am satisfied with everything he told me off the record. But, as your lawyer will tell you, it is necessary to make a court record, which is why I'm calling the man to the witness stand. After he testifies, I will consider whether your lawyer, Mr. Steen, ought to be a witness as well. I'll hold off on that until we get the sworn testimony of the only man that can rightly answer all these questions."

He paused to take off his spectacles and then turned his gaze to his bailiff. The bailiff nodded, turned to me, and gave me a palm's up signal with his right hand. I stood. As I got up and moved toward the witness stand, Judge Blakey announced to the crowd, "The next witness is Deputy United States Marshal Angus Esparazza."

Reaching for the Bible on the stand beside him, the bailiff motioned to me, "Deputy, come on up here and take the oath."

I thought Joe Pete would faint. I got up and squeezed out between Pete and Bo String. They looked at me like a ghost. I hated having to keep them in the dark all this time. Standing in the aisle, I took my badge out of my shirt pocket and pinned it to the leather flap on my vest. Then, as quickly as I could, I took the short walk to the witness stand.

"Raise your hand and take the oath, then just sit down there and tell the judge your name, occupation, and place of residence."

"I am Deputy United States Marshal Angus Esparazza. I'm on special assignment and report directly to the US Marshal in Denver. I live mostly up on the border between Colorado and New Mexico."

Judge Blakey took over, pushing his papers aside. He gave the railroad men a long slow look, then turned to me.

"Yes, thank you, Deputy. Now, how long have you been a US Marshal? And, tell us just what 'special assignment' means."

I tried to give him the short version of a long tale. Last spring, Marshal Ramsey had wired me to come to Denver, where he explained why the federal government was interested in train robberies in Colorado and the New Mexico Territory.

"It was because the US mail car was being looted, along with government payrolls. Mr. Steen had already contacted Marshal Ramsey. The AT&SF's own detective, Captain Plumb, was bogged down. Mr. Steen thought the investigation was at a standstill. This made him nervous so he asked for federal help. That's where I came in."

"Help? What kind of help?" the judge asked.

"I was told to put my badge away and stay away from Pinkertons and local authorities, and—"

"Acting incognito, so to speak, is that what you mean?" Judge Blakey interrupted. "Why not just come out with it and investigate in the open?"

"Because the railroad could not be sure that it was not an inside job all along. They asked to have someone, although they did not know it was me, take a look at their own people. That's how I discovered it was their own man doing the robbing—Captain Standard H. Plumb. He and his man Branson were on every train that was robbed. And, I was on several of those trains, too, although they did not know that."

"How come they didn't know? If you saw them, how come they didn't see you?"

"Well, Judge, I was disguised differently each time. As it says there in my report, once I was a deaf-mute. Another time I was a stove-up rock miner. The last time I was an old coot who smelled up the car. No one took me for a lawman, or a train robber. But, I have to say I didn't know that Branson feller was involved until the last trip."

"You just said 'your' report. Do you mean Marshal Ramsey's report?"

"He signed it. I dictated it to his secretary in Denver."

"So, it is your testimony that Captain Plumb robbed the train, and you found actual proof of it at your cabin up on Bear Mountain, right?"

"Yes, Judge."

"All right, then, go on and tell us how you know."

"So, I told him about seeing Branson drop off the mail car right after I did at the Osier water stop. Then he hightailed it out carrying what I thought was a canvas mail sack. He'd hid a horse a mile downstream; that's why my horse didn't whinny to him—just too far away—a mile upstream. Plain enough that's how the robber got off the train. I figured Plumb, given his job at the railroad, had a mailroom key. He would distract the mailroom guard while Branson snuck up and bonked the poor man with his gun butt. What I didn't know at the time was that Plumb must have spotted me, too. I got off the train at Osier a few minutes behind Branson. I hoofed it to where I'd tied up my own horse, saddled up and lit out. I had a day head start, but left them a decent trail to follow. The next day they gathered up another posse, which included Joe Pete and Alfonso Ganado. Then the four of them—Plumb and Branson plus the first two, tracked me over Bear Mountain to my cabin. I was more or less leading them, intentional-like. You know what I mean?"

"Yes, Deputy Marshal, I see that. But, let me ask you this, for the record. It is in your written report but we need it clear, under oath. Did you find proof of these train robberies at your cabin?"

"Yes, sir. After the shooting, when we were . . ."

"Back up some, marshal, and tell how the shooting came about."

So, I told them what happened. How Branson and his big Hawken tried to blow us out of the cabin, then how he and Plumb planned to burn us out. Then, carefully as I could, I told him about shooting Branson to keep him from plugging me with his pistol. His gun misfired, missed me, and hit Captain Standard H. Plumb in the mouth. Then, I went back and filled in the rest of the story.

"Joe Pete and Bo String heard exactly what was said right before they heard my shotgun blast and before Branson's pistol shot. I told them to come on outside. They did. I was standing in the same spot and the man I shot was on the ground, dead. Plumb was knocked back some, and looked like an upside-down turtle with a bag over his back. His rifle was still snugged to his back on the sling. When Sheriff Pete checked to see if he was dead, he discovered what was in Captain Plumb's canvas rucksack."

"Yes," the judge said, "I read that in your report. Go on, please."

"Undersheriff Joe Pete found a canvas bag marked 'AT&SF Payroll.' He counted it later and told me it had nine thousand dollars in gold coins, and a few hundred paper dollars. It was part of the loot they stole off the train at Osier. Their plan was to kill me, stick the payroll sack in my saddlebag, and make it look like it was me doing the robbin' instead of them."

Mr. Steen stood up, "Judge, do you want me to comment on that, or wait until I'm under oath?"

"Gentlemen, I don't usually like to have a conversation like this, but maybe we can speed this thing up. Raise your hand, Mr. Steen, and swear you will tell the truth, and then speak your piece."

Steen explained how they found the rest of the money. Plumb had twelve thousand dollars in his room at the Exchange Hotel here in Santa Fe, and Branson had six thousand dollars buried under the water tank at his little spread up in Raton. The AT&SF was satisfied that all three robberies were an inside job, just like I said. Steen told the judge his employer was real happy to be shed of bank robbers masquerading as detectives. I allowed as how I was happy to be shed of masquerading as a railroad passenger.

Judge Blakey was decisive.

"Here's my findings," he said,

"First, Branson Chambers died of a gunshot wound to his chest fired by Marshal Angus Esparazza in self-defense. Second, Captain Standard H. Plumb died of a gunshot wound to his face and head fired by Branson Chambers, accidentally. Third, there were no felonious crimes committed at the scene. Fourth, this inquest has no further business to discuss or resolve. This matter is closed. We are at adjournment."

But, that was not how it ended. Alfonso Ganado, from Dulce, New Mexico, stood in the back of the courtroom.

"Judge, I'm Alfonso Ganado. What about me? I got shot, too."

Judge Blakey was already standing and about to go out the little door behind the bench, but he stopped, turned, and said, "I do not mean to be unkind about this, but you lived, Mr. Ganado. So, it is not proper to take up your case at a coroner's inquest. You can file a complaint with the sheriff, if you're of a mind to."

"Can I just say something real quick, Judge?"

The judge let out his breath, but gave a small nod of his head, and squinted at Alfonso over his spectacles.

"It was a misunderstanding, Judge. I thought Mr. String was Mr. Angus, but no one told me there was no warrant for

Mr. Angus. Now that I know he's the law, it changes things. I have no wish to complain about Mr. String."

"Well, that is not before us sittin' at a coroner's inquest, but let me say this, and then we are adjourned for good. The law in this territory is you have to be intending to shoot someone illegally before you are criminally liable. Misunderstanding is lack of intention. That's covered. And, that's my ruling on this. We are adjourned!"

They went out. I stayed behind. Then when I thought they'd be clear of the boardwalk in front of the courthouse, I stepped out the front door. I was wrong. They were waitin' for me.

"I just can't hardly believe it. You are a by-God United States Marshal! That beats all," Bo said.

"Me neither, I thought I was trackin' an outlaw, not a fellow peace officer," Pete said.

"I find it hard to believe myself, boys, but I reckon I'll go back to ridge riding now. I've had my fill of chasing train robbers."

"Where you headin' for, Angus?"

"Maybe I'll ride the Rio Pecos, boys, or maybe I'll head up north to Montclair, Colorado. Cannot rightly tell now, but something will come to me. Keep your cinches tight."

CHAPTER 28
Angus Rides North to Montclair

IT TOOK ME TWO STEADY DAYS riding north, along the Rio Grande, up through Raton Pass, before I spotted that fine little ranch where I'd left Tucson three months ago. The grass, close-cropped within two miles of the ranch house, was a welcome sight. Tucson's ears picked up as I rode toward a hundred-foot corral. He shared the corral with a black stallion and another sorrel gelding. The ranch horses were grazing all around the perimeter, as I nudged Horse down the slope to the road. The closer I got, the more Tucson snorted and pawed the ground.

"Tucson, old son, you're looking fit as a bull elk," I said as I rode the last forty feet toward him.

He squared his ears at me, threw his head, and spun around, moving twenty yards away from me. The wind coming off the prairie spun his black mane in the air. I could sense the tension between the two, as Horse and I rode in close. Dropping Horse's reins, I swung one leg over the saddle horn and waited for Tucson to settle in. It took a minute or two, but soon enough he ambled over and gave Horse a look of horse superiority.

"No, Tucson, old son, I haven't forgotten you."

I swung all the way down, walked over to him, stuck my left arm up under his neck, and pulled him to me. I brushed his mane with my glove and cooed at him a little. It was the best day I'd had in a while, getting close to the best horse I'd ever known.

The rancher, a grizzled old man named Welsh, came over from the little blacksmith shop behind his main barn and we made the trade. I unsaddled Horse and gave him to Welsh. Then I gave Tucson a strong brushing, cleaned his feet, and put my saddle and rig on his back. The long tear in his right shoulder had fully healed, but the scar was still a ten-inch white straggle visible from up close. We headed west for Montclair; I told him we were going to see a lady.

"Tucson, she's not a ranch woman, but don't let that bother you none. You be on your best behavior, now. I want her to like you."

As I rode the last seven miles to Montclair, I tried to settle my mind on what I hoped to do here. I'd promised Marshal Ramsey I'd make my way to Denver right enough after the inquest in Santa Fe. Montclair was seventy-five miles off the trail that ran due north from Trinidad to Denver. This detour would add two-and-a-half days to the trip.

First, I needed to get both of my bank accounts straight with Robert Morton. Marshal Ramsey said he'd deal with the trust account, but my personal account—my so-called salary account—was another matter. Then there was Addie. The thing about women was, you could not just square them away, like a good horse, or a long pull over a mountain range. I tried to think about what needed saying to her. And what I wanted. Both were a mystery. Ten miles from town, I almost turned north to Denver. What 'n hell was I even doing here? Nothing came to me, so I just rode on into town, following the stage road that had brought me here the first time I saw her. I'd only talked to her twice, and my feelings never were reliable when it came to women. That's why I prefer talking to my horse.

Robert must have seen me tying my horse to the hitching rail in front of the bank because he came out the front door before I could offload my saddlebag.

"Angus, it's really great to see you. Especially since you're wearing that shiny nickel badge on your vest pocket. That says a lot about what I didn't know. Come on inside, Deputy US Marshal! We have things to talk about."

Over coffee from his little stove in the back of the bank, we covered my business. He explained that Marshal Ramsey had sent him a telegram confirming the trust account balance was to be closed, and the balance sent to him by stagecoach. That left my personal account. It was not the United States Government's business. Now that the first had been taken care of, I had an idea about the second.

"Robert, I never had an account in a bank until I opened this one with you. I'm a New Mexican by birth and inclination, but if you have no opposition, I'll just keep the account open for a while."

"I'm very happy to hear that, Angus. We maintain several New Mexico accounts. Chama doesn't have a bank."

"Wondered about that. Chama seems as busy as Montclair, and there's a fair number of people down there. Why don't they have a bank?"

"Well, Angus, banking is common in the East and Midwest, but the frontier is slow to accept banks as trustworthy. Most small towns that have banks also have someone local who they think they can trust with their money. Here in Montclair, that became me. Perhaps Chama just hasn't yet found the right man to start a bank. Hard to say. As far as I know, the next closest is in Santa Fe. You don't have to actually be here in person to put money in, or take it out. The US Mail is the most stable institution in the entire West. So, I'll give you some envelopes and we can do business that way, unless you're thinking about moving up here."

"The US mail will be OK by me," I said, wondering how best to get to the next question. Maybe he could see it on my face, maybe not. He nodded at me with the answer before I posed the question.

"Addie is not here, Angus. She caught the stage for San Francisco week before last. Just after I got the call about you from Marshal Ramsey. I thought, perhaps out of place, that she'd want to know who you really were. So, I told her about your real job—Deputy United States Marshal—and what he told me about the gunfight on Bear Mountain. I'm sorry now I ever said a word."

And, there it was. Plain as day. My secret life as a lawman was not something she could bear. She must have thought I lied to her. And, that I toyed with her emotions. "Well," I stammered, "she told me about dreaming of the ocean and getting to San Francisco, but I guess I never figured . . ."

"She left a letter for you, Angus. It's at the house. And, a box, too. Are you staying over tonight? We could have dinner at the café and I'll bring them to you."

"No, I was thinking I would ride to Denver the hard way from here, up past Pike's Peak on the west side and then angle over back toward Denver. If you don't mind, I'd like the letter now."

"Sure," he said, "I understand."

'Course, he did not understand at all. Neither did I. On the one hand, we hardly knew each other—Addie and me. On the other, I was maybe fool enough to think we knew each other in ways that don't take much time, or talk, to understand.

I unhitched my horse and rode to the livery barn. Marse took care of everything, and I walked back up to the street to Robert and Addie's house. He was waiting on the little porch out front with a tan-colored envelope and a small wooden box. It looked like a delivery box—it was marked, FINE CHINA—DO NOT BREAK.

I rode north out of Montclair about ten miles before I came on a little creek, with silver and green water trickling. Good place to camp, I thought. I made coffee and put a nosebag on Tucson with a half-can of grain. I kept the letter in the flap pocket of my duster and opened the box first.

Wrapped in a week-old copy of the *Denver Post* was the little black velvet bag that Addie had showed me at her house. No need to open that, the little note tied to the red ribbon said all that needed saying: "Please Return to Addie Morton—San Francisco California."

All that was on the envelope was my name. It was licked shut but I fingered it open as gentle as I could. She had a fine hand. It came to me as I read the first few lines that this was the only letter I'd ever received from a woman.

My Dear Angus,

I don't know what to say without sounding presumptuous, or foolish. You are the only man I've ever written to, and even as I sit here crying, I don't know why that's so important. But it is.

Robert told me about your secret—United States Marshal. I felt you were hiding something, but at the same time I knew it wasn't any of my business—but I wanted it to be my business. Honestly, learning this was good for me. It pushed me. It freed me. It sunk me.

You love your high mountains. I'm sure you are also committed to your job—chasing out-laws and rescuing damsels in distress. Actually, I know about the outlaws because Robert told me. I hated the fact that you could have been killed. But I'm the damsel in distress. You can't rescue me, can you?

I'm taking your double-eagle with me to San Francisco. My life there is as uncertain now, as yours was to me in Montclair. I'm usually not a fatalist, but I fear that we will always live in our dream worlds—you in the mountains and me by the ocean—never the twain shall meet.

If you're reading this, you know how important my lovely conch shell is to me. But it's yours now. Maybe someday, you'll knock on my door again with my conch in hand. I'll trade you a twenty-dollar gold piece for it. And maybe we will start anew.

Love, Addie

CHAPTER 29
Angus Takes the Badge

"**A**NGUS," MARSHAL RAMSEY boomed when the girl showed me into his office in the federal courthouse in Denver, "get yourself in here. I'm powerful glad to see you. I feared you'd ignore my telegram and keep on riding high and lonesome, down there in the New Mexico Territory."

He poured me a cup of mud-looking coffee and asked, "Want a little sweetener in that?"

"No," I lied. "Too early for me." Another lie, but he had no reason to know all that much about my private life. We talked about horses, weather, and Denver's busting out at the seams. Five minutes of town talk. Then he got down to business.

"Angus, now that we're done with that nasty bit of business with the AT&SF railroad and Captain Standard H. Plumb, I want to talk to you about a more permanent deal. I've talked to the US Marshal down in Santa Fe, and we'd like to take you on as a special deputy for both Colorado and the Territory of New Mexico. How's that sound?"

"Well, I'm not sure. Things are a little upside down right now. I can't quite figure out what I want to do. If the job you're offering won't pin me down to just one place, well, I have to say I'd be interested. But, we'd have to talk some before we could come to a handshake on it."

"Well, if we can see eye-to-eye on it, it'll take more than a handshake. What I'm talking about is a joint offer from two offices of the US Marshal's Service. You'd be answering to both, but not stationed at either one."

"Stationed?"

"You see, Angus, the US Marshal's service is run a little like the Union Army was twenty years ago—military-like. We're federal police doing business in all the states and territories. Mostly we enforce the law for federal judges and lock up scoundrels that break federal laws. So, the old Army ideas like being stationed here or bivouacked there is part of the ways we do things."

"Bivouacked. Now there's another new word—can't say as I've ever even heard that one."

"A bivouac is a military encampment with tents or some kind of improvised shelter—you know, to keep the rain off you or protect you from enemy fire. My last bivouac before I mustered out after the Civil War was a hospital in Northern Virginia. They gave me a stout horse and twenty dollars paper money. I rode from there to Denver, where my horse gave out, and I hired on with the federal judge here, serving warrants, and guarding at the federal jail across the street. I was the first

US Marshal here in Colorado. But, my friend, that's not the job we're offering you."

"So, what would I be doing if it ain't bivouacking, or being stationed?"

"Well, to use another military example, you'd be strictly a field officer. No station, except the back of your horse. And, no more hiding the badge, except in special circumstances. We're thinking you're the man we need for what's going on up here, and down there. Like I said, it's no handshake deal. You'd become a sworn peace officer. You'd have to take the oath with your hand on the Bible—and your badge wouldn't be a temporary one from a drawer in my desk. See, the Federal Department of Justice is particular about who it hires. Taking the federal oath is something no man can take lightly."

"Well, I was thinking about a long ride—from here to the Pacific Ocean. Is this something needs doing now, or would I have a little time to myself before I take the badge, permanent-like?"

Marshal Ramsey studied me a moment, then got up and went over to a bookshelf against the wall. He looked down the shelf and pulled a thin, leather binder down.

"Take a look at this, Angus," he said, handing it to me. If we were preachers, this would be our bible. But, we're peace officers—federal peace officers—so our ten commandments come from Congress, the President of the United States, and this official rendering. The title on this is, *History & Duties of Office—United States Marshal under the Judiciary Act of 1789*. But, the job I'm offering you is not just a title, it's a tradition and we're coming up on a hundred-year anniversary. It's something to think on."

I took the book and was surprised to find that the binding felt like glove leather. Not stiff, but comfortable in the hand.

"Feels smooth, Marshal. I'll read it after supper."

"Actually, Angus, it's a lot more than you'll ever need to do the job. But, it will be of some assistance. We don't do what local lawmen do—keep the peace, mostly in towns and counties. We are here primarily to support the federal system. Our job is to carry out all lawful orders issued by federal judges, Congress, or the president. Why don't you check in to a hotel, read this, and I'll meet you for dinner tonight. You ain't got other plans, have you?"

I checked into a hotel halfway between the public livery and the courthouse. It wasn't much, but I'm not particular. They had a room, a phone in the lobby, a saloon, and a dining room. I called Marshal Ramsey's office and gave the girl the name of the hotel; she said Marshal Ramsey would meet me in the dining room at eight o'clock. I went down to the bar at six figuring it would be a good place to think and have a drink or two.

"Hello again, Angus," he said when he came into the saloon at seven-thirty.

"I thought you might be here and if you don't mind, I'll have a drink with you before we go in to dinner."

"Mighty fine, Marshal. Pull up a chair, the barkeeper will send over a glass."

We had two drinks apiece, talked about horses, what 'n hell's going wrong with people; in time he got back to business.

"Let me sketch out the federal problem we've got down here and in New Mexico. I suppose you've heard of Tom Emmett, New Mexico's most notorious train robber, right?"

"Heard some from bartenders and livery stable owners, but I don't spend much time paying attention to that sort of thing."

"Well, of recent, he's been robbing trains in the northeast corner of the New Mexico territory. But, he's been seen in Colorado, too, although we don't know of any robberies up here, so far. But, there's talk about him and Butch Cassidy's wild bunch. Some say they are on friendly terms. I doubt that, but that's what they say. As Marshal Neis explains it to me, Emmett's got a hideout somewhere in the northeast corner of New Mexico, maybe close to the Texas line. Which I suppose makes sense. He's a scalawag from Missouri that got run off from his home state. He's picked New Mexico to start a new life—one where the law don't pay much attention to what goes on in little one-horse towns. There's a good many in the northeast corner of New Mexico. You ever ridden that part of New Mexico?"

"Some, down the Rio Pecos. But not over to Texas."

"Me neither. But, the Colorado and Southern Railway winds through four states that share a common border. I know the state and territorial lines are not well known. The railroads don't care about that. Kansas, Colorado, Oklahoma, and New Mexico all converge, more or less in the northeast corner of New Mexico, and there's very little law, local or federal there. The railroads carry federal payrolls along with most everything else that folks need. Mr. Emmett fancies himself a gentleman train robber. Along with his brother Neb and a fair-sized bunch of gun hands, they have been relieving that train, and others down south around Las Cruces, of their cash, gold, and paper money, too. So far, there's been no killing, but that can't be far behind. Robbin' and killin' are usually paired up like a shovel and a hole, if you know what I mean."

"I take your meaning, but what's that got to do with me?"

"Angus, the federals in all four states have talked this out, and they've decided to put this Emmett and his gang out of the train robbing business. My boss, the United States Attorney here in Denver, assigned the job to me. We're hoping it's an assignment you'll take on. Based on the job you did for us involving the AT&SF and their Captain Plumb, I'd say this assignment was plain meant for you. It's that simple."

"Well, as I remember it, New Mexico has a mighty fine US Marshal in Santa Fe. Ain't Emmett his problem?"

"Yes, and I've been to talking to the US Marshal down there. You know Joe Neis. He's talked to his boss, a man named Jon Tracta, the United States Attorney for the Territory of New Mexico. You know, this new telephone line between Denver and Santa Fe is damned convenient, but I swear it makes more work for me than him. Neis only has two deputies down there. I've got four here in Denver. We have the same problem—we cannot dedicate a regular, full-time deputy to ride up into the mountain country in Union County, New Mexico. There's been a local posse or two that tried, but hell, they can't even find Emmett's hideaway, much less ride in and arrest Tom Emmett."

"What makes you think I can?"

"Well, Angus, it's because you got an unusual way of seeing things, and places. I mean the way you figured out the train robberies on that last New Mexico case, looking at places no one else thought about. Well, I figured that's the kind of look-see we need again. We got several federal arrest warrants out for him. I think the state authorities in three states probably have some local warrants, too. What me and Marshal Neis need is you. Are you game?"

"Well, suppose I was. I can't say how useful I'll be. The last time you gave me a badge, you told me not to show it off. This time, you're talking about me wearing it. Out in the open."

"Right, and here's the difference. The badge I gave you for that assignment was an extra one I keep in my desk drawer for temporary appointments. But, this one here is what I'm offering now."

He fished a shiny, round badge out of his vest-pocket and pushed it across the table to me. It was bigger than a silver dollar, and had a five-pointed star cut in the middle. US Marshal was inscribed across the top and Deputy around the bottom. It looked brand new.

"Angus, if you take the job, that badge will be yours. The back will be stamped with your name, along with your jurisdictional base. Know where these are made?"

"Nope."

"At the United States Mint, right here in Denver. Now, as I said before, the job and the badge won't tie you to Colorado or the New Mexico Territory. And, of course, I can't officially hand it over until you take the oath of service. But, I thought you'd like to get the feel of it."

"Well, Marshal, no one ever hired me on for a job with anything like this. Like that book you gave me to read, this badge seems to stand for more than just working a job."

"That's how all of us feel, Angus. The badge we wear reminds us of what we do—we serve justice. That's not a job—it's our history."

"How come you didn't mention any of this when you hired me to ferret out Captain Standard H. Plumb down in Chama?"

"Because that was just temporary work. I'm offering you a lot more this time."

We asked the barkeeper for another bottle, and if we could have dinner served in here. He brought us fresh cornbread, a bottle of rye whiskey, and one menu. Neither of us looked at it—just ordered beefsteak, overdone. While we were waiting, I excused myself, went up the stairs to my room, used the copper night-bucket in the corner, and took out Addie's conch shell. Couldn't hear a thing. So, I went back down to the saloon.

"Marshal Ramsey, you don't know all that much about me, and . . ."

"Well, Angus, that's another reason I asked you to come on up and see me. It's true that I don't know much about your life before you took that temporary badge last year. I'll thank you again for that fine job."

"Thanks, Marshal. I felt good once that was all done, but I ain't proud of killing a man, even if he was a disgrace to the Pinkertons."

A boy from the dining room, who looked to be a kitchen boy, brought two dinner trays in and set them down on the table. A bone-handle, cutting knife and a cheap tin fork were wrapped inside white cloth napkins. No salt shaker, so Marshal Ramsey ordered us one. Salt out of a shaker was unusual for me; I usually just took a pinch from a leather salt pouch in my saddle bag.

As we started in on the steaks, he said, "Angus, let's just spend a few minutes on a small matter. I understand you left Montclair a week ago and then got into a fracas of some kind in Pueblo. Mind telling me about that?"

"Not much to tell. I rode into Pueblo from Montclair after getting some gloomy news there. Not something I want to talk about, but I guess I was carrying a load when I found a saloon full of hard cases in Pueblo. They all worked in some kind of cinder plant down there. Anyhow, it got a little unruly. I don't remember all of it—I had a little too much to drink and ended in the Pueblo jail for the night. How'd you come to know about it?"

"The county sheriff down there is an old friend. When they inventoried your saddlebags at the jail, they found your badge. So, instead of taking you before the local magistrate the next morning, they called me. I asked them to just turn you loose, hoping you'd keep on riding north and not bust up any more cinderheads."

"Thanks."

"Don't mention it."

We sat awhile, neither of us moving back to the subject of full-time lawman.

"Hell, Angus, there ain't nothing wrong with a man cutting loose once in a while, as long as it ain't on the job. You don't have a drinking problem, do you?"

"No, it's women that I have a problem with. Women are more dangerous for me than whiskey."

"Well, I know a few things about you. You have a nose for outlaws and you have a keen eye for high ridges and fast rivers. You're pretty much a loner. Strangers can see you're not a man to mess with."

"Well, sir, I don't know that my nose can smell an outlaw any better than the next cowboy, but maybe Montclair and Pueblo have nudged me in another direction. I'm feeling like I ought to take you up on your offer."

"Well, that's fine news."

We cut into the steaks, continued sipping the whiskey and let the talk sit for a while. When the marshal pushed his chair back, he gave me a look.

"Angus, there's something else. Tony Neis said that, for such a young man, you seemed mighty set on avoiding people. His take was you only came to town for supplies. He might have talked to the undersheriff up in Chama. Something about you losing your wife, at a young age. Gave you a heavy load to carry. Memories and all. Maybe ghosts, hell I don't know. How old are you, anyhow?"

"Twenty-five."

"Would you mind telling me about your wife—not intending to pry, but being a US Deputy Marshal comes with responsibility, you know that, right? And, I take pride in knowing how to take care of the men who work for me."

"Yeah. Suppose it does."

"OK, you don't have to tell me anything too close to home. I'm only interested in distress. You know, things might cause you difficulty when you're out on assignment, all by your lonesome. Tom Emmett might be a handful for a dozen men, the way I hear it."

I looked at the last remnant of the whiskey in the glass in front of me and pushed it to the center of the table. Then, I got up and walked over to the window—it was chin-high off the floor and set in a narrow slit in the brick wall. But, it was enough so I could see that the black sky had clouded over outside and there was some rustling of wind in the tree that brushed up against the outside wall. I figured Marshal Ramsey's intentions were good, but he was asking about the worst thing that ever happened to me. He sat patient-like and waited me out. I walked back to the table and took my chair. Nudging it back a little, I took a deep breath. He had kind eyes and seemed settled under a brown Stetson. I looked at him square on and decided it'd be best to tell somebody else. I'd told Addie and it may have pushed her on to San Francisco. But she needed to know. And so did Marshal Ramsey.

"Mazy. That was her name. She was sixteen when I met her, up near Chama. I told her I was nineteen, and I nearly was. But neither of us were grown up. I'd been a top hand at the *Dos S* Ranch since I was twelve or thirteen and there wasn't a horse in the territory I couldn't ride. I knew every water hole and every cattle trail in a hundred square miles, but she was all I could think about. I didn't even know what love at first-sight meant. Truth be told, I still don't."

"Me neither, but my wife did. She spotted me coming out of the herd, dropped a loop around me, gave me a three-legged tie with a piggin' string, and we've been married ever since—going on twenty-four years now."

"Nearly as long as I've been alive, Marshal," I said as I pushed the whiskey glass another two inches away from me.

"Mazy was a rancher's daughter, raised as much in the saddle as I'd been. Her folks were leery of me. And . . ."

Marshal Ramsey was a man with a face that told its own story. He'd once sported red hair, and his bushy eyebrows still showed it. The rest of his head was kind of gray red. He nodded, sipped his whiskey, cut another slice of steak, and gave me time to gather my story. I chewed slowly, sipped my cold coffee, and took my time.

"Well, anyhow, Mazy and me could not wait one minute longer. So, we run off, got married in Aztec, New Mexico, and spent the next year, seven months, and five days living up on a mountain called Ten Shoes Up. We only came down off the mountain two times—on Christmas Day and on her mother's birthday. No one understood us, and no one liked it. But, it was heaven on earth for us. Mazy and me."

"But, what did you do for money—supplies, entertainment, all that? Didn't she get homesick? My wife did. She still does. We left her folks in Kansas, like I said, going on twenty-four years ago."

"Supplies? Entertainment? None of that mattered. I had a stake. And a cabin in the mountains. I'd been punching cattle since I was twelve and saved nearly every dollar the trail boss handed over twice a month. I didn't drink in those days, never understood gambling, and always had my pick of horses from the remuda on whichever ranch I was working. Mazy could hunt and fish and did everything her ma did in the kitchen and around the house. We didn't intend to stay up there that long. But, the months went by and the seasons changed. We were in no hurry to go back to ranching, or the civilized life down in the river valleys."

"Well, Angus, sounds like you made a fine choice. Mazy must have been one in a million. I can see on your face how happy you were; just talking about it makes your eyes light up."

We talked about how federal judges looked at things differently—not from the viewpoint of real people, but too often from a book. Marshall Ramsey confided a view that he said some federal judges might not like; it's how the law is executed, not how it is made that's important.

"So," I asked. "Does that mean that we answer to those who prosecute the law, like the US attorney rather than a federal judge?"

"No," he answered. "It means that federal marshals are the long arm of the law. But, sometimes judges are so tied to the law book that they can't see the eyes of a defendant who is brought in by a US Marshal. It ain't always as clear as the law book says it is."

We sat for a while enjoying the smoke and coffee. Leaning back in his chair, he gave me a wide smile.

"Angus," he said, as he lit a fresh cigar, "I'm glad we're having this conversation. It's important to me. I know you lost Mazy on Ten Shoes Up. If you don't mind, I'd like to know what happened."

"Why?"

"Well, because if it was something that dug a hole in your gut, I wouldn't want to send you out on an assignment that will make the hole deeper; that's about it. If you don't want to talk about it, fine. I still want you to take the badge and the oath."

"Her folks ain't forgiven me yet. That troubles me plenty. And, they got cause to hate me, for carrying her off to the top of a damn mountain and not bringing her back. They got cause . . ."

"What happened, son? I got the feeling you ain't told hardly anyone what happened. Maybe you should."

"Her appendix burst. No reason, no warning. But it did. The pain was something awful, and she could not sit a horse—that's saying something because she took to horses and difficult terrain same as I did. So, I rode lickety-split down to a ranch twelve miles away where I knew the missus was a midwife who doctored about as good as a real doctor. Since I plumb wore out a good horse, they even let me borrow a strong ranch-broke horse for the return spurt back up the mountain. Mazy was alone up there for almost seven hours. I rode into the little clearing alongside my cabin and found her stretched across the open doorway. Dead."

"And this was how long ago?

"Four years and eight months."

"Are you a God-fearing man, Angus?"

"Can't say I am. Don't fear high mountains or fast rivers, neither. My folks weren't church people, but we went once a month. But if I'd had religion, back then, I'd been cursing a god that took Mazy away. So, no Marshal Ramsey, I ain't a God-fearing man."

"Well, I was just thinking . . ."

I cut him off by pushing my plate to the center of the table and pushing myself back away from the table.

"I have just told you more about that day than most anyone else, except for Mazy's parents, and my own mother, whose death came along two years ago this month. So, Marshal, if you don't mind, I'm going to go upstairs to my room. Tomorrow morning, I'll come to your office after I check on my horse at the stable. If you still want me to find Tom Emmett and serve a federal warrant for his arrest, I'm your man."

CHAPTER 30
Angus Riding the Rio Cimarron

THE BREAK OF DAY along the Rio Cimarron is purtin' near as close to heaven as a man can get in New Mexico; cold, fast-running water, sweet grass banks, and tall, sheltering cottonwood trees. Nobody around to mess with you; the day's yours to keep or let go.

Tucson whinnied and gave himself a good shake, stomped the wet earth, and played some with the lead rope I'd looped around a forty-foot-tall cottonwood on the north bank of the river. Stretching my legs out from underneath two Navajo saddle blankets, I hunched my shoulder blades together, brushed off the early morning frost, and put my hat on. The brim was cold, but a man can't start the day bareheaded. It was the first day of spring, 1883, and I was ridin' southeast.

As I stirred a handful of beans in hot bacon grease, the small fire perked up some. The white smoke trailed up slow-like and disappeared into a turquoise sky. Always took my breath away. A sky like this on a frosty morning will make you wonder some. I wondered about how I'd fit in this new job—full-time, sworn deputy marshal. But, it didn't make any sense to wonder about the future. It'll get here when it's of a mind to. This time, my US Marshal badge was pinned to my vest, and I had posters and warrants for Tom Emmett and other members of his gang in my saddlebag.

"All right, Tucson," I said as he turned his neck back my direction, and gave me his good morning, copper-eye look. "I'll drop the reins for you, but don't go sucking up a bellyful. We've a ways to go."

The low, faraway whistle of a train put me in mind of that old bastard, Plumb. "Trains," I said to Tucson, as he slid off the bank and down to the river's edge, "attract two things—outlaws and payrolls. The outlaws are always after the payrolls, and here I am again, chasing after both."

But, he wasn't listening. That cold, clear water had his attention. The smell of running water always puts me in mind of the continuity of life; it wakes a body up in the morning, just like the sound of it puts a man to sleep at night.

"We'd best get moving, old boy. Folsom is a half-day's ride."

I'd begun this ride five days back. Started up high, almost at the twelve thousand-foot level, about fifty miles north of this little bend in the riverbed, on the western slope of the *Sangre de Cristo*. Now, at a more comfortable elevation of purtin' near seven thousand feet, I was just shy of Folsom, Union County,

New Mexico Territory. Folsom was a town just barely getting by, from one day to the next.

"No sense in puttin' it off," I muttered, "we got a job close by and we'd best get to doin' it."

CHAPTER 31
Angus in Folsom, New Mexico

"**M**ORNIN' STRANGER," the man behind the big oak desk said as he lurched up out of the creaky chair, sticking out his right hand. Bony and callused, but a right firm grip for such a little man. He gave me an up-and-down look.

"Sheriff," I responded, feeling like a one-eyed undertaker was sizing me up for a coffin. Sheriff Godfeather's eye-patch was something I'd never seen on a lawman. Could a one-eyed man shoot? He wore a long-barreled Colt revolver high up on his left hip and had an odd holster, fixing the gun almost parallel with the gun belt. The grip was out in front so the business end of a twelve-inch barrel pointed astern, ready for a cross draw. The rack on the wall behind his desk held a new Sharps repeating rifle and a long-barreled, Hawken .50 caliber.

The Hawken looked new, too, and wasn't a percussion cap, like the one that old bastard Branson had tried to kill me with.

Sheriff Godfeather was downright gaunt, with a purple tone to his skin, and nose hair aplenty. He seemed to belong to that old oak desk jointed strong enough to sit a buffalo.

I suppose I was staring at him, because he said, "I lost this eye in a way that no one could ever suspect, much less believe. It wasn't a shootout. Everyone wonders why Union County keeps me on the payroll. I'll be happy to satisfy your curiosity on that right now, stranger. My eye went dark when a cinder blew out of the coalhole on an Iron Horse. What my grandfather called the first steam engine he ever saw. The cinder cooked my eye like an egg dropped into hot grease in a frying pan. Just to set your mind at ease, I can outshoot everyone in the territory. Except maybe Tom Emmett."

A noise, soft but close by, caused Sheriff Godfeather to crane his neck to the barred door at the back of the room. A metal clank or maybe someone dropping a hammer.

Turning his oversized Adam's apple back to the door, he croaked, "You boys don't start a clanging on them bars now. Flora will get your lunch over here when she's of a mind to."

Turning back, he settled back into the creaky chair.

"So. That's why I'm still the sheriff. They all know I can shoot. But, I can't catch no wild-eyed, murderin' Missouri man like Tom Emmett. But, you can, I expect. Otherwise, you wouldn't be sitting in my office. Right?"

"Maybe. Maybe not."

I took the cane-back chair he pointed to as he eased back down behind his desk like it was a fort and I was sitting at his front gate. He waited, polite-like, for me to continue. When I didn't, he tried again. I could tell right off: He was a man with a lot to say and in a hurry to say it.

"Well, stranger, it don't make no never mind. Could be I'm figuring you wrong. But, what the hell, I'll tell you what I know about the man."

What he had to say wasn't all that much. I'd got more than that just by reading the marshal's file about Tom Emmett up in Denver. I knew he was from Missouri, got into some trouble there, and then took to rustling cattle down in Texas. I suppose I looked disappointed to the sheriff.

"All right, stranger, there you have it. You're entitled to your own views on anything. Now if you want to know more, go across the street to the hotel. Talk to Flora, the proprietress, and her hired man, Cipriano. They'll entertain wild stories about outlaws who ride through our little town every once in a while."

"Sheriff, you're making assumptions about my business here, but we've never met. Mind telling me why I ought to be interested in this Tom Emmett?"

"Simple enough. I know everyone hereabouts. Strangers don't come into my office unless they need the law, or unless they are the law. You got that look about you—you got a badge somewhere—whether you wear it or not's up to you."

"Do I look like a lawman?"

"You do. Then, of course, there's the telegram. Came in yesterday from US Marshal Ramsey in Denver, telling me to expect you."

That was news to me. When Marshal Ramsey had given me my own badge stamped with my federal government iden tification number on the back, and my disposition orders, as he called 'em, he didn't volunteer that he'd be announcing my presence here in Folsom.

"What'd he tell you?"

"Not all that much. You're looking into some recent train robberies afflicting the AT&SF over near Grants, and the Southern Pacific down to El Paso. But, mostly he said you'd ask about the Colorado and Southern Railroad here in the best part of the New Mexico Territory. Union County. He didn't say your name, but I been in the lawin' business for a good bit of time. I figure you're on the trail of the Emmett boys. That cover your ground?"

"Could be. Any idea where the man holes up?"

He gave me a grin, then leaned forward and pulled open a center drawer just below his hollowed-in stomach. Pulling out a map folded into twelve-inch squares, he started in.

"Well, whatever your name is, you need to know there's a lot of grass country angled across the northeast part of New Mexico, just this side of the Texas line. My county jurisdiction starts south of Trinidad, Colorado, and moves a few miles east of Cimarron, New Mexico. I don't cover that town myself, and I won't accept no blame for what goes on there. But, I'm thinking your interest lies in paying special attention to what is due north of my little town, Folsom, New Mexico."

"What might that be, Sheriff?"

"Well, two things. First off, there are those pesky S-curves as the railroad tracks make a slow, but steep climb up the mountainside, about halfway between here and Cimarron. The grade climbing up from the Dry Cimarron to the grassy plain—some call that stretch 'Robbers Roost.' And, second of all . . ."

"S-curves? Could you flesh that out a little before we get to your second point?"

"S-curves cut into the side of the mountain to reduce the grade. But, the engine must slow down. That's why they get robbed."

Sheriff Godfeather leaned back in his chair and sucked in his small gut some. He looked pleased at the frown on my face.

"They get robbed because they slow down? Is that what you're saying?"

"Yes, sir, you got it. Slow trains are easy to board. In some places along there, you can just step up onto the platform as the train ekes on by."

"How many times has the Colorado and Southern Railroad been hit there?"

"Twice. It's mighty tempting. You see, we don't have many banks in New Mexico. Ranchers and storekeepers out here deal in cash, not checks like they do in Denver, or over to Santa Fe and Albuquerque. Now, that cash has to move by stage or railroad. And, of course, the federals move their payrolls and money to pay the railroads for their part in building the whole dang system. That pretty much explains why the territorial legislature upped the ante—suppose you heard about that, right?"

"No, can't say that I have."

"Well, sir, let me get you up to snuff on the law west of the Pecos—that'd be what folks back east in St. Louis call the Wild West. The New Mexico Territorial Legislature listens when railroad lawyers are paying for the steaks and fine whiskey and prodding them like cattle in a chute. Robbers are having their way of it on three different railroads. And, Tom

Emmett's gang is gnawing on the railroads like they was big juicy apples. He hits them when it pleases him, and then he and his whole damn gang slap leather and make the climb up to their hideout."

"That would be where, exactly?"

"Well, I'm thinking the federal United States Government hopes you can figure that out for all of us. No one that's willing to talk to local lawmen knows where Emmett and his gang hide out. They must have a camp or a ranch or something, leastways what folks say. That's the second thing I was gonna tell you about."

"This would be a good time."

Before he could begin, the clanging started up fresh from behind the barred door behind me. Godfeather unwound himself from the swivel chair again and moved back to the rear of the room. The floorboards creaked as he walked away from me.

"Excuse me, stranger," he said, cross-drawing the long-barrel colt with his right hand and popping up the bar latch on the jail door with his left. Then, taking one step inside the backroom, he fired up into the ceiling. The boom resounded both ways.

"Goddamn you boys! You're riling me up. No lunch on the county today. When Flora gets here with your lunch, I'll be sending her back across the street. And, if you make me draw on you again, one of you is gonna be short a big toe."

I couldn't help smiling.

"Sheriff, I guess I am in the right place after all. Is that how you manage your prisoners here, by threatening to shoot them in the big toe?"

"Well, the first one was an accident. A drunken cowboy from the Long Branch got to banging on a Mexican through the bars. He'd got hold of him with one hand, and was punching him with the other. I was trying to make him turn him loose with the barrel of my gun, when I accidentally pulled the trigger. The bullet bounced off the bottom bar rail into the Mexican's foot. The local undertaker amputated his big toe. But he lived. So, since then, I been keeping order that way. No one wants to lose a big toe, you know. Makes you walk funny."

"'Spect so, Sheriff. You were about to tell me the possibles that Emmett might be using when he ain't robbin' or stealin' somewhere. A camp you say?"

"Yes, or a ranch run by someone friendly to outlaws. Whatever it is, it's up north of here, maybe forty miles, maybe more. And it's well hid. You can't ride up on it unsuspecting. Not been there myself. Rock country, plumb full of ambush trails. And, easy pickings for anybody with a Winchester to sight down on you."

"You know anybody that's been there?"

"No, can't say that I do. I formed a posse once, but we got stopped short of his hideout. "

"By what?"

"Good sense. You see, there are canyons up there that are one way in, and no way out. That's no place for the law. Outlaws make their own rules when they have this sort of permanent hideout. That's what folks say Emmett has. And, he might be renting it out to other gangs. What I hear, anyhow. So, if you got a federal troop of top riders, with repeating rifles, and a saddlebag full of warrants, then you can give it a try. Otherwise, good sense ought to prevail. You ought to come on home, like I did, a mile short of the canyon entrance."

"Well, Sheriff, what you see sittin' here in front of you is all the federal law that's coming to your fine county. No top riders, but I do have a repeating rifle—just one, mind you. And, I have a federal warrant, but not in my saddlebag. A court warrant can get a man killed if the wrong man was to get a look at it. I have it here in my duster, and I'd like to leave it here with you for the time being. My badge, too. That OK with you?"

The sheriff opened the top left hand drawer of his big desk.

"Pop 'em in there. If you grab aholt of Emmett, bring him down here and I'll stick him back there with those boys looking to get their toes shot off. You can serve him official-like with the warrant once he's in custody."

The door from the boardwalk opened and a girl, maybe nine or ten, sashayed in from the front, carrying a wicker basket with a blue-checkered cloth tucking the contents in, and a tin pitcher.

Ignoring me, she said to the Sheriff, "Flora says you ought not to be shooting your gun just because she's a little behind on the sandwiches."

"You tell her that I was not trying to hurry her none. I was just explaining jail rules to our lunch guests."

The girl went directly to the little table beside the cell door and set her bundles down.

"Uncle, Flora made five sandwiches for lunch. I counted them—two for whoever's locked up—two for you and Bo, and one for this guy sitting right there," she said, pointing a long bony finger at me.

"All right, Nancy," the one-eyed sheriff said, smiling at her. He looked like a different man smiling that way—not so frail looking and more like an uncle which, as it turns out, he was.

"You go on now, and tell your mother we appreciate her food, and I'll remind you that her name is 'Mother' to you, not 'Flora'."

"Thanks," I said to the young girl. "It's kind of you and your mother to send me a sandwich. It'll be a welcome change for me."

"You are welcome, sir," Nancy said to me.

Then, turning back to the sheriff, she added, "All right, Uncle, but she says she don't mind who calls her Flora. So I do."

As the girl left, I asked, "So, you're going to feed your prisoners lunch anyway, Sheriff?"

"No, they ain't getting lunch today. Those sandwiches will be their supper. That's the real price for riling me—Flora usually cooks fried chicken for supper on Fridays; that's what they're gonna miss."

"Who's Flora? You mentioned she ran the hotel, right?"

"Flora's my sister-in-law," he said, as he dug down into the first wicker basket, fished out two sandwiches, and then poured us each a glass of buttermilk from the tin pitcher.

The front door opened again, and a bony cowboy with his hat tucked down tight on his head strode in.

"Sheriff, I saw Nancy come out, just as I was fixin' to report for duty. I sure hope one of those sandwiches is for me. The boys in the back riling you a little? I heard your .45 booming as I was walking down the street."

Then I realized the bony cowboy was wearing a badge on his vest. His grin was a welcome sight.

"Angus! Ain't you a big-ass surprise? I been wonderin' what became of you since you walked out the courthouse door over to Santa Fe. What was it, half a year ago?"

"Hello, Bo. The coroner's inquest was four months back. It's good to see you wearing a badge. You look as skinny as ever. Are you living off one sandwich a day?"

I stuck out my hand to the cowboy I'd more or less drug into my cabin on Ten Shoes Up just before the shoot-out with Captain Standard H. Plumb and his hired gun, Chester Branson.

We filled in Sheriff Godfeather as to how Bo String and I came to know one another. Seems that Bo had two jobs here in Folsom. He was not just, as he put it, "A by-God man of the law."

"Hell no, Angus, I'm working mostly over to the livery stable. It has eight stalls for strangers and traveling folk to bed down their stock. I been here since the week after I last saw you. In all that time, we've never had more 'n five stalls full. So, I do part-time deputy work for Sheriff Godfeather, and I do part-time livery stable work."

"Who is the livery keeper here, Bo? A man I could trust?"

"A man you could trust? Heck, no, seeing as how the livery keeper ain't a man. Flora's her name. She's been real nice to me. She runs the hotel and lets me tend the stable for her."

I turned the talk back to Godfeather.

"Sheriff, that was a fine sandwich, but I think we got off on a side trail. What was it you were saying about a change in New Mexico law?"

Wiping the chili off his chin from the cheese and slab-ham sandwich, he picked up the thread of law west of the Pecos.

"So, on February 15th, a year back, they made train robbin' a capital-by-God crime. I got it right here on the desk," he said, pointing to a leather-bound volume of the New Mexico Territorial Laws and Statutes. "Lemme read it aloud to you. Bo, you pay attention, too. It says 'the Territory of New Mexico will suffer the death penalty upon anyone who should assault any train, car, or locomotive with intent to commit robbery, murder, or any other felony upon any engineer, brakeman, conductor, mail or express agent, or passenger.'"

"Angus, you can't deny the logic in that," Bo chimed in. "Train robbing is a dangerous business done by men who give little thought to dying themselves."

This talk stuck in my craw just a little.

"I suppose you're right," I said to the oak desk and the skinny deputy. "But, if you rob a bank, or a store, or the sheriff's office of something valuable like that Sharps hanging on the wall over there, you would not get the by-God death penalty. Not clear to me that stealing money from a railroad express agent warrants the death penalty."

Sheriff Godfeather gave me another of his up-and-down looks.

"Angus? Your name? Just Angus? Not that there's anything wrong with going by just one name. Now, here's my thinking on our new death penalty law as to train robbin'. Robbing in town is different because there's other people around. Robbing a train out in the country is hardly any trouble at all. And, Tom Emmett's gang has done it three times of late, and twice not twenty-five miles from here, so if you catch him, he'll get the rope. And, that's because he ain't just robbin'; he's killed railroad people, although not around here. That's what I hear anyhow. Taking the money is not enough for him. He comes with a reputation as a rock-hard killer."

"Well, Sheriff, I ain't about to argue with hanging a man who murders someone. But, as you lined this out, it seems the capital crime part—which is what I'm told makes hanging a man legal—ain't dependent on killing. Under the Railroad Act, robbin' a train alone is enough to bring out the executioner's big rope. That puts me in what I'd call a dilemma."

Bo coughed and asked the sheriff for water for his parched throat. After he poured himself a cup from the pitcher, he joined in.

"Dilemma? That's a word I heard some from the pulpit over in Española—Father Dominguez used it. But, I confess to never being sure what he was talking about. What's it really mean, Angus?"

"Well, Bo, I ain't a priest or a judge. The one-room school marm that taught my two sisters and me said it's a choice between two equally unpleasant things. Like making you choose between eating horse turds, and going hungry. Both are unpleasant, right? 'Cept here it's the difference between getting arrested for stealing from the bank, or stealing from the railroad. One gets you sent to prison. The other gets you a rope notched on your Adam's apple. The dilemma's on the man with the badge."

Bo listened and nodded his head my way, but if he had another thought on it, he kept it to himself. Godfeather walked over to the water pitcher shelf, picked out a cup, and poured himself a big gulp.

"Angus, I see the point you're aimin' at, but I got to say that you're riding the wrong horse on this one. Lawmen like you and me ain't got no say in the matter, much less a choice. You got an arrest warrant to serve; you just do your job. A sheriff can't choose who to arrest. He just locks them up. The judge is the dilemma man. He sends the man who robbed the store to the penitentiary. He sends the man who robbed the train to the gallows. Either way, it ain't on the lawman's plate. You want another sandwich?"

"I'm just saying that everybody has choices in life, Sheriff. You're right, lawmen can just do their job and let judges sort out the punishment. I never gave it a single thought before you told me about New Mexico treating train robbing as a capital crime even if nobody got killed. That's all."

"Come on, Sheriff," a gravelly voice called out from the cells in the back of Sheriff Godfeather's office, "I'm sorry about the commotion, but it's been a long time since breakfast."

"Deputy String, you'd best get back on duty monitoring those boys back there."

Bo had been hunkered down on his heels beside the door to the cells enjoying his sandwich. Effortlessly, he rose up, set the cloth napkin back down into the basket, and spun back toward the cell like a cowpony changing direction in a stampede.

"Yeah, Sheriff, it's that Oscar fellow in the small cell. He's steamed up and expecting the worst when the judge gets here tomorrow. That's his three-legged stool you heard. He likes to throw it around—in particular against the bars of the big cell next to his."

The sheriff and I followed Bo back into a large room holding the cells, behind the front office. First off, I noticed a small table and a cane-back chair with a soft cushion. A book and a writing tablet sat on the table, a spittoon was on the floor, and a hat-hook hung on the wall above it. I'd guess the hallway to be ten, twelve feet long. Two cells on one side, and what looked to be an inside outhouse and a storage room on the other. They used three-quarter-inch diameter, black-bone steel to build these cells. The little one had no window, but the big cell had a long slit across the top of the north-facing wall. It let in a little light, although it was too high up to see out. Cold steel bars were affixed to window's inside ledge. This was a tight jail. And smelled like one, too.

Bo was in front of us. He walked to the edge of the small cell. "This here's Oscar," he said pointing to a burly man with snarl on his face. I couldn't guess at his age but he had thick long hair and big ears, one of which had been sliced and scarred. The man's black eyes hid out below big bushy eyebrows, separated by a nose that looked like an acorn stuck between two rocks, all cracked with age and likely rotten inside.

Picking up a ten-inch hickory stanchion, with leather wrapping on the handle and a nasty looking knob on the business end, Bo stopped just shy of the bars. He commenced to slap the well-polished end of the club into his palm. Whap, whap—it sounded like a muleskinner putting the whip to one of his animals.

"Oscar, you'd best quit throwing that stool. I already told you that more 'n once. You want another h-i-c-k-o-r-y adjustment with this stick, or are you behaving yourself?"

Oscar was a dirty little man, pushing two hundred pounds, but no taller than a gatepost. And hairy. Neck and chest hair stuck out of his shirt in front, back hair puffing out over his collar in back. His beard looked like a small coal shovel hanging down from his mouth, tangled worse than a briar patch. Thick hair covered his wrists and the tops of his hands. For a short man, he had arms that didn't fit the rest of him. If he stretched his fingers out, I expect they'd reach his knees, without bending over.

He sounded like a rusty coal bucket, too, "God damned, snot-nosed, pearly skinned kid—that's all you—"

Bo interrupted Oscar's rant by reaching between the bars with the stanchion and whapping Oscar on the forearm.

Oscar yelped and said something in a foreign language, or maybe it was English with some strange accent, maybe German, or other European talk—hard to tell which. He was understandable, but you had to be looking right at him to make full sense of his words. His cord pants hung loose because his belt was hanging on a hook six feet away from the bars, and he was barefooted. I could smell him from ten feet away—the dank smell that comes from months without getting close to soap or water.

"You skinny little bastard," he yelped, jumping backward out of reach. "I ain't afraid of you, or your goddamned stick. And, I ain't fond of stayin' here next to an Indian and a broke-down Mex. Why ain't you got a proper jail for white men?"

I suppose he was white, from the sound of him, but he didn't look white. He looked like a gorilla, nearly black as ones I'd seen in pictures. The Indian, and the one he called a broke-down Mexican, sat on a bunk against the far wall. The Indian got up, turned his back to us, and stared up at the window slit high up on the wall. He had tight black hair, with a long braid hanging halfway down his back. It was oily and wrapped with white rawhide. The Mexican was skinny, like

Bo. He had darting eyes and a pencil thin mustache. He sat hunched over, with his knees pulled up under his chin, and his brown, bony arms gathered around his legs like corded rope. He sat still as a rock and breathing easy. I got the feeling he was enjoying the show between Oscar and Bo.

Only the Mexican looked at Oscar when he spoke. The Indian made his feelings obvious. Neither one seemed much interested in what Oscar had to say.

"Boys, this man," the sheriff said, aiming his thumb at me over his shoulder, "is a federal law officer, but he ain't after none of you. He's got bigger fish to fry, but still it would be in your interest if you made no more commotion back here. Otherwise, I'll think of a federal crime and turn all three of you over to him. You won't get none of Flora's sandwiches in the federal penitentiary over to Santa Fe."

"Sheriff," I said, "these men are of no interest to me. I've had my look at them. You can keep 'em as long as you like."

When we went back into his office, I made plain my position. "Sheriff, I do not appreciate your telling my business to your prisoners. Can't be much good coming of that."

"Sorry, Angus, but it just came out, natural-like. You see, Oscar is a man you might oughta think about questioning. Word is he used to be a member of Butch Cassidy's gang. And, them other two, hell's fire, they could be tied in with Tom Emmett."

"You think?"

"Well, word is that Butch sometimes shares his Hole-In-The-Wall hideout up in Wyoming with Tom Emmett. Some speculate that Emmett returns the favor whenever Butch comes down to New Mexico. Oscar might be your key to the hideout. Them other two scalawags might know something too, who knows? I could bring one of 'em out here to talk, so's the other can't hear, if you want."

"No. Thanks just the same."

"Well, Oscar's doing fifteen days for being drunk and beating on that Indian you saw. I'll have to let him out a week from tomorrow. The other two are in there just on my suspicion. I'll have to let them out before the circuit judge rides back through here."

"When's that?"

"Dunno. But, I got a wire yesterday saying it'd be sometime next week. Maybe longer."

"Much obliged, Sheriff."

CHAPTER 32
Angus at Flora's Hotel and Dining Establishment

LIFTING THE SINGLE REIN I'd looped over the hitch rail at the Union County Sheriff's Office, I swung my leg over Tucson's rump and trotted down to the end of the street where the livery barn beckoned. *Union County Livery Barn—Horses & Mules—Tack & Feed*, the sign said. As I figured, there was no one there since Bo was still at the jail babysitting Oscar and the other two fellers. The double front door was wide open, so I rode on in and nudged Tucson to the rear stall—a freshly raked, twelve-foot square with cut pine planks nailed onto spruce poles. I rubbed him down with a spare gunnysack, gave him a thin sheaf of alfalfa, and a coffee can of sweet grain. Then I walked the two blocks back up the quiet street to *Flora's*

Hotel & Dining Room. Sure seemed a quiet little town—only a few people moving about, stock and wagons rolling up and down the single street, but no one in a hurry and everyone nodding back and forth to one another. Friendly enough, I thought. But still a town. I wondered where the saloon was.

As I walked back up the street, I pondered on my time-table. I figured I had a week to figure things out. At the end of that week, either Oscar, or those other two might find their way back to the hideout, if Sheriff Godfeather was suspicion-ing them right. And, they knew me, thanks to his ill-advised introduction.

Flora's Hotel was the only painted building on the street, and the only one with a second story. And, it was the first building I ever saw with two front doors, set six feet apart. The right-hand door was surrounded by a cut-pine porch and set three feet up off the street. It had a white, two-foot high picket fence around it, with two benches and some pots for growing plants. No flowers, but there were green buds ready to pop out with something. The other door was at ground level, with a rough boardwalk in front. The build-ing had a coat of more-or-less white paint—grayed but white some time back. Up above, on the second floor, I could see six shuttered windows. Four were shut tight, but two on the right-hand corner were open to the late afternoon sun. The right-hand door had fresh white paint, while the other was a faded gray color.

The door with the fresh paint was centered with an oval-shaped piece of leaded glass etched with *Flora's Hotel and Dining Establishment*. You couldn't see through the clouded glass. The other door didn't have a window, but had a small brass plate identifying it as "The Bar." Thought that was welcome news.

Flora was a surprise. She was tall, lean, and very unlike her short, wiry brother. From what I could see of her skin, which was only her wrists, neck and face, she was part Hispanic, or maybe Italian. She read me with her deep-set black eyes. And, as she talked, her auburn hair, cut short, moved with her head and neck. I don't remember ever meeting a woman with a curved set of doubled dimples on her face, but hers seemed to talk with the words coming out of her mouth in a voice nearly as low as a man's was. On the down side, she was clearly the type of woman I'd learned to avoid—a town woman settled in her ways, and under thirty with no wedding ring in sight. Trouble, I thought.

"You must have just come from my brother's office. Nancy said you were nice to her. Thanks for that. How can I help you?" she asked, offering me her hand as she strode toward me.

I was more or less about two feet inside the hotel lobby, "Ma'am," I said, taking off my hat, and nodding my assent to her guess as to who I was.

"Name's Angus. Need a room for the night, a bath, and a sit-down dinner. Your brother assures me that dinner at your place will be a real treat."

Looking around the lobby took a little time because it was not what I'd expected. Instead of a chest-high registration desk and a rack of keys, there was a parlor filled with what looked to be the kind of valuable furniture usually found in a well-to-do banker's home. Two highly polished mahogany sofas with deep red cushions faced one another across a low table with a glass top on which sat a porcelain bowl of water filled with what looked to be small beads and leaves. The north and south walls had oil paintings of mountains, valleys, and clouds. Etched-glass cabinets stood on one side of the room, full of things I couldn't make out from the doorway. A large, circular rug was in the middle of the room.

Instead of a swinging door into the adjacent saloon, there was a short hallway leading to double sliding doors faced in brass. The small sign proclaimed, "Dining Room." And, at the top of a four-foot-wide stairway leading to the rooms upstairs was another set of double doors, closed, with a matching sign that said, "Rooms, Upstairs." All in all, this room demanded good manners.

"Doesn't look like the lobby at the La Fonda, does it?" Flora asked.

"No, ma'am, it doesn't."

"My daughter, Nancy, thinks you're here on business. I'm happy to accommodate you, whether just for tonight, or a future visit."

"Ma'am, I will be moving on tomorrow at sun-up, but I would like a good meal, and if you can spare the time, a little conversation. Sheriff Godfeather sort of volunteered you, suggesting that you have information about a man I'm looking for."

"The dining room's through that door over there. On the other side of the dining room is a door that leads down three steps to the bar. I prefer that bar customers enter from the street. Hotel guests are welcome to use this living room, which is my own. Make it your own, please. "

"I'll be needing a bath, too, but I suppose that's down the street somewhere."

"No, it's behind the bar and has its own outside entrance. A delightful man from Korea, Oh Jin Suh, is the proprietor. He smiles at me when I say 'I love you, Mister Oh Jin Suh.' He runs his little laundry and an apothecary at the same time. He matches the best drugs mixed down the street at Dr. Anderson's little one-room clinic, which he incorrectly calls his surgery. I suggested surgery was what he does, not the room in which he does it. But, he's a man with little use for a woman's opinion. Mister Oh Jin Suh is always open to suggestions. You'll see."

"I'm sorry, ma'am, for not introducing myself. Name's Angus. And, I would be happy to hear your opinions about the town, and about a man they call Tom Emmett."

"Well, Angus, of course you can have a room. You'll be our only guest tonight, so I'll put you in the best room, upstairs on the outside corner."

"That'd be the one with the open shutters?"

"Yes, it is. You are an observant man, unlike most of Folsom's regular visitors. I swear, sometimes I get guests who are surprised to hear, once inside this room, that there even is an upstairs."

"Reckon I spotted it because this is the only two-story building in town, ma'am."

"Please, call me Flora. You've met my daughter, Nancy, our cook is Bernardo, and during the week I do the waitressing. There is another two-story building, but it's back off a ways, next to a one-story church. It used to be a grain shed. Can you guess what this building was before my late husband bought it and we moved here to Folsom?"

"I ain't all that good at guessing."

"It was a brothel, at least the upstairs part was. That's why Nancy and I live downstairs, behind that locked oak door you can see back there. Just so you know, I keep one of my brother's shotguns back there, even though there's rarely any rowdies in town these days. Sheriff Godfeather has culled rudeness and lawlessness by threating to shoot everyone in the foot."

"Yes, Flora, I heard about that. It happens I have a friend here who works for both the sheriff and apparently you. He's Bo String, a man I met over near Chama."

"Bo String's a delightful young man; glad to hear he's a friend of yours. My brother thinks I'm the town librarian and its welcoming hostess. It's a wonderful surprise to have a guest who knows Bo. He has been a godsend to me. My husband had a sizeable grub stake from a silver mine he worked up near Durango. He was smart enough to get out of the mining business at the right time, and he bought this hotel, the livery stable, and he married me eleven years ago. A year after we moved here, from Cortez where my family lives, he died. I had been running the hotel anyhow and took on the livery barn as an extra chore. I've had a half-dozen young boys helping me over the last eight years, but Bo is the first one to both love horses and do an honest day's work. Besides, he seems like a young uncle to Nancy. But enough of me. Tell me something about yourself while I get the guest register."

"Not much to tell."

She smiled at me with those double dimples. "If you come down for dinner at six, we'll feed you as good a sit-down dinner as exists in the entire New Mexico Territory—at least that's what Ira used to say."

"Ira? Was that your husband?"

"Ira is my brother. But, nowadays he thinks his first name is Sheriff. He's a lovely man, but titles are important to him. And your title is?"

"Don't have one. Titles mean little although I respect sheriffs, judges, and doctors. But, sometimes my work is best done by ignoring what someone is called and paying close attention to who they really are."

"Fair enough, Angus. What sort of conversation does Sheriff Ira Godfeather think we ought to be having? I'm always happy to talk with anyone new to town—even if it's only a short stay. But, I have a condition."

I nodded and gave her a longer look than I'd intended. I wanted to talk to her, but was always fearful of conditions imposed by attractive women. So, I just said, "Yes, ma'am. What might be your condition?"

"Flora, please. Do you have time to tell me what's going on outside Union County?"

I stored my kit upstairs in a too-big room with two large windows overlooking the street and a good view of the livery stable, two blocks down. The bath was out back, where Oh Jin Suh held sway over everyone. He ordered people around just by looking at them. A young Chinese boy caught his look after I told him what I wanted and immediately fired up a small wood-burning boiler. Flora had warned me that Mr. Suh's water would take a half-hour to heat up, so I used the time to write some notes in my case log about the men in the jail. I'd developed the habit of making notes because I'd have to write a detailed report to Marshal Ramsey, no matter how the hunt for Tom Emmett turned out. I planned on sticking the notes and my badge in Sheriff Godfeather's desk drawer before I left town.

An hour later, bathed and toweled, and sporting my only clean shirt, I went downstairs for dinner.

The menu offered three choices—beefsteak, pork chops, or chicken. But Flora was out of pork. She said the chicken was fresh-killed and the steak well-hung, but chewy. I didn't tell her that I ate beef, venison, and antelope as my regular fare and thought chicken was a delicacy. She seemed oddly pleased when I said I'd have the chicken. Her cook, Bernardo, was not a fry cook; he roasted everything on a spit, along with potatoes, and green chilies. He basted all three, she explained to me, with a sauce that was a mix of olive oil, mustard, and ground black pepper. Can't say I've ever had a better meal, especially the cold buttermilk served out of a crock pitcher. Water was hard to come by in this part of New Mexico, but there was a small ceramic pot and two small water glasses on the table. You had to pour it yourself. No bread, but she said corn muffins would be served for breakfast. She served my dinner, but didn't sit with me. There was only one other table, occupied by the man and his wife who owned the dry goods store next door to the livery barn. They talked mostly about pounds, containers, and prices of things I never bought or thought about. When I finished my meal, Flora suggested I take my after-dinner coffee in the lobby. More comfortable, she said.

Over coffee poured from a blue porcelain pot into cups too small to keep it warm for more than a few seconds, and held with caution, I learned a lot about Flora and a little about

Tom Emmett. "Angus, you have the look of a serious wanderer who likes what he does and does not come into the company of town folk all that often. Am I right?"

"Well, truth be told, I'm most content when I'm horseback. I love riding ridgelines high in the mountains; it's almost as much fun as running a horse headlong into a roaring river aiming sideways at the bank on the other side. So, talking to a woman in a room like this is a rare treat for me."

She paused, probably expecting more from me than I'd given so far. "And, just what did my big brother Ira suggest that we talk about?"

"Tom Emmett."

"What about him?"

"Dunno. He just said you probably knew more about the man than anyone else in town."

"Hmmm. Well, he's stayed here four, maybe five times. He's a pleasant conversationalist, but clearly a rounder who'd take advantage if he could."

She paused, stirred another teaspoon of sugar into her coffee, and continued. "Which he can't, by the way. He has good table manners, despite his insistence on eating only fried meats and overcooked vegetables. He dresses well, gets the boy who swamps out the bar to shine his boots, and seems to want a level of respect his business does not normally command. Oh, yes, there's the thing you're probably most interested in. He robs trains for a living. Maybe that's why I occasionally enjoy talking to him. He's honest, even about things he ought not to talk about at all, especially to the sheriff's little sister. That's how he sees me. How he sees Ira is entirely another matter."

"Yes, ma'am, it's his train robbing that interests me. I'd like to talk to him about that, but I don't know where he is now. You wouldn't know that, would you?"

Nancy came in from the house quarters behind the lobby where we were sitting for coffee. She had a mischievous look on her face, and took a seat on the piano bench across from us.

"It's time for my lesson, Flora, but I'll wait until you and your gentleman caller are done."

"*Finished*, Nancy; *finished*, not *done*," Flora said to Nancy. Turning to me, Flora asked, "Angus, has any smart-talking ten-year-old ever referred to you as a 'gentleman caller' before? No? I thought not. Please don't take Nancy serious; she just likes to provoke grownups into thinking she's older than she acts, sometimes."

Nancy probably knew better than to engage her mother in front of a stranger. She left the room and Flora returned to our conversation.

"Do you want to catch him, Mr. Tom Emmett I mean, or join him?"

"Yes, ma'am. I'd like to do that."

She gave me a long look. Then, she got up and walked over to a bookshelf on the back wall. She had long wrists, I noticed, and ankles to match. Turning back toward me with a small grin, not yet a smile, she walked back while turning pages in a leather-bound book.

"You are clever, Angus. So's he. Catch him, join him, it's all the same to you, right?"

"Yes, ma'am."

She handed me the book, which looked to be the hotel register. I took it but didn't open it. Seemed impolite to read it right there in front of her. Nancy came back in from the dining room, stopped just short of her mother's chair, and waited, looking at her mother for direction.

Flora took her cue. "Nancy's terribly interested in anyone new to this town, and especially someone who might have traveled to San Francisco, or met the King of Siam. Have you done either of those things?"

"Mother," Nancy exclaimed, "you don't have to tell everyone about that! But, I would dearly love to talk to someone who has been to a city by an ocean, or met the King of Siam. You see, I'm interested in those things right now because—"

Her mother cut her off. "Nancy, Marshal Angus is interested in Tom Emmett, not the King of Siam. After you take the dishes back to Mrs. Delgado, maybe you should get back to your school work."

"Mother, can't I stay, just for a minute? I'll be quiet."

"Can she stay, Marshal Angus? Or, do you have any more questions for me?"

I turned to Nancy, "I haven't been to San Francisco, but I'm thinking that's my next stop, once I finish my business here. To tell you the truth, I didn't even know Siam had a King. Schooling was something I wasn't all that good at. But I bet you are. Maybe you could tell me about the King of Siam, and I'd be glad to tell you about the only two-headed calf I ever saw."

"Really, a calf with two heads? That sounds terrible. The King of Siam would never allow such a thing in his kingdom; he's very serious, you know."

"Well, I hope you find someone who's met the King, but in my line of work, we don't meet kings, or princesses, either."

Nancy dived directly into her chance to talk to a stranger. "Uncle Ira said you were a federal marshal, and I know what that is. But, you're the first one I ever shook hands with. How do you know who to arrest? I mean, you have pictures of outlaws, because I've seen them in the sheriff's office. But, even if you have pictures, how do you know they really did what they say he did on the reward poster? It's very confusing, can you just—?"

"Nancy," Flora interrupted, "Marshal Angus can't answer ten questions at once, and besides, he has things to do and I'm sure there are things he cannot tell you about the federal government's business."

"Nancy," I said, motioning to her to come around from behind her mother's chair and sit on the other end of the sofa from me. "Being a marshal for the US Government is a job that doesn't require me to find the truth, or even to be sure that someone actually is a criminal. Mostly I hunt for outlaws that a federal judge thinks should be arrested, based on what they call probable cause. Do you know what that means?"

"No, I've never seen that on a wanted poster. I study them because sometimes men come into Flora's bar, and they look all scruffy and I look at them to see if they are wanted, or not. My uncle says if I spot one, maybe I could get a reward. But what is probable cause?"

"It's what the judge says you have to have before he will issue an arrest warrant for a suspected criminal. Those arrest warrants are typed up and sometimes they are used to print arrest reward posters, like the ones in your uncle's office. Once the judge does that, a lawman like me or your uncle doesn't have to worry about being right or wrong. We just arrest 'em and bring 'em in before a judge. They take over from there and our job is done, or maybe it's finished; I can never remember the difference."

Flora smiled at me and waved her hand to Nancy.

"But," Nancy paused and frowned, "what if you're not sure they did it? What if it's all a mistake? I mean, what if you arrest the wrong man because the picture was too fuzzy—some of them are just drawings anyhow—and besides . . ."

"All right, Nancy," Flora said with a smile that was half frown, "I think that's enough for one civics lesson."

"Well, Nancy, you ask hard questions. I have to be sure I got the right man before I arrest him. I've never had a case of doubt before, but to be honest I ain't arrested that many so far, for I only do this job on a part-time basis."

"And, what else do you do? Are you a liveryman, like Bo? Or is it something . . .?" With that, Flora shooed Nancy off and returned to our conversation.

"Thanks for being patient with Nancy. As you just saw, her mind works faster than a little mountain goat can run, and she jumps from question to question like one, too. Now, as to Mr. Emmett, the alleged train robber, I'm sorry I can't be informative about him. He's just plain Tom Emmett when he's here, and he's always alone. I've been told his men, or what some call his gang, stay in the rooms over at the Excelsior Saloon."

"The Excelsior? I guess I missed that on the short walk from your livery barn to here. Where is it?"

"It's one of many odd things about Folsom. This town was born when the railroad came through here. But, we're only a mile away from Madison, which was the first white settlement of the state. It had no law, good water, and the Excelsior Saloon, which was on the second floor above the livery barn and black smithy. It's a ghost town now, but the bar remains open."

"A bar open in a ghost town? That's a mystery to me," I said.

Flora paused, brushing the sleeves of her blouse. "That bar caters to men on the run and women of the evening. Not the sort of place I expect you ever visit, right?"

"I've been in bars, saloons, and other places where a man can find trouble of all sorts. But, your establishment is a cut above anyplace I've been lately."

"Angus, you are either a delightful liar, or the only well-behaved guest in this hotel. If you don't mind my asking, is there a young woman over in the Chama area that has your attention?"

"Well, seems like my horses like talking to me more than women do. Can't say as I blame them."

"Lying again, Angus. But, I'll not invade your privacy any more. Today. What else can I tell you about Mr. Emmett?"

"Ma'am, you've already told me most of what I need to know about Tom Emmett."

"That's very nice of you, but I wasn't aware that I'd told you anything of substance about him. I handed you the hotel's register."

"Well, you told me that he was a good conversationalist—that makes him a smart man. You said he's a rounder—that means I'd best not underestimate him. You said he had good table manners—that means he will fit in almost anywhere—makes him hard to find, and you said he's a train robber. I doubt you say that on rumor alone, so he must have told you that. And, you said he gets Oh Jin Suh to shine his boots. He's proud and wants to be seen at his best, even at dinner. I'll be wary of a man like that, because he won't take kindly to any man he thinks is trying to best him, or insult him. I'll make some notes about his visits and return the register to you in the morning. All of that helps me. Thanks."

The next morning, just after breakfast, I saw Nancy doing her figures at a table in the dining room.

"Nancy, it was a pleasure to meet you. You keep up with your schoolwork and pay attention to your mother, and to the sheriff. When I have more time, I'll tell you about a horseback trip I took, all the way west to the ocean, just to make sure it was really there. And, when you don't have homework to do, you can tell me how Siam got a king."

CHAPTER 33
Angus at the S-Curves

Tucson picked up a stone bruise coming up a shale grade. Made him favor that left front hoof some. I got off and walked him a half-mile. When I reached a bluff, fifty feet above the railroad tracks fifteen miles northwest of Folsom, I loosened his cinch, took off the bridle, and tied him to a blue spruce. I pushed some paste liniment up into the frog of his foot and tied a grain bag onto his head, snug behind the ears. He settled in for a long, slow chew. Then, I sat on a rock and studied the train track below me.

The black iron rails and creosote ties seemed to draw up out of the river bottom before angling sideways over to the thick, cedar forest covering this bluff. The ground was a couple inches thick with slick, brown pine needles. High up above me, I could see a vulture, or it might have been an eagle. It spied

Tucson and me as it wove a lazy circle in the sky. It could see everything for ten miles or more. But, all I could see was the riverbed, a quarter-mile away—squeezed down into a twisty crevice between high, sandstone bluffs. Thirty feet above the edge of the river, like a shelf, lay the Colorado and Southern's iron track. The midday sun bounced a blue light off the fast moving water, flashing it up and onto ribbed limestone. The midday train that lumbered through here every other day hadn't yet reached the S-curves that Sheriff Godfeather told me about. I looked at the sun, and at the shadow just starting to form on the east side of a dead, lightning-burned-out pine tree. The train would be coming along here, soon enough.

I slithered down from the bluff to the rail bed following a small arroyo that emptied onto the cinder base of the train track a hundred feet below me. The cinders were cold, and the black rails glistened, as though both were waiting for the warm-up that came every time a train chugged its way through here.

This was the second of six "S"-shaped curves in the track bed. It looked to be just right for what I had in mind. Sheriff Godfeather had put it plainly, "Hell, son, those boys just step out from the crack in the ribbed limestone wall and up onto the lumbering train. Then, once their robbin's done, they step back down, since the trains only doing two, maybe three miles an hour through there. As I figure it, they crawl back up the limestone ridge, where they hid their horses. That's it—robbin' the easy way."

If it was good enough for Emmett, it was good enough for me. I figured in two hours I'd be on horseback again. Tucson's grain bag would be empty, and he'd be ready to ride.

The sun was a quarter-sky off dead center when I heard the wail. Steam engine, pulling four cars, chugging up the grade at no more than ten miles per hour. By the time she reached me, she'd be down to two. Easy enough to climb aboard, I thought.

First thing I saw was the big iron cowcatcher in front. It was an inclined frame made to gently push cattle off the track. Looked like an iron mouth. A big, oversized light spun off light flashes off in every direction as the train wobbled from side to side. She leaned a bit as she hung to the curve of the track. When she was about one hundred feet from me, I could see the engineer leaning out the window looking up my way. Ducking back in, I just let her come on up, hoping I had not stupidly given away my position. The engine chugged on by me, then the coal car. The mail car was hooked onto the butt of the coal car. Once it slithered by me, close enough to touch, and loud enough to hurt my eardrums, I stepped out and spotted the steps up onto the little platform fronting the mail car. Swinging up, in the middle of a blast of steam and a short toot on the whistle, I planted my boots apart and steadied myself. I was pretty sure no one had seen me.

Pulling my bandanna up over my mouth and nose, I tapped on the door three times with the business end of my Colt. Within seconds, the door opened and the mailroom attendant looked at the hole in the end of a blued-black barrel.

"Mr. Angus, is that you?" he asked.

"Yes," I said, holstering my gun. He looked to be in his fifties, with gold spectacles, thinning yellow hair, a black string tie, and a hefty paunch in serious need of the wide, black suspenders he wore over a yellowed shirt.

"Oh, good Lord, this is the strangest thing that's ever happened to me in three years tending the mail for the railroad. I have the telegram from the marshal in Denver, and I've got your special saddlebag right here."

"Give it over."

"Well, sir, I don't understand a bit of this. No, sir, I surely don't."

"Not your concern, Mister."

"Yes. My boss gave me the telegram when we pulled out of Cimarron. My instructions are clear."

"Which are?"

"They said give you this marked saddlebag. We use these for both stage and train runs. It's got eight hundred dollars in currency and two hundred dollars in gold coin. The rest is just newspaper cut and stacked like bills."

The man seemed about to faint, so I tried to ease him some. "Just give it over, mister, and I'll step back off the train. This is all legal, so don't you worry none. When I'm off the train for a few minutes, then you can untie the rope I'm fixing to tie you up with. Easy knots. You run on back into the passenger car. Yell at 'em. Say you've been robbed again. I'll be up the cliff by then. They can't stop in here on account of the grade."

"But, what do I say? I can't tell about the telegram, can I?"

"No, Mister, you by-God cannot. Just tell 'em about my red shirt, black boots, and black hat. And, tell 'em about the business end of this here Colt. See these marks on the butt here? And the copper bead up front? Tell 'em you saw my gun and describe it for 'em, notches and all. You'll be in no trouble over this."

Backing out, I stepped off the train and into another crevice two hundred and fifty feet down the track. I hunkered down tight as I could. The last two cars, with passengers mostly looking out the other side down at the river, lumbered on by me like two buffalo slowly grazing at first light. Paid me no never mind.

CHAPTER 34
Jack Strong

"**J**ACK STRONG," TOM EMMETT ROARED as he stomped into the main room from his bedroom, "you been itching for two weeks now! I got a job for you."

And he was right. Hell of a job. I ain't never been good at sitting back on my haunches when there was robbin' or killin' to be done. Every man in the room could see the boss was fired up about something. Whatever it was started when that rider come busting through the door twenty minutes ago.

"Damn straight, Boss, I'm at my best when my blood's up. I can see yours is, too. What's happened? "

Tom motioned for me to leave the card table, which I was reluctant to do with three fives in the hand that Snork had just dealt. Snork, a red-eyed, scrawny man, grinned through yellow, displaced teeth when I threw my hand into the pot. I stood up straight away; Tom tolerated no tardiness in his house, or his gang.

"I'll tell you what happened!" he screamed as he reached the bar and grabbed a bottle of Texas Jack by the throat. He took a long pull and slammed the bottle down hard. A glass flew off the edge and splattered good whiskey all over the floor.

"Some bastard is poaching my railroad, that's what goddamn happened. Clemson heard about it down in Folsom, when the fool telegraph operator shouted the news out to Sheriff Godfeather in the Bar at Flora's place. So, everybody in Folsom thinks I hit another of their pet trains—but as every jackbird in camp knows, I ain't left here for nigh on two months. Someone's got my money and is making it look like I struck again. I ain't gonna stand for it."

"OK, boss, I'll get provisions and be in the saddle out front in a snap. When do we leave?"

"Not we, goddamm it, I can't leave. Butch is due tomorrow or Friday. Christ all mighty, he's two weeks overdue and I got to be here to settle his ashes about the last split he cheated me out of. You! *You*, goddamn it. You will lead this roundup. Go to the S-curves. Take Wolf and two others. Pick hard cases, men who can stand a long ride at near full gallop. Take an extra horse in case one of the nags breaks down. Just don't take my big grey—you ain't man enough for that horse. Ride all goddamn night. I want you there before sunup. Let Wolf ride point and nose out the sign of that bastard once you're a half-mile from the S-curves. Track that thieving bastard, and whoever's with him."

"Can we hang him, Boss, or do you want me to cut his head off and bring it to you in a gunnysack?"

"Jack Strong, you are a haunch back with no reluctance to kill. But, I worry whether God gave you any brains to go with that vicious streak that runs from your belly to your jaw. You get my money back—that's job one. And, then you bring whoever stole it from me strung across a saddle. Alive if you can, or dead if he insists. I'll give you a bonus if you bring him in alive and full pay if you have to kill him to get him here. But, Jack Strong, don't you fail me. If he gets away, you'll pay for the embarrassment."

"Damn straight, boss. I'll get him for you, don't you worry none. Exactly when did this man rob your train—I mean how much lead-time has he got on us? You got any idea what he looks like?"

The room was so damn quiet you coulda heard a chicken scratching in the pen out back. Nobody dared speak when the boss's blood was up. Then one of his women, Anza, came out of the kitchen door. Everyone looked at her wondering what he'd do with this interruption. But, she walked right past him, looking down at the floor like she always did, acting as if she was alone in the room.

"Clemson said something about a red shirt and black hat, but don't be looking for that. The man's got my money in a railroad sack, and he's riding a goddamn horse, that's what you look for. Wolf will find his track, and if you ride hard, you'll catch him. He'll be riding easy. He can't be more 'n a day ahead, you can make that up tonight when he's asleep somewhere south of here."

Tom took a chair at his table, the only one with a cloth spread over it. His voice ratcheted down, as he sucked in a bellyful of air.

"You got any more damn questions?"

"No, sir."

"All right then. Pick a long-striding pony. Ride fast, I say! Just you leave the tracking to Wolf. He's got a wolf's nose—that's why they call him that—he can smell game two miles off. You are in charge of pushing the men, and you do the hogtying, or killing, if necessary. But do it fast. Word of this is likely spread all over Union County. Once it hits Santa Fe, everyone will think I'm a four-time train robber. I can live with that, but I want the money. It's mine, goddammit. What I won't abide is being made the fool. The very idea of him stealing my money *and* my thunder makes my blood boil. Get outta here."

So, I saddled up the little dun mare with the big heart and picked a buckskin gelding to pony down the mountain on a ten-foot lead rope. Wolf was the only man riding bareback. He had a rawhide strap snugged loose around the horse's withers, down under the belly behind his mount's front legs, and then looped back up over the neck. He tied two small deerhide bags, one on each side of the horse's neck, to that strap. I watched him stuff the little bags with a leather water pouch, a signal mirror, a rabbit-skin bag with his throwing beads, and his prize possession—a pair of official United States Army brass binoculars. Never saw Wolf go anywhere without them. He tied a small canvas tarp, which is all he used for sleeping, to the strap, and then slung his .30-30 carbine around his back on a string of double-braided rawhide. His big, skinning knife was sheathed on his belt. Last thing, even though it was a spring day, with the sun shining in the late afternoon, he put on his usual riding coat. He was the only man I ever saw wear the same coat out of camp no matter the weather—a short canvas jacket with a big collar and no buttons. But, it had something he needed more than buttons—four big flap pockets stuffed with jerky sticks, a flint stone, bags of nuts and hominy corn, and two handfuls of bullets.

The other two men, Jumbo and Snork, were hard cases with small eyes and yellow teeth. These two gave little thought to anything except killing and whoring. Whenever they drank enough to pass out, it didn't bother them in the least whether it was dirt or hardwood. It didn't make no never mind to them. Sober, they were reliable gun hands; drunk, they were either mean or out cold.

The women packed saddlebags for me, Jumbo, and Snork, and a double gunnysack for Wolf. Each man got a canvas tarp and blanket, jerky, soda crackers, nuts, a pound of grain for each horse, and enough water in two tin canteens for three days. We snugged up our scabbards to the D-rings on the saddles and strapped in our .30-30 rifles, checked our ammunition, and tied slickers to the saddles. Last thing before mounting, every man tightened his spurs and cinched up the belly pulls on the riding horses. Just before I swung my leg over the cantle, Emmett, who'd been eyeballing us from the porch, hollered at me and motioned me to come over.

"Jack Strong," he said confidential-like so the others couldn't hear, "the man you're after is a killer, so don't be taking chances with him."

"A killer? Do you know him?"

"No, but my man in Folsom says he has a gun with notches on the butt end. He didn't get those by stealing candy from a storekeeper. Keep your wits about you and stick Jumbo or Snork out front. I'm counting on you to ramrod this."

We rode out in a hard gallop. Created a dust cloud likely visible for a thousand yards all the way up to the hidden mouth of the canyon. This was my chance to become Emmett's right hand man. And, I could feel it deep in my gut.

CHAPTER 35
Angus Leaves a Trail

A GOOD COWBOY KNOWS that ropin' a young steer is the easy part. Then you got to get 'em down, hog-tie 'em, and get your brand on 'em. That takes a mite of work. Getting on the train was like ropin' the calf—the easy part. My young steer was the canvas bag of railroad payroll money that nervous mailroom guard had fixed up for me—it now became the hard part.

First off, I shinnied back up that fifty-foot crevice in the sandstone, untied Tucson, checked the stone bruise in his right foot, and mounted up easy so's to check his left forefoot. He seemed sound enough, so I rode up through the spruce for four hours at a steady climb before I spotted just the right place—a rock bluff with a ten-foot overhang, facing south. Good place to make a short night's camp. I took care to walk him in sandy areas, and into the mud along two streams that we crossed. Good place to eyeball the ground up ahead.

I needed an advantage for this particular camp. Picking a spot on the downslope of a tree-darkened mountain seemed to be a good start. Stay away from obvious game trails and small creeks. Last, find a closed-end space others aren't likely to come on. Tucson always helps me by listening for sounds of unwelcome company. As we rode across a rocky outcrop of shale, populated only by black ants, we only saw the droppings of small critters. No human sounds anywhere. No small animals stirring. No leaves rustling. Best of all, no bent branches. Birds visit every part of a mountain. But, they never disturb the air. The air up here is something that flatlanders never taste, see, or feel. Pay attention to the air, and it'll tell you about game animals, marauders, and storms a comin'. "Tucson," I said, giving the old boy a friendly pat on the neck, "you'd best remember that mountain storms bring life to the ground."

Tucson whinnied back at me, sensing something up ahead, as the incline grew steeper. That brought to mind a time when Tucson became the subject of conversation in a smoky bar in Tierra Amarilla. A mouthy cowhand a few stools down from me guffawed to his friends about a New Mexico man who names his horse after an Arizona town. 'Course, they were no more sober than I was. Featherbrained, one of them replied with a giggle, only he said it in Español, *descabellado*. A man can't allow his horse to be made fun of, so I whacked his right ear with a beer bottle. That should have ended it. Except, I'd already had four or five beers. I counted six men giving me the evil eye. Took me a week to get over the beating, not to mention the hangover. But, a horse's name is as important as what you name a child. Tucson was a teenager now, and didn't get his name from me, anyhow. Old Bob Beasley had given him that name when he was a foal back on the Happy Valley spread he ran. It suited us both. He picked his way carefully among broken rocks. Clumps of grass hung onto the slope like ledges for miniature Ute warriors. His steadiness gave me a peaceful sense.

When we reached the overhang, we both could feel it pushing from behind us—a spring storm. Tucson's ears were up and the hair on my neck was bristling. We knew we'd best pay attention; storms at this altitude were nothing to sniff at. But, the storm didn't come that day—giving us a dry camp for six hours. Before dawn next morning, we headed north-by-northeast for another half-day, where I made a dry afternoon camp. I left Tucson saddled, and hobbled. Then I laid down close by his feet with just my tarp wrapped around me. Had anyone come on us, I coulda jumped Tucson and rode off at the first sound of an approaching horse. Finally, near dark on the second day, we come on the perfect aspen stand.

Actually, it was more than just aspen, although the slim black, white, and green ladies dominated the patch. Flatlanders see only the aspen when they come on a patch of trees like this. But, a man paying attention could see the mixture of beech, aspen, chokeberry, and a few stubborn pines on the southern edge of what looked to be a one-hundred-foot diameter stand. I came at it from the west, circling up and around her top edge to the catty-corner side. Figured anybody looking would come at us from the downslope, not from up above me. So, I took care, and time, to leave no telltale entrance tracks on the downslope edge.

The upper right edge, at about one o'clock on the face of my Hortense pocket watch, had a protective run of chokeberry bush and scrub oak about five feet tall. Just right, I thought. When we reached what I figured was purtin' near dead center of the thick stand, I dismounted from the offside. After gathering up all the tack, gear, and bags off Tucson, I unsaddled him. I'd found a small, maybe six-foot, circular clearing in the middle of the stand and laid both saddle blankets in the sun. Then I hung Tucson's bridle, reins, and breast collar in a crook of hickory six feet off the slope. Finally, I led him upwind to a stand of blue spruce and mixed scrub oak about fifty feet across a clearing, and hobbled him.

A man needs three things to make a camp that others won't see in a good-sized clump of thick, close-in trees: a right sharp hand axe, fifty feet of rope-twine, and the ability to think small. Walking sidewise into the trees, I only cut enough branches to make sure I could pull my horse through to the middle. Once I was inside the stand, I cut ten trees down, but not all from the same space. With these, I made a tree-bed three feet above the slope, by lashing the aspen poles together. This would keep me above the rain that would come gushing down this slope when the storm hit, maybe tomorrow morning.

I notched the poles into V-shaped branches and fashioned a six-by-two-foot platform. I hung the platform three feet off the ground from the crooks of four sturdy hickory trees in the middle of the aspen stand. Two feet above my sleeping platform, I lashed my canvas ground cover to keep the rain off me, and my kit. It was a tight fit, but it had to be small to be invisible from the outside. I hauled my saddle, tack, bags, rope, long gun, and the rest of my kit from the edge of the stand fifty feet to the inside. My little hidden camp was almost set.

Lastly, I walked slowly, trying not to leave a track, a quarter-mile away from the lower edge of the aspen stand to a much bigger stand of spruce and Ponderosa pine. That's where I'd hobbled Tucson. Then I walked him back, slow and easy, in fifty-foot intervals. I dropped the reins to the ground so he'd stand still, and backtracked with a big spruce branch and swept away all sign of us. When we got back to the aspen stand, I eased in slowly, walking backward with Tucson's nose on my chest, as we slithered in. I'd cut a small area for him to stand and to lie down at night, only three feet from my tree-bed. He could see and smell me. It'd be a comfort for both of us.

"Tucson, be patient," I said. "Ain't no telling how long we'll have to wait. We got to let 'em catch us, not just keep on trailing us."

The wind came first, about two hours after sunset. I'd watered Tucson from the two water bags I'd hauled in and stuck a grain nosebag on him. Then I fixed myself a dinner of jerky, shucked corn in thin molasses, hardtack, and cold water. No fire tonight. Maybe not for some time. Then, just like Tucson had been trying to tell me, the rain commenced. Big drops, coming straight down through the leaves. The wind picked up, slanting the rain in sideways. Finally, from all four directions, the wind howled and bashed the trees, ground, and us. Rain and cold don't much bother horses, if they feel safe. The big gelding could see and smell me close by so he just let the water slide on off his back and head. He closed his eyes and waited it out. I tried to do the same, lying on my tree bed three feet off the ground. The ground tarp flapped some in the wind, but did its job. My plan was working. I was high and dry inside a gray jungle of trees, rain, and black dirt. Still, it isn't easy trying to sleep in a sluice slide at a working gold mine.

The rain didn't let up for a day and a half. When it finally stopped, I figured they'd come looking for us, now that it was dry and high time to get the job done. But our track was gone. The last part of my plan never gave them boys a new track to follow. Staying put does not suit most men. But, mountain life was at its best if you made yourself small enough, and stayed quiet enough, to take it all in. So we waited it out. Tucson snorted and stomped his right front hoof on a piece of shale. I tried to hold back a cough deep in my throat, and took a small swig of medicinal whiskey. No more than one every twelve hours. I knew that much about myself. For the rest of that day and the start of the second, we just stayed put, didn't move about, and made no noise. Once a day, real small, I made a fire—with a flame no taller than my glove, and only after midnight. In the dark, hidden by the aspen stand, I had coffee once a night, and beans, but no bacon. The smell of coffee and beans might drift thirty feet, but the smell of bacon cooking will drift a half-mile or more.

Tucson, usually restless when standing, and especially when tied to a tree by a four-foot lead, settled in reluctantly. I cooed to him and brushed him five times a day. Much to my surprise, he took to the quiet like a bat in the daytime. For me, a little jerky and two hardtack biscuits at noon was enough for a sitting-tight man. A coffee can of grain in his nosebag sustained Tucson. That's the thing about a horse that really knows you—as long as you're close by and giving him comfort, he'll stick out anything you will.

I figured that Tom Emmett probably had a paid-man in Folsom. Someone to watch out for his interests. Else, he wouldn't have stayed at a hotel four times in the last eight months. Whoever that was, he probably got word back to Emmett on exactly where the train had been robbed. Likely give up the description I'd planted with the mailroom clerk on the train. That ought to give a tracker a good look at the limestone cracks where I'd crawled down, and then back up, after I more or less robbed the train. If they were serious about their trade, they'd get a good eyeball on where I'd hobbled the mare and nose out my track from there up the mountain. I had their gold. That's how I figured they'd look at it. And, I was messing in their business. So, they'd come get me and teach me a lesson about territorial robbing rights.

Well, leastways, that was my plan. But, plans are like mountain streams. They take on a life of their own. Don't matter who did the planning. Sometimes streams just go off in a different direction. If Tom Emmett gave his men killing instructions, my plan would turn out to be a dry stream. But, if he told them to haul my sorry hide back to him, the plan might be a good one. But, if Tom Emmett was in the group on my trail, he'd likely plant a .45 caliber hole between my eyes.

We out-waited the bastards. Twice, I heard them cross-tracking above and below my camp, looking for sign. Both times, I muzzled Tucson with a gunnysack. It worked. We stayed put, and quiet. They rode in circles and put up a racket.

CHAPTER 36
Jack Strong Hunts Angus

"**W**ELL, IS HE UP THERE, or not?" I snarled at Wolf, the half-Apache tracker that had Tom's confidence.

"Jack Strong, you shut up," he hissed back at me.

Like always, the breed used as few English words as possible. Once he'd said his piece, he went back to his US Army-issue binoculars, spanning the mountain slope up, down, sideways, and every which way.

"Can you see him, or not?"

Finally, without looking back at me, he snarled back, "No."

"All right, then; lemme see if I got this straight. You tracked the fool from his hold on top of the limestone cliff above the train track for one day. Then you lost him the next day. And now, here we are, three days a-ridin', forty miles or more away, and you say he's here, but you can't see him. None of us has seen a single sign of him. Right?"

"Yes."

Jumbo, the old Slovak miner turned bank robber, spoke up. "Well, Jack Strong, or Mister Kansas Gunfighter, whichever you prefer, Tom sent us to find whoever robbed our train, and he put you in charge. Why, I do not know. But, he did, and I'm here for the ride, hoping like you, to catch the fool. But, your grinding away on the boss's best tracker isn't helping none, even if he is a treacherous breed. I been with Wolf for nearly two years now. He's found lots of cold trails since he come to join us. His Apache ways might not sit well with you, but as long as Tom trusts him, we ought to just follow his lead. For as long as it takes."

"You two are a pair to draw to, all right," I said. "So what that I'm new to this territory? I've shot more men in Kansas and Missouri than your whole damn gang. That's why Tom gave me the lead on this catch-the-fool ride. And quit calling me Kansas, or I might just have to push some lead your way. My name's Jack Strong, though there was a time, when I was pushing seventeen, that everybody in Kansas knew me as 'The Kansas Kid.'"

We rode another two miles, up a slope we'd ridden twice in the last two days. After dismounting, Wolf fished out his US Cavalry binoculars again. I pulled up alongside and was just uncorking my water bag, when the breed reached over, grabbed a handful of mane, and swung up and onto his gray spotted horse. He was four lengths away and headed up a slope too steep for a goat before I could get the cork back in.

When I caught up with Jumbo, who was now a hundred feet behind Wolf, he decided to let me in on how Wolf tracks critters and men.

"Jack Strong, you got to be more patient if you aim to be a member of Tom Emmett's gang. He's still alive because he bides his time. On everything. He'll commence to wonder about you if you keep on yapping while his tracker is doing his job."

"Well, now here's the thing. Somebody's got to tell me why we are here riding up this particular mountain, instead of over there, riding down that one. I mean, if he ain't seen track, can't hear or smell anything, how 'n hell can he expect us to follow? Are we tracking a ghost? An Indian spirit?"

We hit a clearing about then, and I could see for maybe two miles up, ten miles across the valley, and damn little behind us. The breed was down on the ground, hunched on his heels, leaning forward toward three stands. A good-sized aspen stand. One higher up, mostly spruce and fir. The third caught his attention. It was a smooth rock outcropping topped by the huge trunk of what looked like a burned-out ship's mast.

"Wolf's hands tell him which way to go. He feels things we would miss. So, he's up there, feeling the ground and looking for what's not there."

"Not there? You're kidding me, right? Hoo hah! How we gonna find a bank robber if we are looking for what's not there?"

Jumbo was twice my age, outweighed me by a hundred pounds, and had more guns lashed to him than any man I'd ever seen. I was upwind of him, a good thing since he wasn't fond of bathing. "Well, Wolf told me on another one of these chases last winter that you have to look for what's not there. That'll tell you what is there. Birds are always in stands of trees unless they've been frightened off by something. Mountain critters are attracted to prey unless the prey's too big. So, if Wolf can't see birds where they should be, or any sign of critters wandering about, he feels the chase. You know, some people love the chase. Wolf puts up with you and me because he don't want to shoot anyone. He's just finds men who don't want be found. We're the shooters."

We caught up to Wolf. When we got about twenty feet downslope of him, he turned around toward us. Without standing up, he motioned with his arms that we should get down, be quiet, and look where he was pointing. A thin brown forefinger pointed at a big aspen stand dead ahead, maybe a half-mile away.

Ten or fifteen minutes passed. The breed never moved. Jumbo sat on a small rock, and I got my own long glass out and studied the stand. Nothing moved; nothing happened. Then Wolf stood up, right out there in the open and walked back to us, leading his horse.

"The man you want is in there. You can't see or hear him. But he's there. He's looking at us. If he's got a long rifle, he might be drawing a bead right now. He's your job. I've done mine. I'm going back to the hideout."

He turned and swung up onto the horse, Indian-style. I drew down on him. Jumbo sat it out. Snork, a stoop-shouldered man with dark, leathery, wrinkled skin, put one hand on his beat-up old Army pistol and the other on the saddle horn of the skinny sorrel he was riding. Both of them had the same look—always hungry.

"Get down, Wolf, you ain't going nowhere. Dismount and I'll let you live out another day. You move that horse one foot, and I'll shoot you out of the saddle."

Wolf looked back at the aspen stand, then at Jumbo, and making no effort to look at me, said, "I'll get down, but I am not part of your shooting gang. Soon, you and I will talk about aiming your big gun at me for doing my job."

Jumbo got up slowly. Speaking low, he said, "Easy now, boys. We all got jobs to do. Mr. Jack Strong, we don't need any shooting except at the fool Wolf says is up ahead of us. I done told you he was never going to shoot. He's got a gun, but that ain't his way. He's a knife man. You ought to be well away from him before he talks to you with that knife. Now, can you holster your gun and focus on getting this job done?"

CHAPTER 37
Angus Spots Jack Strong's Men

FOUR OF 'EM. One sitting on his heels, spreading the dirt around while the other three nudged their horses up behind him. I saw the sitting man point my way and then mount his horse, just after the others dismounted.

"Tucson," I whispered, "we got company."

I took my Warner & Swasey binoculars out to the edge of the trees for a closer look. Because I was worried that the glass might throw off a glare, I shielded the big end with my glove. The man on his haunches was an Indian. It wasn't his looks, or his kit. It was how he mounted his horse. Cowboys mount by sticking one foot in the stirrup and swinging up into the saddle in three movements: knee up, stand up, swing over. We can do it right fast. But, Indians go from ground to horseback in one fluid movement. And, then there was that patient look about him as he studied the trees around me. I knew he could not see, hear, or smell anything from where he was. *Damn, that's it. He knows I'm here because of what he can't see. Tucson and I have spooked the birds. That's his tell.*

"Tucson, it's time for us to get caught. If these boys are working for Tom Emmett, they'll either take us to him, or shoot me. You'll get fed either way."

CHAPTER 38
Jack Strong
Closes In

WITH WOLF BACK WITH US, and Jumbo making sense, I holstered my gun and moved over behind my horse, trying to put him between me and the upslope stand of trees. Standing tall, Wolf acted as if he did not care whether he got shot by whoever was up there in those trees. Jumbo hunkered down behind a fence-gate-high rock while Snork laid flat-out. All four of us studied the trees up above our little dip in the mountainside.

"All right, here's how it's gonna be," I said. "Assuming Wolf's right, the man in those trees has the upper hand for now because we are in an inferior shooting position. But we're changing that. We're out of range here; hell, maybe he don't know we're here yet. So, Wolf, you just stay here and focus your long glasses on him. I don't think he'll shoot you outright until he knows what we're here to do. Jumbo, you and Snork fade back into that other stand of trees—just over there on the right. Then, you work your way slow and easy up through the trees, to where it's just a short run to the fool's hidey-hole."

Snork had a lisp and didn't talk unless someone forced him to, but I could see he was nervous as he asked, "Jack, watch you got in mind?"

"I'll ride out in the open, in clear sight—out of range, and I'll make a big ole circle around his stand. I aim to box him in, so when he tries to escape, one of us will drop him. Wolf, you stay right here. Snork and Jumbo will have the right hand ground. I'll circle the stand from the left and get the drop on him from the top end of his tree hide, or I'll push him downhill into your line of fire. But don't kill him unless you have to. Tom wants me to get our money from him, and he wants to deal with the fool himself, in his own way. So, we'll hog-tie him to his horse and pony him back like a side of Kansas beef."

Jumbo looked at me like I was touched in the head. "We can't see him. He can see us. He will shoot you. Maybe he'll run—out to his left."

He pointed up to a rocky outcrop with the big, burned-out tree trunk on top. "Why you want to split up?"

"Jumbo, it ain't your job to think. I'm ramrod here; do as I say. I'll stay out of range until I'm up above the trees. He can't see me coming in from the top. And, I don't figure him for a bolter, anyhow. Hell fire, for all we know, if he's in there at all, he's taking his afternoon nap. I figure him for a night rider."

Wolf ignored me, but settled himself flat down on the ground with his elbows dug in the dirt and aimed those big binoculars dead on toward the tree stand upslope. He'd said his piece. Jumbo grumbled, but him and Snork mounted up and headed upslope on the right side. I veered as far left as I could. We'd scissor whoever was in the aspen stand.

CHAPTER 39
Angus Studies Jack Strong

I WATCHED AS THE INDIAN hunkered down on his haunches. He was studying me as I studied him. Steadying his binoculars on his forearms, which were notched on his knees, the man seemed motionless. He kept his carbine crooked across his waist and looked more like a tree stump than a man from this distance. Safety off, I bet.

Then, effortlessly, he unwound himself into a standing position, mounted his buckskin, settled his rifle across his lap, and trotted his horse way off to his left, and away from me. The other two neck-reined their horses and made a beeline to the other side of my tree stand.

Splitting up? That's queer, but maybe a break for me.

I moved back up into the tree stand, wrapped a large gunnysack over the lower part of Tucson's head, closing his mouth, so he wouldn't whinny, but not so's he couldn't breathe. As long as he could see me, he'd stand still. I made sure he watched me skinny up into the tree bed. If those boys came in blazing, they'd better not shoot my horse. Hell to pay for any man that does that. More than an hour passed before I heard the first branch crack, near the top of the stand. One man. Trying to be careful, but not good at it. Then, the jangle of a spur. Not smart, either. I knew it wasn't the Indian. And, I couldn't imagine the big guy in the black felt hat either, because of the way he sat as I watched him through my binoculars. He was impatient and would have made more noise. So, it had to be the nervous one, the man who drew down on the Indian.

I tugged my hat down low over my eyes and crooked my right elbow up behind my head. And, I breathed in and out as loud as I could, hoping to sound like I was dozing off. Another fifteen minutes crawled by.

"All right, you bastard, just you hold it right there. You move, you're dead," someone snarled from about twenty feet up above me on the slope. Hoping he'd think he caught me by complete surprise, I acted startled, grabbed at and then lost my hat, somewhere on the ground. Leaning up on one elbow, I said almost in a whisper, "Who's there? I ain't bothering no one here. My gun's in my saddlebag. Don't shoot me."

Once my captor could see I wasn't holding iron, and my long rifle was leaning up against the tree, he stepped into view. He had a flat twang to his voice, but tried to make up for it by sticking his chest out. *Banty rooster*, I thought.

I started to say something else, but he hushed me up by firing his gun. In the air. Not at me. Twice.

"Shut the hell up. You're caught."

Then, he shouted out to his friends. "Jumbo! Wolf! Come on in. I caught the bastard unawares. Come on in."

I just lay there. Elbow cocked, knees locked. And silent, like the man said.

CHAPTER 40
Angus Meets Emmett's Gang

THE KNOT ON MY SKULL had receded some but my disposition was not kindly toward anyone except Anza. She was
a small, dark woman from one of the pueblos over along the
Rio Grande. Her given name was a tongue-twister. The men
called her Anza for short. Her English was fair, for a captured
Indian. Learned it in church school, at the Sandia Pueblo, she
said. And, she was good about bringing me two meals a day.
Sparse, but tasty food. Chili in a small ceramic bowl, something
like shredded goat meat, frijoles, sage, all clouded in a watery,
paste-like, brown stew. Twice, somebody'd thrown in a root
potato. Tortillas and a small pot of water rounded things out.
It kept me alive and helped to disappear the bruises on my
back and belly from Strong's boot. He was the kind of man that
did his best fighting standing up, with the other man hogtied.

I couldn't see outside the adobe room. The lattia door let in light and most of the sounds from the big room on the other side.

Two days before, when they threw me in, they loosened my ropes enough so I could work myself out of them. Then, after Jack Strong came in and gave me a goodnight kick in the ribs, I figured it was a good time to rethink my plan. I'd been assuming whoever came after me would be the gang robbing the trains in Union County. They wouldn't be partial to competitors, but I thought I could convince them I'd be useful. I didn't count on Jack Strong. Now it was clear. Catching me made him Emmett's top dog.

From what I could make out of the whiskey talk in the big room, Emmett had the railroad pay money, the bag it came in, but not my pistol. And, up to this point, I'd made no progress toward becoming a member of his gang. Probably a dumb idea. But, now, listening to Jack Strong bellow through the door, I got the impression he was talking the boss into making sport of me by giving me a *no-law* trial. As best I could parse it through the thin lattias in the door, Emmett was judge *and* jury. Strong was gonna be the lawyer, for *both* sides. Everyone in the gang could give testimony and be a witness. But, I was to shut my mouth and take whatever came my way.

"Anza, how long you been here and how come you stay?" I asked her, not expecting much of an answer.

"Two years. I like it here. No hard beatings."

"Do they pay you or what?"

"They feed me. I have warm bed. Other women to talk to. So I stay."

"Could you leave if you wanted to?"

"Yes. Like my sister did last year. And, my friend Tewassoie left yesterday. They gave her a horse, food, and twenty dollars. My sister got more money, a horse, and a donkey to carry bags of stuff for her people."

"But are you protected here?"

Anza looked away from me and didn't answer for several minutes. Then, still looking at the dirt floor from her stool in the corner, she explained life inside this hidden canyon.

"Emmett is good to all of us. He doesn't let the men hurt us. He asks when he wants something. So, it's OK to stay, and then go when we need to see the world again. My sister will probably come back for the winter."

CHAPTER 41
Angus Gets a No-Law Trial

HOOWEE! OUTSIDE LOOKED real good to me.

Long about noon, Anza came to my room. I'd begun to think of it as my cell. She said, "Go outside. Wait on the porch."

"For what?"

"For Emmett. He said no-law trial is today."

So, I went to the porch. Nobody paid any attention to me. Off to the right, past a little arroyo, the cookhouse chimney was throwing up smoke. Behind that was a fallen-down barn, chicken coop, and pig slop. It smelled rank, but better than the outhouse. Women of various sizes and ages were about; some working, some sitting, smoking on little cottonwood benches made from tree stumps. Two kids chased a dog across the creek. I couldn't tell whether they were boys or girls. One of the women hollered at them in Spanish. There were stacks of old dynamite boxes, tool chests, buckets, and barrels. And something strange. Gunnysacks, some full, most empty, hanging on nails under the eastside eave.

The main building, where I'd been for three days, was a log fort, plastered with adobe mud, with slit windows on a sandstone foundation. Lodge-pole-sized vigas, topped with small lattias made up the roof, which was covered with mud and grass. A dazed rooster looked down at me like I was a worm, ready for snatching. Two heavy, fir-slab doors lead out onto the sugar-pine porch. Both doors were wide open, cooling the adobe down. They would be closed mid-morning to keep the cool air in. On one end of the porch, someone had built a makeshift hitching rail. The other dropped down into a five-foot deep arroyo full of sage, Chamisa, stubby pinion, and junipers—can't have piñion without junipers.

Anza told me about the building, which looked to be about forty-by-forty. The central portion of the building had four add-ons, like the claws of a desert turtle, thrown out on each side. Now that I was out, I could see that my cell was one hind leg and the other was where Anza and two other women slept. The front leg on the west side was more substantial. It had framed windows, which, at one time, probably featured blown glass. But, nowadays, they were stuffed with butcher paper. It was Emmett's counting room.

"What's a counting room?"

"Where they keep the whiskey and the dynamite. Emmett has the only key. Sometimes, Emmett lets me clean up in there, but no one else. Sometimes. He sleeps in the other room on that end."

The main room was for sport, drinking, and gambling. There were two bunkhouses for the men, but they were behind the main house. I couldn't see them from the front porch.

"So, is this Emmett's porch?" I asked, just to pass the time.

"Everything here is Emmett's. Only over there, down the hill, is where he lets Butch Cassidy and his night women stay when they visit us. There's a bunkhouse and cook shed, too. But, we don't have to clean that up. It's a mess."

All the adobe buildings looked to be forty, fifty years old to me. Anza said this was a Mexican village before the Utes attacked, killed the men, and took the women away as slaves. I gathered from her clipped English that other outlaws, before Emmett, had stayed here from many years. They left when someone with more guns wanted the place. Simple things made it all work, as a fort, or a hideaway. It was remote. It had natural springs that supplied plentiful clear water out of the rock face, and a stock pond. There was only one way in. A handful of men with the right guns could hold off an army troop.

Anza went quiet, "Wait on the bench. Don't look up too much."

Over the next hour, a dozen men ambled up to the porch, gave me a curious look, and then went on in. Anza sat on the other end of the porch studying the boards like they were telling stones out of a Shaman's bag.

Jack Strong came out, looked at me, and then walked over to her. "Bring his ass in here. Emmett's ready to start."

She looked at me, nodded, and pointed to the other door, not the one I'd come out of. It was a door with a twelve-inch-wide leather hinge and a rifle slot cut in the middle. Inside, I discovered a room about the size of a small saloon. A bar made of two heavy planks nailed onto the tops of fifty-gallon oak barrels formed the back of the room. Corked and uncorked bottles of whiskey, cider, and a collection of small and large glasses were layered out across the top. It was about fifteen feet long. A beer barrel with a brass spigot had its own stand behind the bar.

There were four round tables—two big ones with six or seven chairs and two smaller ones with just one chair on each side. The two smaller tables had ten-gallon barrels for stools, with gunnysack pads. The big round table closest to the bar had chairs that looked to be stolen from a wagon train of settlers headed for the gold rush up north. Every table was in use. Every man had a drink, was heavily armed, and looked at me more curious than threatening. I didn't count them, but I'd say there was about fifteen hard cases, and none too clean from the rank odor.

Strong told me to sit on a tin washtub in the middle of the room. I sat; he walked past me up to the bar, where he poured a water glass full of whiskey. Taking off his bowler hat, he turned around to face me with his elbows propped up on the oak slab. He fished a gold watch out of a chest pocket and took his time counting something. Then, with a scowl on his face, he motioned the room quiet. My no-law trial was about to commence. A couple minutes went by before Tom Emmett strode in from his office.

As Emmett moved toward the bar, Jack Strong took a chair at the table closest to the bar. A little one. He sat by himself, ten feet opposite of where he'd told me to sit, on a damned washtub. *Humiliating*, I thought. The room went still, with most of the men sitting at tables, and three women at the back standing like stone columns. Most of the men seemed either half-asleep or tuckered out from a night's drinking. But, Strong was powerful hopped up—pushing up his left shoulder, and flexing his right hand, down at his side alongside his tightly strapped, quick-draw holster. He wore a leather vest, but had it tucked inside his pants. His gun belt, half-filled with brass cartridges, was tightly slung around his waist.

Emmett gave me a long once-over before turning his giant head in Strong's direction. "Is this here the sumbitch you been telling us about, Mr. Strong?"

"It's him, Tom. Sumbitch robbed your train, stole your payroll, and is trying to oust you as the head of this fine group of gentlemen. I say let's give him a mule-hide whipping, a belly full of eight-gauge buckshot, and then a long, slow hanging. Nothing too good for a no-account thief."

Turning his slow gaze back to me, I noticed that Strong's eyelids were unbalanced. One was half down, the other cocked open, as wide as a fisheye. He cupped a mug of beer in his left hand; his right arm hung down, outside the armrest on the chair. He just kept on flexing the fingers on his gun hand like he had a sore neck or something. Or maybe it was a nervous tick. Whichever, it was hard not to stare at it.

"You got a name?" Strong asked, more or less in my direction.

"I been called 'Sumbitch' for the last few days. I reckon that'll do."

Emmett smiled, and then bellowed. "Hot Dam, boys! We got us an honest man for this no-law trial. He's owned up to his name and his heritage. Now, seeing that this is the first no-law trial held in the New Mexico Territory, far as I know, I'll give you boys a taste of how I been thinking on this. First off, the bar is open today just like every other day. Drinks on me, as usual. Second, no card playing during the trial. Every one of you is a witness, and we might be calling on you any time, so don't be poking your nose into no playing cards. Third, I am the by-God judge and by-the-devil jury, and I will pronounce my judgment on Sumbitch here anytime I feel the urge. Jack Strong, because he brought the defendant in, is gonna be the poor bastard's lawyer."

That brought a guffaw from the crowd, and a sour look on Jack Strong's face. Holding his hand to show they ought to be quiet, Emmett continued.

"And, by God, he is also going to be the prosecuting attorney in this no-law trial. You all know how I hate lawyers, so I cannot stand the thought of there being two of 'em in my house. Could be I'll shoot both lawyers by the end of the day. Jack Strong, you know that, don't you?"

Strong rose, puffed up, and started to talk.

Emmett thumbed him back down. "Jack Strong, don't you start yet. I was just making sure you knew what's at stake here. I might have to hang the defendant on the strength of your case against him, or I might have to let him off if your defense compels me his way. Either way, I might shoot you. Just wanted you to know the odds. I'd call his odds at fifty to one against and yours at even money."

"Ah hell, boss," Jack Strong wailed, "you don't need to go to picking on me that way. I rode my ass off with Jumbo and Wolf to catch this here sumbitch, so I ain't gonna be no goddamn defense attorney for him. How come Jumbo can't be appointed to that job? I'd shoot him for you at the end, if you want."

The men in the room laughed, causing Emmett to ask whether they had fresh drinks.

"Boys, no need to be thirsty, or shy. If you feel the need, come on up to the bar and pour some. We got all day. In an hour or so, I'll get the women to make us some eats so we can enjoy this no law trial."

I decided that I might as well join in, seeing as how I was hoping to become one of the boys. I got up off my upside-down washtub and pushed my way through a half-dozen, well-armed men, finding myself an arm's length away from the famous Tom Emmett. Not paying him no never mind, I reached for an empty whiskey glass.

"Happy to meet you, Mr. Emmett. I'm told your given name is Tom. I'm the sumbitch on trial. I suppose that entitles me to a drink, don't it?"

"Sumbitch!" Emmett said. "If you don't take all! Might be I've underestimated you. You got sand in your craw. I'll give you that. Wasn't planning on lettin' you say much in your own defense, so I might as well let you drink some. What'll it be?"

"Well, sir, how about a shot of Colorado Red Eye, with a beer chaser. About my defense, I'd be pleased if your man Jack Strong accepts that appointment. Judge Emmett, as long as we're having a no-law trial, could I ask your indulgence on something?"

Emmett, wiping a fleck of something off his chin with what was likely the only clean handkerchief in the room, stared at me for a full one minute. Then, appearing satisfied I was no immediate danger to him, said, "'Bout what?"

"Well, your man Strong might have filled you in on what happened when your boys came on me three days ago. Or maybe not. Maybe I could talk to him in your presence—hell 'n the presence of all your men right here. That might be a conversation you'd enjoy. You could call it a pre-no-law, lawyer-client conversation. Whadda you think?"

"I think maybe your craw will get you gut shot by Jack Strong and your blood will mess up the floor of my house. He's heavily armed, and you ain't got no gun. But, if those odds don't bother you, go right ahead. Ask him whatever you want."

The crowd peeled away from the bar. I turned to look at Jack Strong. He was enjoying himself. Smirking at me, he leaned way back in his cane back chair. He had one spurred boot propped up on the table and the other tapping the floor. Not a patient man. He'd quit flexing his gun hand because he was gripping a half-full beer cup. He drummed a little tap-tap on the table with his left hand, as if he didn't have a care in the world. I was standing up, unarmed, with a smile on my face, six feet away. Damn fool thought I was just messing with him.

"Good morning, Jack Strong," I said, stepping two feet closer. "As you can see, and the boss confirmed, I don't have a gun. But, three days ago, I was armed with both pistol and rifle. I ain't worried none about the rifle; just another .30-30. But I'm partial to my Colt. Did you tell Mr. Emmett you stole my pistol?"

"What 'n hell you implying, sumbitch? I could shoot you where you stand for your insolence and . . ."

"Insolence? That's a two-dollar word from a two-bit gun hand. Are you afraid to tell the boss about my pistol? Is that it? Did you notice the scribes on the butt? They mean anything to you, Jack Strong?"

It took three seconds for my insult to boil over in Strong's mind. He tried to put down his beer, get his boot off the table, and lower the two front legs of his chair to the floor. But he was too late. I was on him quicker 'n a diamondback coming out of its coil. Kicking the chair out from under him with my right boot, he crashed to the floor. I reached down and fished his gun out of the fast-draw holster, butt first. Flipping the butt up in the air, I grabbed the twelve-inch blued barrel, and whacked him on the head with his own gun. He rolled over onto his belly like a pig in its holler.

Every man in the room drew down on me, but Emmett was standing behind me, right in the line of fire from the crowd. They froze. I spun around on my left boot, stepped back to the bar, and laid the gun down. I placed it with the barrel facing me and the butt toward Emmett. Smiling, I eased it on over to him slow and careful-like.

"Now, Mr. Emmett, I've paid your man Strong for his rudeness by a return crack on the top of his head. You'll recall the goose egg I had atop my own head three days ago. Strong gave me that, *after* he hogtied me. Cannot abide a man that strikes an unnecessary blow. Can you?"

No one moved. No one said anything. Emmett had not moved a muscle and his face bore no indication of his mood. But, within seconds, a grin swelled up from the corners of his mouth, and branched out to the big cheeks on either side. Then, he threw back his head and bellowed, "Boys, I'm rethinking this man. He got the best of one of us, and I might say, he did it with style."

Turning back to me, he said, "Now, sir, let's start again. You got a name?"

"Angus."

"That's it? I like that. A one-name man is good enough for this place. Let's you and me get a table and share a bottle of the best in the house. You rob trains, but do you play cards?"

CHAPTER 42
Jack Strong Plans His Revenge

"**T**HAT DIRTY BASTARD TRICKED ME," I told the boys on the porch, after they revived me by throwing a bucket of water on me. Jumbo laughed like hell, but showed a little pity. He got Big Enough, a midget-sized Welshman, to help him carry me outside and tend to the blood on the top of my head. They got a clean rag, watered it down, and wrapped it across my head, and down underneath my jaw to come up the other side.

"You're still leaking a little blood, so you keep this wrap on till tomorrow," Big Enough said.

I tried to stand, but my knees had jelled. There was a mighty wind blowing in my head, and my eyes were blurry. They told me I'd been knocked out for a half hour, at least. Didn't know if I'd come out of it, they said. I told them I just needed a shot of Mescal and a gun.

"Then I'm going back in there to fill that brazen bastard full of lead. I intend to empty my pistol. Then, I'm gonna get me a double-barrel shotgun and blow him into about a hundred chunks. He's got it coming."

Jumbo and Big Enough took aholt of my elbow and eased me back down onto the bench. Big Enough did the explaining.

"First off, Jack, your pistol's inside. And, the man we been calling Sumbitch has another name. Name of Angus. He and Tom Emmett are having a good ole time, drinking the best whiskey in camp, telling lies to one another, eating Anza's good chili, and talking, mostly about you. Second, you ain't in no shape for a gunfight, especially with a man who done bested you without a gun. Hell, you're lucky he took pity and just banged you, instead of shooting you dead with your own gun. Last of all, where did you put his gun? The boss told me to fetch it for him. He wants to see those notches on the handle."

"He does, does he? Well, that gun belongs to me. I fought the sumbitch for it, remember? I already gave the boss the bag full of money and explained how we came on him, hiding out in a stand of aspen. What's he want with the gun, anyway?"

"Don't know. But it don't matter. Either I give it up to him, or he comes out here on the porch and gets it from you himself. Not a good choice, Jack."

"Well, hellfire! This is a turnabout for me. I think I'll just quit this outfit and find me a better class of train robbers."

Jumbo was a cowboy who could get drunk on his own words. He gave me more of them than I needed.

"Jack Strong, you maybe need to go to the bunkhouse and stay in bed for a couple of days. You're gonna have a headache that will feel like your horse stomped you. And, you won't be thinking straight at all. But, mostly, you ought to stay out of the boss's way and plenty wide of this man named Angus. I watched him with the boss; he's a man to reckon with. And I seen those notches on his gun. They ain't there 'cause he hit lard cans on a fence. Them are kill scribes. Hell, anyone knows that."

"Any damn fool can notch his gun handle. Don't prove nothin'."

"You ain't gonna listen, are ya? It's why the boss wants to see the gun. If I was you, I'd tell me where the gun is at. I'll give it over to him. Ain't you got enough knots on your head, without riskin' another from him?"

Jumbo and Big Enough were my friends. So's I told 'em where I'd hid the sumbitch's gun. They fetched it to the boss. I went down to Butch Cassidy's shack and asked an old Mexican woman who was sitting outside if I could stay there a few days. They said it'd cost me two dollars a night and I'd have to clear out if word came that Butch was headed back.

Next day, coming on sundown, Big Enough came down to check on me. I was a lot better, and my plan was to ride out right after supper. I told him my decision. He went back up to the bunkhouse and brought me my bed roll, saddle bags, and a gunnysack with my winter coat, extra shirt, my other pistol, and two boxes of ammo. I saddled a good young gelding and hightailed it up to the crevice. By morning, I intended on crossing the Rio Cimarron and be shed of everyone up here. *I'll get even with Angus or whatever his name is later,* I thought. *And, Tom Sumbitch Emmett, too.*

CHAPTER 43
Angus Makes Friends

Tom Emmett had everything a man like him could want in that hideaway, except for one thing. He had no one he cared to talk to. His men were not interested in talk. The women knew better than to talk to him. Everybody in camp liked his jokes and stories. They could listen, as long as they were sober. But, Emmett missed talking about the goings on in the outside world. Are we at war? Why is the government giving away land to pilgrims who can't even load a gun, much less fire one? And, are there any new women at The Excelsior Saloon?

Late the next morning, two women in black shawls served up the noon meal on the long bar. I was playing a card game called Three-up-and-Two-under-the Table with Jumbo, Big Enough, and a young gunhand name of Félix Onchero Gomez.

Félix was a handsome boy, except that a bay mare had kicked all four of his front teeth out when he came off her in the bucking pen. When he smiled and took in a breath, he whistled like lard pail on a campfire. Tom Emmett came into the big room just as I was peeking at the best hand I'd been dealt all day. With *my* gun in his hand. And, the canvas Colorado and Southern Railroad pouch with all that money in it slung over his shoulder.

"Angus, you interested in explaining the notches on this gun? And this railroad payroll bag?"

I nodded respectfully, folded my cards, and pushed my chair back. He had a glint in his eye I could not make out. Curiosity, maybe. Or, on the other hand, it might have been the start of an outlaw investigation. I chanced it.

"No, sir. I'd rather not, if you don't mind."

The room went quiet. Félix whistled, and Jumbo and Big Enough decided they needed to visit the porch. Two women, jawboning in Spanish in the back, quit their jabbering. The three men at the big round table eating tortillas, black peppers, and hogback bacon froze to the bottom of their chairs. Their eating knives now held stone still in their hands. Everybody took to studying whatever was in front of their noses.

In the short time I'd known him, I had no way of gauging his temper. Others talked about his harsh bite and how slow he was to smile. He just sat there for a minute. Then, as though a storm had just passed us on by, his stern look faded into his swooping mustache, and his eyes glistened.

"We got rules here, Angus, and you just invoked one of 'em. No man has to speak about his past exploits, if you know what I mean. But, hell fire, we like stories, so while I'm getting me some eats, why don't you and I talk about the geography of New Mexico. I'd be interested in your views on riding ridge lines and things I expect you know a lot about."

So, I joined him at the long bar and spooned some chili paste into a little ceramic bowl. Breaking off a hunk of bread to dip into the chili, I was surprised when a man poured me a beer in a tin cup. Slid it down the bar with a smile. Turns out, we had some common interests. And some differences. He was as handy with a rope as I was with a branding iron. He liked being alone, but often felt the need for conversation with new people. We differed there. He was never bored, and could live almost entirely in his mind until someone interesting came along. I could live that way a lot longer. His older brother, Neb, more or less gave over the running of the gang to him. Neb was a man of few words and even fewer original thoughts. I had no brother. Neb, he said, had gone back to Missouri to look in on their folks. Said he'd be back in a day or two.

"How'd you get in the train robbing business?" I asked.

"Easier than dirt farming, more fun than chasing beeves up and down arroyos, and it don't really harm anyone."

"How's that?" I asked, "You're taking another man's money, ain't you? Ain't the owners of that money harmed?"

He gave me his long view of things. They'd robbed a Santa Fe train down near Deming a summer back. That had been the first of a half-dozen trains that seemed easy pickings. "You see, Angus, there ain't really any harm in this. Its banks and big ass mines that put their money in the mail cars. They use it to make more money, and they hardly miss the occasional sack or two I take out of a mail car on a lonesome stretch of track. You know how easy it is for banks and mining companies to replace the money I take. For them it's like buying new shovels in a hardware store. Hell, they might have money-printing presses in the back of the bank, for all I know."

I didn't want to press the man. So, I volunteered something about myself. Figured talk was as cheap as hardware store shovels.

"Mr. Emmett, I figure most things out here in the New Mexico territory are free to those who roll up their sleeves. Land can be had by staking claims. Gold can be dug the same way. But, there's no charge for riding ridgelines, catching fresh trout in the morning, and using windfall trees for night fires. Barbed wire's coming, hellfire; they already got it all over Texas. But, for now, I can ride anywhere I take a mind to."

"Ain't you got anybody you need to take care of, Angus?" he asked.

"No. It's just me, a saddle horse, and often a packhorse or mule. We keep one another's company. And, when I feel a need for it, which ain't that often, there's always a town within a day or two's ride."

"Well, how about money? You gotta need that. Tobacco ain't free, and grain for your pony's nosebag costs some, right?

"Sure, but that's the thing about money. I can ride fence for forty dollars and found in the summer and during fall round up. I can do scout work for the army, or even guard work for freighters, railroaders, and mine crews. And, I can work both sides of the law, if it comes to that. Is that what you're getting at, Tom? Do you mind if I call you Tom?"

He pushed his tin plate away, shouted for Anza to bring us coffee and a little sweetener. She brought two tins of coffee, and two shots of Taos Red. The rest had already let out a collective sigh, and was back to whatever small business they had to conduct. Overall, they seemed a peaceable bunch, now that I wasn't on trial and Jack Strong wasn't around to poke at me.

Turning back to me, with a smile on his face, he said, "How's that work, riding both sides of the law? You mean you are a deputy at sunup and an outlaw at night? Whowee! That's rich."

"It ain't all that mysterious. I'm not parcel to heavy drinking, although I enjoy good whiskey occasionally. I can shoot straight. So, town marshals and county sheriffs sometimes ask me to help them out between hiring full-time deputies. It's mostly posse work, or helping to guard a special money stage, riding shotgun. And, I got a head for observing things and picking out easy ways to work the other side the law, long as there's no killing involved. I can step up onto the mail coach, like I did down to Folsom, but I would not rob a man of his hard-earned pay. That's different, like you said. I ain't up to robbing people, just banks, or railroads."

Just then, a commotion started up at the big, round table. Two men were claiming the other was cheating at cards. But, the third man, the one with the most money on the table, was chewing on both of them. Emmett told them to either kill one another or quit interrupting the peace and quiet of the room.

Emmett was a man who liked to pause and think about the conversation every once in a while. So, he sat there for going on five minutes, while I nursed my drink. Finally, he came back into the conversation, "Angus, you thinking about joining up with me?"

"Well, now's you ask, I ain't inclined to take it up as an occupation. I got some time on my hands. And, have a need for a little stake in a venture up in Colorado I'm thinking about."

Joining up with him? Emmett was making this easier than I'd thought it would be. On the ride down here from Colorado, it had seemed obvious. A one-man posse wasn't going to pull Emmett out of his gang. The only way to get close enough to separate him was to be one of the gang. I figured I'd have to beg for the job. Now here he was plain out offering it to me. Not wanting to appear all that eager, I got up, and walked outside to the porch for a smoke in fresh air.

He came out to the porch later. "Why don't you tell me how you came by that gun? In turn, I'll tell you what I think about the habit of notching them. Then, if you're of a mind, you can join up with my boys and me. We'll talk about splitting the money in that canvas pouch you found in one of my mail cars."

"The gun ain't really mine. It belonged to a Chama man I admired some. He died five years ago, peaceable. Dave Wilder was his name; he put it in his will I was to have his gun. I don't know the story behind the notches. But, old Dave was a wild one. Might be he did some notchin' in his day."

"Fair enough. What's the story on the moneybag?"

"You mean how come the bag had cash, gold and stuffed newspapers?"

"Yep."

"I was in a hurry. Expect they knew that. So, I didn't check to see how much was in the bag—just looked at the top. Fooled me. Expect that's a risk in the train robbin' business."

"Being in a hurry is good. Don't give it no never mind," Emmett said, as he slid my gun across the table at me. Then he opened the bag and took out the cash and the gold coins. He took his time counting, and then he pushed four hundred dollars in cash and half the gold coins across the table to me.

"Seein' as how you did all the work this time, you get half the take. Next time, you get the same split as the rest of my men. I take two shares. Everybody else gets one share. Ain't something I negotiate. You in?"

"I'm in."

CHAPTER 44

Angus Leaves Camp

EXT DAY, I TESTED MY FIT as the newest member of Tom Emmett's gang. After I brushed and saddled up my mare, I asked Anza if she wanted to go for a little stretch-out ride with me. Like I figured, she was befuddled.

"Watch you mean a stretch-out ride? I don't leave the camp. What's the matter with you, gringo?"

"Thought you said you could leave anytime you wanted?"

"I can. But only to leave, you know, leave for good. The women don't go riding."

"All right, but there's some real pretty country outside this little canyon. Think I'll just stretch my saddle legs a bit."

"You better ask Emmett; don't think he'll like it."

"Good idea. I'll see if he needs a little stretch-out ride himself."

I waited a spell, then led my horse from the barn to the hitching rail on the west end of Emmett's big house. He was sitting on the porch, with a man I had not seen before.

"Good morning, Tom. I suppose Anza told you I was thinking about a little stretch-out ride this morning. Might come across a whitetail deer. Fresh venison for the camp. Care to come along?"

"Angus, I said it before. You beat all. Sit down and meet my brother, Neb. Neb, this here is a man who brought us a little rent money and will ride with us for as long as it suits him. He's different. Give him a Missouri hello."

Neb Emmett didn't smile, but he rose to his full six-foot-three-inch boot height. Stickin' out a hand, he said, "You the damn fool that conked Jack Strong with his own gun?"

"I'm the one, but he was rude. Thought he deserved a time-out in the sick house."

"Well, hello, then. I'm from Missouri, and I'm the brother who remembers his place and his friends. Jack Strong was due. I'm just surprised my brother put up with him long's he did. But, you ain't proved yourself yet, and this gang's half mine. You'd best remember that."

"Angus," Tom said, "suppose you heard Jack Strong's gone. Headed out last night. Took a little filly, and left his jug-headed horse in the pasture. But, that's all right. We're shed of him. Means you probably won't have to kill him to make him shut up."

"Nah, he didn't need killing," I said. "Probably, I'd of had to just keep whacking him on the head until he quit bellyaching."

So, we sat the porch for the better part of an hour. Neb Emmett was Tom's older brother, and they hailed from the Missouri delta country. Tom'd hightailed it out of there three years back and Neb followed him two years later. He was just in time to take part in Emmett's first train robbery, down near Las Cruces, on the Union Pacific line. After spending an hour jawing about St. Louis women and New Mexico opportunities, I tested my luck.

I leaned over in my chair and tucked my pants into the tops of my boots. Snugging my hat down on my head, I looked at Neb as I got up.

"Neb, it's been good talking to you. Expect I'll be back by lunch. I'd be pleased if both Emmett brothers wanted to take a stretch-out ride with me this morning. You boys are the bosses here. Do you need one another's permission to break camp? Maybe we can talk about an idea that's been buzzing around in my brain. You might like it."

Emmett gave me a quizzical look as though he was trying to decide. Then turning to his brother, he asked, "You up for new ideas, Neb?"

Neb allowed as how he'd just spent three days horseback, and needed to see to his horses and repair some tack. So, Tom stood up, hitched up his pants, and told a young Mexican boy sitting on the far edge of the porch to saddle up his big, gray stud horse.

"He needs to get out of the corral anyhow; we got two mares in heat and it's gettin' his thunder up. I'll sweat him some and he'll settle down."

We rode down out from the big house, and turned onto the trail leading up the invisible crack in the canyon wall. We worked our way up two switchbacks to the narrow rock ledge that fronted the crevice from the inside. The outside world was just forty feet from here.

"Angus," Emmett said, as we moved onto the hard scrabble, "be honest with me; have you ever seen a better hideaway?"

"Can't say as I have, Tom. I'm curious about something. How'd you find this place, anyhow?"

"Butch Cassidy told me about it once, when I was up at his hideaway in Wyoming. He called his place up there the 'Hole-in-the-Wall.' I suppose you could call our little hidden canyon the 'Crack in the Crevice,' or something clever like that."

"I heard something about him. Guess it was not too complimentary. Are you friends or competitors?"

"He has men loyal to him, just like I do. We have done no outlaw work in the same patch, if that's what you mean by competition. We just stay out of each other's way outside this hideout. And, outside his, up in Wyoming."

"Well, it's a right pretty place inside and damned hard to see from the outside. How'd Butch Cassidy come on it?"

"I think I got this right. He had a nighttime woman from the Taos Pueblo. Related to Anza. Anyhow, they knew about this place because their people used it to hide from the Apache whenever they marauded over from Arizona. Their people knew about this place a hundred years ago. Or, maybe more, who knows? I had to turn out a few dozen scalawags misusing the place. That's another story. This is a lucrative business, Angus. You got any idea how much we take in?"

"Can't say as I do, Tom."

"Well, it's us that's done the most, but Butch's well-dressed crowd also brings in a good share. The measure I think is the most accurate is reward money."

"How's that work?"

"Well, you can measure a man's worth by how much the United States Federals are willing to spend to stretch his neck with a government noose. In my case, the posted reward is probably north of fifteen thousand United States dollars. Haven't seen the latest poster, but that's a fair estimate."

"Well, I'm impressed. Hoowee, fifteen thousand dollars! That'd buy a fair sized ranch."

"True, enough," Tom said, as he turned his big grey stallion off the little trail to relieve himself.

I sat on Tucson and pulled a chaw of venison jerky out of my duster pocket. There was a cool breeze coming from the southwest, and some clouds building up north. Good day to get away, I thought.

"You know, Tom, I stopped by the sheriff's office in Folsom before I hit the Colorado and Southern train at the S-curves last month. There was a poster 'bout you and Neb tacked on the door. It said you might be found in the mountain country north of the Cimarron River. Can't say I read the flyer all that close, but seems like they put it in a canyon in what was called Table Land. Another put it closer to Catalpa. That's a fifty-mile stretch of open ground. Is that why you are still hid from every lawman who's ever tried to find this place? "

"Nah, that ain't it. We're still hid because we're careful. And, because the federals do not have the manpower to track us. The locals like sitting beside their wood stoves, or fishing the creeks in the summer time. This is a good time to be an outlaw. Long as you don't hurt local folk, or get the federal government's dander up."

"Safe and warm, that's your secret?"

"Well, the hideout's safer 'n hell, but cold in the winter. I prefer a ranch down near Deming for my winters. What took you to the sheriff's office in Folsom?" he asked given me a queer look.

"I'd done some posse work for the undersheriff in Chama a year or two back and one of his deputies got hired on in Folsom. So, I thought since I was over this far, I'd stop by and say hello."

Changing the subject, I asked, "How do you keep your men quiet about the camp's location?"

Tom didn't answer, so I neck-reined Tucson down onto a flat shelf a quarter-mile down the outside trail. We rode quiet for some time.

"Fear of retribution. That's how. I bust a head once a month or so. Keeps a man on his toes, watching another man hit the dirt. But, you know, we share the canyon with some other law-disobeying friends. And, some of them ain't actually all that friendly. Best as I can make it out, this sweet hidden canyon was first used when the Wild Bunch was running from a posse. Name of Elzy Lay, as I recall. Butch told me he'd left Kid Curry, whom I do not like, wounded beside a stream down in the bottom of that canyon over there."

Tom pointed to a sharp drop off from the mesa we were riding, over to the east. I pulled off the trail, and told Tom I needed to check Tucson's left front shoe.

"He picked up a stone bruise a while back, and it may have worked that shoe loose a little."

I dismounted, checked Tucson's hoof and felt the frog for tenderness. He didn't wince none, so I got back up and touched his belly lightly with my right spur.

Tom continued his story. "Anyhow, as Butch tells the story, Elzy hid out for a day, then ventured out and rescued Kid. Should've let the no-account bleed to death, I thought. Anyhow, we do no business together, but we respect those who ride outside the law and who want shelter. 'Course, we charge them rent."

"Rent?"

"Sure, you don't expect a room in a good hotel for free, do you? Same thing for a shack inside the canyon. Everybody pays except Butch and me. We're the landlords, don't you know."

"That's rich. Rent a hide out! Too bad you don't have copper piping for hot water like Flora does in her hotel down in Folsom."

Tom tensed up some, gave me a squint, and asked, "You met Flora?"

"I did. Seems nice. We only talked a little, but I did discourse at some length with her daughter, Nancy. She's mighty curious about what's outside Folsom. And, she mentioned something about the King of Siam."

"Well, I'll be damned. She asked me the same thing. Or was it her mother? Can't exactly remember, but people ought to be curious, don't you think? Keeps a body interesting, don't it?"

"Yep."

"So, Angus, here's a curiosity I got about you. You robbed one train, but I ain't got no insight about what else you might have done outside the law. Anything interesting there you'd care to share?"

I let that go unanswered, and spurred Tucson up ahead about twenty paces.

We rode in silence for ten minutes or so, until Emmett couldn't stand it. "So, Angus, I guess you ain't going to satisfy my curiosity, are you?"

"You told me one of the rules was that a man don't have to talk about what you called past exploits, right?"

"True enough."

"Well, my past exploits is best kept quiet—some are down-right embarrassing, others dull as Oklahoma farm land. And, none of them match up to your colorful career, Tom. Let's let it be; OK with you?"

"Yeah, but you did not come here exactly volunteer-like, now did you?"

"No, your man Jack Strong ambushed me. On your orders, he said. Was he right?"

"More or less. I was unhappy that some interloper from who knows where was treading on a business opportunity I created. So, I sent him to the S-curves. I got a man in Folsom that keeps me one step ahead of the law."

"Who's that?"

"Ain't none of your concern, Mr. Angus."

I took that as a sign to ride quiet for a while. We rode the better part of five miles down and across a neighboring canyon before nature called Emmett. So we found a little flat spot with heavy oak brush and a damn near fifty-foot ponderosa pine holding center stage. We dismounted and tied off; I watched Tom Emmett walk into the brush with some paper strips he'd fished out of his saddlebag. When he finished his business, he came back to the horses. I was standing on Tucson's far side with my left hand lying across his back. He couldn't see my right hand.

"Damn, I'm feeling fine now, Angus, can I have a pull on your water bag?"

"Sure, Tom," I said, lifting the bag off my saddle horn and flipping it over to him.

He caught it, uncorked it, and took a long pull of sweet stream water. When he looked back in my direction, he saw the open snout of my Colt staring him dead-on.

"Tom Emmett, I'm a United States Deputy Marshal, and I'm placing you under arrest for various crimes committed in the New Mexico Territory. Take this quiet-like. Drop the water bag with your right hand, then lift that pistol with your left hand and pitch it behind you. I already have your saddle rifle over here."

His eyes narrowed and he tucked his jaw in tight. Staring at me like I was the devil himself, he said, "You are a sumbitch, after all."

But, he knew I'd drop him and was figuring the odds of living another ten seconds. He lifted the pistol, left-handed, and let it fall to the dirt at his feet.

"Now back up, steady-like, to that big ponderosa behind you."

He did, all the while boring holes in me with his eyes slit together, and his jaw so tight he had to breathe through his nose. I retrieved his gun, and motioned him to turn around. He did. But he would not stay quiet. He muttered assorted curses. Claimed he would not soon forget my treachery. I slipped a piggin' string out of the mule hide pocket in my chaps, looped it over his neck, and jerked him to the ground. He tried buckling over onto his back, but I used my boot to convince him to lie belly down. Then I tied the piggin' string from his neck to his belt and snugged it down. Once it was tight enough, I turned him over, used another piggin' string to tie his wrists to his belt buckle, and looped it up to the one around his neck. Then I jerked him back up, more or less gentle.

"I'll help you mount your stud horse, Tom. Let's hope we don't come across any mares in heat between here and Folsom. I'm tying your hands to your saddle horn. You won't be able to control that cayuse, but you can hang on, if need be. The neck loop running from your back belt to your saddle horn will keep you upright in the saddle; it's none too comfortable. I intend to execute your arrest warrant in front of a federal magistrate before noon tomorrow."

CHAPTER 45
Jack Strong Meets Up with Oscar

I CURSED ANGUS, EMMETT, AND every other bastard in that camp. It took me near twelve hours on the borrowed horse to make it down the mountain from Emmett's hideaway to the outskirts of Folsom. Damn skittish horse dumped me twice. Once when we forded the Cimarron, which was raging down the mountain in full spring runoff. Like to froze us both. Second time, just a mile out of town when he bolted as a polecat crossed our path. By the time I got to the outskirts of Folsom, I'd calmed down some, but something told me I'd best not stop there. So, I pushed on to the old town of Madison where the only thing still standing was The Excelsior Saloon.

The bartender remembered me, "Evening, Jack Strong. Whiskey?"

God, I needed this saloon. Dark, a mile away from Folsom, and a bartender who knew to serve a bottle without sticking his nose in your business. This one, whose name I recalled was Ike, had good reason not to ask me any goddamn questions except what I'd be drinking. He'd been here for years and had served the whole gang on our last trip out of the big house at the hideaway. That was the time that Jumbo, Big Enough, and Oscar had gotten mean-ass drunk. They busted up one of the few decent tables in the joint, and a stray cowboy. Fool had come along just in time to break his nose for a crude remark about Big Enough's manhood.

Not even the weak light from three gas lanterns could soften the dreary feel of the twenty-by-twenty room with two doors and three windows, one of which was boarded up. There was a hole, roughly cut into the rear wall with a double-canvas tarp nailed to the beam over the top of the hole. It led to an outhouse. As I walked through the side door, I remembered the unwashed smell and the feeling that this was just another hideout. Only dynamite could improve this place. The clapboard building sat between two boarded-up, single-story buildings with false fronts. One had been a dry goods store and the other a land office. It felt like a damn cave, one where derelicts and men on the run would come in from out of the cold or away from almost everything else in the whole miserable territory.

"Yeah," I said, "whatever passes for your best—a clean glass—leave the bottle—and a beefsteak, one that's been on the stove for at least an hour."

I didn't give a good goddamn about the other customers. Paid no mind to the two quiet men at the back in the corner table. I'd tossed back two whiskeys and the bartender was bringing my burnt black steak to the bar. He carried it on a tin plate crooked in his arm. There was a basket full of sliced bread, a little pad of butter, and a peppershaker. I'd just cut into the steak when one of the men at the back table got up. Before I knew it, he was behind me, with his pistol stuck to the back of my neck. Then he clomped a meat hook of a hand on my shoulder and bellowed.

"Jack Strong, you still ain't got no manners. How come you're standing up here at the bar instead of joining us at our table? You forgotten how much fun we had the last time we busted up this joint?"

"Oscar? What 'n hell you doing here? We lost track of you a month ago—thought you'd gone soft, or got shot, or something. I'm glad to see you. I'm gonna start a new bunch and could use you, and that Indian back there I see you got with you."

"Well, I been around, but there was a misunderstanding over in Folsom. Short of it was the judge gave me thirty days. Soncho and me. Sheriff Godfeather lied to the circuit judge about us. We just got out this morning. We're headed back up to the camp tomorrow morning. Come on back and sit with us. Bring that burnt log you got with you, and your bottle. We're running a little low on ours."

So, I sat with them and eased into why I'd left the boss's gang. I told them about catching the bank-robbing bastard who poached on the boss's patch. And, I told them how the bastard tricked me during the no-law trial we'd set up for him.

"Watch you mean, somebody robbed the train that wasn't Tom Emmett? We never heard nothing about a train robbery for the last three weeks in jail. The deputy, Bo String's his name, cannot shut up about anything. If there'd been a robbery, he would have bragged to us. And, if it was just one man, he would have laughed at us. Something's screwed up in your story."

"No, Oscar, I'm telling you straight, this bastard Angus he robbed . . ."

"Angus, you said? Angus, a man with notches on his gun? Tall, bony guy with blue eyes and a gray hat?"

"Yeah, that's him. He robbed the boss's train. And he . . ."

"Jack Strong! Are you crazy? Angus ain't no train robber! He's a Deputy United States Marshal from Colorado. He came into the jail with the sheriff. He was by-God introduced to us as a federal marshal. What do you think about that? And Bo String, Godfeather's deputy, hell, he knows this Angus from over by Chama. They was having a good ole time catching up with one another. He would have busted a gut telling us about a robbery. I'm telling you, something's screwed up."

I could not believe what Oscar said. I filled him in on what happened. We agreed we'd head back up to the hideaway at first light. We'd warn Tom that he had a goddamn US Marshal in camp pretending to be an outlaw. He was probably after Tom. Jesus Christ! He must have faked the train robbery to get inside Tom's camp. Goddamn, whoever heard of such a thing? Oscar looked at me like I was the crazy one, not that bastard Angus.

CHAPTER 46
Angus Fords the Rio Cimarron

I'D STUCK A TEN-FOOT lead rope in my saddlebag and used it to pony Emmett's horse. I'll say this for him, he sucked up his rage so's to maintain his balance in the saddle. Riding a stallion is always a handful, and Emmett's hands were tied. I hoped the big gray wouldn't spook at bushwhacking, but I had no intention of following the little trail down off the mountain. It wouldn't be long before one of Emmett's gang figured that something was amiss when we didn't come back by midafternoon. But, in the haste of catching up, they might miss where we turned off. I used a big acorn bush to hide our marks as Tucson led us, weaving in and out of scrub oak, pine, and big rocks.

The brush was thick with thorns, bristles, jagged rock, and loose shale. Broken tree limbs posed threats to both horse and rider. Once we left the natural game trail, the trees, rocks, and crags were a challenge. And, I was leading a stallion carrying a big man strapped to his saddle. The only sound was the wind whistling above and the clink of hoofs on the loose, shingly rocks. I angled us south by west down toward the Cimarron River. I knew it'd be a difficult ride down a steep mountain, and an even more difficult river crossing once we got there. Tucson's toughness came out as he maneuvered us through narrow spaces, down off slippery rock ledges, and around mountain obstacles of every kind. Emmett had no control of his horse, and didn't dare use his spurs. Dead branches scratched him, since he didn't always duck at the right time, and he had trouble weaving to one side of his saddle. We navigated through heavy timber, windfalls, and blind rock slits. Then, it got worse. A cloudbank rose up in front of us, driven by a southwesterly wind that smelled of rain, and commenced to flash and buck in our direction.

I was using dead reckoning because my compass was back with my kit in Folsom, at the livery stable. I had a slicker slung across my saddle, but Emmett hadn't thought to bring one. One of us was likely to get wet. The river, at least according to my rough guess, was maybe eight to ten miles away. The ground was hard granite shale, with spots of black thick turf beneath a spread of big trees, prickly acorn brush, and bands of lodge pole pines. As the horses slithered downhill, both of us fought whipping brush that latched onto stirrups, spurs, and slammed our knees all to hell. My shoulder joint near got torn off every time Emmett's horse balked, or Tucson jumped over a barrier or a log.

Finally, with an hour to spare before sundown, I heard the crash of the river. Soon enough, we could see and smell the foam crashing and swirling around the big rocks in the Rio Cimarron. I'd forded this fine river six or seven times in the last ten years, but never before in full spring runoff. I knew just from the sound of her there'd be white water aplenty. The banks were steep and the water level near flood stage. The current would be as strong as a runaway steer. But I couldn't see it yet. We'd been following a fifteen-foot wide steep cut down the mountainside, and it blocked our view of everything except straight up. The blue sky of noon had turned grey and then black, with heavy water just waiting to drop down on us like a ten-foot chute at a railroad water stop.

Emmett had been mute for almost three hours. But, he could smell the river and hear the sound of rushing water crashing over boulders.

"Sumbitch, you don't intend to drag me across the Cimarron River tied to my saddle, do you?"

I figured it was best to ignore him until he used my proper name.

"Hey, you treacherous bastard, are you listening to me?"

I gave him a backward look at my head moving from side to side. He got it.

"OK, Angus, you're the law. I ain't got no choice but to accept that. But, even outlaws got the right not to be drug across the Cimarron at high water in spring runoff. You want me to hang, not drown, right?"

He had a point.

"I intend to do my job, Mr. Emmett, and you'd best pre-serve your strength by holding your breath. Crossing rivers is something a mountain man has to do to get down to civilization. If it comes to dragging, well, I'll see about those ropes. We got to get to the north bank first."

Coming out of the steep rock chute, we happened on a small herd of mule deer grazing near a dirt-roofed log cabin in a bad state of repair. One end had collapsed down into the single room, and the short rock chimney on the other was crumbling. The deer spooked, and Emmett's horse bolted. But, Emmett held on to his saddle horn as the big gray tried to pull loose from my lead rope to get to the river. These horses had sweated up some, grinding down the mountainside, switching back and forth sideways to angle into the decline. Now they had a powerful thirst and the swift, churning water of the Cimarron was less than a hundred yards away.

We held the nags back, or at least I did, and I spotted the rocky edge of the riverbank—eight-foot drop off at a steep angle. On the opposite side, maybe forty, fifty feet across, it didn't look too steep. I figured if I angled down and to my left, and if I gauged the speed of the river right, we might make a landing over there. I put the angle at forty-five degrees and the water at, well hell, who knows how fast? We would get powerful wet; that was plain enough.

Emmett's horse had pulled around me to the lead position as we came in sight of the river. I gave the lead rope from the big gray a tight turn round my saddle horn, and stuttered him to a stop. Tucson held his ground like an anchor. We ground to an agreeable stop, twenty feet from river's edge. I stepped off, flipped the onside stirrup up over the saddle, and took a firm hold onto Tucson's breast collar. I pulled him toward me to get us into a circle with Emmett's big gray. They followed suit, and we formed a little knot—two horses, him up in the saddle, me with both feet planted on solid earth. I loosened the cinches on both saddles, which wasn't all that easy on the big gray stud, since I had to take care not to let Emmett give me his boot in the process. I untied all the loose rawhide strings on both saddles in case one or both of us went off the saddle midriver.

A minute later, the rain came down on us in buckets, not little drops.

"Here's our crossing, Emmett. I expect you made enough crossings in fast-moving water to know about loose cinches and low reins, don't you?"

"I ain't a shopkeeper, Angus, you treacherous bastard. I've crossed bigger rivers that this in Wyoming," he said in a voice that belied his confidence.

Fast water does that to some men. And, with water coming down on you from the sky, and flying up at you out of the river, it dampens more than your clothes. It's like swimming under water on the back of a horse that ain't acting like a fish. Horses take to water natural, but not with heavy saddles and big men astride them.

"All right, but this crossing looks to be more 'n four feet deep. So, I've loosened both cinches. And, I untied the rear cinch on both horses. If you go off, try to grab the rear cinch, or one of the saddle riggin' strips. These horses need lots of lung room when they hit this cold water. I'll take you at your word, but do not pull up, or tighten your bridle reins when your horse hits swimming water. The smallest pressure on his head will make him roll over on top of you. Got that?"

"Angus," he said, as he studied the swirl and looked for water pockets to gauge speed, "you are gonna give me my hands back, ain't you?"

I pushed Tucson over closer to the upper edge of the riverbank, looped the reins over his neck, and tied them with a half-eight loose knot. I cut the piggin' string on Emmett's hands and the string looping his neck to the saddle pommel.

"Pull your boots full out of the stirrups and flex your knees backward. Knot those reins and drop them over his neck, before we hit the water. After that first big splash, bend down and grab ahold of his breast collar. You and this stud horse are about to go swimming with me and Tucson."

A flash of lightning lit up the sky across the river. Five seconds later, the boom hit us. Tucson held his ground, but the stud was already up on his toes, and he tried to spin up and to Emmett's right. But, Emmett showed he was still a cowboy and held fast while leaning forward and getting ahold of the gray's ear. He settled the big gray down right smoothly.

"Emmett, there's nowhere to go from here except back up that rock chute, or across this river. I will shoot you out of the saddle if you misbehave in any way. You got three choices: behave, get shot, or drown."

"And, I'll drop you on the other bank. Just you wait," he growled.

I took that as bravado because I could see him studying the crossing and gauging the power of the water. He snugged his hat down, looking miserable without a slicker. He could reckon the crossing on his own. We'd get pushed downriver maybe two hundred yards and make our landing on the other side. I could see a small level spot. We'd be in the cold water for five, maybe ten minutes. Emmett would have no opportunity for misbehaving out there. Swimming horseback across a roaring mountain river would take all his attention.

I took off my chaps, strapped them over the pommel of my saddle, and tied my saddlebags down tight. Then I swung up into the saddle, being careful because of the loosened cinch, centering myself and the saddle. Sticking only the tips of my boots into the stirrup irons, I loosened the lead rope from Emmett off my saddle horn, held Tucson's reins high up with my teeth, and gave him a little spur to get him into the rushing water. Just before we slid down the bank into the water, I gripped a handful of Tucson's mane. I knew better than to hold onto the saddle horn with a loose cinch. Holding onto his mane was a comfort to us both. Tucson had crossed more rivers than any other horse I knew of, but even well-broke mountain horses are skittish about rushing water.

I eased both horses up to the edge of the bank and sucked in a big breath. Kicking my boots out of the stirrups, I let out a great big "Hoorah!" Tucson took the plunge. Two seconds later, the lead rope pulled taut and I held on just long enough to be sure Emmett's horse was in the water behind me. We jerked that big gray down into the thunder of the river with us.

The bitter sting of the cold water hitting my face, and his, startled us some. Both horses crashed loudly off the bank. They clawed down with iron-covered hooves for the bottom, and we swung to my right and out into the downstream river flow.

"Hoo wee, Angus," Emmett yelled, "I'm about to be a free man, you . . ."

Whatever else he said was lost in the roar of several tons of roaring water swirling around us pushing us downstream faster than a train coming across a downhill trestle. But once we hit mid-river, the pull lightened up. Tucson found the bottom and gained some purchase. He strained mightily, and we found the natural pull down and over to the opposite bank. And that's when I saw them.

Three men. Coming out of the trees about fifty yards downriver and pulling up their horses when they spotted us midriver. One good look and they pulled their rifles out of their scabbards. It seemed like we were in slow motion while those boys were at double speed. We drifted toward them. They agitated and pointed at us. Now, at about forty yards, as we drifted by them, I got a first look at their faces.

Jack Strong. Cocky and still wearing his black hat with the long eagle feather sticking out the back. Behind him, swinging out of his saddle, rifle in hand, was a man I'd only seen once before, in the Folsom jail. Oscar. The third man, still mounted, wheeled his horse around, giving me a head-on view. It was the tall Indian with the long braid. He'd turned his back on me in Sheriff Godfeather's jail a week before. But, here he was, partnered up with Jack Strong.

CHAPTER 47
Jack Strong Meets Angus Once Again

"WELL, I'LL BE DAMNED," I said to Oscar. Even though dark was coming on, we could see them clearly. They were only fifty or sixty feet away, but the river was moving them quickly past us. One of them sat tall in the saddle, with his legs swinging free of the stirrups. The other one, closest to us, was out of the saddle and hanging on to his horses' rear cinch. He looked weak, about to go under.

Oscar squinted at them and then screamed at me, over the roar of the river, "Jack Strong, it's the boss! He's riding with that lawman I was telling you about. That's the man who was standing in the jail hallway with Sheriff Godfeather. What 'n hell's goin' on?"

While it was a little hard to make out, I could see some kind of small rope swinging free around Emmett's neck. And he didn't have his vest or gun rig on.

"I'll tell you what's going on, Oscar. That sumbitch Angus is tugging on a lead rope from Emmett's big gray stud! Jesus H. Christ, that Angus bastard has arrested the boss. How, I do not know, but shoot him out of the saddle right goddamned now!"

Just then, Angus pulled that Colt out of his holster and fired over in our general direction. He missed, but the shot spooked the Indian's horse and he bucked. I fired at Angus but my shots went high. I realized I might shoot the boss, so I holstered my pistol. Just then, my horse pulled away, banging into Oscar's young mule. We were in the middle of a horse wreck on the bank. And, Angus and Tom just drifted on by. I scrambled toward the bank, as the horses were stomping and kicking at one another amid the gunfire.

As I looked at Angus, I could see he was aiming high on purpose. He didn't care if he hit us; he just wanted to spook our horses. The next three shots plinked off the tall rocks to my left and made all three horses think we were in some kind of war.

Oscar didn't care none about horses, much less the young mule he'd rode on this trip. He jumped out of the saddle and jerked his mule to a standstill. Ripping his saddle gun out of its scabbard, he jacked a .30-30 round into the chamber. His first shot hit a tree branch across the river. Then, he dropped to one knee, steadied his aim and fired, jacked a new shell, fired again, jacked another cartridge, and hit Angus with his fourth shot. He must have grazed the horse because he almost turned over backwards. But, even from this far off, I could tell that Oscar's bullet slammed into Angus' leg. There was a spurt of blood high in the air as he tumbled off the horse's rear. The horse, now with a black red flow coming down his neck, righted himself and turned away toward the middle of the river. Angus, without his hat or pistol, grabbed the horses' tail and hung on with his left arm. But his head went under water. Oscar took two more shots, but there was nothing to shoot at now. I thought he was drowned, and his horse just floated away from us.

We all kept a close bead. About a minute later, we saw him. Hanging on with one arm, but with his head above water. Floating like a log in the middle of the river. But there was no shot to take. We watched as the horse drug the rider past a bend in the river three hundred yards below us. That's the last I saw.

Emmett had regained his saddle as his horse neared the waterline. Coming out of the shallow water, he spurred the big stud horse up the bank, even though he'd completely lost his reins and his stirrups. His saddle was snug way back from the gray's withers, but had not turned off to one side or the other. He'd kept a wet, loose saddle centered. How he stayed on is a mystery.

"Strong, you bastard! I never thought I'd be glad to see your sorry ass again. But I am in your debt."

Oscar was dumbfounded. And, dripping wet because he'd fallen in the shallow water at the edge trying to grab ahold of the big gray's lead rope. He mumbled, "Boss, damn it's good to see you. We was coming to tell you that that man weren't no train robber—he's a United States Marshal with a warrant on you."

"Yeah, Oscar, good to see you, too. But you got off some shots. Did you kill him? Is he drowned? He arrested me, then he hogtied me in the saddle and was taking me back to Folsom. The goddamn nerve of it all! Is he dead, or was he just playacting out there in the river?"

Oscar answered for us, "Can't say. I hit him and his horse. Saw blood on the horse's neck spurting out. I blew him out of the saddle with a leg shot."

The rain had come full-on now, and we moved back off the riverbank under the partial shelter of tall cottonwood trees lining the bank. After quieting down the horses and taking a pull on Oscar's pint of warm-up whiskey from the inside pocket of his duster, Emmett told us the story of how Angus tricked him into going for a short, stretch-out ride. I'd never seen him this mad.

"I got to dry out before I freeze, but Oscar, you and the Indian mount up and head downstream. Find Angus. Bring me his body, no matter what. If he's still breathing, it'll be my pleasure to put six shots into his windpipe. If not, I'll throw him back into the river to rot in a beaver dam downstream. Strong, you stay here. Build us a fire and get a canvas over my head."

So, I built a fire from windfall timber up on a small bluff about ten feet off the bank and got some hot coffee into Emmett. Three hours later, Oscar and his Indian came back. The rain had let up. It was pitch black now. We could see they didn't have a body slung over either the mule, or the Indian's horse. Oscar's grim face told it all.

"I'm betting that he bled out, or drowned hisself," he muttered, wiping wet slime off his face with a rag he dug out of his saddlebag. Between swigs from his whiskey pint, he told the story.

"We rode the south bank for more 'n five miles and found no trace. I kept a sharp eye on the north bank and could see no place where horse or man came up out of the river."

"Oscar, you're beginning to rile me again. Don't you be telling me he's plumb disappeared! If he drowned, he'd show on the bank, or get himself hung up on the rocks, or in a fallen tree branch in a pool somewhere. If he lived, he'd pull his sorry ass out of the river just to get out of the cold. That damn river is near froze over with ice."

"Boss," Oscar pleaded, "we looked. A strong man might be able hold on to a horse being drug mid-river. And, that big bay of his was a real sight, floatin' along fast with the pull of the water. The current gets even faster a half-mile down below us, because the channel narrows. As long as that horse stayed mid-river, they could be ten, twenty miles or more downriver by now."

"So, you're saying the horse is smart enough not to try for the bank because he knows you're following him? You're dumber than I thought. If there is no trace of him for five miles, then Angus got aholt of his saddle horn and kept the horse calm enough to float ahead of you. Come first light, you and the Indian will track both banks, side by side for as long as it takes. Find his body or his tracks up out of the river. I'll kill you both if you fail. Bring him back and you each get a bag of gold coin. Now you'd best lay down beside the fire, because I want you on that mule at first light."

CHAPTER 48
Bo String Rides to Find Angus

"**D**EPUTY BO STRING," Sheriff Ira Godfeather began, all formal-like, "you are now a go-get-'em, one-man posse. I want you to saddle up your best, long-stepping horse. There's three outlaws on the loose. You follow them."

"Three outlaws. Me, a one-man posse. Sheriff, I ain't no such thing."

"Shush up and listen to me. The bartender over in The Excelsior Saloon sometimes tips me off to keep me from arresting him for crimes I know he's committed. He just told me that Jack Strong, Oscar, and that Indian were in his place last night. This morning, at first light, they lit out headed north. He overheard them talking about Tom Emmett and Marshal Angus. He was sketchy, like always, but said enough to tell me those three were up to no good."

"All right, Sheriff, I'll be mounted and on the trail in half an hour. But, I don't have no idea which way to go. I ain't never been up into the mountain country north of here."

"First off, Bo, you go over to The Excelsior and talk to the bartender. He'll know which trail they took out of what's left of that sorry little town. You can pick up a trail of three horses easy enough, I'd guess. But, anyhow, you'll reach the Rio Cimarron north of here, say fifteen, twenty miles. Just ride the south bank of that river until you can see where they crossed. It's in high spring runoff this time of year, so it's a wild and mighty cold river. When you see where they crossed, follow that track. They'll be headed to wherever Emmett is hiding out. If you can find that, you'll probably find Angus, too. 'Cept there'll likely be a shoot-out or a hangin'. Try to get there before either one commences."

"You're sending me to try to rescue Angus, is that it?"

"I'm sending you to do what I can't do. I wouldn't be of any real use to Angus on account of my one-eye vision. It ain't as good as I make it out to be. Don't tell anyone that. Besides, I'm too old to be busting brush, climbing a mountain, and crossing a wild river this time of year. You go on up there, and give Angus some help."

"I'm obliged, Sheriff. He's my friend and I already did this once before."

"All right, then. You can take that Sharps repeating rifle there in my case. Cartridge belt's in the lower drawer. Pack light—you might have to run fast."

"But, how'd you figure this all out, anyhow?"

Sheriff Godfeather leaned back in his creaky old cane back chair, like he was studying the question. He tapped on the desk for a minute or so.

"Bo, here's how I reckon we got to this point. Oscar's jail sentence run out three days ago. His Indian friend got out the day before and probably stayed at The Excelsior till Oscar could catch up. That new feller, his name is Jack Strong. Well, he rode through town on the way to Madison and The Excelsior day before yesterday. Flora told me she heard all this from God-knows-where. That woman has a gossip ring big as Union County. Anyways, she said those boys were whiskey-talking about getting even with Angus. She said the man, Jack Strong, rode with Emmett."

After I saddled my best horse, got a week's worth of grub and grain tied on with my saddle bags and rifle scabbard, I lit out and found their trail, pretty much where Sheriff Godfeather said it would be—a half-mile out of Madison on a north-by-northeast track. I trailed them more or less fifteen miles up towards Colorado, but lost them yesterday afternoon. Now, I'm on the south bank of the Cimarron River where the sheriff told me I'd find some track or some evidence of them crossing over to the other bank.

Last night was more or less miserable. I snugged up against a damn tree, sitting on a rock, hoping to keep from drowning in the damn rain. My little bay two-year-old, who I named Tecalote, got a five-inch gash along the top of his right rear leg on a jagged piece of rock as we skinned down a crevice trying to get to this powerful river. But, he was all right—not too much blood and a long way from his heart. I didn't want to lame him, so I unsaddled and rubbed some lichen moss and creek mud onto the frog of his foot. Then the damn rain came on us, and here I am.

"How you doing this foggy morning?" I said to Tecalote, chewing on sweet grass with no never mind about yesterday's cut.

The Cimarron River was something to see this high up. She was a good thirty-foot across, black in the middle, gray on the banks, with white foam swirling in circles. In places, the middle of the river had giant boulders and all kinds of trees and dead logs stuck up, down, and every which way. She was running like there was no tomorrow after that rain last night. I could hear her gurgle and splashing the rocks on the bank all night long.

I brushed, bridled, and saddled Tecalote and was about the business of strapping down my duster, bedroll, and saddle-bags when I heard a horse. A high whinny. Up river. *It's them,* I thought. I stepped up into my McClellan saddle, gave Tecalote a slight tap with my right spur, and pulled Godfeather's Sharps repeating rifle out of its scabbard.

"Easy, son," I cooed to the little horse as we trotted through the trees along the bank toward the whinny, "I ain't got no idea of what's coming. Let's us do the surprising, not them."

After about ten minutes of slow-going, I spotted Angus's big bay horse. He looked a mess. His saddle was half-down on the off-side. Somebody'd knotted the reins up tight around his neck, and he was shaking like a hound dog at the end of a nine-mile hunt. I could see a hump of gear alongside the horse, but couldn't make it out. First thing I thought of was a bear, or maybe a dead beaver. Except for the shaking, the horse was calm. If it was a bear, he'd never stand that still, unrigged saddle or not. I knew the horse had been in the river because he was all slick and glistening in the early morning light. And, there was river moss and mud all over him.

I rode up slow-like, not wanting to spook him.

"Easy, horse," I said, giving him a friendly click with my teeth. "Easy, easy, I ain't intending you no harm, now. You just stand while I . . ."

The hump moved.

"Hold on now, what in tarnation you got with you here?"

I swung down and stepped into the frozen water. I moved slowly up to where I was ten feet away from that poor horse, leading Tecalote. I reached out and took hold of the bay's breast collar. I felt him dig in and pull his head up, jerking me around on the lead rope. Good God almighty, it was a man! Rolled up like a big ball, covered with blood, mud, muck, and river debris, and most likely dead. But, something was moving on the other side of him. I stopped still, bolted a shell into the chamber on the Sharps rifle, and forced myself to take a pause and reconnoiter this situation.

"Hee, yaw, you goddamned little varmints," I hollered at what looked to be two small muskrats chewing on the man's leg. The shaking horse was drained of all his energy, but he managed a little flinch. He just didn't seem to fathom the muskrats. They slithered out over some moss-covered rocks and disappeared into the debris along the riverbank. The man had a big bunch of leather wrapped around his right shoulder and arm. Stepping in close I realized it was a pair of chaps, with leggings still square-knotted to the saddle. I reckoned the man was astride his horse when they stumbled, or hit a rock out in the middle of the river. When the river was tired of hauling them, it washed them ashore. My mind was racing some as I tried to guess how long they'd been in the river, or where upriver they'd tried to cross.

I couldn't make him out for all the mud. His clothes were in shreds; he was more rags and mud than human. Somehow, he'd managed to wedge his right spur between two big rocks on the river's edge. But, his horse wasn't going anywhere. It could have kicked loose, but it didn't. It stayed with his rider. *My kind of horse*, I thought.

"Damn, horse, are you trying to tell me something?"

It took me a while to untangle everything once I felt the downed man's heart. There was a beat there, not much but just enough. It was like he didn't have a face—just a head so covered in moss and mud, it was only vaguely human. I could not see his throat move, and his mouth was full of moss and river root. I uncinched the saddle and unwound the bay reins. Then I moved him ten feet up the bank and dropped his reins. He wasn't going anywhere.

Then, I loosened the man's knee out of the rock and took off his tangled spur. The spur itself was bent at the rear arch and the rowel was gone. *Wow*, I thought. It took a powerful blow to knock the rowel off a handmade spur. It was a chore dragging him up onto the grassy bank. After looking him over a little closer, I was even more sure that he'd hit a rock or half-buried log. His left leg was bloody all the way down into his boot, and his head had a right nasty knot, covered with mud-mixed blood. I cut his pant leg down some to get at the wound. Christ almighty, he'd taken a bullet. It was a through-and-through shot with a larger hole on the backside of his thigh. His head was a real mess, with a big knot stretching from his right cheekbone to his ear. He had three deep cuts across his face and jaw. Probably from hitting rocks and trees as they were swept downriver, I thought.

But, while he didn't look it, he was alive, with a faint whisper of breath. His breathing was so shallow I could not detect it by just looking. I put my ear on his mouth and could hear a little wheeze, but not anything resembling human breath. When I'd got him laid out flat, I tried to get some river mud off his face.

"Angus! Angus, by God, it's you!"

He didn't respond to my outburst, but both horses flinched. Flabber-damn-gasted was what I was. Boy, oh howdy! Angus lying on a riverbank in front of me. The same man that Sheriff Godfeather had been so all fired worried about.

"Eye God, Angus, you are some kind of messed up," I said, knowing that he couldn't hear me.

After building a fire, I stripped him down to his long underwear, laid him on my canvas ground cloth next to the fire, and let the heat and smoke do their work on him. He coughed, sputtered, and trembled. His limbs started to tremble, then I could see purposeful movement. He was trying to move, but he could not open his eyes, or talk. He was conscious for about a minute, and then he went all limp. I kept checking his pulse up along his throat. It was weak. Good, I thought. Not too fast. Finally, his skin temperature seemed about right. Truth be told, I'd never taken a man's pulse before. But, on the ranch we always felt for a pulse and a temperature on foals and calves. If that was all right, we figured they'd grow up to be horses and cows. As long as he wasn't burning hot and had blood running in his veins, I figured his faculties would come back.

The clouds got heavier, but there was no more rain. By noon, I could see that it was gonna rain again. I went to work settling his gear and hobbling the bay. That's when I discovered a rifle ball wedged into the pommel of his saddle just below the horn. Another was snugged tight into the left stirrup leather. It musta been the one that went plumb through his leg.

Once, when I was working the *Dos S* brand on fall roundup, I'd been riding drag with a cowboy who picked a fight with a midsize brown bear and lost. The bear mauled him something awful and knocked him off a cliff. He fell more than ten feet onto a flat granite shelf. The man was unconscious for nearly a week before he just woke up one day and asked about his horse. I was hopin' this was how Angus would turn out.

It took two days. About noon the next day, he woke up. Slow, like he wanted to talk, but couldn't. He gazed around like he could see, but not much. His first words were, "Who are you?"

"Angus, it's me. Bo String. Damn, Marshal, you ain't forgot me, have you?"

He looked like he was hearing me, but then he closed eyes again and just lay there. I quick-like poured a half-cup of hot coffee in my only tin cup and tried to get some down him. He balked. So, I tried to dribble a little water into his mouth from my water bag. He swallowed some and tried to get me in focus. Then, several hours later, he woke up.

"Bo String, I believe you ain't no ghost after all. I've been laying here trying to remember what happened before you came along. How long have I been here? Where 'n hell are we?"

Turns out that when men get their heads banged hard enough to go all unconscious, they take their time remembering things. My old partner from the *Dos S* took several weeks to wrap his mind around things tight enough. It only took Angus two days. Finally, with lots of coffee, some beans, and a few sips of my warm-up whiskey, he told me the story, in little bits and pieces.

Seems he'd fooled Jack Strong into thinking he was dumb enough to get up in a tree bed after the phony train robbery. He'd hoped they'd take him to wherever Tom Emmett was. They did. He confused me some when he said he'd talked by-God Tom Emmett into leaving camp. Then, even more confusing was how they made it down to the Cimarron River before he got shot off the saddle by the three men I'd been trailing.

"Bo, you seem to be in the habit of chasing me up one mountain or another, and then getting yourself involved in the business of chasing train robbers."

"Well, Angus, I do not know what it is about you. Are you good luck, or bad? I don't rightly know. But, I am just proud as I could be you're on the mend, and that I had a hand in getting you off that river bank."

"Well, Bo, if you hadn't've come along, I dunno. Suppose Tucson would've shuck loose of me, and the saddle rigging, and then made his way down to some ranch. Fish and critters would've gotten fat on me."

"You're welcome, Angus. But, that fine steed you're riding would've just stood there by you in the river waitin' for the two of you to die."

CHAPTER 49

Angus Back
at Folsom

THEY SAY IT WAS NEAR on five days before I talked sense.
Can't say myself. But, I remember Bo String dragging me
out of the Rio Cimarron and down off the mountain in a travois. I don't remember getting here to Flora's hotel in Folsom.

"How long did you say I've been laying here in this bed?"
I asked Flora when she brought in a plate of hot bread, fried
eggs, and coffee.

"Well, Bo and my brother carried you up those stairs
on Wednesday, a week ago. You mostly slept until Sunday,
and then refused to get up and go to church. I suppose that's
because you are not a church-going man, are you, Angus?"

"Don't remember the last time I was in a church. It wasn't
something I took to as a kid."

"Where'd you grow up?"

"Ranch country over in the Chama Valley and some down into Española near the Rio Grande."

"Hmm. Mostly Catholics there, Spanish people and all. The church is a real strong presence in their lives."

"Yes, Flora, and now that I think on it, I can't say why I never took to it—church and all. But, it brought those people a good deal of peace."

I ate my breakfast in bed, leaning over on my elbow, forking the eggs onto the little round biscuits, and sipping my coffee carefully. Flora tended to my room with her broom, wet mop, and feather duster. There was almost nothing to clean because she did it every morning. The chest of drawers held what'd been in my saddlebags, which she'd scrubbed and oiled for me. My other clothes, the ones I'd left here a month ago, were stacked neatly behind the dressing curtain in the corner. She'd told me my saddle was a mess, but Bo String was rigging it. Sheriff Godfeather cleaned and oiled my guns. Flora stacked them on the corner table, by the window. She watched me take my morning inventory of my surroundings.

"Everything still to your liking, Angus?"

"It surely is. This room has been a comfort. My mind seems to be up and ready to go. But, I ain't got the strength of a day-old calf just yet."

"Well, here's the wound count. You got shot in the leg. You have a banged-up shoulder. Your left wrist is sprained. The river rocks knocked your head so hard you were dumbstruck for the better part of a week. Bo says you talked without connecting thoughts to words all the way down the mountain."

"I don't see how he managed it, yet."

"Well, I can tell you this, that Indian travois he made is a fine piece of work. It's hanging up on a hook in my livery stable. Might be handy if we get called out to rescue any other hapless critter that gets shot off his horse in a mountain river. Oh, and he said he'll be by after he finishes the morning routine at the livery stable. There's no prisoners right now in the jail, so he's got his afternoons more or less free. You talked to him about it day before yesterday, he said. But, you don't remember that, do you?"

"I remember talking to him, but I ain't clear on what we said. Remembering the talk, not remembering what 'n hell really went on for however long it took to drag me down the mountain. "

"Well, it was a sight for all to see. Especially Nancy. She cannot stop talking about her friend, Bo, sitting astride your horse, leading his horse, with four fresh-cut, green aspen saplings strapped to either side of your saddle. Good thing you had that big ole Texas Jack roping saddle on Tucson. He'd've never strapped a travois on his McClellan army saddle. There was a web of rope and ground cloth sagging in the middle of the travois, with you wrapped in it like a sausage in a big tortilla. Made big ruts in the dust we call Main Street, as he rode in with you. It was a parade, for sure. Folks all over town are still talking about it. They were real impressed with Bo, and wondering about you. Still are."

CHAPTER 50

Angus Rides to Cimarron, New Mexico Territory

"**A**NGUS, I'M MIGHTY GLAD to see you up and about again," Bo said, jumping up as soon as I hobbled into the sheriff's office.

I finally felt strong enough to make the trip downstairs for breakfast and to walk across the street to the jail. The sheriff and Bo were having their own coffee inside, and I helped myself to another cup, my third of the morning.

"Morning. I'd like to thank you both for what you did."

"Don't mention it again, Marshal," the sheriff said, in an official law kind of voice.

"But, Angus, if you're of a mind," Bo chimed in, "I think I'd like to hear how 'n hell you managed to get Tom Emmett

out of his hideaway. And, you drug him all the way down to the Cimarron? How far did you get before his boys shot you in the river?"

We jawboned it for half an hour. I told them how I'd talked Emmett into a stretch-out ride, then hogtied him to his horse for the eight-mile ride down to the river. I admitted Jack Strong had shot me out of the saddle halfway across the Cimarron. Bo filled in some holes about how he followed Oscar, his Indian, and Strong from here in Folsom up to the river. He described the place where he found me and Tucson on the river bank. We commiserated on the good and bad of the situation.

"Well, it's been two weeks now," the sheriff said, "and there has been no word of any more train robbing . . ."

A boy, about twelve, burst in the room all out of breath.

"Jimmy, take a breath," the sheriff said. "It probably ain't the end of the world being announced in that telegram in your hand. I presume it's for me; give it over."

"Sheriff, the station master told me to run here as fast as I could. Wait till you see the news! Tom Emmett's been caught for robbing our train. They got him over in Cimarron. And . . ."

"You been reading my telegram, Jimmy? That ain't your business, is it? Give it over, you scalawag!"

Sheriff Godfeather read it aloud for Bo and me. His grin grew with each short declaration:

TO ALL LAW ENFORCEMENT OFFICERS AND AGENCIES IN THE NEW MEXICO TERRITORY—STOP—FROM TOWN SHERIFF CORNELIUS O. COOGAN—CIMARRON NEW MEXICO TERRITORY—STOP—HAVE TOM EMMETT AND TWO OF HIS GANG INCARCERATED MY JAIL—STOP—

EVIDENCE OF TRAIN ROBBERY NEAR FOLSOM TWO MONTHS AGO —
STOP — JUDGE SIMON QUINTANA AND RAILROAD CHIEF OF DETECTIVES
TO ARRIVE THIS WEEK — STOP — EXPECT TRIAL SOON — STOP — SEND
COMMENTS AND ANY EVIDENCE YOU HAVE TO ME YOUR SOONEST — STOP

"Evidence?" I asked, looking at the boy and talking more to myself than anyone else. "That don't make sense."

Later that afternoon, back at Flora's hotel, I was sitting on the porch taking in some afternoon sun when the sheriff and Bo brought me more news. Godfeather was beside himself.

"I talked to that old coot of a sheriff, Coogan, over in Cimarron, and we exchanged words back and forth all day. You know that new telephone line is only about three months old. One phone is all we got here, and they put it in the telegraph office. But, anyhow, here's the story. I already told you Sheriff Coogan runs a poor operation, but he's crowing about this. He says Tom Emmett, along with Oscar and Jack Strong, were in town drinking, gambling, and visiting the upstairs ladies in a sporting house. A commotion broke out between Strong and Emmett. Both drew down and shots were fired. Minor wounds were inflicted to both and . . ."

"Minor? What does that mean?"

"Can't say, Angus. Coogan is not only a poor excuse *for* a sheriff, he ain't all that good at relaying the facts of a crime. Anyhow, here's the nub of it. Emmett shot Strong, but didn't kill him. Apparently, both were too drunk to shoot straight. One of them shot the deaf bartender in the foot. Don't know the particulars of that, but hell, he was deaf so he probably didn't even hear the muzzle blast that propelled a bullet into his dang foot."

"Sheriff," I interrupted, "I don't care about the deaf bartender. What about Emmett?"

"I'm getting to that, Angus, but the story came to me a slice at a time; that's how I'm relaying it to you. Now, as I was saying, Oscar entered the fray, trying to protect Emmett. He knocked Strong out of his chair—seems both men were shooting from a sitting position during a card game. Then, while Oscar was tending to Emmett, who suffered a bullet wound to his thumb, Coogan came in on them. They were at the saloon at the St. James Hotel. Coogan sort of lives there. You ever been there, Angus?"

"No, I ain't. Stick to what happened."

"So, seeing as how both were wounded, making 'em no threat, Coogan arrested Emmett and Strong both. He says he found evidence against 'em they must've robbed *our* train, the Colorado and Southern, here in Folsom six weeks ago."

"But, Sheriff, you and I know that is not the case," I said. "You know Tom Emmett never robbed that train at the S-curves. Coogan's got that backwards. He can't be much of a sheriff."

"Well, didn't I just tell you that?" Godfeather said, like he was put out that I wasn't listening carefully enough.

"'Course he ain't much of a sheriff. But, he told me, and says he also told the United States Marshal for the New Mexico Territory, Jon Trachta, that he has solid proof. One, he has the railroad bag. Two, he has almost three hundred dollars in gold coin and paper currency, along with some clippings that seem to be from newspapers in Lincoln County and from Santa Fe."

Bo shouted, "Jesus, Mary, and Joseph, Angus, they got him cold as a frozen fish. Hoowee, he'll taste the hangman's rope in his mouth for this!"

"Well, boys, they got it ass-backward. Emmett never robbed that train. I did. Strong knows that for sure. I had that railroad canvas satchel up there as bait; it was bait to get me inside Emmett's hideaway. Strong took it when he banged me on the head. He gave it to Emmett up at the big house after they hogtied me to Tucson. That's the truth of it."

Sheriff Godfeather looked at me bug-eyed.

"Angus, seems like you been taking a lot of bangs to your noggin of recent. Now, I believe you, but I know Cornelius Coogan for an old fool. He will see this as his one chance in life to be a hero. He'll crow about this all over town and at Emmett's trial."

"Well, boys, I'd best get my gear," I said to the sheriff and Bo as I eased up out of the chair.

"But, Angus, you're just getting well," Bo chimed in. "Flora says you're in need of another week resting. Your leg wound is fine, but your head is still hurtin' you some, she says. Is that right?"

"Don't matter. They cannot try Emmett for something he never done. I'll be on horseback come sunup tomorrow. Cimarron's a one-day ride, if I trot all the way."

CHAPTER 51

Angus and Sheriff Cornelius Coogan

THEY WERE RIGHT. The sheriff of Cimarron, Cornelius Coogan, was a fool. Hunchbacked from sittin' behind his desk for ten years. Skin nearly bleached white from staying inside every day. Ventured outside to walk from his office a half-block to the saloon, at the St. James Hotel, and usually only at the crack of noon after he'd shaken himself awake. I confronted Coogan in his office as soon as I arrived in Cimarron. I knew he was worthless as a sheriff, right off. I told him Emmett was being falsely accused. But, Coogan was closed-eared to boot. He just would not listen to what had really happened. "Don't matter," he said, when I explained that I'd faked a robbery on that train, following the orders I got from the US Marshal in Denver.

"Ain't you hearing me? I got Emmett locked up in my jail. The evidence is in a locked drawer in that cabinet over against the wall. He was caught with a Colorado and Southern moneybag, more than three hundred dollars, a bag full of gold coins, and papers proving it was him. Judge won't be of a mind to listen to anything but the evidence, no matter what you or Emmett says. And, it sure as hell don't matter to me what some marshal up in Denver says about it. This is my town and we don't cotton to outsiders like you or a marshal in Colorado. This is New Mexico, by God!"

We were in Coogan's lean-to office tacked onto the adobe jail in Cimarron. This was no one-horse town. Smack on the Santa Fe Trail, Cimarron had a history of catering to fur traders, then miners, then cattlemen. Finally, it welcomed outlaws. Maybe more so than Dodge City back east or Tombstone over in Arizona. The Earps had stayed here, and so had Kit Carson and Buffalo Bill. And, of late, so had Emmett's gang and others from Wyoming all the way down to Texas. Coogan let them be even when they were shooting up the ceiling in the St. James's dining room. But, he was of a different mind this time around. I tried another tack.

"It does matter, Sheriff. Don't you see? I planted that evidence myself to catch him, and I did arrest him, three weeks ago. But . . ."

"Well, there you have it. He's been twice arrested. Judge Quintana will make short work of the trial and give him the rope with two arrests and a bagful of evidence. Besides, there's the man's history to consider. And, I ain't never heard of Judge Quintana feeling sorry for no train-robbin' bastard."

"History? The law says you can't hang a man on his history. I will explain all of this to Judge Blakey in Santa Fe. You got one of those new telephones in town, don't you? Let's call him right now. "

Coogan puffed up his scrawny chest and wheezed at me. "You listen to me now. We don't call no judge in Santa Fe. We wait for the regular judge, Judge Quintana, to come to town. He's a man who loves being on horseback, and he ain't fond of long trials. He'll listen to my evidence and then give Emmett the rope, so's he can get back on his horse. He don't even like to preside over a hanging, but this 'un'll bring a crowd from hell all over the place. Good for business, too. I don't know about the law in Colorado where you come from, but down in New Mexico, we take our history serious. Emmett's been robbing and killing for longer than I want to admit. He should be swung for what he done. Hell, I'm a rhyming man."

It was hard to figure Cimarron out. It had a sheriff partial to men who lived by their own codes. Now that same sheriff was trying to jump his own barb wire. Law-breaking and law-abiding coexisted here. Somehow, Coogan fooled the locals into making him sheriff. Instead of enforcing the law, he got drunk every night at the St. James Hotel. It was a place that catered to travelers. Wasn't particular about their habits, as long as they could pay the rate. Leastways, that's the truth before Tom Emmett went on a two-day drunk and made the huge mistake of telling a nighttime lady she was ugly.

Her name was Conchita Gurgenswarten, a hard-to-pro-nounce name even when sober, which she rarely was. Coogan said she was from Paraguay. She'd been married to a German tool and medicinal peddler, but he died, poisoned by his own medicine. Anyhow, Conchita took to entertaining men in her room on the ground floor, just off the rear door to the facilities out back. Before they shot one another, one of them insulted her. It could have been Strong, she wasn't clear. Anyhow, she was upset with the situation. When she found the moneybag in Emmett's personals up in his room, she sent a boy to fetch Sheriff Coogan, figuring he'd split it with her. Emmett was passed out at the time. The only hard part about the arrest was lugging him from the St. James across the street to the Cimarron jail. He and his two deputies drug Strong along since they'd shot each other, and he hadn't fixed the blame for that. Oscar didn't shoot anyone, although he might have been the one who knocked Strong out. Anyway, he let Oscar go, and stuck the other two in one cell. It took a half-hour for Coogan to sketch this tale together for me.

I spent the next morning thinking and scratching out a plan in my room on the top floor of the St. James. You might say I looked over everything in town. This hotel was the only three-story building for nearly fifty miles. It took until almost nine o'clock at night, but finally I got the telegram back I'd been waiting for. I found Sheriff Coogan in his usual spot, hanging onto a bar stool downstairs, and gave him a different nut to chew on.

"Extradition? What 'n hell you talking about, Angus?" Sheriff Coogan said when I showed him the telegram from the United States Marshal's office in Santa Fe.

"This is now a federal matter, Sheriff Coogan. You no longer have jurisdiction over the case. Emmett did not rob the train you arrested him for—it was me who done that—as a ruse to catch him for other robberies down in the southern part of New Mexico. But, he has federal crimes and judicial warrants against him for other robberies in at least two states.

The US Marshal for the State of Colorado has prior right of extradition. I'm authorized to act on this Extradition Order. The original, signed order is on file in the federal court in Santa Fe. So, you turn the prisoner over."

"Well, I never heard of this before, and Judge Quintana won't be here for another week. He rides a five-county circuit, you know."

"Don't matter. Judge Quintana don't matter. It's federal now. You have an order from a higher authority right there in your hand. It's also a federal offense to interfere with lawful extradition orders."

"Well, your order don't say nothing about Jack Strong, does it? He's also in my jail, and there's some figuring out to do about who shot who—on my head as the only law here. I figure he was in on it with Emmett, and I intend to try him as Emmett's robbing partner. The judge will set his bail next week; it'll be too high for such a man to come up with."

"Well, he wasn't a robbing partner, any more than Emmett was a robber. But that's no never mind to me. What you do with Jack Strong is your business. He ain't been extradited."

"I tell you I ain't never heard of extradition before. Why ain't this come up before?"

"Well, Sheriff, why don't you ask Judge Quintana for a little lesson on federal law when he gets here next week? How many federal warrants have you been involved with, Sheriff? That's the question. If this is your first, then you ought to let me save you some embarrassment in the federal court system. I'm expected to carry out the extradition order by-God forthwith. You see the word right there in the order—*forthwith*. That means today, not next week."

After another drink and a few minutes to think about which was the easier trail to take, Coogan cut a deal. He'd release Emmett under what he called "partial custody." He'd hold on to Strong. I told him I intended on taking Emmett before the federal magistrate in Santa Fe in two, maybe three days.

"And, there's one more thing, Sheriff Coogan. You're going to have to ride shotgun with me over to Santa Fe with the prisoner. We'll execute the extradition order together. Suit you?"

"But what about Emmett's gang? Word is they're coming for him soon. And what about that big Mexican, Oscar? He sobered up yesterday. Since I had no reason to hold him, he lit out."

"I see. Well, that supports our bargain. I'd appreciate your gun hand and your keen observation while I'm transporting the federal prisoner to Santa Fe."

Coogan threw down the last shot of strong-smelling whiskey, wiped his mouth with his sleeve, and gave me his best opinion on the matter. He studied the table and likely gave some thought to how comfortable he was.

"No, I don't see it that way. I got Jack Strong locked up, and I'd best stay in Cimarron guarding him till the Judge gets here. And, besides, if Emmett's gang gets here to bust him out, the town will need guarding. You just go on and pony Emmett down to Santa Fe. Make sure you report to the US Attorney, Jon Trachta that I cooperated and expect to be compensated by the federal government for my expenses in catching their prisoner."

I was sure that Coogan never met Mr. Trachta and that he'd refuse to do anything that took him away from the bar at the St. James. The sooner I got Emmett into the federal system, and away from Coogan and his go-along judge, the better I would feel. Emmett was decent to me up at his hideaway. He ought to get a fair trial for actually robbing trains, not one I made up as a ruse.

"Sheriff, I think it's best that I take the federal prisoner off your hands tonight on account of his gang might stir up trouble tomorrow. They've had two days now to stew about this. You wouldn't want them riding into town and shooting up everything, would you?"

"Guess not. All right, let's do this. I'll come over to Santa Fe on the stage three days from now. We'll sort this juris—whatever you call it—problem out over there."

I saddled Tucson and arranged to borrow a horse for Emmett to ride from the livery stable. Then I headed to the Cimarron jail. It was getting full-on dark.

CHAPTER 52
Jack Strong's Jail Break in Cimarron

"**J**ACK STRONG, JACK STRONG," someone was whispering outside our jail cell. I couldn't believe my ears when, right after sundown, I heard Oscar's soft whistle outside the jail window in our cell.

"Oscar. Am I ever glad to hear your voice," I whispered back.

"*Si, compadre.* They told me over at the saloon that you and Tom were in the jail. I got a gun for Emmett. We can pull these bars out with my horse. You ready?"

"Damn straight. But first lower that pistola down here. Emmett's still groggy from the bar fight. I'll pass it to him soon as you pull the bars off this cell. We're gonna need that gun soon as the bars go. You ain't got two of 'em, do you? 'Cause someone's gonna come a runnin' when the commotion starts."

"Is Emmett in your cell?"

"Yeah, they double-bunked us. Just quit jawboning and throw me a gun. When there ain't no bars between us, we'll both come on out. I got to warn you though; Emmett is dead asleep on account of the sheriff gave him a bottle to suck on. I guess he figures a drunk outlaw is less troublesome."

Three minutes later, the jail cell window, bars and all, went boom as Oscar's big chestnut gelding jerked it like a five hundred-pound longhorn at the end of the dallied riata on his saddle horn. I figured everybody in town heard. This was my chance. The second Oscar flung the pistol inside our cell I scooped it up and aimed it at Emmett's forehead.

"Emmett, get your sorry ass up, so I can shoot you standing in your socks."

Trying to shake himself out of his drunk, the old bastard stumbled to his feet. It didn't make sense to him at first, but quick enough he figured I had a gun and that I intended to take over his gang. We were staring at one another in the dimly lit cell. The door from the front office flung open, and I could not believe my eyes. Angus and the broke-down sheriff came a runnin' into the hallway, guns drawn, but the other side of the bars from us.

"Tom Emmett," Angus shouted through the dust, "I have an order of extradition issued by a federal magistrate in the Territory of New Mexico's Santa Fe District! I have served it on Mr. Coogan. I'm taking you to Santa Fe to answer for numerous crimes. Get yer boots on."

The sheriff and Angus were looking at Emmett. They didn't realize I had a bead on him myself. I pulled the trigger, but a half-second before that, Emmett had moved a foot to his left. It was enough. My bullet whizzed on by him and hit the adobe wall with a thud. Another puff of dust.

Sumbitch faced me through the bars; him outside in the hallway, and me inside the cell, but with a wide-open wall behind me, thanks to Oscar.

"You up to killing your boss to take over the gang?" Angus asked, over the snout of his .44.

"You got more lives than a wounded cougar," I hollered back at him. "I shot your ass out of the saddle in the middle of the Cimarron just a few weeks ago. How'd you survive that?"

"Lower that hogleg, Strong, or take your last breath."

Before either of us could react, Oscar and the Indian half-fell, half-climbed into the cell from the outside. They got the surprise of their lives when, from the yellow light of the sheriff's lantern, they saw Angus and me staring one another down over our gun barrels.

Oscar carried a double-barreled scattergun and let loose in the general direction of the hallway. He was shooting birdshot at close range. No one got hit. Angus turned his gun barrel away from me and square at Oscar. The tip of his barrel blew hot fire three times. Oscar flew outside like he'd been jerked back with his own rope. But, as he did, his trigger finger touched off the second barrel of his shotgun. Right at me. Birdshot blasted into my right shoulder and gun arm. I dropped Oscar's gun on the cell floor. Couldn't feel pain in my arm, but I could not move it. Looking down at my gun arm, I was surprised to see holes in my coat sleeve. My arm hung useless as a dead turkey on a cold spit.

The Indian disappeared outside, and quick as a flash, I heard the other boys slapping stirrup leather, and spinning their horses right behind the little arroyo ten feet from the rear wall of the jail. They were firing and spinning; I suppose they hoped we'd scramble through the hole in their direction. I could see they had my horse, and an extra one saddled for Emmett. Both horses were twisting and rearing up something fierce.

In the smoke and confusion, Emmett crawled over to Sheriff Coogan, who had drawn, but hadn't fired his old Peacemaker, a single-action Colt .45 caliber. Coogan was down on his hands scrambling back out of the hallway, but instead found himself tangled up against the front bars of the cell. Emmett just reached out through the bars, calm as you please, and unwound Coogan's trembling hand from his gun. Then he shifted the tip toward Angus and pulled the trigger. The bullet hit a steel bar dead-on, then ricocheted off somewhere, and Emmett cocked the single action and stuck the gun through the bars for his second shot.

Angus returned fire and hit Emmett's gun hand. Coogan's gun blew up and Emmett squealed. Now he had two worthless hands. With Emmett out of the fight, Angus surprised me again. He took one look through the big hole in the jail's rear adobe wall and dove for cover on the floor. In seconds, a screaming hail of bullets from outside rained down on us, as the boys slapped leather and fired at anything moving inside the jail. It only lasted a few seconds, then they held up; I suppose because they knew Emmett and me were in the line of fire.

"Don't move," Angus said to me. Then he fished the key to the cell door from Coogan' s belt, opened it wide, and grabbed Emmett's shirt collar with one hand. Calm as a storekeeper at closing time, he holstered his own gun and used the other hand on Emmett's belt to haul him up off the floor. Last I saw of either one was Angus dragging Emmett through the office and on out the front door.

Coogan, now unarmed and unnerved, crawled toward the door between the cells and the front office, hollering bloody hell for help. Then I heard the fool screaming at Angus, "Hey, you goddamned federal marshal, this ain't right! You come on back here!"

I just slumped to the floor, holding my arms tight against my chest as best I could to staunch the blood. A minute later, Coogan stumbled back into the hallway, followed by a wide-eyed barber in a striped apron from next door. The barber was carrying a .30-30 carbine. I held my hands up, but he looked right past me at the big hole in the rear wall of his jail.

"Where's Emmett?" I asked Coogan.

"He's on the back of a borrowed horse from the livery, in handcuffs. That federal marshal has arrested *my* prisoner and has a tight hold on Tom Emmett's lead rope. They are in full gallop headed to Santa Fe. Damn his rotten hide!"

Sumbitch had captured the boss again.

I hollered to Big Enough, the Indian, and the rest of the boys. "The front! Angus has the boss. They're headed out the front!"

I heard the pounding of horse hooves banging down the pathway between the jail and the general store next door. Then they thundered up, onto, and over the boardwalk in front, with pistols blazing. The Indian and Big Enough were hot on 'em. I thought. Angus's big bay was a fast horse. The dude string saddle horse he'd thrown Emmett on had been grazing on fresh grass beside the river for more than a week. The gang's horses were bone-tired after a six-hour ride from the lower shelf of the mountain trying to get here in the dark of night. So, they lost them after a two-mile chase, leastways, that's what Big Enough said when he came back into Cimarron an hour later. Coogan let him talk to me while they nailed some boards over the hole in the adobe wall.

"Dammit, Big Enough," I roared, "what 'n hell happened?"

"Last I saw was their dust over the cut in the river. They headed south toward Santa Fe."

CHAPTER 53
Angus and Emmett Take a Ride

TUCSON NEEDED A LITTLE BREATHER after the four-mile climb up off the grassy plain outside Cimarron to this gap between two stone towers. I swung down and motioned to Emmett he could do the same. He just sat the horse; out of stubbornness, I suppose. Cimarron Canyon ends the tedium of the reach upward. The mouth to this canyon felt like a nature-formed terrace, with a drop-off to our right and an upslope to the left with no top-off in sight. I figured we'd lost Emmett's gang about fifteen miles back. He had ridden the last two hours quiet-like. Tiring of my silent treatment, he gave me a piece of his mind.

"Goddammit, Angus, I just do not understand you, or anything about you. First, you rob my train, and then arrest me for it. Now you break me out of jail and shoot Jack Strong. You're a hard man to figure."

"Not what I arrested you for."

"Well, why 'n hell did you shoot Jack Strong then?"

"I didn't shoot Strong. Oscar did. I shot Oscar."

"But you broke me out of jail. Drug me right out the front door, not the new one Oscar made of the back wall."

"Wrong again, Tom. I extradited you from custody of that fool Sheriff Cornelius Coogan under a federal extradition order. Damn sight different from breaking you out of jail."

After a six-hour ride, the eastern sky was just coloring up some. I stretched my legs, saw that both horses were breathing easy now, and swung back over the saddle, clicking to Tucson to lead on out. We rode another three miles up into the canyon.

A little stream glided over a hard outcropping of rock and formed a small pool. Tucson and Emmett's horse pushed at one another seeking purchase on the slope alongside the stream.

Leaning back in my saddle, I could see the switchbacks that would take us up and over the last mountain pass between us and the Santa Fe Trail due south. Holding up my hand, I eased Tucson down from her trot into a slow walk. Then, tugging him back evenly, I loosened the dally on the lead rope to Emmett's horse, stopped, and swung down.

"We'll stop here. I'll boil some coffee and I've got some biscuits in my saddlebag. We'll let these horses rest for a couple hours and then start the pull over the top and on down the other side toward Santa Fe. We ought to be there by nightfall."

"So, you're aiming to take me all the way down to Santa Fe. Is that it?"

"Tom, if you'd do me the favor of not predicting me, I'll return the favor by making this ride easier on you. We got some talking to do."

I led Emmett over to a fifteen-foot juniper that'd wrapped itself around a young two-foot piñion. I untied the lead rope I'd looped over his handcuffs. Then I hobbled his horse on the far side. He just studied me.

Digging into my offside saddlebag, I pulled out a lard pail and some coffee grounds and started a small fire with windfall twigs and dead piñion bark. Soon enough, the fire was hot enough to boil water in the lard pan, and the coffee grounds sizzled up from the bottom. Emmett had shut his mouth. First smart thing he'd done since I met him a month ago.

I'd been watching the night sky all the way across the prairie and now gave some attention to the full-on dawn giving us a warm-up from head to boot. We'd entered a long, winding canyon that strained itself against the low-hanging sunlight like the folds in a blanket. Night riding always gave me a sense of peace and quiet that daylight seemed to hold back.

"Tom," I began as I handed him a tin cup brimmed with hot coffee, "I ain't got all of this figured yet, but here's what I thinkin' now. The two warrants out on you in the federal system are from two robberies you done down in the Las Cruces area, some years back. The train you robbed down there was the Union Pacific. The money you stole was for Army payroll in the Arizona territory, down Tombstone way, near Fort Huachuca. But, as I recall the actual warrants, the evidence was thin and mostly based on your reputation for other train robberies in southern New Mexico."

"Well," he said, pursing his lips on the edge of the hot cup, "those were some time back and I cannot be expected to remember every detail, can I?"

I looked at him, sitting there drinking *my* coffee, after riding a horse *I* was paying for, with a guttural snarl to his voice telling me he hated my guts. I didn't relish telling him what was troubling my mind.

"This ain't about that. This is about what Coogan and his ride-into-town-and-find-'em-guilty judge are fixing to do to you. Coogan's set on swearing in court you robbed the Colorado and Southern Railway train just a few months ago on the S-curves near Folsom. They plan to stretch your neck for it. Make 'em both big men in New Mexico, if they carry it off."

"But you did that, God damn it! You had the money on you when Jack Strong took you prisoner. He tracked you and ambushed you sleeping in some goddamned tree stand."

"You got it about one-quarter right. I had the money tucked in convenient-like, stuck in a Colorado and Southern Railroad bag, but the whole deal was a setup, just to get to you. My boss, the United States Marshal for Colorado, arranged it. So, I let Jack Strong, who claims to be a Kansas gun hand, follow my well-marked trail and then let him think I was sleeping unawares that he was sneaking in through the trees."

"Well, that beats all. You were salting me with easy money, is that it?"

"You could put it that way. But, I didn't figure on him conking my skull the way he did, or that he'd just hand over most of the money to you. Then, I had to improvise and get you to join me on a little stretch-out ride outside your hideaway. The rest of the story you already know."

Emmett finished his coffee, banged the tin cup on a rock, and rubbed a little sand 'round the bottom. He threw the cup to me and smiled.

"So, are you a United States federal lawman, or not? 'Cause, if you are, I reckon you know you cannot give me back to New Mexico law. They ain't got the shine on things you do. They don't care which robbery they try me for, as long as they get to rub my neck with a New Mexico rope. I'm thinking you already told Coogan I did not do that Folsom job. And he did not care one whit. Am I right?"

"Yeah. That's pretty much it."

"So, you ain't aiming to pony me all the way to Denver, are you?"

"I don't see how that would help the federals, or you. There is no warrant up there. The warrants are from down south of here, Las Cruces way. But, like I said, the evidence supporting those warrants is mostly reputation. The problem we both got is that the evidence in Coogan's lockbox came from me, but points directly at you. No one seems interested in what I have to say about it."

"Where's that leave us?"

"I ain't lined it out yet. But, for now, I'm gonna unlock those cuffs on your wrists, and I'll let you rein your own horse. I ain't setting you free, and I ain't taking you to Santa Fe."

Rubbing his wrists to get the blood running again, he asked, "What in tarnation were you taking about in the jail— something about an extradition? What's that mean?"

"The extradition letter was a law trick to get you out of Cimarron. When the judge in Santa Fe gets wind of it, he'll stomp on it. I only got it by ginning up a telegram to the

prosecuting attorney in Santa Fe. He knows me. I said I needed
a telegram back confirming an extradition in order to prevent
manifest injustice. You know about that, don't you?"

"There's two things I don't know about. What's extradition mean, exactly?"

"Didn't know myself until a few weeks ago. My boss,
Marshal Ramsey, gave me a book on the authority of the US
Marshals Service. I read it quick. It gives US Marshals the
authority to take a prisoner from one jurisdiction and deliver
him over to a different authority if a judge gives the order."

"Well, why would they do that?" he asked with a puzzlement on his face.

"I suppose in a situation like this one. It just came to me
when I was trying to figure out some way to get Coogan to
turn you loose."

"Ain't making sense to me."

"Well, like I said, it was not much more than a trick to
get that old fool to hold his horses a little. It came to me as I
realized the punishment for train robbery under New Mexico
law, which is a damn sight different than under federal law."

"Different how?" he asked, signaling that I had his full
attention.

"Well, according to Marshal Ramsey's book, the extradition authority goes to either trial or punishment. And, it's the
damn punishment that's got my gut in a twist. I just added
in my mind what Marshal Ramsey told me to what Sheriff
Godfeather told me about punishment for train robbin' in
New Mexico. Hell, did you know it's a capital offense in New
Mexico, but only if you're tried in a state court? Ain't so in a
federal court, that's the nub of it."

Neither of us said much for five minutes. Emmett got up from his haunch and walked around and around the little fire looking up at the sky and then back down at me. The horses had finished the grain I'd spread on the ground in front of 'em. Tucson was dozing off, standing up with one eye closed. He was good at that.

"Angus," he said, stopping and giving me a look from ten feet away, "you are a thinking sumbitch, ain't you?"

"Well, it ain't giving me all that much clarity at the moment. I'm half-way one direction on account of my badge, and I'm half-way the other because manifest injustice is something I can't be a party to."

"Hoowee," Tom said. "Manifest injustice! That's some kind of poetry to an outlaw. My pa, who was a law-abiding man, would be right proud to hear you saved me from such a thing as manifest injustice. But, what's a prosecutor in Santa Fe gonna care about me?" he asked as he spit downward.

"He knows where the money really came from. And, he ain't Coogan, or a circuit judge looking to bag a big name and string your neck."

CHAPTER 54
Angus and Manifest Injustice

WE'D TALKED OURSELVES OUT, so we saddled up and rode five straight hours in silence. The trail was as old as the Rocky Mountains themselves. It spilled out of Colorado, meandered down through Taos, New Mexico, and bottomed out in Santa Fe. This was the hard way to get to Santa Fe, but it was a trail that avoided purtin' near all the little towns and stage routes that marked the Santa Fe Trail from Kansas.

We came abreast of a gap in a high granite and lava wall about fifty miles southwest of Cimarron. Few riders had ever ridden through here; there was no sign of a trail or a human touch. No horse droppings, or stray bits of leather or cloth. Just clean, high desert country. We rode along the screes of a rock tower rising steeply on our left. Beyond a spinney of juniper and creosote, the climb flattened out some.

"Best get down and check your cinch," I said, more to myself than to the back of the outlaw riding ten feet in front of me. I'd given him some slack by taking off his handcuffs and letting him take control of his borrowed mare. But, it occurred to me that he might spur his horse and get clean away once I was on the ground. It didn't seem to have occurred to him. And, I was thinking that maybe I didn't care if he did.

The ride from Cimarron had taken the hump out of our horses, but a man ought to pay attention to his tack in steep country like this. I stepped off, threw the left stirrup leathers up over my saddle, and stuck three fingers under the cinch strap. No wonder I was feeling loose in the saddle for the last half hour.

"Lawman Angus, you're a puzzlement to me," he said as he dismounted and threw his own stirrup over the cantle.

"Puzzle? Well, that's one way to call it. Another might be my gut's in an argument with my head. You ain't a man that ought to be set free, but you ain't guilty of what they plan to hang you for."

"Well, Angus, we ain't gonna get to wherever you plan on taking me before that big storm that's aiming at us down there in the south. You got any coffee left? Break it out, and your lard pail. This time, I'll build a fire and we can look at the pieces of the puzzle together. I got the feeling I am not your prisoner at the moment. And I like the cut of your jib."

So we did. Instead of riding four more hours to round out the day, we sat across the little cook fire from each other, him on a rock and me on my heels. The coffee tasted bitter. Probably the bile seeping up from my stomach to my head. Or was it the other way around?

An hour and then some passed with no talk between us. But there was sound all around us. The wind had picked up, not exactly roaring, but blustering. It kicked up dust, which bounced off the lard pail. In the distance, a pack of coyotes yipped. Close by, we could hear the cones in the pine trees letting loose with that little shrill they do when evening starts to lay down on the ground. The horses snorted, farted, and pawed the earth around them. And, a varmint made a hasty retreat through some scrub oak twenty feet downwind of us. While the day was still open, I knew darkness would come early, riding over on that approaching storm. The mountain would come down on this trail soon enough, and us.

Emmett broke the silence.

"Here's a piece you can chew on, Angus, if you're of a mind. I took to outlawing reluctantly, if you can believe that. You see, wrangling another man's cows is an honorable way to make your way across Texas unless you hire onto a brand that ain't worthy of your respect. That's how I got my start. The foreman on the *Triple J* was inclined to borrow strays from every which direction and brand 'em with that runnin' iron he carried in his bedroll."

"I didn't know you got your start rustling cows."

"I didn't. Them five bony cows were Big Nose Ned's handiwork, not mine. He told me to take them to the railway holding pens. I led them right into the hands of the stock buyer down Amarillo way, who sent for a deputy sheriff. They looked closely at the brands. Then, without so much as asking my name, he arrested my young ass and threw me in jail. I spent two weeks waiting for the circuit judge to ride in."

"How'd you end up?"

"On the run. There was a for-sure outlaw in the cell with me. He had a gang—two worn-down drunks. They saw a hole through the floorboards under the jail. Never found out where they got that little handsaw. So, we just crawled down and out underneath the floor, punched a hole in the clapboard between the footings, stole two horses from the hitching rail, and lit out. I been on the run ever since."

"Four of you on two horses?"

"Nah, he pointed me to one horse, jumped the other one himself, and yelled, 'See you boys,' as we run off and left his gang. That's how I became the gang of one. He led, I followed."

"How come you didn't wait for the judge and tell your side? Most judges at least listen to an innocent man."

"No, not in my experience. You just broke me out of a jail in Cimarron that could have been anywhere in West Texas. What'd you say the judge over there was named?"

"Quintana. I'd seen his name on several wanted posters tacked to Coogan's door."

"All right. Judge Quintana might be a man who gives a damn about justice, and he might not. He might be like that judge over in Amarillo, one that judges a man by his circumstances. Mine were no good back then, when I first lit out of Amarillo, and they ain't all that good now. I only told you because it's part of the puzzle you're trying to figure out about me."

We sat there until the little cookfire went out. Didn't seem like more words needed to pass. I leaned back on my boots, keeping one eye on that dark cloudbank coming at us from the southwest. It resembled a black wing, torn from the shoulder of whatever giant bird it'd been attached to. A wounded bird,

I thought. That thunderhead towered miles up into the western horizon where the sun would be trying to set before long.

"Angus, you had any experience with the capital offense—that is, executing men for crimes?"

"No."

"Well, we had a judge in camp for a month last year. He'd been struck off the list in Oklahoma for sleeping with a lawyer's wife, and taking bribes, too. But, it was the hanky pank with another man's missus that got him run out of town—they paid little attention to his bribe-taking. He said he didn't get due process. That's the way he put it. Mighty bitter about it, too, being a judge and all. It was winter, and we had some time to pass in the long nights, so I asked him what exactly he meant by due process. Know what he said?"

"No, what?" I said, stirring the ashes in the fire with my boot.

"He used legal words. But it came down to fairness. The government must be fair to every man, even one that's committed crimes. That's because government is a burden on us. They turn honest citizens into outlaws. That's how I became one. They just would not listen to my truth. I told them about the running iron the foreman used. They jumped to the conclusion it was me. Well, by-God, it was not. Those cows were evidence, they said. But they were not mine. I drove them cows to town. So I did not get due process of law. That broke-down judge in my camp clarified it. That's what you're doing now, clarifying things."

I pointed up to the thunderhead headed our way.

"What do you think that black wing is trying to do? Is it pulling that thunderhead, or being pushed by it?" I asked Emmett.

"Can't say. But, either way, it's free."

"It ain't for me to say whether you got due process back then. Or if you're getting it now. That's what's twisting me like loose wire on a fence gate. We ain't in court now. You might get due process in a court, but we're on a mountain top, and I'm sworn by the oath I took to bring you in."

"In? In for what? In for robbing a Las Cruces train? All right then, slap them handcuffs back on me. Or, are you sworn to take me in for what you did? Is that what you swore to do? Arrest the wrong man so you can say you abided by your oath?"

"You're muddling this up, ain't you, Tom Emmett? The issue we got is bigger than you or me. The issue is liberty. You're free to defend yourself in a court of law. I'm free to turn you over, so you can do that however you damn please. Hell, man, if I could get you to the right court, your evidence would be listened to. You can see that, can't you?"

"Tell you what I can see. Coogan and his store-bought judge were going to string my neck. That badge on your chest is rubbing up against your brain. You are thinking about the law. But I'm thinking about what's right. Angus, I respect your oath and that badge you're wearing, but let me tell you what every innocent man knows. Just because it's law don't make it right. It ain't right to hang one man for something another man did."

I got up and walked out into the high desert. A half hour later, Tom was still sitting there. Hands in his lap, looking up at the sky.

"Tom, here's the truth. There never was a train robbed at the S-curves. I cannot be a part of hanging you for something neither one of us did. This ain't about you getting off your horse in Amarillo on the wrong side of the law. And it ain't about me doing my job. It's about what we see right now, right here. Pulling or pushing don't matter none. Right or wrong is the answer. So, you just tighten your cinch and ride on out of here."

He did. Riding due east, he never looked back. I waited till the storm passed me by, not long after sundown. The black wing, and the thunderhead chasing it, skirted on past. In its wake thunder rumbled, and I could see faint lightning strikes far off. Tucson took to pawing the ground again. I'd done the right thing. I cinched him up, snapped up into the saddle, and headed north, along with the coming storm. I was gonna see a man about a badge.

The End

Made in the USA
Middletown, DE
05 January 2017